SONIC ATTRACTION:

GRACE NOTES

SONIC ATTRACTION:

GRACE NOTES

BY:

LAURA CHRISTIAN AND GIHAN SALEM

RAMBLING RHODESY

PUBLISHING

ISBN: 979-8-9871415-4-0 (Paperback)
ISBN: 979-8-9871415-5-7 (E-book)

Rambling Rhodesy Publishing
PO Box 3164
Sugar Land, TX 77486-3164

www.ramblingrhodesypublishing.com

First printing, July 2024.

DEDICATION

For the dreamers, the fans, and the kids hiding out in adults and gasping for breath…

Revel in those dreams!

Live those fantasies and make no apologies!

And to all the artists that have inspired us:

Thank you for living your lives out loud.
Thank you for all the interviews you've done,
for the creative contribution you've made to the collective psyche,
and the impact you've had on our lives.
Thank you for giving us a place to escape from the real world.

Lastly, a special thank you all of the people in our lives who have loved us through the crazy stages of this writing process and have listened to us yakking for hours on the phone debating the plot. Your support was a critical part of this writing process.

BONUS EXPERIENCE

Listen along to some of the music that inspired this story.

BONUS EXPERIENCE

Listen along to some of the music that inspired this story

ONE

Grace was weaving through heavy pedestrian traffic, hands full of shopping bags, and had nearly reached the parking lot when her left hip pocket started vibrating. She stepped out of the flow, dropping her bags at her feet to pull the device free. It was Sunday afternoon, and she could guess who was calling her work cell. The smooth marble blocks of the storefront were warm against her back in the LA afternoon sunlight.

"Good afternoon. Mr. Meyer's office," she greeted.

"Ah, Grace! Glad I caught you!"

"Mr. Meyers," she acknowledged, groaning inwardly at the sound of her boss's voice. "How can I help?"

"What's on my agenda for Monday?"

Grace hadn't thought about the office since 4:00 on Friday, and she struggled to remember what was coming up for the week. She also wondered why he hadn't simply opened the calendar on his phone that they'd confirmed was working before he left for his trip.

"Nothing too important," she answered. "I believe you *do* have a meeting." She pressed an earbud into one ear and opened the app to review his appointments.

"Right—lunch," he agreed. "Anything else?"

His tone was brusque, and she nearly bit her tongue in her haste to reply as she scrolled through the day. "No, sir. Nothing I can't reschedule for you."

"Great. Listen, I'm going to be here for another day. But I'll be back Tuesday. So, if you could reschedule that meeting and extend Oscar's boarding arrangements, that would be great."

"No problem. Enjoy your son's wedding." She began looking up the boarding facility to find their number.

"I will. Thank you."

The line went dead, and after a quick call to the boarding agency, she tucked the phone back into her pocket. When her new boss had presented her with an iPhone three months ago, she'd been very excited. People had stood in line for days to get one of these, and someone handed it to her for free. The feeling of importance had lost its luster quickly when she realized it simply kept her on call 24/7.

Grace collected her shopping bags and headed to her car. The information she needed to reschedule wasn't available through her phone or laptop, and she would have to go into the office to complete the requested tasks. She knew when she took this job that it had potential for after-hours work, and that in Hollywood, this was considered paying her dues, but she couldn't help grumbling as she pulled onto the freeway. At least the office would be empty.

Once seated at her desk, she loaded the email and calendar. She cringed as she reviewed the lunch meeting he'd asked to reschedule. She couldn't wave this client off. If the meeting didn't happen Monday, it wasn't going to happen. Jacob Hunter was a new client, and Meyers had made a big deal about the size of the fish he'd caught when he was making the appointment.

She stared at the monitor, crossing her arms over herself and leaning back in her chair to plot. Everything was arranged: the time, the place, and everyone had agreed. Mr. Hunter was leaving town on the redeye Monday night and setting up the meeting had taken Meyers some time to pull off.

Grace wasn't familiar with many musicians, but she was once a card-carrying member of Jacob's boyband's fan club before they'd splintered and gone their own ways.

Filled with dread, she rang her boss, turning her chair to stare out over the LA skyline.

"Meyers," he answered.

"Mr. Meyers, it's Grace. Sorry to bother you," she apologized.

"What do you need?" The question was terse, but she had come to learn that this tone was unintentional. It simply meant he was distracted.

"I'm rescheduling tomorrow's lunch, but I'm afraid we really can't cancel this one."

"What?" he asked. "Why?"

This time, his shock and unhappy tone meant she had his full attention, and she squirmed uncomfortably, twisting the phone cord around her index finger.

"You're scheduled with Jacob Hunter." She waited while the client's name set in before she continued. "We set the appointment for lunch because he's leaving town Monday night, and he really wanted to meet with the producer you found for him."

A noise akin to a sailor who'd lost his rum sounded. "Okay, this is highly unorthodox, but here's what we're going to do. You're going to meet them at the restaurant in my stead."

She gulped. "Me? I could reach out to Monica—"

"No. Monica will try to poach my client. And this is above her pay grade. This meeting will take care of two pains in my ass that I don't want to be chasing down for weeks. Take the company credit card—you have one, right?"

Grace choked on her, "Yes."

"Just get the table and let the waiter bring them to you," he emphasized. "Pay for the meal. Say almost nothing. Listen and send me an email after to let me know how it went."

Grace felt like a two-year-old being told not to touch something hot. Swallowing hard, she licked her dry lips. "I don't see the producer's name in the appointment, and his email is like producer72@yahoo or something."

"Oh, right. Reed. Tell the host at the restaurant you're with the

Meyers Agency, and they'll find you at the table. Don't worry. Neither of them is shy, so you won't even have to introduce them."

"Yes, sir," she replied, attempting to force confidence into her voice. Her knees and thighs were trembling as she started panicking about what to wear, what to say, and most horrifyingly, what she could possibly eat in front of two celebrity strangers.

"Great. Send them a note that you're taking over for me so there's no surprises. Reply to the evite and copy me on the message," he replied and hung up the phone.

Grace stared at her desk phone long after the screen had turned dark. She was certain this was the most money she had ever earned. She was also certain that she was completely underpaid.

Monday afternoon, Grace was confident that choosing what to order wouldn't be an issue as she stared at the lunch menu where she awaited Meyers' clients. She wouldn't be able to eat regardless of her order. She glanced at the empty doorway again before looking back at the lunch specials. She was familiar with one of her lunch guests: Jacob Hunter. Like many other women her age, she owned all his boyband's CDs and his single solo album.

She considered her other guest as she settled on a tuna salad and tomato plate. Reed. The way her boss had thrown it out, she felt as though she should've known it. But she didn't. Her love for music barely extended to the performer's name, let alone the producer's.

She giggled to herself, smiling as she reached for her water glass, thinking of the only Reed in her memory banks. However, she hadn't heard *anything* about him in years.

Swallowing her water, Grace froze. Perhaps the Reed she knew was not so far-fetched. At thirteen, Grace had laid eyes on the seventeen-year-old, red-headed boy who became an immediate obsession: Derek Reed.

He was a member of a made-for-TV boyband canceled after one season, but Grace had recorded the entire series and memorized every moment of every episode. She knew all the jokes, all the songs, and to a startling level of detail, the way Derek's heavily styled hair dangled over his cerulean eyes. She bit her lip happily to prevent squealing.

Ten years ago, she had stumbled onto a tiny group of fans who had arranged a "convention," if five girls gathering to meet their teen idols could be called a convention. It was merely a dinner with Derek and his band mate, Peter Day, but it had meant the world to her.

A fresh sweat broke over her forehead, and her chest tightened as she scoped out the restaurant. Was this a heart attack? Surely her boss hadn't meant *Derek* Reed. All the musical credits she had found through internet stalkery began rolling through her mind. He *had* been songwriting lately for some big names and showing up on other people's albums as a producer. Was he big enough to work with Jacob Hunter? How had she not known he was Meyer's client?

The answer was simple: her job was to be discreet, and pawing through files in hopes of finding a name she recognized would be a terrific way to lose her job. She had no reason to suspect that Derek might be connected to Meyers. And if she had, she wouldn't have wanted to invade his privacy.

She gripped the arms of her chair, shifting as she scanned the restaurant's entrance, but no one fitting his description appeared. Meyers couldn't have meant Derek. Reed wasn't a terribly uncommon name, she rationalized. Hosting Jacob Hunter was a big enough mind bender, but to have to do so while also in the presence of the man who'd dominated her daydreams for two decades? Grace chewed her lower lip, heart pounding in her ears.

She was so busy convincing herself this was not happening, that she missed the waitress approaching her table until she arrived. Grace released the breath she had been holding and smiled, recognizing the tall man with the server instantly. Jacob Hunter.

"Your table," the waitress announced, beaming at the man beside her.

Grace knew from the magazines that Jacob was about six foot two, but while she was seated, he looked ten feet tall. Her eyes roamed from his loose jeans to his casual T-shirt tucked under a pinstriped, black sports coat. The sleeves were rolled almost to his elbows, and he combed one giant hand through his dark locks. He was every bit as delicious in person as he was in print. She sprang to her feet to greet the incoming celebrity.

"Mr. Hunter. I'm Grace, Mr. Meyer's assistant." She extended her hand, preparing herself to shake professionally.

Jacob squeezed the appendage firmly without breaking her fingers. His lips turned crooked, and Grace fought the urge to squirm under his scrutiny.

"Pleasure to meet you. And please, call me Jacob. I'm not old enough for a mister yet," he offered before taking a seat. "Where's the boss man?"

She cleared her throat, smoothing the skirt of her lavender suit as she sat back down. "Unfortunately, Mr. Meyers was detained out of town. He knew how important the timing of this meeting was to you, so he hoped you wouldn't mind my stepping in to facilitate."

"Not at all," he answered. "It's about time Meyers got himself an assistant, and it's nice to be with someone closer to my age for a change." He shook the linen napkin into his lap and settled his silverware in its correct placement on the table.

"I'm incredibly grateful to be working for him."

"So, you're new to the industry, I'm guessing. How long have you been with Meyers?"

Grace wilted. "Only a few months. What gave me away?"

He chuckled. "You've been nothing but professional, but the last time I saw a suit at a meeting like this, there were lawyers involved."

"Oh no," she mumbled, suddenly uncomfortable in her fitted business suit. Meyers wore a suit to all his meetings, she'd reasoned. She had hoped to exude professionalism and confidence in her business attire, but as she looked at her dining partner, she realized how grossly overdressed she was. She wished she was wearing any kind of camisole so she could remove her jacket, but she wasn't, and her discomfort tripled at the notion of being naked under her jacket.

He laughed. "It's okay. You look very professional. I'm not used to anyone taking us so seriously anymore. It's refreshing."

Her cheeks warmed. She glanced at her cell clock and started to frown, mentally preparing an apology for their late lunch guest. "It appears that perhaps our…" she trailed off.

Across the room near the entrance, she spied a man of average height and above average build topped off with a buzz cut, which did not suit him, in her opinion. Even after more than a decade and from across the room, Grace would recognize Derek Reed anywhere. From the way he was gesturing toward the hostess, she assumed he was looking for them.

"Never mind," she continued. "It looks like our producer has arrived."

Holding her breath, she watched Derek being led to their table. She and Jacob stood as he arrived, and she extended a hand to him.

"Welcome, Mr. Reed," she greeted. For a brief moment, Grace allowed herself the fantasy that he would recognize her but pushed it aside.

Derek returned her handshake slowly, eyes squinting as he looked her over. "Thank you," he mumbled, adjusting the small satchel in his hand.

Before he could introduce himself, Grace took charge. "I'm Grace. Allow me to introduce Jacob Hunter. Jacob, this is Derek Reed, the producer Mr. Meyers wanted you to meet."

Derek's head snapped toward her, halting his motion briefly before shaking Jacob's hand. "Great to meet you."

Grace gestured for everyone to sit and rubbed the hand he had shaken against her thigh, trying to erase the tingle in her palm. *Keep it together*, she scolded herself. *Be the wallpaper.*

As they took their seats, Grace and Jacob politely looked away as Derek fumbled himself and his bag into position.

Grace pretended to peruse the menu. In truth, she was sneaking glances at the newest arrival. He was thinner than she remembered, in his face and legs, but she could see the hours he'd spent at the gym bursting out of the caps of his short-sleeved heather gray Henley. The small buttons at the collar were straining, the top one having given up the ghost and exposing his smooth chest. A few freckles dotted his skin, and she imagined counting them one by one.

Derek began reaching for his bag again, and Grace cringed, waiting for more of the same scrabbling that had accompanied his sitting down. This time, however, the motion flowed smoothly as he pulled out an iPod complete with a set of over-the-ear headphones.

"I brought a demo of my studio work if you're interested," he offered, holding the equipment out to Jacob.

Jacob grabbed the headphones as Derek queued a song on the player. There was silence at their table, Grace waving off their server after water had been deposited. She squeezed her fingers together beneath the table, listing in Jacob's direction in hopes of an errant sound bite. The headphones were high quality, keeping all their secrets to themselves.

Jacob's eyes closed, head leaning forward as he listened, fingers tapping on his knee. Derek's eyes were glued to the man, the corner of his jaw twitching.

"Wow! This is you?" Jacob questioned, pulling the headphones free and passing them back. His eyes were wide, mouth set to catch flies.

Derek began absently winding the cords to stow in his bag and eased back in his chair. "Yeah, I was just noodling."

"Dude, that music's got some chops. I really like that electro trance direction you were heading. I've been wanting to experiment more with that myself. And that bass line..." he shook his head, rubbing his hands together. "So catchy."

"You can thank my studio tech Rae for that. Phenomenal bass player. I'm open to all kinds of music: pop, hip hop, EDM, K-pop, you name it. I'm really inspired by all kinds of music. I like to think my flexibility is an asset. I truly believe that each artist has their own unique sound, and I really want to showcase their vibe, whatever flavor it is."

"He's so modest," Grace cut in. "You should see his resume." She ticked off a handful of the dozens of well-known artists from his catalogue. Realizing that they were both looking at her now, she stopped, folding her hands in her lap and staring at her kneecaps. This was not what Meyers had told her to do, but she had been so caught up in hoping Jacob said yes, she hadn't been able to remain silent.

"That's right," Derek confirmed. "Someone's done her homework."

Grace shrugged at him, blood thrumming in both ears now. And then he winked at her, and she wanted to fall out of her chair. But she had already said too much, and she gulped down her water instead.

Jacob's posture inclined toward the other man, one hand on his chin. "I feel like we might be speaking the same language. I've got a few tracks I've been kicking around...some lyrics...but it feels incomplete. I should've brought it with me." He frowned, leaning back. "I'd like to move fast if you have some time. What's your calendar look like to fit in a collab?"

Derek beamed as he tucked the gear back into his satchel. "Let's compare calendars, and we'll see what works." He reached for his cell phone. "I transferred mine to the phone last week. There's an app."

Once they had nailed down a date, Grace allowed the server to take their orders and listened to the guys bantering about the music industry and eventually the project Jacob wanted to pursue while they picked at their lunches. If it wasn't for their impassioned faces as they discussed the latest specs on microphones, mixers, and software, she might have fallen asleep. The two of them diving into the minutiae was endearing if dull. They went on for over an hour before Jacob glanced at his cell phone.

"Hey, dude, I've really enjoyed meeting you. Meyers was right about us," Jacob proclaimed. "Let's get this going. Grace can get you all my contact info. Shoot me a message. I've got a place in town where we can work so we don't have to worry about booking a studio."

"I'll plan on it," Derek agreed. He deftly extracted a paper CD sleeve from his bag. "I brought a demo with some samples if you wanted to listen to it later. See if it jives with what you had in mind."

"Awesome!" Jacob exclaimed. "I'm really digging this. I'll listen on the plane today. I'm so sorry to cut this short, but I can't miss my flight."

Derek waved him off as all three stood. "Never apologize for your success."

Jacob held up the CD, shaking it gently for emphasis. "It has been so cool to meet you, man. I'm looking forward to working with you." After a quick shake with Derek, Jacob turned to her. "It was a pleasure meeting you, Grace. Tell Meyers I said you are always welcome to take care of my business. Great to have you on the team."

She shook his hand. "He'll be pleased to know you're so happy with the agency."

Jacob didn't let go of her hand and met her gaze as he repeated himself. "No. I mean, tell him that I liked working with *you*. *You* were the perfect combination of facilitating and staying out of the way. Meyers gets too involved. But don't tell him that last part." He patted her hand as he released it finally, flashing a too-bright smile, and walked out.

Derek's gentle laughter brought Grace back to earth as she tracked the pop-star scurrying past the host station.

"I'm so sorry I was late," he gushed when they were alone.

Grace dismissed his apology as she took a seat again. "You were right on time. We were early," she replied graciously, accepting the check from their server. She was so busy studying the totals and calculating a tip, she almost didn't hear it when he spoke again.

"So, you're Meyers' new assistant."

It was a statement more than a question, but she looked up to meet his deep blue eyes. "That's right."

It didn't matter how many times she had stared at his pictures; Grace was still overwhelmed seeing his face less than three feet from hers. She felt hot suddenly and took a deep breath. The pause felt too long, and she rushed to cover it up. "He knew Jacob had the flight today, and he didn't want to reschedule, so he asked me to stand in for him."

Derek nodded. "You mentioned that."

Grace felt herself shrinking under his gaze, despite the inviting upward curve of his mouth. Anything else she wanted to say was unprofessional, and she held her tongue.

"So, you knew an awful lot about me for a last-minute understudy. I'm not sure Meyers himself ever stepped in like that for me before."

She gulped. Something about his friendly words carried an accusatory tone, and she reached for her empty water glass hoping enough ice had melted to give her a sip.

"That's my job," she chuckled, nervously thinking that it had actually not been. Meyers had specifically warned her to say almost nothing. All she was supposed to do was pay for lunch, and she fretted about what Meyers would say when he found out she'd spoken.

Derek eased back in his chair, eyes on the credit card awaiting pickup. "Then you're the best assistant I've ever met." He squinted at her. "Have we met before?"

She hesitated, contemplating the best answer. Honesty was certainly the easiest. "Yes. For a few hours one evening."

Color drained from his face, and his brows knit. His eyes raked over her, head tilting to one side. "Oh…I…was it a long time ago? I'm so sorry I didn't remember."

Grace mimicked his expression. "Why would you remember? I was a fan. You're the celebrity. I didn't expect you to remember. I doubt you remember all the fans you've met over the years."

His sigh of relief drew onlookers, and he reached for his water. "Thank God," he murmured. "When you said it that way…I thought we…" He gestured between the two of them awkwardly. "You know."

She blinked rapid fire as her brain short circuited when understanding dawned on her. She licked her dry lips.

"No! Nothing like that." Did he do things like that? Did she look like an option for a one-night stand to him?

Grace could feel the heat roiling off her skin as she attempted to look anywhere but at him. Where was their waitress? Where was *any* waiter? Seeing no help but to confess, she did so.

"It was a reunion, kind of. Peter Day was there, and I was one of five girls you were having dinner with. The other three guys from your band couldn't make it." Grace wanted to melt under the pavement and ooze into oblivion.

"No way," Derek mumbled. "You were at one of those *conventions*?"

"One of?" she asked, straightening and meeting his eyes. Her embarrassment disintegrated instantly as indignance took over. "You mean there was more than one? How could I not be invited? I totally would've been there. I'm the one who copied the video tapes for all those girls."

Derek laughed heartily. "There were only two," he reassured her. "The last one was about five years ago." He crossed his arms over his chest. "So…you're a fan, huh?"

Grace rolled her eyes. "Apparently I'm not much of one seeing as how I missed half the reunions."

His eyes narrowed, thumb and forefinger gripping his chin before his eyes widened, and then he pointed at her. "Wait. Wait. Were you *my* fan? The one with the lunch box and the T-shirt I didn't own? Pretty impressive, by the way. I am the keeper of all things me-related."

She fanned herself and looked away again. He remembered her…or her collectibles at least.

"Please don't tell Meyers," she begged, watching as their check was collected. "He didn't tell me you would be here, so it was a total fluke. I didn't even know you were one of his clients. I promise I had no hand in orchestrating this because I'm some obsessed fan."

"How could I ever jump to that conclusion?" he teased. He patted the table as though a great matter had been settled. "Well, I'm glad you were here. This could be a very big deal for me, and you jumped in at exactly the right time."

Grace swallowed the comment and let it roll around for a moment in her brain. "Thank you."

"That first reunion," he confessed, "It came at a really important time for me. I was feeling pretty low, and when you guys reached out— it was good to know someone still had faith in me."

Grace's embarrassment faded almost instantly. While she had

been hiding her fandom since she'd seen him walk in, his admission switched her into full confession mode.

"I've been randomly searching you on the internet for years in the hopes of finding out your next project was a solo album or you were performing live somewhere, especially since I moved to LA earlier this year," she burbled.

"I've been staying busy with song writing and producing. It's really fulfilling, actually."

"I'm so glad to hear it."

"It's unusual to run into fans these days. My bass player, Rae? Had a thing for Leo. I should introduce you some day."

Grace remembered Leo, the handsome Latino member of the group and his master level dancing skills. "My best friend had a thing for him too back then."

"At any rate," Derek went on, "what do you think about Jacob and me cutting an album together? From a fan's perspective?"

She tapped her bottom lip as she evaluated the pairing, then replied. "I think your styles would blend well. You're both super passionate about music. I think there's a lot of similarity in your careers."

He chuckled. "That's generous."

Grace's head tilted to one side. "It's true. You've both been in boybands, you've both had solo careers, you are both amazing dancers, singers, and songwriters."

"I hadn't looked at it quite that way." He glanced at his watch. "Well, I'm glad Meyers couldn't make it. It's hard to talk around him."

Grace slipped her credit card into her wallet as Derek stood. Before she could do it herself, he gently pulled her chair out and helped her up. She schooled her features, as though this was a totally normal thing that happened to her—handsome men pulling out chairs and assisting her to her feet.

Trying not to gawp, she pulled her handbag strap over her shoulder. Why wasn't he backing away? He was incredibly close now that she was on her feet, and then he tucked her arm against his side.

Her entire body puckered as she felt his hard muscles against her forearm, and he led her out of the restaurant.

"Where'd you park?" he asked when they reached the sidewalk.

Lifting a finger, she gestured in the appropriate direction. "I'm not far," she answered, thinking he would let her go and preparing to disengage.

"Me either," he added He patted her hand against his arm and started down the street as indicated.

Grace hung on for dear life to keep up with his stride.

When they reached her car, he released her hand. "Tell Meyers I'll be in touch with you soon."

She tsked at him. "I'm not sure that will work out well for me if he thinks I'm after his clients."

"Trust me—he has bigger fish to fry than me. He'll be relieved to have you handle the paperwork. Man still tells me to fax stuff." He held up a hand and waved. "Talk soon, Grace."

As he pivoted to walk away, Grace couldn't believe her audacity as she called, "Derek?"

He stopped, twisting toward her. "Yeah?"

"You wouldn't happen to have another copy of that demo I could steal for my own personal use?" She bit her lip, afraid that she had overstepped. And if he said yes, would Meyers accuse her of accepting benefits or bribes from his client?

"Not on me. But I can get you one."

"Really?" She felt herself nearly stumble but adjusted before he would notice. She hoped.

He nodded. "Sure." He waved then turned and sauntered away.

Grace watched him go for far longer than necessary, head tilting to one side with a lopsided grin as she stared at his back side. While she would be thinking about every word they shared for days, at the moment, she was enthralled by the sight of him walking away. Whatever he had been doing at the gym had worked for him. He looked like a firefighter, muscled and lean. Ready to whisk away a damsel in distress at the drop of a hat. With any luck, his hair would grow out. Thoughts of running her hands through his auburn mane gave her a shiver, and she squealed in the privacy of her vehicle. With a flick of her wrist, she revved the car to life and headed back to the office where she was pretty sure no work would get done.

~ ♫ ~ D E R E K ~ ♫ ~

Inside his car, Derek laid his head back and exhaled. He had been working on this demo for a solid week at the studio with his tech/bass player Rae. He'd been lucky she turned out to be more than a tech. He may never confess to her, but the addition of her bass and vocals as well as her encouragement to force him to play the keyboard had taken the track to new levels. Inspired, he had recorded three tracks with her to demonstrate a broad range of styles and skills.

He drummed his hands against the wheel, allowing himself to shout out a cheer before calling Rae and inviting her to meet him at their favorite watering hole near the studio where they'd recorded together. He needed to tell someone who would understand how important the meeting with Jacob was. Bragging by phone wasn't good enough. This celebration required line of sight.

Replaying every detail in his mind as he drove, he was on autopilot. Jacob Hunter's boyband career had been astronomically more successful than his own. The rug had been pulled out from under Derek and his friends after just one of the multiple years they'd been promised. Derek had spiraled when nothing materialized immediately and all the people he considered friends had disappeared.

But Derek wasn't focused on that now; he couldn't be. In the last decade, he had worked like a fiend to get to this moment where someone with Jacob's credentials was ready to collaborate with *him*. And he couldn't lie; it felt good.

He whipped the car into a spot half a block from the bar then jogged toward the front door. He spied Rae in the distance swaying lightly from one foot to the other as she waited outside the front door.

She hadn't seen him yet, still scanning the crowds passing by. In the year they'd been working together at Lakeshore Studios, she had become like his little sister to his actual sister's chagrin.

Rae barely measured up to his shoulders which compounded the feeling of being siblings. Her chocolate brown hair was braided loosely today, and she was decked out in what he had dubbed her uniform: a long halter top and jeans rounded out with a pair of cheap flip-flops. She took her comfort seriously.

A pang of sadness washed over him. Rae had been laid off the day he'd asked her to record his demo for Jacob. He'd possibly overpaid for her time and flaunted her around the same studio that had done her dirty, but it was worth it to see the looks on their faces when he'd asked the staff to bring snacks and bottled water for them both. She'd gone from coworker to client, and his altruistic side basked in it. He hoped his news about Jacob would pick up her spirits.

He slipped behind her undetected, snaking his arms around her waist and lifting her off her feet to swirl her in greeting.

"Holy crap!" she yelled before wriggling out of his embrace. She whirled around and socked him lightly on the arm. "No sneaking up on me!"

The smile on her face belied her scolding. "Sorry. It was too perfect a setup," he excused as he pulled the door open wide for her.

Per their standing agreement, Rae searched for a table while he ordered drinks. He studied other bar patrons as he waited, not recognizing anyone. He preferred being in a place where no one would be intentionally eavesdropping. He was buzzing as he set down a whiskey, a cocktail, and two shots in front of Rae.

"Oh my! Is this a celebration?" she asked, dividing out the drinks as he slid into the booth opposite her.

Derek nodded, anxious to drop the information bomb on her. He had withheld the identity of his potential client while they were in the studio, afraid of jinxing the opportunity. Mostly, it was because Rae was a fan of Jacob's, and he was afraid knowing would detract from her performance. Now that it was all over, he could tell her everything. He opened with the most trivial piece of information to torture her.

"So, I have another fan," he blurted.

Rae giggled, lifting her shot glass in salute. "Your artist is a fan?"

"Hah, not the artist," he corrected, lifting his own glass. "My agent's assistant. She filled in at the meeting." He slugged his shot. "Still not important enough for him to show."

Rae shot her drink as well, toying with the small glass between her fingers. "So *now* can you tell me who this big star is that we gave up last week for? I've never seen you nervous before."

Derek stared back, lips curled upwards. He leaned forward, meeting her eyes and pulling his whiskey back protectively. "Jacob Hunter."

She froze. The grin on her face slid slowly down. Fingers statue-like, the shot glass suspended in an awkward half turn between them. It slipped from her grasp, clattering and rolling until it met his. Finally, she blinked and cleared her throat as she righted the cup.

"Excuse me?"

Sensing her wheels turning and the accusation looming in her eyes, he held up both hands briefly.

"Okay, at first, I didn't tell you because I thought you'd mock me until the end of time. Then…I didn't want to jinx it," he expounded.

Rae inhaled deeply and exhaled shakily with excruciating slowness. Her eyes closed, hands making tiny, rhythmic motions on the table's surface. He guessed she was counting to a number higher than ten.

"Can you forgive me?" he asked.

Rae didn't answer, her stare piercing.

Derek fidgeted in his seat, hoping he hadn't made a mistake they couldn't move past. He liked Rae. She was a great tech and an even better bass player. However, she could be incredibly sensitive. He took another fortifying sip of his top-shelf whiskey.

After what felt like more than five minutes, she finally spoke. "So…this fan of yours. When do I get to meet her?"

He barked out a laugh at her change of subject. "Never! I don't need the pair of you ganging up on me! It was nice to be recognized again. I thought you were the last one."

"Is she cute?" she questioned, hiding behind her drink.

Derek couldn't say he had given it much attention during lunch, not allowing anything to distract him from talking with Jacob. In retrospect, he had noticed a few things while walking the trembling woman to her car. She was tall, almost taller than he was. She wasn't thin or especially distinctive, but she had been well coiffed and even more buttoned up than her perfect hairdo. But she was well named, in his opinion, recalling how her slim fingers had negotiated the check. Every ounce of her was controlled. Measured. Graceful. He didn't want to live up to that kind of pressure. Perfect people didn't like him for long.

"Yeah, but not really my type." He shrugged. "I mean, she was wearing a suit! A freaking lavender business suit!" He gestured to his knees, indicating the modest skirt length and picturing the curve of her calves all the way down to her pumps.

Rae's pensive smirk unsettled him, and he frowned.

She leaned against the table and crossed her arms. "Your type? What is that, exactly?"

Derek shrugged, unsure how to phrase it. He wanted someone that was maybe a little bit of a hot mess. Someone not afraid to show some skin—get messy when it counted. Someone who would grind with him on the dance floor until they were both breathless, regardless of who was watching.

"Christina Aguilera, Fergie, Carmen Electra, Kim Kardashian. Girls like that are my type."

"And how's that going for you?" Rae's arched brow emphasized her chuckle.

"What's that supposed to mean?" He ran his palm across the dark wood table. The lights were too bright, or he was too sober, because he could see everything clearly: the clapboard walls, sticky smears of spilled alcohol on the floors, and the train of mockery barreling toward him.

"Sex symbols," she spelled out. "Are those few minutes of

satisfaction all you're looking for?"

Derek had heard this particular accusation from people more often than he cared to admit. Didn't he deserve someone who set all his nerves on fire with a mere glance? He'd worked hard to look like he did now, compared to his skinny, teenaged self. He had earned a traditional sex-kitten. Rae had no right to call him shallow. Of course he wanted more than good looks, but he had to start the judging somewhere—a sexy exterior was as good a place as any.

He rolled his eyes, leaning back in his seat to maximize the distance between them.

"What? You think I should date someone more like you?" he countered. He gave her a cursory glance.

"God, no!" She laughed. "We'd kill each other in less than a day! I meant that maybe you should widen your parameters."

"Most people call that settling," he retorted.

She smiled ruefully. "All I can tell you is that since my divorce, I have no interest in giving someone that kind of emotional access based on simply a pretty face."

With those few words, Derek withdrew. He remembered the aftermath of her divorce. He didn't know all the details, only that Rae was willing to work long and weird hours to keep herself out of the house which had worked to his advantage more than once. He knew now that she was being a decent friend, and his best friend and former bandmate, Pete, had said something similar.

By way of apology, he turned the conversation back to work. "Well, I plan to keep you busy with this Hunter project," he promised. "And any other project that comes my way."

She focused on her glass and waved a hand in the air as she spoke. "You don't have to—"

"I know," he cut in. "Just…let me do this, alright?" Considering the matter closed, he lifted a hand for another round from a passing server and filled Rae in on the details of his new project.

When Derek woke at noon the following day, he wondered if he'd fallen asleep sucking on a cork. His whole mouth was dry, and his head throbbed with each heartbeat. After a grumbling sigh and stretch, he stumbled to the kitchen and chugged two bottles of Gatorade. He knew better than to drink like he had the day before, but he'd been in the moment celebrating with Rae, and he didn't regret it.

He slipped into loose clothing then jogged the three blocks to his gym to sweat out the toxins and do a few laps at the pool. Feeling more or less human, he wandered home to check his email.

There was a message from Grace to him and Jacob sharing contact information. It was short and to the point, and every bit as professional as her prim business suit. He remembered the way she'd chewed her lip as she'd asked for his demo. It did not match her strictly business email at all. When talking about *his* music, she looked more like she wanted to get down to business.

Her contact prompted him to email his availability for the next week-and-a-half to Jacob.

He was about to log off and call Pete when a new message popped into his inbox from Jacob.

> *Obsessed with the CD! Listened to it the whole flight. I'm back in town Thursday. Can we do lunch Friday and plot to take over the world? Must have your musicians on this project. Whoever's in your back pocket is magic—bass, keyboards, and all the vocals. Pretty sure that's your voice too. Let's do a duet if it is. Bring all your people to lunch Friday if they're available. Drum machine is a no-go. I want a live drummer and a guitarist to get those old-school tasty riffs. That work?*

Derek stared at the screen happily, sitting up straighter as he read the praise on his vocals. He'd always been shy about them. He could hold his own in a room full of semi-talented people. And he could outwork them all, of that, he was sure.

Sighing relief, he hit the reply button, keys echoing through his apartment as he hammered out an answer.

Glad you're stoked. Lunch Friday is great. Yeah, that was me on the vocals. I'll bring my bass player Rae. I agree about drums, and guitar would add a whole other level. We can check with Meyers about the drummer and guitarist. I'm sure he's got plenty to choose from. See you Friday!

He almost felt guilty for committing Rae's time without asking, but it dissipated quickly. He was more afraid she might kiss him when he told her Jacob had requested her too.

He lifted the cell to call her but imagined she was still sleeping off their celebratory liquor and texted instead.

> **Derek**
> Jacob wants to meet Friday. He demanded to use my bass player. YOU.

Satisfied, he eased back in his chair, waiting for her reply. He didn't have to wait long, and a quick succession of questions followed. Now that he knew she was conscious, he opted to answer the deluge of replies with a phone call.

In half a ring, she answered with a whisper. "Talk softly. I'm mostly recovered, but my brain's still tender."

He chuckled. "We've got a brainstorming session with Hunter," Derek murmured.

"Good for you." It came out as nearly one word, then she paused. "Wait. *We?*"

Derek laughed at her sudden coherence. "I was wondering if you'd catch that. Yes, *we*. He asked me to bring my bass player to meet him. Best to get introductions out of the way early and make sure we can all work together."

"You think we won't get along?"

Sadness filled her voice, and he replied quickly. "No, didn't say that. Just confirming. It's always good to introduce everyone early."

"Isn't he out of town? So, do you mean this Friday? Or next? And is he coming back here? We're not going to have to like hop a private jet or something, are we?"

Derek disliked her litany of questions mainly because he did not have answers. "Um, this Friday, and he said he'd be back in town. No jet hopping. We're not there yet. I guess we need to pick a place. I didn't really expect him to respond so fast, and I was excited to move forward. Lunch on Friday sounded like a great idea."

"Devil's in the details," she slurred.

"I'll work out the plans and let you know. We can carpool." Rae refused to drive in LA, and he knew the offer to chauffeur would sweeten the deal.

"Great. What time?"

Derek faltered again. "Um, we didn't discuss that either. Lunch is you know…lunch time."

Rae snickered. "*You* need an assistant," she suggested. "Or he does. 'Cause you both suck at making plans."

Derek laughed as well. "I can't afford an assistant. I'll manage. I'm not completely incompetent."

They said their goodbyes, and the phone had barely disconnected before Derek hurried to scoop up the laptop from the couch. He sent an email suggesting a time and place to meet Friday. Once he'd pressed send, he stared at the computer, waiting. He glanced at the clock on the corner of his screen, then checked the sent box to make sure the message had been sent. He checked his social media accounts, then refreshed his email again. Nothing.

Derek went to his fridge, pulling out a bag of sliced apples.

This project was going to be a big deal if he played his cards right. He was doing fine. But working with Hunter would increase his street cred and open doors he hadn't been able to break through yet. Several dozen more checks of his email yielded no new information, and worry creeped in as he re-read the message he'd sent. He'd asked to meet at the Thai place on Sunset. But—maybe there were other Thai places? He mapped it all out, discovering his error, then groaned. Maybe Rae was right.

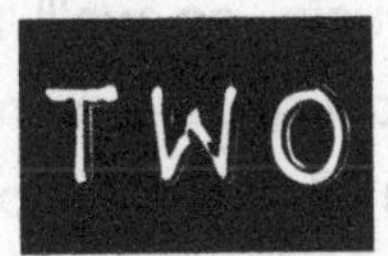

It took three rings for Grace to wrestle her cell from her purse without jerking her car into other lanes of traffic before she answered breathlessly, "Hello?"

"Hi, is this Grace?"

She assessed the familiar but indistinct voice, trying to trigger some recognition in her brain.

"Yes, it is," she replied, settling her phone in the cup holder and securing the left ear bud in her ear. She inched the car forward on the freeway, braking again when she ran out of space. Pulling over in the heavy traffic would be virtually impossible at the moment. "How may I help you?"

"Grace, this is Jacob Hunter. We met at lunch last week."

She checked her rearview mirror and scolded herself for not recognizing his voice. "Yes, sir. I remember you. How can I help?"

"Well, I need your help setting up another lunch for me and Derek…and his bass player. It's become incredibly clear to me that neither of us have your skill for arranging lunch meetings. Meyers said you were a whiz at that."

She chuckled. "That was kind. I'd be happy to coordinate. When do you want to meet?"

"This Friday for three," Jacob replied. "No—four with you. See? I can't even tell you who's going to be there."

"It's not a problem," she excused. "I'm happy to help. Would you like something casual or formal? Any dietary restrictions I should know about?"

"Definitely casual. We need to hash out some scheduling details and the direction of the music, so we'll need space to lay out our laptops and stuff. I don't know about any restrictions. I eat everything. Derek mentioned something about a Thai place on Sunset?"

"I'll take care of that for you. I'll send you an email so you'll have all the details in writing. Is noon okay?"

"Spectacular," he replied. "I really appreciate it. We've traded like four emails, and we couldn't get it done. It's nice to have it all taken care of."

"You're in luck. I excel at lunch," she proclaimed. "I'll have that for you this evening. I'm actually in the car right now, and I don't have a way to—"

"You're driving?" he interrupted. "Hang up now. No sandwich is worth risking your life for. I'll look for your email later tonight."

Before Grace could protest, the line went dead. She glanced from the road to her cup holder, verifying the call had ended, then back to the road. She blinked in surprise.

"That was weird," she mumbled to herself.

When Grace finally reached her apartment, she sighed with relief. Turning the key in the apartment door exhausted the remainder of her strength, and she leaned against its surface as the tumblers aligned.

She kicked off her shoes neatly at the entrance. Remembering her promise to Jacob, she hurried to her laptop to plot. Roughly twenty minutes and two phone calls later, she sent an email to Jacob, Derek, and her boss with the details, then answered the call of her growling stomach.

As she nuked some leftovers, her work phone trilled to announce a text. She grinned at Jacob's polite request that she call him when she was not operating a motor vehicle. Armed with a beverage and leftovers, she nestled behind her coffee table to return the call. Normally, she would finish eating first, but he had been so nice that she refused to make him wait. The call rang in her earbuds as she uncapped her soda.

"Grace? Not driving?" Jacob asked.

"No, sir. How can I help you?" she countered. It was nice to have someone ask after her safety.

"Please call me Jacob…or dude, or anything other than *sir*. That's…you know, my dad," he stammered.

"Of course." She liked his warm and friendly tone that made her feel like part of his team. Her own boss didn't give her that feeling.

"I need a drummer and a guitarist," he announced. "I was hoping you could get with your boss or someone at the office and give me a list of about five recommendations for each. I would be super grateful. Especially if we could have it by Friday's lunch."

Grace stared at the phone, digesting the verbal barrage. Now she was a talent scout? She rubbed her forehead. "I don't know how…what I mean to say is, shouldn't you talk to Mr. Meyers?"

"Well, the last time I asked him for help, he sent me to you," Jacob reasoned. "Figured I'd go straight to the source this time and skip the middleman."

"Well…yes, I…" she ventured carefully.

"Thanks, Grace, you're a peach! Remind me to buy your lunch when I see you on Friday!" Jacob hung up.

Grace stared at her phone again as she started to eat. Why would he expect her to be there for the luncheon? Was she supposed to deliver the list he wanted by hand? Shaking her head, she went back to her meal. At this rate, she'd be spending all her time working for both Mr. Meyers *and* Jacob with no time for herself.

The following day, Grace stared restlessly at her office computer, trying not to spin anxious circles as she waited for her boss to arrive. Meyers should be home from the airport by now, but she debated if it was too early to call or if it was worth risking his wrath for calling at the wrong moment. He could be anywhere, and he seemed to get extra cranky if she called while he was in transit.

Attempting to be proactive, Grace sifted through her boss's

contacts, trying to determine which of his clients were drummers or guitarists. She was afraid he would view her search as overstepping her bounds and stopped before she could get caught. Her search netted a total of one name she recognized as a drummer. By lunch, she couldn't put it off any longer and dialed her boss's number.

"Meyers," he answered on the first ring.

"Hello, it's Grace," she replied.

"Grace. What's up?"

He sounded busy—distracted. But then, he often did. It wasn't her place to question. She answered as succinctly as she could.

"So, Jacob Hunter called me last night—I guess you must have passed my number to him. He asked for a list of about five guitarists and five drummers to consider for the project he's about to do."

"Project?"

"Yes, sir. The one he was meeting with Mr. Reed about yesterday. I guess they've decided to move ahead."

"Oh—right. Right. He told me about that when he called last night. Did you put that lunch on my calendar?"

Grace hesitated. "No, sir. He didn't tell me you would be there. I can adjust the reservations."

"Grace." He sighed her name like he was getting ready to scold a silly child. "I'm not going, but I want it on my calendar. I need to know where my clients are. And if you're setting this up, it's my business."

"Yes, sir," she replied. She chided herself for not guessing he would want to know. "I'm putting it on your calendar as we speak. I've started looking through the client lists, but I only found one drummer. I wasn't sure how you organized them..."

"Don't," he interrupted. "I'll take care of that."

Grace blinked. "Okay. Jacob asked that I bring him the list at lunch on Friday."

"Bring it to him? At lunch?" he repeated. "Why would you go to lunch with them? Just email him the list I give you."

"Yes, sir. Thank you."

"That all?"

"Yes, sir."

"Grace, I know you're new. But don't forget who the agent is here. I've been doing this for thirty years. You've been a great addition to the team, but if I needed an A&R team, I'd hire one."

"Yes, sir. I understand. Sorry for the confusion."

"You work for me, not them. Good work setting up the lunch. Put it on my calendar." The line went dead, and Grace stared at the phone long after she rested the receiver in its cradle.

Calendar modified, she grabbed her purse and headed out. It was time for lunch, and while she wasn't sure where she would be spending her allotted hour, she knew it wouldn't be in the office.

~ ♫ ~ D E R E K ~ ♫ ~

At midday on Friday, Derek glanced at his watch as he ushered Rae ahead of him into the restaurant where they were meeting Jacob. They were five minutes early and found Jacob sipping a glass of water and perusing the menu at an enormous table tucked into a semi-private corner. His pea green sweater vest nearly glowed in the dark.

After introductions and orders, they got straight to work.

Jacob reached for his water again. "I'm a little surprised you haven't invested in a home system. It's life changing," Jacob noted as they discussed how Rae and Derek had met at Lakeshore Studios.

Derek shrugged. "I'm working up to it." He pulled a notebook and pen from his satchel. "What do we need to get this ball rolling? Drummer and guitarist?"

"Yeah, Grace sent me a list of prospective musicians," Jacob replied, handing over his phone with the aforementioned email open. "Meyers wouldn't let her come with us today."

"Grace?" Rae asked, as Derek accepted the proffered item.

"Our agent's assistant," Jacob explained. He turned his eyes on Derek. "I know a few of them by reputation."

Rae's face lit up, and she clasped her hands together. She leaned forward on the table between them. "Oho! Is that *the* Grace? Your fan?" Rae cooed as she poked Derek in the ribs.

"That explains so much," Jacob exclaimed. "And here I assumed she was just well-prepared! So, Grace is Derek's fan?"

Derek opened his mouth to speak but his bassist rushed in first.

"And he thinks she's cute," Rae cooed.

"Well, she hid her fandom well," Jacob replied, shaking his head.

"Only until you left, and then it all gushed out," Rae explained. "Derek told me all about it after your meeting."

He was certain he didn't like the two of them ganging up on him, and it was clear from the way they were hedging closer to one another and speaking around him, they were barely getting started. He eyed Rae, hoping she would get the hint. This was not the sort of professionalism he liked to show his clients. He didn't talk about his personal life. He would talk about theirs if they wanted, but never his.

Licking his lips patiently and taking a deep breath, Derek tried to steer the conversation away from himself.

"So, I know of a few of these musicians by name, but none personally. You?" Derek interrupted.

Jacob continued looking at the bass player as if Derek wasn't even there.

"Cute, huh?" Jacob repeated, bumping shoulders with Rae companionably. "Too bad she couldn't come today."

"Well, she's not his *type*," Rae stage whispered, holding a hand to cover her mouth. She put it down as she continued, glancing distinctly away from both her table mates. "Although... you know what they say about those straitlaced girls..." Her eyes darted around the room.

Jacob opened his mouth to speak, then looked at Derek. He sat up straight and reached for his water.

"So, getting back to the music," Jacob continued. "I've been so inspired by the sample you gave me that I was thinking I'd shoot for a whole album instead of a single. And if that goes well, and we get to the tour stage, I'd like for whoever cuts the album with us go with us, too." He looked directly at Rae. "Would you be okay with that? I mean, sharing a bus and stuff?"

Rae blinked dumbly and looked to Derek.

"I'll share a bus with Rae and make sure she behaves," he teased.

Jacob raised an eyebrow at them both, looking back and forth like it was a tennis match.

"Are you two…" Jacob trailed off.

Derek felt his brows thatch, and he had to fight to close his mouth. He glanced at Rae, seeing horror written over every wrinkle in her face as she drew back from them, mouth agape.

Rae shuddered. "Ewww. He's like a brother to me."

The server arrived with three large entrees, and they spent several minutes tucking into their meals.

"So, I was thinking maybe Monday we could hold auditions for the other two band members," Jacob mumbled around a bite, hastily chewing and swallowing. "Just see who meshes."

"Fire," Derek agreed. "I like that you're going after a four piece. Very traditional."

If Derek didn't know better, he'd swear Rae was blushing as she stared at Jacob. Food was in her mouth, and she was chewing but not swallowing. As though she'd forgotten what she was doing.

"Five-piece," Jacob corrected. "You'll do keyboards, right?"

Derek set down his silverware. He wasn't sure he was ready to tour. It had been fun when he was seventeen, but he was nearly forty now. Wouldn't that be something? At his age to be the main act again?

"I hadn't really planned to. Do we even need them?"

Jacob's eyes were wide. "Come on. It'll be fun."

He wasn't sure how to answer. He'd been under the impression that he was being contracted as a producer and to contribute some writing as needed. He had never played keyboards for an audience. And he wasn't sure if he'd call what he did playing as much as pressing buttons at the right time.

"Why don't we play that by ear," Derek suggested. "If it needs it, we can decide in the moment."

"Fair," Jacob consented. The ideas began to fly, and Derek noticed that Rae had picked up his notebook and was writing furiously. He had planned to do that, but she seemed content to continue, and Derek allowed himself to focus on the music as he and Jacob spitballed. It wasn't until Rae started shaking out her hand and flexing her fingers that he realized how long they'd been at it. He took the pen and notebook back, assessing her work.

"You need a secretary," she grumbled to them both.

"Sorry," Derek and Jacob apologized in unison.

Rae threw up both hands. "Never apologize for having so many great ideas. Taking notes isn't my strong suit."

"You're not wrong. We couldn't sort out lunch. How are we going to arrange auditions by Monday?" Jacob agreed.

"We're grown adults," Derek reasoned, but they were right.

Jacob's face brightened, and his shoulders squared. "Maybe we could get Meyers to loan Grace to us? Rae's right about us needing an admin for this project at least till we get it off the ground and find our own team. Can't have our bass player ruining her grip taking notes."

"Maybe you should seriously consider *hiring* Grace away from Meyers," Rae suggested. "She made an impression on you both."

"She *is* easy to work with, but are you really sure you want to work with a fan?" He looked to Derek.

"Plenty of bands do it," Rae retorted. "Fans are the most loyal employees you'll ever find."

"Whoa!" Jacob held up his hands defensively. "All I meant was that fans aren't usually objective."

"That depends on the fan!" Rae snapped, crossing her arms over her chest.

Derek watched the exchange with trepidation. They had been getting along so famously, but this turn of events didn't look promising. He jumped in before Rae could react further.

"She's our agent's new secretary. Are we sure we want to risk pissing off Meyers?" he posed.

"Oh," Rae replied, arms loosening around her body until she rested her hands at her sides. He watched her face struggle over the very real idea that they couldn't take what they wanted without consequences. She picked up her fork, pushing food around her plate. "I hadn't thought of that."

"Well, let's think about it," Jacob conceded.

"Can't we talk to Meyers and borrow her for a little bit?" Rae pleaded. "The auditions need to be set up, and I can't be notetaker for all these brainstorming sessions. "

Derek recognized the motive couched in her request. He fought not to scowl, thinking she needed to butt out of his personal life.

"I'll give him a call later today and see what I can hash out. At the very least, I'll ask him for a short-term loan till we can get to the recording stages," Jacob promised.

Rae sighed. "Well, I hope he says yes, because how else am I going to meet her?"

"You could always meet with Meyers about taking him on as your agent," Jacob suggested.

She scowled. "No thank you. I don't need an agent. Besides, how much do you get to know about a person when you walk by them to talk to someone else?"

Chuckling, Jacob set down his fork and folded his napkin on the table beside it. "She has a point." He took a long drink of water. "She could be faking all that niceness."

All three nodded, and Derek debated whether to speak up. He was far more concerned about the three of them getting along than their admin needs. Deciding to ask forgiveness from his friend Pete later, he voiced his idea.

"Actually, if you're in town, my buddy Pete and his wife are having a cook-out tomorrow. We could invite Grace and hang out with her there. I'm sure they wouldn't mind three extra people."

"Pete?" Rae gasped. "As in, Peter Day? Will Leo be there, too?"

Derek groaned inwardly. This was exactly why working with fans wasn't an idea he relished. They could be wonderful and competent and in the next moment, gushing like kids and strapping him firmly in the past when all he wanted to do was move forward and be known for something else. He was waiting for Grace to have a similar fallout.

Maybe inviting her to Pete's house wasn't his best plan. He saw the confusion over Jacob's face.

"Who's Leo?" Jacob mouthed.

"Pete and Leo were two of my bandmates from a million years ago. We still hang out sometimes," Derek expounded. He turned to Rae, adding, "And no, Leo's still in the Big Apple. You know I'm never gonna subject him to you!"

"Well, now *I* want to meet Leo," Jacob mocked. "It's been a while since I got to hang out somewhere. It sounds like fun. Count me in."

Derek chuckled. He liked this new partner. He was funny and friendly, and most importantly, he was talented and had the bankroll to do this project right. He had never anticipated having a bigger role in this project than writer/producer.

"In that case, I will send you the details, and I'll copy Rae and Grace so they can meet."

"Yeah, that's a great idea," Jacob encouraged. "It's smart to get to know people before you hop into bed with them."

Derek suddenly pictured pulling Grace into his bed, and his scalp started itching as he tried to tune out the image.

Rae burst out laughing. "That's a *proverbial* bed, Big D," she pointed out, squeezing his arm. "Oh, come on. We're teasing you. You're a big, strong guy. You can take it."

They departed soon after, and Rae took the opportunity to rib him all the way to the car. It was nice to watch the lighthearted way she pranced from foot to foot, skipping along. He held the car door for her when they reached it.

"After you, Sunshine."

Rae thanked him by sticking out her tongue.

~ ♫ ~ GRACE ~ ♫ ~

The feeling of thrashing and thudding to the ground between her coffee table and couch was surprisingly the second feeling Grace noticed as she startled awake. The first was lukewarm soda running down her scalp to her nose, off to one side and toward her ear. She swiped the trickle away, sputtering and gasping as she looked for the item that had started it all. Half under the couch, her phone was lit up and blaring the most annoying ringtone in the world.

Ignoring the pain from where she had body slammed the coffee table, she reached for the offending phone.

"Hello, this is Grace," she answered feeling a half-eaten ravioli squish under her palm as she pressed herself to her knees. She gripped the phone between her shoulder and ear before scraping what she could back onto the plate.

"Grace, it's Jacob," the caller announced. "Not driving I hope?"

She swallowed a yawn and answered, "No. How can I help you?"

He chuckled. "I wanted to thank you for that list of musicians you got for me and for setting up the lunch. Perfect choice. And I wanted to give you a heads up."

"Oh?" she asked, shuffling to the kitchen with dirty dishes in hand.

"Yeah, I met with Derek and his bass player Rae today. And we really are hitting it off. So, Derek invited us to this barbecue thing tomorrow, and we're hoping you can go, too. It's not a work thing—just for fun if you don't have plans."

It was hard to have plans with her schedule, but it was even harder without friends in the area. She had gotten to know some of her coworkers' names, but she felt insulated from them in her office next to the company president. Being new to LA isolated her even further. If left to her own devices, Grace realized she might never make friends. Despite being excited to receive the invitation, she was worried that these super cool people would be disappointed in her company.

She withheld her excitement. "Um, yeah, I could do that," she replied noncommittally. "Have you got the details?"

"That's what I like about you, Grace! Coordinating in your sleep. But I, uh, don't have them. Derek's gonna send you an email with the finer points. That's why I'm calling: to tell you to watch your email."

"That sounds great," she said, wiping her hands on a paper towel in disgust then carrying the roll to the living room. "Thanks for the heads up."

"Sure. I think it's a good idea to have a little fun before all the work gets started."

"Right," Grace replied. It was comical the way he talked about the work not having yet started. She'd already completed her part of the task. In fact, she'd had "a talk" that afternoon about what tasks to be proactive about and which to leave to her boss before he released her for the weekend.

"Cool. Well, see you there I hope."

The call disconnected, and Grace sighed as she set to cleaning up the spilled food and drink. It had been difficult to concentrate on what he was saying with the smell of soda and ravioli clinging to her hair. It was bad enough that Meyers had her cell number. Being on his clients' speed dial was going to turn her hair gray.

Although, none of Meyers' other clients had ever extended a friendly invitation like this before. In fact, most of them treated her like an answering machine—a piece of equipment. Most of them expected her to know everything by osmosis. One had asked her to walk his dog, but Meyers had intervened on her behalf. She wasn't paid to handhold his clients—*he* was, and he wasn't keen on handling his client's day-to-day activities. He was paid to facilitate their careers, not their lives. Or so he had reminded her in their uncomfortable conversation that afternoon.

However, Grace knew that the moment he needed to go out of town again or *his* dog needed walking, she'd be the first person on his list because her job was to revolve around him. She grumbled all the way into the shower, frustration growing.

It wasn't as though she hadn't known what the job was when she took it. What she hadn't realized was that the person making the requests would be quite so condescending. Maybe she was being too sensitive, and she pushed down the aggravation. It was a great job that a thousand other people would mow her down to get. And her lack of connections in the city made it imperative that she plow through this particular irritation. There was no slush fund to dip into if she lost this job. And it was this or work retail or food, neither of which appealed.

Fresh from the shower, head cleared, Grace checked her email. As promised, a message from Derek was waiting for her inviting her to a friendly potluck barbeque, and Grace began mentally rummaging her cabinets to think up a side dish to bring. Maybe it would be fun. She may not be particularly good company, but she could make up for her lackluster social skills with food. She hoped.

THREE

erek paced his apartment, pressing his mobile phone to his ear as it rang. "Hey, man," he greeted the moment his friend answered.

"D! How's it hangin'?" Peter replied.

"Long and strong," he answered, laughing when Peter groaned on the other end.

"TMI!" Peter groused.

"You asked," Derek said with a chuckle.

"What's up, dude? We're kinda in the throes of it over here. You know how Nancy gets before a party."

Derek did, in fact, know how she got, which was why he'd been making excuses to put off the call for half the day. "Yeah, that's kind of why I'm calling. So don't freak out, but I kinda invited a few more people for tomorrow."

He heard his name being grunted. "How many is a few?"

"Three, and I'm not sure that they'll all even come."

"Oh," Peter blew raspberries on the other end. "Three's not a big deal. I was afraid you were gonna say a dozen or something."

"I'm not that kind of jerk," Derek retorted. "Do you need me to grab some burgers or something? Anything? Beer? Soda? I don't wanna get on your wife's bad side." Peter had been married for ten years and with the same woman for longer still, and Derek had only needed one taste of her bad side to not want to be on it.

Peter chuckled. "You know she plans for a small army."

"And she does a good job, and everyone she invites shows…it might *be* a small army."

"So, who's worth risking the wrath of Nance for?" Pete questioned.

"Some people from my new project: Jacob, Rae, and my agent's assistant."

"Not your agent though, right?"

"Right. Just his assistant."

"You're not selling me on this, bro. You don't hang out with people you don't want to—and you certainly don't invite them to my house. What aren't you telling me?"

Derek squeezed his eyes shut. Peter knew him too well. "Well, you're always telling me to bring Rae by some time. What better time than this?"

"Uh-huh. Why bring the client?"

"Jacob?" Derek repeated, playing dumb. "He's wanting to hang out with everyone and make sure we gel. He's already talking about touring, and we haven't recorded a single note yet."

"Okay. And why invite the agent's nameless assistant? Isn't that his way of keeping tabs on you?"

"No. It's in a friendly capacity. Rae's begging to meet her, and Jacob is thinking of hiring her for the admin stuff."

"And she's interested in the assistant why?" Peter pressed.

Derek cringed as he replied, "Oh. She's a fan of ours too."

"I thought Rae was the last," Peter laughed. "Is she safe?"

"Oh, yeah. Had to drag it out of her."

"Does assistant/fan have a name? Or should I call her Agent Assistant the whole time?"

"Grace," he answered, realizing that Pete had also met her eons ago. "You remember that first reunion we did in a past lifetime? The one with like three people?"

"It was five," Peter corrected. "We gave them a ride to their hotel. You had to climb in the cargo space."

Derek had nearly forgotten that. The fuzzy details began filling in around the memory. "Right."

"She was one of them?"

"Yeah. The one with the cool merch that told me what a mess my solo CD was."

Peter's laughter halted the conversation for a few minutes. "You're kidding? And you want to hang out with her?"

"Well, she's nice enough. It's really for Rae and Jacob. I can tolerate it. She's fun to tease," he confessed. "Turns cherry red."

Peter laughed again. "If you say so. Okay, I gotta go. See you tomorrow. Bring extra sodas."

Seeing Grace again wouldn't be the worst thing. Derek wasn't convinced there was much to the over-dressed woman besides her fandom, but he had enjoyed the ego boost she'd given him. Right now, he needed all the confidence he could muster.

They exchanged their goodbyes, and Derek dragged himself out to buy soft drinks and a few chairs for his extra guests. He tried not to be too irritated by the families rushing around him, a few wild children screaming in the distance.

This was the reason he cringed whenever he thought about having a family. The commitments, the errands, the screaming kids, and the chaos. He dreaded having to sacrifice his career for his kids the way his father had. But, if he was honest, he was growing tired of coming home to an empty bed. Or worse, having the awkward conversation where he had to kick someone out or sneak out of their place. It would be nice to have someone to wake up to.

Fortunately, his parents hadn't been hassling him to have children. Peter, on the other hand, was actively encouraging him to find a wife. Part of him guessed it was so that they could double at parties and maybe even vacations.

A family was a fine idea for someone who had a normal life. But Derek didn't see how his sporadic income and all-night recording sessions could be construed as anything close to normal. Somewhere in the back of his head, he always assumed he'd end up with someone. But with his career, that had gotten pushed to the side without him even noticing.

He had an endless stream of women available—everyone in LA wanted a producer for a boyfriend, especially with some of the contacts in his little black book. But the last thing he wanted was to be some woman's step ladder to the top. Having to figure out a new woman every time he needed satisfaction was not only exhausting, but it was also starting to take some of the joy out of an act he otherwise loved. It would be nice to have a partner who could anticipate what he liked without having to give instructions every time.

He wheeled his cart into a long checkout line, leaning over the handle. This barbecue was exactly what he needed to clear his head before his stress reached a fever pitch. And if it inspired Jacob to engage him for a longer project…his feelings wouldn't be hurt.

The following day, Derek was glad he had arrived early. No one was there to see him fumble getting the lawn chairs out of his trunk. Putting them in the car had been easy enough, but now, parked bumper to bumper with the cars around him miraculously only a few houses away from Peter's place, he struggled to wrench the orange webbed frames from their resting place. Finally, he freed the fourth one in time for the three that had been propped against his leg to slide to the ground. Peter arrived on the scene as he wrangled two in each hand.

Derek rolled his eyes as he passed them to his friend. "Five hours a week at the gym, and I can't manage ten pounds of chair. What's that about?"

Peter hid his laughter, slinging all four over one arm. "Gimme a bag of ice before it completely liquifies," he offered.

Without protest, Derek accepted the help, managing to get all four cubes of soda under his arms.

Peter shook his head as he walked back to his place with two ten-pound bags of ice in each hand. "That's what five hours a week at the gym gets you: the ability to carry four cubes of soda like a maniac."

Derek tried to laugh, but nearly lost his concentration and instead focused on not dropping the carbonated can-bombs. The threat of disaster hurried his pace until they reached Peter's gate, and they stared at each other for a moment before Pete's wife appeared and rescued them.

"Stubborn as always, I see," she teased, yanking a case of soda from under each of Derek's arms.

He sighed relief. "Nancy, you are an angel," he murmured.

The postage-stamp of a backyard had been transformed with hanging paper lanterns, tiki torches, and coolers spaced evenly around. A colorful paper tablecloth was fluttering on a long table held down with various covered dishes, plates, and plastic tableware.

She directed them where to unload their burdens and then skittered back up the stairs to the kitchen to continue her mission.

"It looks great, Pete," Derek complimented, shaking out his arms once they were free.

"It's all her. I have no talent for this." He arranged Derek's chairs while Derek dumped ice into empty coolers.

"PETER!" Nancy's voice carried for nearly the whole block.

Derek stumbled in panic, but Pete waved him off.

"She's fine. This is not the *I've-broken-something* cry. I'll be back." Peter trotted toward the back stairs and launched himself up.

Derek busied himself finding tasks he thought needed to be done before sneaking into the shade with a cold beer. Someday, he'd throw a party like this, and someone would be yelling his name like a drill sergeant. And he wouldn't be standing alone sipping a beer to pass the time.

~ 🎵 ~ GRACE ~ 🎵 ~

By the time Grace arrived, she was beginning to regret her decision to join the party. The small grassy area was veritably swarming with strangers, and a cursory glance did not reveal any familiar faces. She did not want to think about walking into an unfamiliar place and having to explain who she was and why she was there. She wasn't entirely sure that she knew how to answer the question.

Laden with one of her favorite summer salads, she had parked three blocks away, grateful to find any parking at all. She looked at the sky, thinking perhaps she should make a point to leave before the sun set so she didn't have to walk back in the dark.

There was no doubt she was in the right place, listening to the music pumping out of the speakers. She let herself in, assessing the situation quickly. No one seemed to notice her weaving around them to the buffet of goodies where she deposited her meager looking addition, pulled away the cling wrap and dipped a serving spoon into the bowl. She was looking for a place to dispose of the wadded-up film when she heard her name called from the direction of the house.

"Grace!"

She recognized Derek's voice easily and fought back the squeal that rose in her throat. This was not the time for silly old fantasies. She cleared her throat and straightened up before turning to see Derek about two feet away and closing. She reached out a hand in greeting.

He shook it strongly, using it to pull her closer. "Glad you could make it. I never saw your reply."

Grace was caught off balance by the warmth of his welcome. He seemed genuinely pleased to see her, though she couldn't guess as to why. She was merely the assistant to his agent. An outed fan.

"To be honest, I hadn't really made up my mind till this morning when I found pineapple on sale," she confessed. She felt her face get hot again at the admission when she realized that it sounded like she was serving expired food, which she hadn't meant at all.

He laughed, peering behind her. "You'll have to point out what you brought so we can all marvel at sale-priced pineapple," he joked. He snatched the ball of cling film from her and tossed it deftly into a nearby trash bin at the end of the buffet.

"Well, it will be the thing with the pineapple in it," she explained, her cheeks heating.

"Duh, Derek," he scolded, tapping the side of his head and rolling his eyes.

Grace's shoulders began to relax until he cupped her elbow with his tingly palm. She had to swallow hard to keep from squeaking as he eased her away from the food and led her to the nearest group of guests.

"Hey, guys, this is Grace."

Everyone waved and smiled but did not stop their conversations for a longer introduction. It seemed Derek didn't think this was unusual as he looked across the yard to another group. He called out as he began moving Grace again.

"Hey, Pete, come meet Grace."

Grace froze at his words. Her brain insisted that Peter was not an uncommon name, and surely Derek knew more than the one from his former band. But when her eyes followed his and landed on Peter Day, the one Peter she had hoped not to see, her chin dropped.

It was as though almost no time had passed since the fan dinner as the pair waved at each other. When she had mapped the address the night before, she didn't realize that Peter would be there. Was this his house? Before panic could finish strangling her, the man in question jogged toward them.

Unaware of her angst, the tall, dark and perfectly coiffed man shook her hand with both of his and beamed at her.

"Grace, I'm Peter. Derek says you're his agent's assistant and a fan. I'm glad to hear someone's got my bro's back." His cheeks dimpled as he spoke.

Grace squeezed his hand gently. "Thank you so much for having me. I hope I'm not imposing."

"Neh, any friend of Derek's is a friend of mine. I'll have to introduce you to my wife. She'll love knowing someone's keeping D in line other than me."

"I look forward to it," she replied, and before the conversation could go further, another voice called Derek's name over the crowd.

"Big D! A little help here!"

Grace followed his gaze to see a diminutive woman at the gate, attempting to open it with an elbow. She was cradling a giant aluminum pan that must be heavy from the way she was teetering. The woman's hair gleamed in the midday sunlight.

Scurrying behind her was Jacob.

"Excuse me," Derek murmured quickly, letting go of her elbow. He jogged away before she could reply.

Grace looked to her remaining companion. "Who's that?" she asked.

"I'm guessing Rae and Jacob from what Derek's told me," Peter replied. "As host, I think I'd better go see if I can help."

She nodded quickly. "Of course. Of course." She blinked, mentally confirming that she was in the backyard of the members of the boyband who changed her young life. Was she dreaming?

"I'll catch up with you later. I want to talk more." With that, Peter dashed off, and Grace watched as he relieved the newcomers of their burden. She sighed happily at the comfortable way that Derek greeted Jacob, as though they'd been friends for a lifetime instead of this being their third meeting. She might be biased, she knew, but something about Derek drew people in. She counted her blessings as she watched the transaction.

Peter hauled the pan to the buffet, towing the new woman behind him by her hand. She was veritably skipping, and Derek and Jacob trailed slowly behind, chuckling over what looked like an inside joke. At this distance, Grace felt safe to stare openly at Derek's tight jeans and his two-toned blue shirt sleeves stretched over his biceps. She had thought he was beautiful as a teen idol, but now, before her in all his masculine glory, she thought she might have to change her opinion about preferring skinny men. Her brain treated her to the mental image of him throwing her over his shoulder and absconding to a remote location. Her hands formed excited fists at her side. If she squealed, she'd have to abandon her favorite serving dish and spoon and ride off into the sunset possibly over a cliff to avoid embarrassment.

For the first time since starting her job, she was grateful to hear the ding of a text message from her phone, and she pulled it out to read.

Working in her off hours was not fun, but it was certainly less embarrassing than having a daydream about one of the other party guests. Her boss was asking her about the status of his dry cleaning and demanding to know if she'd remembered she had to pick it up.

Grace was tapping out an answer to him when her phone disappeared mid-word, and she gasped as she looked up to find Derek with her phone pinched between his fingers.

"Gimme that," he demanded, shutting it off.

She thought he was looking pleased with himself, and she frowned. He was adorable, but it wasn't enough to squash her concerns about the work phone. If it had been anything else he'd snatched, she'd have willingly surrendered. However, Grace grabbed at the device instinctively, worried that if Meyers didn't hear from her soon, there would be another conversation about not answering when he texted, and then she would have to tell him who she was with.

Derek held it barely out of her grasp. "Is there another one?"

"I'm not sure I should tell you," she snapped, looking to Jacob for backup.

Jacob stood beside him, his expression reflecting her apprehension. In an instant, he plucked her phone from Derek's hands and leaned in to hug her lightly. "Grace, so glad you could make it." He beamed.

She felt the weight of her phone dropping discreetly into her purse as he pulled away. "Thank you," she whispered in relief.

Jacob held her at arm's length. "You look lovely." He grinned, waving a hand at her pale purple sundress dotted with tiny white flowers. "Derek, shall we escort this lovely lady over to the grill?" Tucking her arm in his, he led her in the direction of the food.

Grace followed along, glancing over her shoulder to find Derek right on their heels.

As they walked, Jacob spoke quietly to her. "Today is your day off, right? We invited you to have fun; not to work."

Grace replied with a tight smile. "Technically, yes. But when Meyers speaks, I respond," she replied. "Everyone is replaceable."

"You're among friends," Jacob reminded.

Worried about the fallout, Grace shook her head. "Thank you, but don't worry about me. I knew what the job was when I signed up."

Jacob cast a sidelong glance at her. "Well, at least *try* to enjoy the day. I got your back."

"Thank you," she murmured.

Derek was suddenly at her other side with the newcomer right behind him, her hands full of beer bottles.

"Grace, this is Sunshine," Derek introduced.

She inched closer to Jacob momentarily as Sunshine elbowed Derek sharply in the arm.

"The name's Rae," the woman corrected, meeting Grace's eyes as she passed out beers.

Grace smirked between Derek and Rae. "I see what you did there. Ray of sunshine."

Rae bit her lip, and Grace felt suddenly as if she'd said something she shouldn't have. She pulled the beer to her chest, ostensibly to keep it close. In truth, it gave her a way to hide.

"Cool to meet someone else who remembers this one from back in the day." She patted Derek's arm and cozied up to her. "We're thin on the ground anymore."

Grace shook the proffered hand as she disengaged from her safe zone with Jacob. "Nice to meet you, too." She stared at the beer in her hands, wondering how long she could hold it without drinking before anyone noticed.

Rae beamed. "I hear you're responsible for introducing these two?" She gestured between Derek and Jacob.

"Nah, I just paid for lunch." Grace shrugged. "My boss gets the credit for hooking them up."

Rae hummed, stretching up on her toes. Her arms twined above her head, her shirt rising up and threatening to expose her belly. She froze, exhaling and suddenly dropped her arms to her sides. She swirled to face Grace with a devilish grin.

"Miss Grace, we are being summoned! Let's go!" Without waiting for a reply, she hooked her arm through Grace's and dragged her away.

Grace followed Rae's gaze and spied Peter laughing as he watched their jogging approach.

"Hey, I'm in a dress here," she groused and did her best not to stumble as she and Rae came to a stop in front of Peter.

"So, Derek tells me you're both fans. Is that true?" Peter asked, smiling down at them both. He folded his hands in front of himself like a carnie about to sell them tickets to an exclusive show.

"Well, yeah," Rae answered. "Saturday mornings were never the same after you. At least for me. I can't speak for Grace."

Peter beamed at them both. "Grace?"

She felt herself go hot from head to toe at the direct address. She squeezed her arms around herself. "I wasn't supposed to be a fan, but I caught the pilot by accident," she added. "I was home sick from my piano lessons, and I never looked back. Recorded them all…watched them on repeat till my whole family was sick of them."

Peter's face was like a star beaming across the neighborhood. "I love that!" he exclaimed.

"I have so many questions," Rae gushed, dancing in place like an excited kid.

He waggled his brows. "Okay. Consider me your guru for the day." Peter escorted them through the buffet and found a quiet, shaded space where he regaled them with stories while they ate.

Grace focused on not spilling her plate all down her knees and let Rae take the lead, raining down questions on Peter about the good old days.

She was a little jealous of the way the other woman attacked her plate of barbecue without any apparent concern over anyone watching her. She had good questions, pulling plenty of funny stories about the show and their touring days out of their host.

"I heard you were a fan, Grace," Peter egged. "You've been awfully quiet."

Her eyes snapped up, hearing her name. She had been perfectly happy listening to the stories. She clutched her bottle and willed herself not to say anything too stupid. "Oh, I am. I freely admit it. It's that I can't think of any burning questions that wouldn't be wildly inappropriate."

Peter barked out a laugh then smirked wickedly and met her eyes. "Boxer-briefs. No, he does not shave his chest. And, yes, he's single and very straight."

Grace dropped her fork into the grass and barely kept her napkin between her fingers as Rae belly laughed, first grabbing Grace's arm, then reaching for Peter's.

"I adore you," Rae cackled.

The laughter was infectious, and Peter joined her. "He's really like my little brother, you know? I want to see him happy. It's weird. I remember running into him at auditions. I did not think I was going to make it when I saw the competition. But we really clicked the first day, and here we are all these years later. We got pretty lucky. It's rare to find that sort of friendship in this town."

"Or anywhere," Rae added. "It looks like you got double lucky between Derek and Nancy."

Peter beamed. "D introduced us. He met her when he was a waiter over at Planet Hollywood."

Grace arched an eyebrow, wondering how Derek had gone from teen idol to waiter and now producer extraordinaire. Her stomach rolled, realizing the importance of this collaboration for him.

"I guess the universe isn't always out to destroy us," Rae offered.

"It's a roller coaster," Peter agreed. "It's sure easier to hang on when you've got someone in the car with you."

Grace felt her phone buzz and glanced at it. Junk mail. She returned to the conversation.

Rae shook her head. "Are you always on?" she asked Grace.

Grace shrugged. "It pays the bills. And I don't always have to be in an office at eight."

"Sounds like pretty steady work," Peter complimented. "That's hard to find around here."

The conversation steered into more mundane small talk before Peter's wife called him away for a bag of ice.

Grace looked around the party, in a little bit of shock at her present situation. "Should we find the guys?" she asked her new companion.

Rae scanned the back yard, until her finger jutted in the direction of a pair of chairs under a tree where Derek and Jacob were hunched over plates on their knees. They appeared to be pulling food off each other's plates like teenage boys and laughing.

"What on earth are they doing?" Grace whispered.

Rae giggled, staring. "Look, Jacob's taking all my cobbler."

Grace watched as Derek stole what looked distinctly like her Jell-O salad from Jacob's plate. Although, at this distance, she might be kidding herself. For a moment, she didn't know whether to be offended that Jacob didn't like her salad or pleased that Derek did. The competitive side of her was frustrated, but she took one look at the other woman's face and was happy for her.

"Good for you." Grace gave her a confident nod.

Enjoying the stolen moment they witnessed, the pair ambled toward them. Grace was in the middle of thinking up ways to ask him about the sale-priced pineapple when Rae derailed her thoughts.

"He thinks you're cute, you know," the shorter woman whispered.

"What?" Grace blinked, taking a step backward. She wasn't at all buzzed, not nearly drunk enough to be discussing men thinking she was cute. And which he did she mean anyway? Jacob or Derek? She needed a lot more alcohol to contemplate either.

Rae steered her to the makeshift bar Peter's wife was manning, laughing as she passed out beers and waved bottles of liquor enticingly at her guests.

"May I, Mrs. Day?" Rae asked. "Miss Grace needs something stronger than beer."

Two pairs of eyes assessed Grace, and she closed her arms over her waist defensively.

"You're the pro, sayeth D." Nancy set down her bottles and

stepped away. "Give me a yell when you want out."

Rae gave her a thumbs up. "So, you're an assistant to a talent manager," she murmured to Grace, smiling as she started mixing a fruity drink. "What's that like?"

The question felt completely out of the blue, but she welcomed the otherwise impending tailspin thinking that one of her boss's clients thought she was cute.

"Exhausting, but occasionally cool," Grace replied, gesturing to their current location.

Rae began picking bottles and mixing drinks as though it was breathing. She was passing them to random guests. Rae set down a solo cup and a shot, pushing it in front of her.

"What is it?" One of her eyebrows lodged firmly in her hairline.

Rae tapped first the solo cup and then the shot. "Daquiri and a vanilla Stoli. And from the look on your face, you could use it. Trust me. Drink up." Rae patted the impromptu bar top for emphasis.

After a moment, Grace took a deep breath, braced herself, and knocked the shot back. The initial vanilla flavor was welcome, but when she swallowed, the burn began. Her whole body shivered as she grimaced and gasped for breath. "Oh, that was strong!"

Rae chuckled, taking the shot glass back and tapping the solo cup. "You're not done yet."

Grace sipped the drink and hummed in delight, savoring the mouthful. Fruity goodness flooded her senses, extinguishing the fire in her belly. She took another quick sip then eyed the woman who was already mixing another drink.

"You're good at this," Grace complimented. "It's like watching *Cocktail*."

Rae chuckled. "I do work at a bar, you know. This bass thing is a hobby."

"Do Derek and Jacob know that?" Grace wondered aloud.

The other woman shrugged. "I don't know. Derek should." She was lining up cups on the bar and pouring drinks from a shaker rapid fire.

"How did you end up a bartender and a bassist?" Grace asked.

She listened to Rae's condensed version of her move to LA and her divorce as she made drinks for other guests as they wandered up. It sounded horrible, and not for the first time, Grace wondered if she was lucky never to have been married. Rae's cheating husband baggage sounded incredibly heavy.

"So, he traded me out for a fancier model, and I have no idea what he's up to now," she concluded. "I'm glad he's gone."

Behind the other woman, Jacob and Derek approached Grace schooled her features.

"He sounds like an idiot," Jacob murmured, stopping behind her.

"Well, he thought he was marrying a future rock star," Rae shrugged.

"Ah but you *are* gonna be a rock star!" Derek laughed, throwing an arm around her and squeezing her shoulder. "And *then* he'll be sorry!"

Grace's stomach churned as she listened to their banter and followed their familiar touches. She had her answer: Rae must have been talking about Jacob earlier because Derek was all over Rae. She wished she were anywhere else as she saw the man in question hedging closer to the group. She was flattered that someone as attractive as Jacob found her cute, but he didn't give her the fluttery feeling Derek did. She forced a smile on her face as her brain spun out of control, piecing together the information she'd gleaned.

Hadn't Peter said Derek was single? Right after he'd told her what sort of underwear the man wore. Did Peter not know about Rae? Was that why Derek had invited Rae? To meet his best friend?

Her thoughts were interrupted as Jacob jumped into the conversation, laughing as Rae stuck out her tongue and pushed Derek away.

"You two are worse than my sister's kids," he commented.

Derek snickered, leaning childishly toward Rae, his words coming out in a sing-song voice. "Jacob wants to whisk you away to make him cobbler forever." Edging around the bar, he draped an arm around Grace's neck and stage-whispered into her ear. "I don't think we should let him, do you?"

It took every ounce of poise in Grace's body not to shiver as she felt Derek's breath hot against her neck. She could smell him for a moment, like soap and barbecue sauce assaulting her all at once. She controlled her breathing but couldn't help her eyes slamming shut. She had no idea how to answer.

She was saved as Rae drawled, "There will be no whisking."

"Hey! How long have you been behind this bar?" Nancy asked, shooing her away. "Go, mingle!"

Rae scooted out from behind the bar, Jacob right behind her. They found a shady spot with four chairs and hid there, sipping their cold drinks.

Grace was grateful for the reprieve. Her cheeks were burning from the shot Rae had insisted she take, and she sipped her remaining drink slowly. She did have to drive home, after all.

Derek, Jacob, and Rae started discussing the newest music they'd heard and which songs they liked best. Before long, Derek pulled out his iPod to play snippets of songs, and Jacob produced his iPhone, and it became a battle of the clips, each one trying to outdo the other.

Grace grinned at the joy on their faces. She glanced at Rae, assessing her as the guys talked. Rae was nodding furtively and occasionally interjecting. Grace relaxed, slipping into her usual silence. She could listen to Derek talk about music—or anything—forever.

The sun lowered in the sky as they talked, blinding them for a while, before the sky faded to crimson. Acutely aware of the walk back to her car, Grace was starting to feel restless, and she began plotting a way to excuse herself.

Before she had finished scheming, the music and conversation ceded to the distinct clinking of silverware on a glass. Everyone looked around for the source and found Peter standing precariously on a cooler that was a little less than level. Nancy turned down the music and joined him.

"Get down from there before you break more than a bottle," she teased.

When everyone laughed, Peter hopped down and raised his bottle to everyone. "I wanted to thank everyone for coming. I know some of you have other obligations, but while we're all gathered, I…well, Nancy and I…wanted to share some news."

"And I got tired of everyone trying to push a beer on me," Nancy added.

The guests chuckled again, but Grace gasped. Peter Day was going to have a baby! She knew it instinctively and leaned forward in her chair.

Peter wrapped an arm around his wife's waist and pulled her gently to his side. "Which will remain off limits for at least eight months."

Everyone cheered, and there was a rush of guests around the couple, hugging them both and freeing Nancy from Peter to gaze at her belly. She waved them off, but her downcast grin belied her annoyance.

Grace squirmed uncomfortably, watching as Derek launched out of his chair toward the couple. He nearly knocked Pete down to wrap him in a brotherly bear hug.

Seeing her opportunity, Grace picked her way to the buffet to collect her dish while the crowd was distracted. Amazingly, her bowl was empty, and she wiped it free of any remaining debris with a handful of paper towels. She contemplated making a run for it without a word, but after the hospitality that Pete and the others had shown her, she couldn't be that rude, despite her desire to run for the hills. Bowl tucked against her hip, she made her way to the shady spot where Rae and Jacob remained.

"I've had a really great time. I don't remember the last barbecue I went to." She smiled at the pair then glanced over her shoulder to where Derek was still enmeshed in the congratulatory throng. "It's getting dark, and I should get going," Grace murmured. "I wanna get to my car before dark. You know how it is in LA."

If she was honest, there was also a growing pit gnawing at her stomach at how long it had been since she'd looked at her work phone. Meyers might have sent her twelve emails, despite not hearing the special ding or feeling the vibration it made whenever he did.

"Oh!" Rae exclaimed, hopping up, face flushed. "Would you mind giving me a ride? I'm sure Derek'll wanna stay, and Mr. Hunter's driving kinda scares me."

"Hey!" Jacob pouted. "I'm an excellent driver!"

"For the Indy 500," Rae jeered, poking him in the shoulder. She turned to Grace. "Please? I'll gladly give you gas money."

Flustered, Grace tried not to stammer. "Oh, well. I don't need gas money," she eschewed. She pulled her phone free. "Let me get the address typed in, I guess. What part of town are you in?" Every word that came out of her mouth felt awkward, and she stopped herself before more could follow.

Today felt completely upside down. This morning, she had been bemoaning her lack of a social life, and now she was giving rides to her crush's girlfriend as if they were old buddies. She hoped Rae didn't live far out of her way.

Jacob popped up from his chair as well. "Oh, I'm not letting you ladies walk to the car alone. It's LA," he added. He gestured to Derek. "D! I'm walking them to the car. They're leaving."

Derek looked startled. He held up a finger to his friend then trotted over to join them. "It's so early," he cajoled. "Are we boring you with the music talk? I promise we can stop."

Grace couldn't believe herself as she replied. "No, you can't. And honestly, that's not it. I have things I have to get done before getting to the office tomorrow, and I don't really like to drive around here in the dark when I don't really know where I am." The words were out now, and she groaned inwardly.

"On a Sunday?" Jacob and Rae balked in unison.

"It's quiet. I get more done," Grace explained.

"I'll walk with you," Derek answered. The four made their way to Grace's car, waving and exchanging pleasantries. This was the second time Derek had escorted her to the car, Grace realized, and she quite liked it.

It was a quick exchange, unlike the first time, and Grace fought the urge to sigh dreamily as she slipped into the driver's seat. She kept one eye on the men as she negotiated the car into traffic.

"Here's the deal," Rae bubbled, facing her, "not only does Derek think you're cute, he and Jacob need a manager for this project in the *worst* way. What would it take to woo you away from your current job? Salary, perks, staff, whatever. If we leave it up to them, it will take forever."

Grace didn't know what to say, so she kept her mouth shut. Who the hell *was* this woman? She was like a tornado, whirling in and scattering everything about. There was so much to unpack in her hastily worded statement.

"Did they put you up to this?" Grace questioned, eyes focused on staying in her lane.

"No. Of course not," she scoffed. "But I've been planting a seed. I'm gauging your interest, so I know how to water it. At lunch Friday, I had to sit there taking notes, and they couldn't stay on topic."

"What makes you think I'm good at herding cats?" Grace wanted to ask what made the other woman think she liked taking notes either, but she refrained.

"You're just—calm. But you're on top of it. I've never seen anyone manage two phones the way you did all day."

Grace took a deep breath. "I'm not in the job market," she explained. "I'm sure they can find someone with more experience. I'm a dime a dozen in this city."

Rae arched a brow. "You're telling me if they offered you a permanent job, you'd say no?"

She hadn't expected the question, and her mouth froze in the open position, but no answer escaped.

The other woman giggled. "You'd say yes. How could you not? This barbecue today was so surreal sitting at Peter Day's house with Derek. When you throw in Jacob, I keep pinching myself thinking this couldn't possibly be real. Except, who would ever cross fandoms like this? Only in Hollywood, right?"

Grace nodded, her mind drifting briefly to imagine working with Derek every day. Of hearing all the outtakes and bloopers. Getting the true "fly on the wall" view she'd always dreamed of as a fan. She wondered what it would be like to know him up close. Her brain went down a million rabbit holes at once. Rae had no right to plant this seed in *her* brain, she thought. It was downright cruel.

As she recounted the day, her heart stung as she recalled the obvious flirting between Rae and Derek. Her thoughts twisted up, recalling the words Rae had uttered minutes ago that *Derek* was the one who thought she was cute. How would she even know that? There was a comfort level between them that hinted at having spent at least a few naked nights together.

She wanted to be wrong. She recalled the way Rae had looked at Jacob, like he was the lone glass of water in the Sahara. Not once in a while, but every time she looked at him. Whatever had transpired between Rae and Derek was either open or over.

She realized Rae was still talking, and she hoped she hadn't missed anything critical.

"I hope they hire you," Rae murmured when they stopped, idling in front of the apartment complex. "And I hope we can be friends. Derek has all my contact info."

"Okay," Grace replied.

"Think about what I said. About working for them. I'm going to check up on you in about a week."

"It's a plan," Grace accepted.

As she drove away, she considered the prospect and thought she had already given it too much credence. Until Jacob or Derek made the offer, she still worked for Meyers. Now, she had to dream up something to forestall the conversation with Rae. She had a week. She was sure she could conjure up something.

~ ♫ ~ DEREK ~ ♫ ~

As the party died down, Peter pulled Derek into the living room. "Can we talk for a minute?"

Derek rolled his eyes and smirked. "Yes, *DAD*?" he razzed, easing onto their small couch.

Peter puffed out his chest and grinned widely before taking the seat across from him on the sofa. "That's me, feel free to wear it out!" he laughed. "On a more serious note, I want to talk about your new friends."

"What's to talk about?" Derek blinked, frowning and picking at the tab on the can in his hand. "I've known Rae for a couple years, and you both have been bugging me to meet each other. Jacob is my new partner in crime, and Grace is—"

"Your agent's assistant," Peter cut in. "Why invite her? Look, I like her; she's very sweet. Maybe a little sheltered, but a nice girl for all that."

He had been asking himself this same question for most of the afternoon. She had been so kind at the lunch with Jacob, and she made the perfect bridge between them. Any time he worried he wasn't good enough, one look at her bolstered his confidence. Her quiet presence reminded him that he *had* been someone, and as far as she was concerned, he still was.

He avoided eye contact as he answered. "She's...I dunno," Derek winged. "She was so good at selling me to Jacob. I could see how new she was, and I figured she needed to meet some LA people to acclimatize. She's...she—"

"Oh my God, you like her!" Peter crowed.

Derek drew back, brows furrowed. "She's *so* not my type," he grumbled. "I mean, she's way too...neat and tidy and sweet. I'd break the poor girl! And she's a fan! I mean, come on, bro!"

"Oh wow, wow, wow, you are *bit*," Peter badgered. "If it weren't so funny, I'd be worried."

First Rae and now his own best friend? They were practically brothers, and while he appreciated having a groupie around again to stroke his ego, it didn't equate to being smitten. Had Pete not seen the hot chicks he could pull with a lot more self-confidence than this mouse?

"I don't—" he protested feeling a hand on his shoulder and seeing

Nancy joining them.

"Oh, stuff it, D," Nancy interrupted, sitting in her husband's lap. "Nobody's buying it except her and you."

"But I—" Derek tried again. He wasn't enjoying their dual-pronged attack.

"But you what?" Peter asked wryly. "You don't like beautiful women? You don't like smart women?"

"Man, you guys are worse than Rae," Derek grumbled. "Look, of course she's beautiful and smart. She's just...too buttoned up for me. I need someone who knows how to have fun. Relax. You know...live for something other than the job."

He thought of how many times Grace had checked her phone during the party. He'd assumed she might network a little. But she had been glued to their sides. She'd barely said two dozen words! Even as the criticism occurred to him, he recognized how unfair it was. It was hard to get into a conversation between two music buffs. Even Rae had struggled, he recalled.

"Dude, how do you know she doesn't?" Peter pointed out. "You made a snap decision based on how she dressed and how dedicated she is to her job. Because you're so free spirited when it comes to work."

Derek recognized his friend's tone and shook his head. "Even if...and that's a big if...even if you're right, she works for my *agent*. She has to report to the man in charge of getting me gigs. We hook up, and anything goes wrong: I'm hung out to dry." Derek held up his hand in protest. "No. Besides, remember how we promised never to hook up with fans?"

"Okay, I give," Peter sighed. "For the record, though? I like her for you. Not Rae."

Derek groaned. "Oh, gross. She's like my little sister, man."

"You actually *have* a little sister," Pete pointed out.

"Same thing. Rae's..." The mention of a relationship with her was akin to hugging a cactus. "No."

"Good," Nancy praised. "Because that girl is all over your singer.

You'd be disappointed."

"I'd probably kill her. We do not get along that way," he grumbled. Rae was his wing man when they went to bars. She'd helped him bag a fair number of phone numbers since they'd started drinking together.

Nancy tapped her fingers on Peter's shoulder as she leaned toward Derek. "Remember that *Jacob* reached out to *you*. Don't be a 'yes' man to him. He needs your guidance. Mentor him."

"I knew I loved you for a reason." Peter grinned, kissing her neck. "You're going to be the best mamma!"

Derek warmed at them tangled together in a single chair. They were good to and for each other. He wanted that, too. Some balance in his life—a real partner to fly with him inside the eye of the hurricane. But it wasn't Grace. He hadn't met his perfect mate yet, and he had other things to do besides worry over it.

Maybe he never would meet that perfect woman. He hadn't exactly been known for his success in life. Who would want to be with a man whose backup plan was waiting tables? He might be pretty, but he could only count on that for a few more years. The music was enough, he told himself. It had to be.

The weight of their conversation had drained his energy.

"It's late," he announced. "I'm too tired for this. When I find the right woman, you'll be the first to know."

Nancy smiled knowingly. "They're all welcome back here at any time. Any guests of yours that bring food to a party last minute and help serve are my people."

Derek laughed, congratulated them both once more, and then headed home. He had barely made it half-way when Jacob called to invite him to work on their new project at his home studio. Eager to distract himself from analyzing his conversation with Peter, he jumped at the chance and sped toward his client's house.

When the text dinged on her work phone that night, Grace was pulling her covers up in bed. Between socializing at the barbecue and driving Rae home, she was exhausted. It was after ten, and she fought the urge to grumble as she reached for the cell. As expected, the message was from Meyers.

Meyers
Report to Hunter tomorrow. He has the address. Says you are sending paperwork. Looking for it tomorrow. Call in the morning.

Grace froze, re-reading the message twice. Part of her wanted to jump for joy. The rest of her was terrified at what had happened. In shock, she nearly forgot to reply. Her fingers fired rapidly over the digital keyboard.

Grace
Yes, sir. Will call first thing in the morning.

She watched the phone for ten minutes before convincing herself no reply was coming. Sleep evaded her for nearly an hour as her brain fretted over what she had done to be sent away so summarily. Was it a good thing? Was he mad at her? He'd never sent her to work with a client directly before. How had Jacob managed this feat?

Then she stewed over how the call with Meyers would go in the morning. His moods were so difficult to anticipate in the mornings, never knowing if he'd had a good night's sleep or what fire he'd been putting out the night before.

After setting a reminder to call him and another to call Jacob for details, she forced herself into sleeping…if her stress-dream induced tossing and turning could be called sleep. Half the sheets, including the fitted one, were in a wad attempting to wrest itself to the floor when she gave up on the endeavor around four in the morning.

She stirred up a dark chocolate milk for herself as a consolation prize before booting up her work laptop. She began searching for generic contract blanks that fit the scenario, adding the standard clauses for writers, producers, and musicians. Putting together contracts was one of her least favorite jobs. She always had a sense of dread that she was leaving out something or else putting too much in. She was sending the compilation to the legal department for confirmation when her cell rang. She glanced at the microwave clock. 6:07 a.m. She recognized the number and answered immediately.

"Good morning," she greeted.

"I have a busy schedule today and couldn't wait around for your call," came Meyers' gruff voice.

"Yes, sir," she acknowledged. "I've sent a contract over to legal for review. As soon as—"

"Good," Meyers cut her off. "Get them both to sign today and get that back to me. Send me a report this afternoon with all your billable time. Hunter says he needs you for a week while he's in town recording."

"Oh," Grace kept her voice neutral. When Rae had suggested that the guys might need her, she had never considered it would come to pass. A week in an alternate location sounded like a vacation.

"Listen Grace, I'm going to allow this, but you're my assistant first. I don't know what you said to give them the impression that I would be okay with this, but I would appreciate it if you would refrain from making yourself available in the future. I hired you because *I* need your assistance. I'm glad you're so nice to everyone, but I need you to keep a distance between you and my clients."

"Yes, sir, of course," Grace answered. "Honestly, I said nothing, I swear."

Meyers seemed to mull over her answer. "Well, I'll chalk it up to pop stars being demanding. I told him you'd help him for a week however he needs. Take the laptop and the cell. I've put some things on the calendar for you as well. And don't forget the cell, I'll need to know I can reach you."

She wondered if he realized he'd repeated himself. "Yes, sir," she answered.

"And don't forget the report. I'll have accounting invoice him for your time."

She swallowed uncomfortably. "Will do."

"Good. Talk later. Check the calendar."

"Yes, sir." The phone had already gone dead before she'd finished speaking. She stared at the phone, dismissing the 7 a.m. reminder to call her boss. Grace grimaced at her milk. It was no longer a treat, ruined by the call. It was pre-sunrise, and she had already pieced together a contract, and Meyers had acted as though she hadn't done anything. Not a hint that he noticed her early hours. In fact, she thought he sounded a little disappointed not to be able to lecture her for her laziness any further.

She focused her attention on the new to-do list he had put into her calendar. By the time Grace's phone alerted her to contact Jacob for location details, she had already made several online dinner and lunch reservations, an appointment to take Meyers' dog to the groomer, and was collecting his dry cleaning.

She sent Jacob a quick text, asking for an address, then hopped out and paid the meter before stepping inside. The older lady behind the counter scowled at her.

"No more mustard," she scolded as she set the first load of clothes on the counter to wrap a rubber band around the hangers.

"Yes, ma'am," Grace smiled. "I'll tell him."

The woman reached for the basket that went with the order. "Ticket," she demanded.

They went through this routine every Monday. Grace produced the tiny claim ticket and held it aloft between her fingers.

The woman grunted, snatching it to compare to the stub on the order. She turned to the register and rang it all up. Grace handed over the company credit card then lugged the lot out to her car. At least she'd remembered to wear her low-heeled shoes on laundry day.

She checked her phone for Jacob's reply, but nothing had come. In fact, it showed that he hadn't even read the message yet. Frowning, she pointed her car in the direction of the agency. She could check the records there for an alternate phone number and also drop off Meyers' clean clothes.

Grace spotted her boss' car in his reserved spot—crooked and occupying the one to its left as well. She pulled herself up to her full height and straightened her jacket before buttoning it. At least she wouldn't have to lug his laundry up to the third floor. She hurried up to the office, working on her most neutral smile. When she rounded the corner of her desk, she heard Meyers in his office.

"Grace?" he called. The word sounded like a curse on his lips.

"Yes, sir?" she replied, setting down her purse. When he didn't respond, she entered his office. "Good morning."

"I thought I was clear that you were supposed to be with Hunter today." He looked up briefly from the paperwork on his desk.

"I am, but he hasn't responded with his address yet. So, I picked up your laundry. If I could get your keys, I'll transfer it to your car."

He lifted half of himself off his seat. He fished for his keys in his back pocket before tossing them to her. "Call Hunter. Don't wait on him."

"Yes, sir," she replied, feet already carrying her to the door.

"And Grace—I've got that meeting today at ten. I don't want laundry inside the car."

"Yes, sir. I was going to put it in the trunk," she replied.

He waved her off with a gesture that she had learned meant she was giving too much detail.

She swallowed, silently fuming with a tirade about what he would do without her. She wanted to drive off without transferring the clothes and without returning his keys. Maybe never come back. This thought comforted her until she realized her clearance-priced, outlet-mall Kate Spade handbag was still on her desk, along with her driver's license and credit cards.

She shook her head and set herself to the task at hand. Once finished, she hurried back upstairs, setting the keys lightly in his inbox.

"Call Hunter yet?"

"No sir, that's next. Just finished with the dry cleaning."

She didn't wait for his acknowledgement, excusing herself from his presence and going to her desk. She dialed Jacob's number, cringing on the third ring. She was mentally preparing to leave a message when a groggy voice answered.

"Mr. Hunter," Grace greeted. "I hope I'm not calling too early."

"A little, but it's my fault for working so late. What time is it?"

"About 9:30."

"Wow, okay, what's up?"

"Well, Mr. Meyers said you requested my services for the week. I wasn't sure where to meet you."

"Right, right," Jacob yawned loudly, then gave her an address.

"Perfect. Is it okay if I head over?"

"Oh, sure."

"Shall I bring breakfast?"

"Ooh, yeah, coffee would be magical. You're an angel!"

"How do you take it?"

"Three sugars and about half cream." He laughed. "I think Derek takes his black. He'll be here at some point."

"Perfect, I'll see you soon," she promised.

"Well, not like ASAP. Take the scenic route so I can be ready when you get here." They hung up moments later, and Grace started mapping the address into her cell phone.

Meyers interrupted, calling her back into his office and told her to shut the door. She blinked, screwing up her courage and heading his way. She waited for the door to click shut before she spoke.

"Yes, sir?"

"The contracts you sent over this morning are all wrong. You left out the new language we added last week to protect the firm."

"Oh." Her words about not being aware of the change died on her lips, as well as the growing concern about why he was reviewing them in the first place.

"I asked Casey to correct them and send them to you. Just print them and don't make any changes."

"Yes, sir." She took a seat in front of his desk, sensing that there was more to come.

He looked at her fully now. "How is it that Joe Andrews made the audition list you gave to Hunter?"

She held her breath, trying to look natural as she realized why he was asking. When she had started looking for guitarists and drummers on his client list, she recognized the name. He had filled in with Rebel Gloss, one of her favorite bands, for about four years. He was an excellent drummer, and he might fit well with whatever Jacob and Derek were planning.

"You gave me four names, and Mr. Hunter had asked for five. Since we'd talked about Mr. Andrews, I assumed he was the fifth."

Meyers shook his head. "It's unfortunate that you misunderstood. Next time, ask me. I don't want surprises. You know that."

She nodded. "Yes, sir, I'll do that."

"And what's this I hear about you hanging out with two of my clients over the weekend? Didn't we talk about that after the incident with Friday's lunch?"

She gulped. LA was a smaller town than she thought. Who would have told him about the barbecue?

"Well, it wasn't business," she began. "My friend Rae invited me." As the lie escaped her lips, she instantly regretted it but doubled down anyway. "She knows Derek from the studio where he records. It was coincidence."

Meyers digested the answer. "Try not to let the lines get blurry."

"Absolutely not," she agreed.

"I don't want you to get confused about who the agent is. As my PA, you are deeply woven into my life. You'll need to show better discretion. Be more careful in the future."

"Yes, sir."

Sensing she was dismissed, she rose. "I made an appointment for Oscar at 4:00 today. I'll be by around 3:30 to get him and bring him back when he's finished." She hoped the appointment for his dog's grooming would placate him, but he had already turned back to his paperwork.

"Great," he replied. "Don't forget to put it in my calendar with the receipt."

"Yes, sir," she replied. The appointment had been on his calendar since 7 a.m., but she let it go. It was his way of feeling in control of his own life, and in part, hers. She printed out the contracts and breezed out the door. At least she wouldn't have to see him again for a week. It very nearly warded off her tears of frustration as she climbed into her car and peeled out of the garage.

Upon arriving at what she now realized was Jacob's home, Grace searched for a doorbell. At first glance, his home was modest and unassuming. Its façade was highlighted with stone facing, enormous glass skylights surrounding the front door, and no obvious doorbell. She sucked in a deep breath and shifted the weight of the breakfast food, coffees, and her work gear to one side to grasp the understated knocker.

The door opened several minutes later to reveal Jacob sporting a thin white vee neck T-shirt and sleep pants hanging askew around his hips. He was mid-scratch across his chest as he looked back at her without a word. His smile was sleepy but friendly as he shuffled backward, pulling the door wider to grant her access.

Grace stepped delicately over the threshold, laden with gear. The entryway was a shiny white tile leading to a mid-toned hardwood floor that stretched across the entire front room, dining room, and through the kitchen where she glimpsed a pair of sliding glass doors leading to the back yard. The home that had appeared so modest from the outside now revealed its understated wealth unabashedly. She wondered how much a designer had charged him to set everything so perfectly from his mid-century couches to the enormous art deco chandelier. Her shoulders and hands ached from her balancing act, and she proceeded inside.

"We can set up in the kitchen," Jacob directed.

"Thanks," she replied, navigating through the open concept floor plan to the kitchen island. She set a giant striped catering bag on the table next to the pair of fancy coffees in their trademark carrier. The moment her hands were free, she felt the shift as the bags slung over each arm fell to her elbows. The motion had surprised her, but she eased both to the floor soundlessly.

She twirled to face him as she began opening the breakfast bag and laying out its contents.

"I had them label your cups," she prattled as she worked. "I'll put Derek's in the microwave so it will stay warm. I brought warm and cold food since I wasn't sure what you'd like. If you point me to where the plates and silverware live, I'll lay it all out."

Jacob blinked, hands still resting on the doorknob at the front door. "You're like the Energizer Bunny," he accused, his voice thick with sleep. He pointed to a drawer and the cabinet above it indicating the location of the requested items. "Did you drink more than one espresso on the way here?"

She grimaced. "No. I hate coffee. I'm a morning person."

He frowned as he made his way toward the caffeine. "Inhuman. I restate my case for Energizer Bunny," he replied, greedily reaching for the cup with a giant J on the side.

"So, what can I do for you?" She expected he would be slow and began unloading her laptop at the opposite end of the island where a convenient outlet and stool were located.

"Um," he replied. "Well, I haven't really gotten that far. I doubt Derek's awake after the all-nighter we pulled. But—I haven't checked my texts yet."

Grace's mouth twitched, but she continued smiling. "Okay. Well, I'll handle a few business items until you need me."

"I'll be back," he called to her as he padded out of the room.

When he returned, his sleep pants were pulled up, the tie knotted neatly at his waist. He seemed slightly more conscious as he bellied up to the breakfast bar, picking up a plate to fill.

"D's on his way," he announced. His hand hovered back and forth over several items before he rested it on the counter. "So, I didn't realize when I asked Meyers yesterday morning if I could borrow you for the week that he was going to send you over first thing," Jacob began, taking another sip of coffee. "Derek and I lost all track of time last night, and we were working 'til like after four."

Her head snapped up. Why hadn't she thought to ask him what time he'd want her to arrive? She knew why—Meyers had nearly thrown her out of the office.

"I had no idea. I'm so sorry," she apologized.

He waved her off. "No, no. You're here, and you are the hero of the day with the coffee run alone. And actually, I think we probably ought to get those contracts together before we do too much more work. It's never cool to get dicey about terms after the work's already done."

"That's smart," she agreed. "It so happens I printed the finalized documents from legal at the office this morning." She reached for the laptop bag and drew out a long folder with three thick stacks of paperwork and a pair of pens. "Meyers has reviewed these and approved them for signature, so whenever Mr. Reed arrives, we can get this show on the road."

"Excellent." Jacob picked up the top copy, eyes roaming through briefly. "Any chance you have an electronic version I could send to my lawyer first?"

She nodded. "Since I'll be here for the week, I'd like to create a contact sheet for all of us. I might set up some distribution lists too to keep us all in touch."

"Oh, hadn't thought of that. Great."

Grace felt her face relax at the genuine look of appreciation. It was nice to feel like she was contributing and not playing go-fer. "And I was wondering what you had in mind for me to assist with this week."

"Well, I figured we'd have a lot of logistics to coordinate, and you make it look so easy I figured you'd be the best person for the job. Auditions, contracts, lunches, and some scheduling. I was hoping you would schedule the auditions with the musicians that Meyers suggested. Once we find the band, we'll need more contracts, but I can get my legal people on that. Don't need to go through Meyers for most of it. Stuff like that as it comes up."

She nodded again. "Great. I'll coordinate some supplies like water and snacks too."

Jacob's eyes were wide. "Yeah. That would be super helpful."

Grace wrote a reminder in a spiral bound notebook. "How soon would you like to start auditioning?"

"Well today seems ideal. If there's a space available. But tomorrow would be fine too. I know it's short notice."

She shook her head, thinking that tomorrow was equally short notice, but she already had an idea on where she could find space. "Let me see if I can find a space. I'll get back to you on that."

"Hey, Grace, before we get too much farther…I wanted to let you know that we're totally casual here, so no need to dress up. So, you know, be comfortable the rest of the week."

She looked down at her navy pants. She had done it again—overdressed for the occasion. She realized with a start that she was wearing a full business suit sitting in Jacob's kitchen, and he was in his pajamas. "Oh. Okay. Sorry. I'll do better tomorrow."

Mollified, Jacob turned to the food she'd laid out. "This food looks great. You went all out." He didn't give her a chance to speak as he finished loading up his plate.

~ ♪ ~ DEREK ~ ♪ ~

It was almost 10 a.m. when Derek slid open the patio door from

Jacob's backyard into the kitchen. As soon as he'd cracked the seal, he announced himself.

"Hi! It's me," Derek called.

The first thing he saw was an assortment of pastries, fruit cups, and what he assumed had been hot sandwiches set out.

"Ooh, a buffet!"

He hoped no one heard his stomach growling. His apartment pantry was sparse, and the sight of sandwiches of any temperature gave him a little thrill. He played it cool, closing the door and setting his gear nearby before sauntering toward the stack of plates on the counter.

With a start, he noticed Grace sitting at the opposite end of the kitchen island, in front of an open laptop. She was halfway to her feet as she said good morning, and he felt a breeze flutter across his face as she hurried to the microwave.

"You're here early," he noted.

She shrugged in reply and extracted a white and green cup. The side was emblazoned with a giant D scrawled in black magic marker.

"This for me?" he asked.

Grace nodded. "Yes. It's black, but there's sweetener and sugar here, and some cream in the fridge."

Derek began dressing his coffee. "Food and coffee. Day's starting on the right foot," he said. "Where's Jacob?"

"He disappeared a bit ago. Not sure, but he's somewhere around. Sorry."

"Why sorry?"

She shrugged. "I'm supposed to be assisting, and I don't feel very helpful. And...to be honest, I don't really even know where the restroom is. I'm pretty much limited to the front door and the kitchen."

Derek laughed. "I don't think he's fully awake yet. Come on. I'll give you the tour," he offered, coffee in one hand and a lukewarm sandwich in the other.

"I'll heat that up for you if you like," she offered.

"Thank you, but it's fine." He gestured for her to follow him and pointed out first the powder room before leading her to Jacob's studio. He found the other man damp headed and slouched into the couch. Large black headphones were fitted over the top of his head, and the glare of the laptop balanced on his knees illuminated his face. The room was otherwise dark, and he seemed oblivious to the fact that he had company. Derek flipped the lights on and off.

Jacob nearly dropped the laptop, clutching the machine to his chest and tugging the headphones off. "You scared me!"

"Clearly." Derek stepped into the room gesturing for Grace to follow. "You realize you left her out in the kitchen and didn't tell her where anything was."

It was Jacob's turn to flush. Derek wondered if he'd ever met two more sensitive people.

"My mother raised me so much better than that," Jacob groaned. "Sorry!"

Derek laughed, easing in and taking a seat at the console.

Jacob patted the couch next to him for Grace to join them as he straightened up.

"So, who else is joining us today?" Derek asked as he flipped switches to the console. Tiny lights began flickering across the board.

"Just you," Jacob answered, snapping his laptop shut. "Why did you think it was someone else?"

Derek shrugged. "Lot of breakfast."

Grace opened her mouth, but Jacob spoke first.

"A good host lays out plenty so no one feels shy about eating." He winked at Grace and bounded up toward the other chair at the console. He spun once for good measure, stopping himself with his hands on the padded edge.

"Let's review the whole mix now, then I want to run an idea past you I had this morning about the bridge that was missing. Maybe it's the chorus—I don't know. And Grace is going to find us a place to have some auditions today. Or tomorrow."

It sounded like a tall order to Derek, but if anyone could accomplish it, it was the suit sitting on the couch. "Sounds great. Should we call

Rae?" Derek asked.

"Yeah probably. Is she still working that bar job? Do you think she's awake yet? Those go kinda late sometimes, right?"

"Yes," Derek agreed. "But if I know Rae, she'd want to be here. We should at least ask. Plus, it's always fun to have someone validate your work."

Jacob smiled. "True." He turned to Grace. "Any luck on those auditions?"

"I think so," Grace replied. "You gave me an idea. I assume one of you has Rae's number?"

Derek pulled his iPhone from his pocket and tapped the screen until it woke and handed it to Grace. He watched as she paced away, phone pressed lightly against her face. She tucked completely into herself as she spoke. It was as though the mere conversation took all her focus. How in the world did a mouse like her handle Meyers?

Jacob handed him a pair of headphones, and they dove into the music. It wasn't until Jacob pulled off his headphones that Derek realized Grace had returned and pulled off his own.

"Sorry. We were really into it," Jacob apologized.

She was all business, shoulders square, face neutral. "I'm going to pick up Rae. I'll be back shortly."

"She doesn't drive?" Jacob squawked.

Derek chuckled, remembering the way he had sneakily sent Jacob to pick her up for Pete's party over the weekend. "No, she doesn't. I pick her up when we go anywhere." He rested his headphones on the console and stood, reaching for his keys on autopilot. "I'll go get her. And I'll make sure she gets coffee so she's human."

Grace held up her hands. "You're working. This is what I'm here for. If you leave now, you'll break your concentration. I'll be back, and hopefully when I return, I'll have Rae and a venue for the auditions. As long as the candidates are free, we should be ready to rock and roll."

Jacob shook his head. "It's been like, five minutes. Are you made of rocket fuel?"

She chuckled. "I wish, and it's been close to an hour. See you in a bit." Without further ado, she was out the door.

Derek watched her go with a laugh. "Well, she's not wrong about breaking the mood. Let's get back to it. We should have at least the skeleton of each song before we go auditioning band members without anything to play."

Jacob agreed, and they slipped on their headphones in unison.

FIVE

Grace turned on her flashers near the front of Rae's complex, grateful for a spot near the front door. She wished she'd copied down Rae's phone number from Derek instead of using his phone.

Her eyes fluttered shut at the memory of him passing her the device. He had simply handed it to her as though it was nothing. As though his phone wasn't warm from his touch and smelled faintly of his cologne. Remembering the vague location of Rae's apartment after dropping her off over the weekend, she leaned toward the passenger door and stared up to the second floor. She was not disappointed, watching the other woman locking her door. The confidence in her walk as she sashayed toward the car was nearly unnerving, especially with a soft guitar case slung over her shoulder. Grace had never felt that much self-confidence even on her best day.

Her back passenger door opened, and Rae tucked her instrument expertly in the backseat before dropping into the front. She flashed a bright smile after closing the door and reaching for her seat belt.

"Good morning."

Grace turned off the flashers and glanced at her GPS. "Is it still morning?" she chuckled.

It was starting to feel like evening, and Grace was flagging. It would be after eleven a.m. before she got back to Jacob's home, and her four a.m. wake time was taking its toll. She felt like she'd spent her entire day driving back and forth across LA. When she remembered the contracts she still had to tell Meyers weren't signed yet, her shoulders sagged.

"Oh, stop." Rae smiled.

"Did you have a chance to call your friends at the club?" Grace asked anxiously. When Jacob mentioned Rae working at a club, she remembered the expert bartender skills she'd exhibited over the weekend. Suddenly, finding a venue for auditions same day seemed possible. It was the whole reason she had gotten to use Derek's cell.

"I talked to Suzie, my manager, and she said they are cool to do the auditions there today. There's a basic drum kit setup and a few amps on stage, so we can use that. However, she did have one condition."

Grace cringed. "What's that?"

"That we play our first gig there."

She sighed relief. "I think we can swing that," she replied, already plotting their launch party and reminding herself to make note of it when they arrived at Jacob's house.

"So, Jacob got you for the whole week, huh?" Rae queried.

Grace nodded, navigating the streets. "He did. What's your coffee of choice? I got coffee for the guys."

Rae blinked. "Nectar of the gods. I am not that picky. Wherever," she replied. "And thank you! How did you know I'd be desperate coffee?"

Grace smirked, thinking a morning caffeine addiction was incredibly common. "Derek told me. He said it would quote, 'make you human.' End quote."

"Rude," Rae groaned. "True, but rude."

Grace sneaked into a high-end coffee bar's drive-through and ordered the caramel macchiato Rae selected then snaked around the city 'til she reached Jacob's house. She shook her head as she slowed to turn into the circle drive.

"When Meyers told me I'd be working for Jacob last night, he did not tell me that I'd be working out of his home," she mumbled.

Rae chuckled, half of her coffee ingested by now. "That must have been a surprise."

"Yeah, I thought I had the wrong address. Never been so freaked out by a front door in my life."

Rae chuckled. "I can imagine," she consoled. "So…I gotta ask." She circled the air around Grace with her index finger. "What is this business suit thing about?"

Grace frowned, looking down at her sensible slacks and flats. "I took the jacket off," she complained. "How did you know it was a suit?"

"Derek mentioned your suit from your first lunch."

She cleared her throat to dislodge the imaginary tennis ball.

"I'm trying to look professional. Like Meyers. He sets the tone, and all the women at the office—they're always super put together. It's what you do." She paused. "If it makes you feel any better, Jacob already had a talk with me this morning."

"It does," Rae replied. "I can't imagine your dry-cleaning bill."

Grace shrugged. "I don't take them very often for myself."

A wicked grin split Rae's face in two. "You should slip them into his order and pull them out before he sees. He'd never know."

"That's completely devious. But I couldn't do that." She wondered for a moment if she could but then eschewed the idea. "I have great laundry facilities at my complex. I don't need his charity," she added.

"Mine suck," Rae complained. "I've actually bought new clothes before, so I didn't have to go down into the skeezy laundry room. Half the machines don't work, and I think it doubles as someone's money laundering facility if you know what I mean."

Grace knew enough. "You could always use my facilities if you needed. They're nothing special, but it's clean and well lit, and all the machines work."

"I'll definitely take you up on that," Rae promised.

Grace slipped down the circular path to the back patio door where she spotted Derek's black BMW wedged into the end of the driveway and gleaming in the Los Angeles sunshine.

She had barely rolled to a stop as she heard Rae's seat-belt unbuckle. The moment she threw the car into park, Rae burst out and moved to retrieve her instrument.

Grace gestured to the side of the house. "We should be able to get in around the back. It was unlocked for Derek this morning and probably still is. We'll go into the kitchen."

By the time they reached the studio, the guys were firmly enmeshed in the work. Derek was at the console, hands on two different sliders, eyes closed and head listing to one side as he listened. Jacob was in the recording booth, eyes also closed and belting out a note into the microphone.

Rae and Grace stood frozen in the doorway.

"Should we tell them we're here or wait for them to see us?" Grace asked.

"We might not live that long," Rae teased. She stepped into the room, setting her bass on the couch and slipping into the second chair at the console. She rolled over until her chair gently bumped into Derek's.

He turned to see her and grinned. "Morning, Sunshine. Give us a minute, 'k?"

Rae nodded and rolled to the couch to begin unsheathing her instrument in reply.

Grace watched from the doorway, feeling like an interloper and looked at Rae. "I'll be in the kitchen if anyone needs anything."

"No, don't. It'll be nice to have an audience," Rae elaborated. "Someone who could maybe see the forest for the trees."

"I have to call all the musicians," Grace argued. "See if they are free today. It's super last minute asking them to be at the club at 2:00 today." It wasn't that she didn't want to stay, but if Meyers caught her sitting on the job, he'd be furious. Plus, she wanted to impress Derek and Jacob.

She watched the words land on Rae's face and heard the loud zip of the guitar case as she yanked it open. She realized that the other woman was trying to make a connection ever since the barbecue.

Grace didn't know why she was holding back except that Rae was a little bit of a chaos bomb in her otherwise organized world.

"I'll be back in a bit," Grace conceded.

Rae's face softened as she strapped on the bass. "I'll hold you to it," she vowed.

The firm expression on Rae's face left no question about her intent, and Grace scampered to the kitchen. Her first priority was calling the musicians. It took some cajoling, and she encountered a fair amount of complaining about the last-minute invitation. By the time she finished, she had decided that whoever complained was ungrateful and didn't deserve the opportunity to work with her people.

The tune escaping the studio was fast and beat driven, and she felt her toe instinctively tapping along. She could sort emails equally as well from the studio couch as she could the kitchen counter. Armed with her laptop and power cable, she trotted down the hallway to fulfill her promise to the bassist.

Derek was perched at the console, fingers poised on one knob twisting almost imperceptibly before he withdrew. His head was bopping gently in time with the beat, and he appeared completely oblivious to anything but the music. Grace noticed the length of his slender fingers, and her insides quivered at the sight. She had always had a thing about his hands and how precisely he placed them on things. She imagined how sensitive they must be after having made so many miniscule tweaks.

Quietly, she stood behind him, watching Jacob belting out the lyric and Rae practically humping his leg with her bass. They stopped abruptly, Jacob pulling the pen from behind his ear and producing a small blank book from his back pocket.

"Sounding good," Grace murmured.

Derek glanced over his shoulder with a smile. "Thanks."

"Rae asked me to sit in and listen. Is that okay?"

"Yeah, it's good. We're probably about to get stuck in, so please don't be offended if we kinda forget you're back there."

Grace held up a hand. "No problem. I'm here if anyone needs

anything."

Derek gave her a thumbs up, eyes on the recording area where Rae was now settled near an amp and Jacob was scribbling in his notebook. "You guys ready?" His voice echoed over the speakers.

Jacob looked up promptly, holding up a thumb. "I'm gonna go for it here. Let it all out."

Derek worked his wizardry, and Grace watched with fascination as he prepared the computers and began to record. She had no idea what he was doing, but he drummed silently along the padded edge of the console. He rolled back and forth as it started, tapping different buttons and adjusting faders and slides. He was in his element, and Grace bit her lip. She reminded herself that this would all come crashing down if Meyers thought she was ignoring his needs and turned her attention to deleting incoming junk emails from his inbox.

Her toe was tapping as she listened to Jacob singing. It was all very romantic for a moment, and then she caught the true meaning of his lyrics. He was singing about holding himself together during foreplay, and she watched in horror as Jacob turned his lustful gaze on Rae. She couldn't stop picturing him doing the things he discussed, and she clenched her jaw to keep it shut.

The bassist appeared to be in a tractor beam, sliding closer to him every few notes. Her instrument lowering till it looked like she was acting out his lyrics! Grace swallowed hard, looking away. She told herself that adults had these feelings, and that they were perfectly natural. It was known as "sex, drugs, and rock and roll" after all.

However, when she imagined listening to this song in the company of her boss or her parents, shame washed over her, curling her into a tight ball around her laptop.

As the last note played, Derek held a hand to all to remain silent. The duo in the recording area froze, catching their breath and shaking with the effort of remaining silent. He tapped one button to end the recording then clapped. "That was fire! You guys definitely fed chemistry into that beast," he said into the microphone.

Behind the microphone, Jacob threw his hands in the air and

turned to Rae. "You killed it. You were all the way in the groove."

Rae was walking in small circles, not making eye contact for a moment. "That was amazing. You," she pointed one hand at Derek and the other at Jacob, "are both amazing." Her eyes lingered on him. "Those lyrics," she whispered.

Jacob smirked back at her. "It's not too much?"

She bit her lip. "Not at all."

Grace felt her jaw drop open. Not too much? It was like porn. Her whole body was cringing at the thought of high school kids singing along with the lyrics. She bit her tongue, reminding herself that her opinion was not valid. If this was what they wanted to record, that was their business. It wasn't her place to judge. She was there to set schedules. Send emails. Get contracts signed. She blinked, noticing that Jacob was making eye contact with her.

"Grace?" Jacob asked.

She blinked, uncomfortable as all three of them turned to her. Arms wrapped around herself, she cleared her throat and relaxed her facial muscles. "Yes?"

"What's wrong?" Jacob asked.

"Nothing's wrong," she answered. Her voice cracked, coming out octaves higher than it should have. She popped up from the couch. "Anyone need anything?"

Inches away at the console, Derek pinned her with his gaze. "We need the truth, Grace."

She gulped, looking away from his deep ocean blue eyes. She didn't want to talk about this with anyone, let alone her boy crush. She wasn't even sure if she could say the words out loud in mixed company.

"Well," she began, taking a deep breath. Maybe if she said it fast enough, they wouldn't hear her or be offended. "It's very… well, it's all sex! You can't play that on the radio." She exhaled like a deflated balloon.

Jacob shook his head, clearly not understanding the problem. His hands fell to his hips, and his head cocked to the other side. "Not every song has to be played on the radio," Jacob pointed out.

He was right. This could be a secret B-side or buried deep in the album. Not everyone was as uptight as she was.

"I get that," she said, nodding feverishly. Derek had said he wanted the truth, and she glanced at him as she clarified, "It's just…it's strong, guys." She hoped her expression conveyed the apology she felt for saying something negative about work they obviously felt passionately about. "It just… it kinda sounds like a soundtrack for porn."

All three gaped at her.

Grace backpedaled. "I shouldn't have said anything. I'm sorry."

Derek laughed and turned back to the console.

She felt her heart break. She was stuck being a little girl, she realized. Stuck in a perpetual state of pleasing her parents who she hadn't even spoken to in years. They would have told her how unholy this was and how she was guilty by association.

"Too much for you?" Derek asked, looking over his shoulders and staring directly into her eyes.

Breath caught in her throat, Grace broke eye contact to avoid the disappointment on his face. Tears threatened to spring forward at any moment. *Pull yourself together,* she threatened herself. How ridiculous she was to harbor all these intimate feelings about him when she couldn't even admit it. All the times she'd daydreamed about running away with him for a lifetime of passion, and she'd flipped out at the mere suggestion of sex. She was a fool.

Rae interrupted her inner monologue. The bassist was practically pressed to the glass with her bass slung over her arm, and her voice sounded tinny through the studio speakers. "This is exactly why I asked her to join us. I like something sexy as much as anyone, but she's right. We don't have to give it all away at once. We've gotta appeal to a wide audience to be successful."

Derek scoffed. "Because sex doesn't sell?"

Rae flipped him the bird before turning her attention to Grace. "Subtlety, right?" she clarified. "It should be more like…foreplay instead of the main act. Leave them wanting more, yes?"

Grace fought past the tightness in her throat and avoided looking at anyone other than Rae. "Something like that," she mumbled.

After a moment, Jacob conceded. "That's fair."

Derek sat back in his chair, staring at the monitor and working through a variety of screens in multiple succession, mouse racing across the screen.

Grace cleared her throat and pulled her arms from around herself. She looked at Jacob and Rae. "I confirmed the place and time for auditions. Thanks to Rae's connections, we can get rolling in an hour to find a drummer and guitarist at *The Oubliette*. The caveat is that they want to be the first place you play live."

"Oh. Right. Auditions," Jacob mumbled. He scratched the back of his head. "Well then, I guess we'd better go."

Grace wished she hadn't burst their bubble, despite Rae's valiant efforts to defend her position. She should have told them it sounded great and moved on. Meyers would have her head. She wasn't a consultant. She was a coordinator—a facilitator.

Rae rested her bass in a stand and breezed out of the room, Jacob not far behind her.

Needing space, Grace rushed toward the kitchen, packing up her gear. She felt Rae's eyes on her as she worked.

"You were right to tell us what you thought," Rae encouraged.

Grace glanced at her before yanking an open case of water out of the fridge and plopping it on the counter.

"No, I wasn't," she contended. "I have no expertise. The music was great. The performance was great." She felt like she'd gotten caught watching porn in front of a group of strangers, and she turned to the kitchen sink to wash her hands furiously.

Rae turned off the faucet, handing her a towel. "That took courage. And you're right. As musicians, we get lost in the raw power of a song, when a bit of tempering is what it needs to make it really shine. And don't forget—we asked. If we couldn't handle the truth, we shouldn't have asked."

Accepting the towel, Grace dried her hands slowly. "Well, you are always welcome to ignore me." She frowned, looking at Rae's hands leaning on the edge of the sink. "Are you bleeding?"

Rae pulled her hand toward her face to inspect it. "Huh. It's from playing. I hate using a pick, but it's murder on my hands. I'll toughen up," she promised. "I've got a band-aid in my gear."

"RAE!" The voice was Derek's shouting all the way from the studio. Both ladies jumped at the unexpected shout.

"I better pack up," Rae chuckled, darting out of the room.

Grace leaned against the counter, grateful for a moment to herself. "Grow up," she chided herself quietly.

Instinctively, she moved to the bar stool at the end of the counter, throwing her suit coat on like armor. She was not like the three people in the studio discussing equipment and chord progressions. The jacket gave her some comfort. It was okay to be different. It's not like she had any chance with Derek or wanted one with Jacob. It was a paycheck, she reminded herself. It was a *good* paycheck.

She pushed her hair over her shoulders, collecting her gear. She saved her laptop, abandoned in the studio, for last. She could hear the men talking and the distinctive zip of Rae's instrument case as she approached.

Grace slipped in the room silently, snatching up her laptop and jerking the cord from the wall. She scolded herself for the immature behavior and gathered it more delicately until it was neatly bound.

"I'm driving," Jacob announced.

"Why are you driving?" Derek demanded. "My car's comfortable."

"We could drive separately," Rae suggested, and Grace felt Rae's eyes on her.

Jacob and Derek both rolled their eyes.

"Don't be stupid. We'll easily fit in one car," Jacob reasoned. "No reason to burn more gas." he smirked. "Rae, you can sit in the back so my driving doesn't scare you."

Rae flipped her braid to the other side as she hefted her case over one shoulder. She steeled both men with a chilly expression. "Cool. Grace and I can whisper about y'all." She stuck out her tongue.

Grace stopped short, calculating timetables in her head and frowning. "Actually, I need to take my car," Grace mumbled. "In case it runs long. I have errands for Meyers this afternoon. I'll meet you there." She started to the door, laptop snugged to her chest.

"Yes!" Rae crowed. "I'll join you. This way, we won't even have to whisper!"

Grace had hoped for some peace to let the sting of their recent exchange roll off her back, but to ignore the excitement on the other woman's face would be heartless. She consented, and Rae blew raspberries at the guys.

Once on their way, Rae began telling her about their recording in the studio the night before. She was practically bouncing in the passenger seat as she recalled the night. They were about halfway to the club when Grace's phone rang.

There was no time to pull over, and she tapped the phone's speaker button to answer the call. "This is Grace," she greeted.

"Grace, have you got a minute?" It was Meyers, and if she didn't know better, he sounded almost jovial.

"Certainly. How can I help?"

"Well, I wanted to check on how it's going and how those contracts are coming along. It's after noon, and I wanted those back by close of business today."

"Right, yes, I recall," Grace replied, glancing at her phone for the time. "I spoke with Mr. Hunter first thing this morning, and he's passed them to his lawyer to review."

"Did you relay to him the timeliness of this? They shouldn't be working today until they're signed."

"Yes, sir. I did."

"Well, what are you doing right now? Are you even with Hunter?"

Grace took a deep breath. "I'm on my way to coordinate the auditions I set up this morning. I'm meeting him there."

"Where did you find space on such short notice?"

"*The Oubliette*," she answered proudly. "Rae works there part time, and they said we could use the space if the band would play their first gig there." When she was saying the words, she intended to prove to him how she'd been doing exemplary work. But now that they were out, she worried it sounded like she was overstepping again. Wasn't she supposed to learn from her mistakes? Not her, apparently. She was doomed to continually find ways to make even bigger and more insolent errors.

His reply came on top of her last word. "Grace, you didn't tell them yes, did you?"

"No, no, of course not. That's always up to you to work out the best plan. That's not my place."

"Right. And the musicians were available?"

"Yes, sir. I called and spoke to each of them. They confirmed they'll meet us there."

"Great. Also, when you come to get Oscar this afternoon, there's a bag of clothes at the back door to drop at the cleaners. We need it to be done by Thursday, okay?"

"Yes, sir. I'll get it back to you by Thursday."

Rae looked at Grace, chin virtually in her lap. "Today?" she mouthed.

Grace nodded, focusing on the left turn she was making.

"So, you'll get those contracts today?" Meyers pressured.

"I'll do my best. It all depends on Hunter's lawyer."

"Good. Good. Call me tomorrow morning. You have my schedule."

"Yes, sir."

The call disconnected, and Grace exhaled gently.

"Who the hell is Oscar and why are you doing his dry cleaning?" Rae snapped.

"Oscar is a French Bulldog who pisses all over everything when he's nervous. And I always do his dry cleaning. It's part of my job. About three or four days a week."

Rae frowned. "How are you supposed to get Jacob's lawyers to get through this faster? And what about Derek's? And do I need one?"

Grace shrugged. "I'll figure it out. Or I won't, and he'll either fire me or make me wish he would." The car was noticeably quiet without Rae interjecting, and she glanced at her passenger who was studiously staring out the window. Grace worried she'd done something wrong.

"He does this," Grace excused.

"And you're okay with it?" Rae's attention spun from the passing scenery squarely onto Grace.

"I don't have a choice," Grace defended. "I'd make a terrible waitress, and I'm not an actor or a musician. I don't know what else I'd do. And I can't stand the thought of failing and having to go back to Chicago. I keep hearing that this town is going to either make or break you, and I'm not too crazy about being broken."

"Does Jacob know about this dog thing?"

She shook her head. "Not exactly. It's not like he'd know to ask. And I'm a temp for Jacob. I'll be gone next week, and it'll be like I was never here."

"Grace? Do you not see what you did today alone? There was breakfast, and contracts apparently, and you coordinated a full audition in a single morning, *and* we're going to be on time in a city you barely know."

Grace shrugged. "It's my job." She left out all the things she had done before she got to Jacob's home. "And I'd have done some of this earlier, but I didn't know 'til about 10 last night that I would be here today."

Rae drew back. "He calls you at 10 p.m.? You work weekends?"

"No, no. Banker's hours. Weekdays from 8 to 4:30."

"But he called on the weekend," Rae protested.

"Sometimes," she confirmed. "He only calls in the evening if something's up. It's a good agency. Big. Job security. And sometimes it's a good thing. If he hadn't called last Sunday, I wouldn't have ended up in the middle of Derek and Jacob at a restaurant. It's hard to complain about that."

Rae offered a chuckle of agreement and a tight smile.

At the club, Grace stationed herself near the door to greet each prospective member as they arrived, corralling them in the vestibule.

Some of the contenders milled about. She could tell they were nervous, even the few who were playing it cool. They were wrapped around themselves or obsessively tuning strings and tapping out rhythms with their sticks. She recognized one of the potentials—the drummer she had recommended despite her boss's disapproval.

She grinned to herself at having slipped him onto the list. Meyers had been furious when he saw the fifth drummer, Joe, on the email to Jacob. He had a reputation for being mellow and incredibly talented during his years filling in for Rebel Gloss before their original members reunited. Meyers had let her know in no uncertain terms that he did not approve of her intervention, stopping short of calling it deception. Despite the stern talking to, Grace did not feel guilty as she watched him from the corner of her eye. She enjoyed knowing that she had the ability to at least give him a chance. It was up to him now to capitalize on it.

When the group was ready to begin, Grace called the drummers alphabetically. She stood near the door, listening to each performance. No matter how she felt about Meyers, she couldn't deny that he had selected a top-notch group of performers.

She refrained from showing any special treatment to Joe when she called him in, fourth. She listened closely as she took a seat at the check-in table. His playing was precise and fast without being rushed. She heard Rae's bass joining in, recognizing several of the songs they played. She was doing her best to be impartial, or at least to not show the last remaining drummer who was now slumped in his chair that she guessed the contest might be over.

When he finally finished, the cheers inside the club were earsplitting. The last applicant stood, tucking his sticks into his back pocket.

Grace held up a hand to him, begging him to wait as she stepped inside the room.

"This is it," Jacob called to her. "Send in the guitarists!"

She returned to the waiting area, frowning apologetically at the last person. "I'm sorry. The position has been filled."

He flipped her the bird and barreled through the front door, daylight temporarily blinding her in his wake. The door slammed shut with a reverberating clank in its frame.

She sighed, then smiled encouragingly at the guitarists. "Looks like you're up next." She sent the first person through the door to meet with the others.

Anything else she was about to say died on her lips when the front door swung open again. She believed she was having a nightmare for a moment. She would recognize the bald silhouette of that man anywhere: Bruce Romano. He had worked with Joe in Rebel Gloss for years. However, the former guitarist had ended his engagement with them as a weaselly, over-muscled oil stain in her opinion. His bald head shimmered in the sparse lighting, and he tugged large sunglasses off, shoving them deep into the pocket of his skin-tight leather trousers. Crow's feet pinched his face, and liver spots stretched from his scalp down his neck, leading into a skin-hugging white T-shirt beneath a black leather jacket.

"Is this the audition Meyers set up?" he asked the room in general as the door slammed shut behind him.

Grace blinked, straightening up. Every muscle in her body tensed at the sight of him and the insinuation that Meyers had done anything to facilitate the auditions.

"I'm sorry, this is a closed audition," she replied. "I'm from Meyers' agency, and I'm—"

"Perfect." Bruce had already moved toward the door to the audition area, and Grace raged internally when she saw him begin to unzip his guitar case. "Is there an amp I can plug into?"

"I'm sorry, Mr. Romano, but you are not on my schedule." Grace stood in front of him, crossing her arms over her chest.

"Right, right. That's cool. I talked to Meyers. He said you were looking for former members of Rebel Gloss, so here I am." He stood, throwing the strap of his guitar over his shoulder sland shrugging it into place.

Grace's chin dropped. "You cannot go in there."

He waved her off. "It's cool. Meyers called me directly and told me to come right over."

Speech left her as all the pieces clicked into place inside her head. His comments about adding Joe to the list. Checking up on her on the drive over. She wondered if he even had any dry cleaning for her to drop off, or if he'd used it as a cover to pry the details from her to throw in this surprise attack.

"I'm sorry," she continued, "but I don't think this is appropriate."

"Why not? Meyers is my agent. Not you."

They stared at each other. Grace was not going to back down. In the next moment, his smirk reached his ears, his chin tilted down, and for a moment, she thought he was going to charge her like a bull.

Grace clenched her fists at her side to remain professional. "You must be desperate grabbing at this. They may not know your past, but I do, and don't think I won't tell them how you ruined that band's reputation with all the gross things you did to their fans."

Bruce rolled his eyes. "That's your opinion. And they were consenting adults. I'm going in. You can take it up with your boss."

Before Grace could stop him, he side-stepped around her and strode brazenly through the door. She scrambled after him, deciding if she should grab him. She felt a little barf in the back of her throat at the notion of touching his skin and raced to get in front of him. She'd back him out of the room if it was the last thing she did. She wasn't ready for her new friends to think she was responsible for him.

He had barely made it two steps in before the commotion began.

"ABSOLUTELY NOT!" Rae screamed.

Bruce did not stop walking forward, but his swagger faltered. "I beg your pardon?" he asked.

"No snakes on our team!" Rae snarled, launching herself into his path, bass bouncing against her body in her haste. "I know what you did, you creeper! Making porn with fans is as gross as it gets. Walk away now before I really decide to embarrass you."

"What's wrong with porn?" Bruce demanded, hands raised in confusion.

Grace had never felt prouder of the people she worked with when she saw both Jacob and Derek stand behind Rae. Joe was trapped behind the drum kit, and she saw him cover his face with one hand.

"He's not on the list. I tried to stop him," Grace called to Jacob. She was inches behind the man, hands poised on her hips to emphasize her point. Her eyes flicked to the guitarist who was plugged into the amp beside Joe.

Jacob didn't cross his arms or barrel forward in response. He simply stared, all six plus feet of himself, arms slack at his sides as though this short body builder of a man was a gnat.

"If Grace says you're not on the list, you're not on the list. We're in the middle of an audition and barging in here is incredibly rude," Jacob admonished.

"Meyers said you were looking for someone like me, and I know Joe," Bruce countered, pointing at the drummer.

"We're looking for *our* sound," Derek replied easily. "And you're not it. We do have security if you'd like an introduction." He lifted a hand toward the staff milling around the bar.

Bruce mumbled a string of curses, about to protest further, but Grace was having none of it, stepping between him and Rae.

"This way," Grace encouraged, gesturing toward the doorway.

Bruce opened his mouth to protest, but then flipped the bird to all of them with both hands as he turned toward the door. Grace followed him closely holding the door open for him as he collected his case and shoved past her.

The door slammed shut, and Grace locked it behind him. "Sorry, everyone," she called, scurrying to the audition space. Rae was seated, crumpled over herself with her bass at her feet. Jacob's hand rested on her shoulder, squeezing lightly.

"I'm so sorry, Rae," Grace apologized as she bridged the distance. She stopped in front of the other woman, crouching down to her level. "He passed me before I could—"

"Not your fault," Rae cut in, leaning into Jacob's hand. "We saw how he barged in."

"He's always been that way," Joe murmured. "He has a reputation for taking advantage of fans and screwing over his band mates, then bragging about it."

Derek whistled. "Bullet dodged."

Grace was trembling, and she inhaled deeply as the adrenaline began to dissipate.

"It's okay, Grace," Derek assured, touching her arm.

She shivered, her worry replaced by hunger at his touch. "Thanks," she replied. She caught herself before she could over-explain and focused on the guitarist who had been interrupted instead. "I'm so sorry you got interrupted."

He shrugged then folded his hands over his guitar, surveying the others as he leaned back against the stage.

Wiping the back of her hand over her cheeks, Rae joined them, hugging her bass to her chest.

"You going to be okay?" Grace questioned gently.

At Rae's nod, Grace jogged toward the bar for water and a clean towel for the bassist to wipe her face. When she returned, they were chatting with the candidate politely, still gathered around Rae in her chair with Jacob's hand resting on her back.

She pressed the cloth and a cold water bottle into her friend's hand and took charge. They were floundering, and she could help this much.

"Well now that that's over, should we get back to business?" she asked the group.

Her words prompted them to action, and as she retreated toward the vestibule where the remaining guitarists were waiting, she heard the beginning of a guitar solo. She wasn't sure what they were looking for, but the heavy metal vibe she heard blaring through the room didn't last long before they stopped. They asked for the next candidate and the next.

After the fourth hopeful departed, Grace began to worry that they were going to have to ask Meyers for more musicians. She smiled optimistically at the woman still waiting her turn. She had been sitting by Joe and seemed completely unphased by the process as she pulled a turquoise guitar from the soft case at her feet. She tuned a few strings gently.

"I love your guitar," Grace complimented quietly.

A smile warmed the woman's face, and she picked a note on each string. "Thanks. It was a gift from my Tia," she explained. "Music runs in my family."

Grace liked the sentiment. "Good luck in there. It has to be hard to be last."

The woman shook her head. "No. It's the best place. I've heard the competition, and I have the advantage. Last is always best."

Glancing at her sheet, she read the woman's name: Carmen Luz. She looked back at the woman's severe ponytail brushing against her tawny shoulders and thought she would certainly be the most attractive candidate they had seen for the day. "Well at least you're not going in alone," she encouraged, gesturing at the woman's instrument.

The other woman stared at her blankly until understanding dawned. She patted the guitar body. "You're right."

The previous candidate bolted out the door without a word to either of them. Grace rose, holding the door open for Carmen who needed no guidance.

With no one left in the waiting area, Grace followed her, leaning against the door frame as Carmen strutted toward the others, her guitar over one shoulder, amp balanced in her opposite hand. Her tight, red tank top and dark jeans were in stark contrast to her retro guitar, but Carmen made it look natural. If she felt any fear, it didn't show.

Carmen introduced herself, shaking everyone's hand and congratulating Joe.

From her place at the back of the room, Grace could see that they were tired. Jacob could barely form a smile for the newcomer, and even Derek's handshake looked limp. His usual bouncy nature was subdued after the previous auditions.

Rae plucked strings anxiously as she paced in circles.

Carmen plugged in her amp, tested the volume and turned to face the band. Bold notes rang through the club, and Grace noticed that the staff had stopped working, staring as Carmen played. She started with some classic pop slipping into rock with a hint of heavy metal ballads and then a very smart rendition of one of Jacob's pop songs. She had barely made it into the second song before Joe and Rae joined in.

Given Rae's earlier break down, Grace was thrilled to see the bass player smiling and bounding toward the other woman. When Jacob started singing along, Grace was fairly sure she was looking at the band's final member. And then she saw Derek hop up from his seat to out-sing Jacob, and her heart melted. He threw his head back, belting out a note. Before her eyes, the guys started competing for who could transition the quickest and knew all the words.

Carmen finally ended her performance with *Bohemian Rhapsody*. Grace tried hiding her giggles behind her hand as their antics ramped up, bouncing up and down with the vocal changes. Joe banged out the end, rising from his seat as Rae and Carmen pounded the strings to keep up. Jacob was headbanging to every last beat, Derek beside him twirling and shaking his hands rhythmically.

As the last note ended, everyone was hooting.

"We've got our fifth!" Derek announced, looking to Jacob for confirmation.

"Hell, yeah!" Jacob and Rae yelped in unison.

Grace had not expected the tightness that squeezed her chest seeing this band solidify in front of her eyes. She hugged herself, watching as they shared high fives and Carmen sagged with relief.

She was also not expecting Rae to unplug her instrument and sprint toward her. "Come on, silly," Rae scolded. She grabbed Grace's arm, dragging her to the stage with the others to celebrate.

Grace wriggled through the heavy front door of the dry cleaners, clutching the second heavy laundry bag with both hands and praying it didn't get caught on the door frame and split open like the last bag had. Dealing with laundry was depressing after the excitement of the auditions. The band was currently celebrating at Jacob's house, and while they had invited her to join, she was very nearly late picking up Meyers' dog, Oscar, for his grooming appointment.

Meyers had told her that there would be laundry, but she swore he found every article of clothing in the house to send her way. At least she was almost finished with this task, she consoled herself, dragging the bag inside.

When her phone rang from her purse, she cursed under her breath and prayed the lady watching her from the front counter didn't understand. She scowled as she dropped the bag in the doorway to fish out the phone.

"Meyers' Agency, this is Grace," she answered. "How can I help you?"

Jacob laughed. "You are always on. Where are you? I heard you were taking a dog to the groomers."

She grunted. "Yes, well it's part of my job. Sometimes." Grace pressed the phone between her shoulder and her ear as she hefted the bag and waddled to the counter with it. "I'm at the dry cleaners dropping off Mr. Meyers' order for *tomorrow*," she explained, directing the words to the cranky woman across from her.

The clerk grimaced at her, recognizing the request. "No tomorrow. Thursday. Too late today." She scowled at Grace.

Grace grimaced back and held up her index finger. "What's up?" she asked Jacob.

"We're celebrating, and we all think you should be here. Wanna join us?"

Grace closed her eyes. What she wanted was to go to bed. She reminded herself that she wasn't done yet anyway. She still had to pick up Oscar and take him home when he was finished.

"I can swing by. Maybe we can get that contract signed? Meyers was hoping to get it today."

"Actually, I did hear back from my lawyer. She says it's good to go."

Grace's heart calmed at the news. "Great. I'll be by in a bit. Should I bring anything?" She waited for him to give a dinner order.

He laughed. "Just you. Unless you're anywhere near the iPhone store, Because I sort of ordered three for the band, and the one near here has them in stock right now."

"I'm sure it's not far," she answered. "Did you pay already?" she asked.

"Yeah. I'll send you the invoice with the address."

"Great. I'll pick them up on my way."

"Perfect. We'll see you then."

Grace finished arguing with the clerk at the cleaners, offering to pay double to get the order completed by the next afternoon before she tucked the claim ticket into her handbag.

When Grace arrived at Jacob's house, she let herself in through the unlocked patio door. She would have to talk to him about that. She could imagine the havoc a rabid, stray fan could cause, let alone someone who meant him harm.

Empty beer bottles were strewn across the kitchen, dining, and living rooms. She heard music from a distance and assumed everyone was in the studio. If they weren't a band, she might be offended that they had invited her over and were nowhere in sight to greet her.

She locked the patio door before cleaning up after them and finding her way to the studio with Jacob's phone order in hand. She swung the paper bag gently on her finger as she watched them fooling around in the studio. Rae and Carmen were in the booth playing their instruments together to no tune in particular and laughing while they did it. Joe was adjusting the toms and kick drum behind them.

Derek was the first to notice her, and he waved her in. He and Jacob were at the console debating microphone placement, and they stopped to welcome her.

Grace set the bag next to Jacob before easing herself onto the couch.

He bounced, pulling all three phones out of the bag with a grin that required sunglasses to view. He nodded to Grace.

"Thank you!"

Jacob looked like Santa Claus, dropping a phone first in Joe's hand and then bounding out of the control room to present the remainder to the ladies. Rae grabbed Jacob in a tight hug, and Carmen planted a kiss on his cheek before box lids and packaging started flying.

Standing behind Derek, Grace listened to the exchange through the console speakers.

"Do they need to be charged?" Rae asked.

Grace felt everyone's eyes on her as she answered. "Yes. The guy at the store said you should fully charge them before turning them on. It could damage the battery otherwise."

The four on the other side of the glass stared at her dumbly, gesturing that they hadn't heard her, and Grace frowned.

"I answered," she mumbled.

Derek smiled at her over his shoulder. "They can't hear you. Come. Sit here, and I'll show you how to talk to them."

She looked at the seat he patted before joining him. She could smell his cologne, and she inhaled deeply.

"Here. Press this," he pointed to a button, "then talk into this." He touched a microphone that looked like a long metal stick on a square base. "Easy."

She blinked at him, then relayed her message to the others as instructed.

Jacob gave her a thumbs up, and Rae and Carmen nodded. Joe was already plugging a cable into the phone.

Grace smiled back at them, backing away from the microphone, then looked to Derek. "It's kind of fun to be the voice of God."

He winked at her. "It is a little addictive."

She choked back the tingles running through her. The gesture scrunched his face and lips and hinted at a promise that she was sure he hadn't meant to send her way.

~ ♫ ~ D E R E K ~ ♫ ~

At dinner, Carmen raced around the table, pressing Joe into the chair between herself and Jacob, until Derek found himself wedged between Grace and the singer. He ignored the glances Rae kept tossing at him, choosing to focus on the tangled flurry of hands passing white waxed boxes of sushi, dumplings, and a variety of chicken dishes across and around the table.

He passed a container to his right, surprised at the spark he felt as his fingertips grazed Grace's as she accepted a box from him. He didn't dare look at her for fear she might have noticed and reached promptly to steal a container from Carmen.

The guitarist snapped her jaws at him, nowhere close to his hand but enough to indicate her intention. He chuckled at the antics, grabbing a different box instead to fill his plate.

The chaos was friendly, and he thought of his siblings growing up. It felt like a birthday dinner for one of them, which reminded him that his birthday was around the corner. He wondered if Pete and Nancy would allow him to invite his new friends to the dinner they insisted on throwing.

A quick glance around the table filled him with an unexpected sense of comfort. He could share a tour bus and live out of these people's pockets, he thought. They were practically siblings already.

"So, Grace, what brought you to LA?" Jacob asked as the last container was settled in the center of the table.

She shrugged and reached for a fork. "I wanted a warmer climate than Chicago. I always thought being a personal assistant might be more fun than an office assistant."

"Is it?" Carmen asked, scooping a forkful of noodles to her mouth. The unabashed way she sucked up the food reminded Derek of Pete shoveling down a carb loading meal before a workout.

"Well, it's certainly the best pay I've ever had," Grace confessed. "Weather's great. Still not sure where everything is. Thank God my work phone has GPS. I don't know how I got around without it all my life."

Joe laughed, shaking his head and holding out a fist across the table to bump hers. "I spent so much time lost when I first got here, it was a miracle I ever made an audition. But I can read a city map now like pissing off a bridge."

"And now we all have GPS thanks to you picking up the phones," Jacob acknowledged. "That was above and beyond."

Grace waved a hand. "It's no big. It gives me a place to be until Oscar is ready."

"Wait, what?" Jacob questioned, fork stalled mid-way to his mouth. "It's six!"

"And?" Grace questioned. "Some days I'm at it late, and some days I do almost nothing."

"Name the last time you had a whole day off," Jacob challenged.

"Last Saturday I…" she answered quickly, then stalled, setting down her fork and tapping her chin. Her eyes rolled skyward, then her mouth puckered. "No, wait. No, the Saturday before last. I spent the whole day running errands for myself." She relaxed after her statement, her neck elongating as her chin rose proudly.

Derek stared, transfixed at the sight.

"Well, that sounds like fun," Carmen teased, swallowing her food. "You sure know how to party." She shoveled in another bite.

"Oh, come on. You guys all work all the time," Grace insisted. "Didn't you pull an all-nighter a few days ago?" She sucked a noodle delicately from her fork.

"Musicians work best at night," Derek interceded. "And we might work for three weeks solid, but then we'll take a month-long break."

"Lies," Rae scolded. "Lies. This one never stops working. He's always at the studio."

Derek studied her, as she spoke. He'd known her long enough to recognize her tone as she built him up, and he sensed her about to continue. He stuck out his tongue at her, hoping to skate past the compliment.

To his good fortune, Jacob chuckled. "Makes a good producer. Gotta love what you do." Jacob turned back to Grace. "But dry-cleaning and pet care? Surely you could find something less demeaning."

Grace's brows arched. "It's honest work. And someone's got to do it. We can't all be pop stars."

Derek felt her words like a bite to the jugular. He was sure she hadn't meant to inflict the judgment on everyone at the table, but the damage was done. She was twirling noodles around her fork harshly, and Derek shifted in time to miss a sauce fleck that flew from her plate.

"Ouch," Carmen exclaimed. "Draw back the claws, girl. I think he's saying you work really hard, and he thinks you're getting taken advantage of."

Jacob pointed at the guitarist. "What she said. It's important to know your own value. It's honest work, but you're smarter than that. Look at the auditions today!" he pointed out. "Leave the dog delivery to someone else."

She shrugged, and Derek thought she actually looked relieved when her cell phone dinged, and she grabbed for it hastily. "I have to go," she announced. "Oscar is ready."

"It's a dog. He can wait," Jacob assured, gesturing for her to sit back down. "I bet no one's even home, and they won't have any idea when that dog gets back."

"True," Grace conceded, then countered, "However, if the groomer calls Oscar's family when I don't respond, I'll be in the soup. It's a lot of responsibility, but I knew that when I took the job, so can't much complain, right?"

She was answered by a series of grumbles.

"Can you at least finish dinner?" Derek asked. She looked like she had finally started to relax, and he was enjoying the smile that squished her eyes into happy slits.

She stood with her plate in hand and turned to Jacob. "Sorry. I'll put it in the fridge and have it tomorrow if that's okay."

"Sure. Sure," Jacob agreed. "There's some plastic wrap in the drawer next to the fridge. I think."

Everyone turned to watch her escape. There was a brief noise of drawers being opened and cling wrap screeching out of the roll before the fridge opened and closed.

"Thanks!" she called. Her head poked around the door jamb. "Bye!"

She was already in motion, waving and spinning to the back patio door.

"Grace!" Jacob called.

She whirled again, pausing, ankles crossed and toes lifted. Derek swore he saw her top flutter around her torso and come to a stop a moment after she had.

"Yes?"

"Let's start at ten tomorrow morning," Jacob suggested. "Real casual. Like T-shirts."

Grace blinked. "See you then," she called back. With one more wave, she was gone.

It had been like watching a whirlwind from table to fridge to door and then gone.

"Wow," Derek mumbled.

Carmen laughed, reaching for her beer. "Who let the air out of your balloon?" After a swallow, she pretended to wilt and mimicked Derek's voice. "Can't you stay for dinner, Grace? I want to watch you put things in your mouth." Carmen sighed, flicking her tongue around her lips outlandishly.

Everyone else at the table burst out laughing, and Rae's squeal rose above the cacophony as she clapped a hand over her mouth.

Derek's first thought was to protest, but he recognized the teasing for what it was. And, truthfully, she wasn't entirely wrong. He held up a hand to quiet them.

"I think Rae's got the right idea on this one. Don't shit where you eat. All it takes is one bad date, and she'll have Meyers drop me."

"There are other agents in this town, man. Like—thousands of them," Carmen pointed out. "Get yourself a piece if it looks good."

In Derek's experience, agents were all as difficult to trust as Meyers. But unlike anyone he'd gotten offers from in the past, Meyers acted on his promises, and he could put up with most anything in exchange for follow through. Everyone in this town was riding someone else to the top of the food chain. The next guy might be worse. At least he knew what to expect from Meyers.

"Maybe. But who's got time?"

"Well, me," laughed Rae.

"Don't do it," Carmen implored, reaching for the bassist's free hand. "We'll help you vet someone when you need one." She turned to Derek. "And maybe we'll all migrate."

"He's really not that bad," Jacob defended. "He gave me Grace for the week."

"You know he's going to charge you a few body parts for the privilege," Joe pointed out.

Jacob shrugged. "You get what you pay for."

"It would be cheaper to hire her," Rae suggested.

Derek cast a glare at her. She needed to back off. They had barely started the recording process, and they couldn't afford to take on any expenses yet. He would have to talk to her about this later privately.

"Let's get through the week before we start hiring staff," Jacob compromised. "You're upset because she's doing laundry and pet services for Meyers. But right now, she's scheduling and ordering food for us. We're no better than him."

Derek bit his lips to keep from bursting out laughing at the sour expression on his friend's face. Maybe Rae had finally met her match. He cleared his throat and began making suggestions for what he thought was missing from the track they'd been recording. Like moths to a flame, they immediately glommed onto the discussion, and Rae's lemon face disappeared.

He had no time for drama, or women, or anything besides music and his career.

When Grace wandered into the studio the next day, Derek almost didn't recognize her. She sported a black Rebel Gloss T-shirt tucked into dark jeans with sensible white canvas shoes. He and Jacob looked up from their place on the couch at her approach.

Jacob lifted a hand in greeting, his face splitting into a grin. "I knew you had it in you," he praised, clapping.

Derek joined him.

Grace flushed at his words but curtsied with her T-shirt. "Are you sure this is okay? Meyers would not approve."

"And he's not here. We'll be hanging around the house most of the day. You're fine." Jacob glanced at his laptop and gestured to a chair at the console. "In fact, we were going over the schedule. Can you help get us sorted?"

Grace nodded eagerly and swooped into the chair. She pinpointed their goals with a rapid-fire inquiry to create a working schedule then stood.

"Before I go, I wanted to mention that the patio door was unlocked when I got here."

Jacob shrugged. "I left it open for D this morning, and the others should be here soon."

Grace frowned, toying with the pen in her hand. "I'm worried that anyone could wander in, and if we're all back here, we'd never hear them. I'd be happy to man the door each day and let everyone in," she offered.

"I appreciate the concern, but I've never had any problem. We're fine. It's my friends and family policy," he explained. "Don't worry about it."

Grace slipped out the door wordlessly.

Derek had remained silent during the exchange. Grace's questions had cut right to the heart of the schedule, and all the waffling he and Jacob had been doing that morning felt like a waste of time. When she spoke, their album felt concrete. She took their venture seriously, and her determination to be professional was an unexpected boost to his confidence in the project.

He admired her hustle, he realized, recognizing a bit of his own drive in her. He needed to focus on the task at hand. He did not need the distraction of a woman right now. He had work to do, and BMW payments to make.

Jacob was still staring at the door in her wake. "She's like a tornado."

Derek agreed. "Meyers hired her for a reason."

"Do you think she really got all that? It was a lot...and I'm not even sure I told her everything."

"She'll get it. You watch." Derek stared at his companion for a moment.

Jacob smirked at him. "You're biased. What was it Carmen said last night? You just want to watch her put things in her mouth?"

"What?" he snapped. "That's not a thing." Derek frowned, and heat rushed up his neck as an image of Grace putting...*him*...in her mouth filled his head. Clearing his throat, he eyed his new friend.

"Not like you and Rae sexing each other up in the booth yesterday," he jibed, enjoying the bright red flush that flooded Jacob's face. His own mental image fizzled as he turned the tables on the other musician.

"She's not...I'm not...there's no..." Jacob stuttered, "...sexing..."

"Uh-huh," Derek dismissed.

Jacob's face looked like he'd swallowed a hot pepper, and Derek thought he might have seen an actual trickle of sweat on the man's forehead. A moment later, Jacob half ran out of the room.

Derek moved to the console and poured himself into the mix, tweaking the levels and plotting the backing vocals. He began making notes about where Carmen and Joe needed to add to the track.

One by one, the others joined him, all of them on autopilot as they tuned their instruments and plugged in. Joe took turns poking the girls in the sides randomly and turning away before they could catch him. Derek watched their antics with relief. It was so much easier to get synergy on a recording when everyone was comfortable. The late night had nearly set him out on the wrong foot that morning, but watching this new band gelling righted his path.

He was surprised when a neat stack of papers appeared on the console to his left. He found Grace beside him, her face neutral and hands behind her back as though she was waiting to be acknowledged before she would speak. He met her cool gaze.

"I drew up a schedule based on our conversation earlier. Let me know if I need to make any changes."

Derek glanced at the papers. It was a good thing he didn't have time for anything besides his career, he thought, because the frosty figure next to him seemed less than receptive.

"Thanks," he replied.

She stared at him awkwardly for a moment, and he wondered how long he could stare back before she would either crumple or turn tail and run.

Jacob rejoined them, making a beeline for the paperwork to Derek's relief, and he tuned out their exchange in favor of readying the tracks for the day's work.

"I took the liberty of adding in some breaks, and if that's okay, I'll set some alarms to keep you on schedule. Any requests for lunch? I'm about to order delivery."

Jacob blinked. "Thank you. That's…perfect."

Grace nodded. "I'll be back. Let me know if you need anything." Grace rushed out of the room.

"Told you," Derek teased, looking back at the younger man.

"You did. What else can you tell me about life, oh swami?"

Derek rolled his eyes. "Shut up and get in the booth."

Jacob complied with a smirk, and they were off to the races. The first track was taking shape, and he was pleased at how quickly they'd begun building the track based on Jacob's original melody. It felt like only a few minutes had passed when he caught sight of Grace waving from the doorway.

He blinked rapidly, as if waking up. He eased away from the console, slipping the headphones off one ear.

"Oh, hi." He smiled at her.

She returned the gesture. "It's sounding good," she complimented. "Which is why I hate to interrupt, but lunch is here. And it's hot, so time is of the essence."

"Ah." He glanced over his shoulder, then back to her. "I didn't realize it was that hour. We're actually close to a stopping point. I'm about to do the play back. Wanna listen?"

"Yes!" she yelped.

Derek chuckled at her enthusiasm and gestured for her to join him, patting the chair on his left. He focused on the music from the tracking room as the song ended, hovering his fingers over the stop key waiting for the right moment. He tapped the button as everyone sagged behind the glass and opened the mic.

"Guys, come out here and listen."

Rae, Carmen, and Joe crowded onto the couch behind Derek, squishing and pushing like siblings. Jacob remained standing, arms crossed over his midsection and bouncing gently from one foot to the other.

Derek pressed play and leaned back in his seat, scanning their faces as the music filtered through the speakers. He wiggled anxiously in the seat, twisting the chair back and forth as they listened like statues.

Carmen was the first to begin clapping as the sound faded away, and they congratulated themselves briefly, hugging and cheering before Grace announced that their lunch was getting cold in the dining room.

Joe was on his feet in a flash. "Food! Lead the way!"

There was an amicable bubble of excitement mixed with spells of quiet as the group devoured lunch. Rae and Carmen had teamed up again to keep seating arrangements the same as dinner the night before, but Derek didn't mind. Grace was nibbling at her food, cutting each bite delicately and chewing slowly.

Jacob and the others were rehashing the recording, suggesting changes and discussing tiny noises most people would never even hear. He joined in the debate and was in the middle of a suggestion about additional strings and vocals when the sound of the patio door sliding open halted the conversation.

Every head snapped to the doorway, some with forks halfway to their mouths and others in mid-chew. Grace craned her neck leaning forward toward the door.

Meyers turned the corner into the kitchen with a friendly wave and jaunty, "Hello!"

SEVEN

Grace should have seen this coming. Of course, Meyers was here. She had, after all, allowed herself to relax to the dress code Jacob set. That's how Murphy's Law worked, wasn't it?

Jacob was on his feet instantly, heading into the kitchen and intercepting the agent's path.

"Meyers," he called out. "Surprised to see you. I didn't realize I'd left the patio door unlocked."

Meyers smiled. "I saw all the cars and assumed it might be. Common thing in this town. I hope you don't mind."

"Um, sure," Jacob replied, leaning back against the kitchen counter and crossing his arms over himself. "What's up? Everything okay?"

Meyers nodded, eyes roaming over the table of artists and landing on his assistant.

His eyebrows rose.

"Grace, you look…comfortable."

There was a clatter of forks on plates as Carmen and Rae cleared their throats loudly in near perfect unison.

Grace swallowed, not trusting herself to say anything as she sat up straight in her chair. She felt Rae's hand on her knee under the table. Her best course of action was to have no reaction. Pasting a hint of a smile on her lips, she folded her hands in her lap and smoothed out her expression.

Jacob followed the man's gaze. "Yeah. We insisted. The suits were making us uncomfortable."

Meyers stroked the lapel of his suit coat like a nervous tick. "Ah. I see. I wouldn't want anyone to be uncomfortable," he conceded, as he surveyed the group at the dining table again. "How's the recording going?"

Derek rose, joining Jacob in the kitchen, answering as he walked. "The collaboration is everything we hoped for. We're right on track to finish up as planned." He leaned against the counter next to Jacob, effectively blocking Meyers' view of the dining area.

Grace could barely see her boss between Jacob and Derek now, and she held her breath. Her head slanted to one side as her eyes landed on Derek's backside. His acid washed jeans suited him, and she traced the lines of his pockets. She licked her lips, remembering abruptly that her boss was present. Meyers met her eyes between the guys' heads, and she blinked slowly, keeping her expression smooth as though she had not been ogling his client.

"Great! I'm glad to hear it," Meyers continued. "Any chance I could hear it?"

There was almost no pause between Meyer's last word and Derek's reply. "Oh, no. We're not ready for that. I don't want to jinx anything by playing it too soon. Too many cooks in the kitchen and all that. You understand."

Jacob looked at the producer and back to Meyers. "Yeah, we're a little superstitious about that. Playing it close to the vest."

Meyers nodded. "Well, that's why I introduced you. Kindred spirits." He looked around the guys to the dining table again, but when neither Derek nor Jacob invited further discourse, he lifted a hand. "Let me know if you need anything."

"Will do," Derek answered.

"Yeah, we've got Grace. We're good," Jacob announced, breaking the wall he and Derek had put between the agent and the dining area. He slid the door open, reaching to shake Meyers' hand. "She'll reach out if we need you. Thanks again for the introduction and for Grace."

Breath caught in her throat, Grace's eyes narrowed in on her boss. After Jacob's answer, he was going to accuse her of stealing his clients, but he wouldn't do it now. Not in front of them. She prayed that between now and Monday, he would get distracted by something and forget to give her another stern talking to. Or worse: a pink slip.

Meyers accepted the platitude, and Grace felt Rae's hand release under the table as the man stepped out the door.

Jacob waved, closing doors behind the agent. The distinct click of tumblers locking into place echoed across the silent house. No one spoke until the crunch of tires in the driveway signified that they were again alone.

Leaning against the patio door, Jacob shook his head and met Grace's eyes. "You were right. No more leaving the door unlocked."

Her vision was blurry, and she blinked to clear it. Normally, she would have quipped how she was glad to hear him say she was right. But she was at a loss for words at the way everyone had defended her in his presence and swallowed back the tears threatening to unleash themselves. She picked up the fork to push around the food on her plate, unsure if she was ready to eat again.

"Yep," she finally rasped and took a bite.

"Okay, I'll say it," Carmen grumbled, leaning her elbows firmly on the table and half laying over her plate. "What a fucking ass! What was he doing here? He's only our agent, right?"

Joe shrugged, already plucking another dumpling from the middle of the table. "He does this."

Jacob's brow thatched in wrinkles, and he squinted at the drummer. "He's done this to you before?" He and Derek reseated themselves at the table.

"Yep," Joe confirmed.

"How long have you worked with him?" Carmen asked, leaning toward Grace.

Her voice was shaky as she answered. "Almost four months now. It's still new," she explained. She sucked in a deep breath and smiled at the others, then stared at her plate. The last bite felt like lead in her stomach.

"Quit!" Carmen yelled. "Quit now. And sue the motherfucker. How dare he say *anything* about what you're wearing?" Carmen's knuckles were white around her fork.

"He's my boss," Grace sighed. "It's his purview to set the dress code."

"And this week," Jacob interrupted, "I'm your boss. And I say anything goes."

"So, ass-less chaps tomorrow?" Rae suggested brightly.

The group screamed in laughter, and Grace joined in, grateful for the break. She wiped the corners of her eyes as she began clearing her plate. In silent accord, the others followed suit. She waved off their help, gesturing for them to set down the dishes.

"I've got this," she promised, tapping her wrist where a watch should have been but wasn't.

"We don't mind," Joe offered.

She plucked the plate from his hand.

"Thank you, but I'm good. This is how I contribute. I can't play an instrument or sing, but I can clean up. Go strike while the proverbial iron is hot. Please. Derek's about to wet his pants waiting to get back in there," she mocked. She worried briefly that she'd overstepped her bounds, but his laugh set her at ease as she picked up his plate next to hers.

"The woman knows what she wants. Let's leave her to it," Derek ordered. He winked at Grace and led the way from the kitchen toward the studio.

Grace was frozen to the spot. The others filed out, Carmen grumbling to Joe about their nosy agent. Rae smirked at Derek and then to Grace before skipping behind the others.

As the room went quiet, Grace allowed herself to set the load in her hand on the counter. Her hands were shaking, and she collected them against her chest, turning to face the back yard. This was the second time today she'd received the knowing signal from him, and her legs were like jelly.

Working near Derek was becoming a problem. Every word and look directed toward her set her brain to goo mode. She had very nearly dropped the plates because he winked at her. Every teen dream and wistful thought she'd ever had came oozing through her pores.

What had she been thinking moving to a city of celebrities? She had known somewhere in the deep recesses of her brain that Derek lived in this city, but the possibility that they would ever cross paths had never seemed remotely plausible.

She sucked in a breath and looked at the remains of lunch spread across the kitchen and dining room. This was normal, real-life stuff. She eyed his napkin wadded on top of his plate, thinking that she had watched him eat. Like they were friends or at least colleagues. She pushed the romantic whims away and set to the task at hand. An unexpected thought popped into her head, and she skipped to the sink.

"I'm with the band," she squeaked to herself.

The rest of the week flew by in a flurry of breakfasts, lunches, and dinners, and as Grace gathered her things from Jacob's house on Friday evening, the entire band watched her like *she* was the celebrity. Her skin prickled at the sensation as Carmen and Rae kept hiding her power cables or her phone, and Grace chased after them good naturedly.

"What am I gonna do next week without you?" Jacob groaned. "You can't leave me alone with all these mongrels."

She chuckled as Carmen slapped his arm and Joe made gnarly faces behind him, exposing as many of his teeth as he could bare.

Jacob spun on them. "See? They're already attacking me." He made faces back at Joe.

Grace laughed, waving him off. "You'll be fine. You're traveling Tuesday anyway, and I know 'cause I booked the ticket! You won't have long to miss me, and you'll be gone."

He rolled his eyes. "Well, yes. But…"

"But nothing," she silenced. "You're great. It's not like you've never done this before."

He shrugged. "Okay. But maybe I want you to understand how much you were needed here and how much you contributed."

Grace smirked. "Put it in the liner notes," she bantered.

"Liner notes," Jacob laughed. He turned to Derek who was joining them from the studio, one of Grace's computer cords dangling from his fingers. "Do we do liner notes anymore?"

"If we have a shred of dignity left, yes!" he affirmed.

"Who needs dignity?" Carmen interjected.

"Quit acting like we'll never see Grace again," Rae insisted. "She's family, and I *know* she'll come visit when she can," she added, eyeing Grace.

"Yes!" Jacob agreed. "You'll stop by in the evenings, right? You could listen to it then."

"Um," Grace hesitated, thinking about her schedule. She hated to commit this far in advance.

"Yeah," Derek agreed. "It's kinda nice to have an outsider's perspective."

Rae growled, punching Derek in the arm. "*Family* is not an outsider. Aren't you listening?"

Derek groaned, rubbing his arm. "You can't hit old guys, Rae. I meant as someone not directly involved in writing or performing the music. Geez," Derek grumbled. "Could you lighten up?"

Rae squinted one eye at him, then relaxed her face. "It's a good thing you're pretty," she acquiesced.

"You are," Carmen pestered, hanging on Derek's good arm and making kissy faces at him in one moment, then pushing him away in the next, laughing all the while.

Jacob pressed past the others, leaning against the kitchen counter where Grace's laptop bag rested.

"I've really enjoyed having you here. And I've got some ideas." He turned on one elbow for the full effect of his serious stare to engulf her. "If this really goes where I think it could, I'm hoping you might be open to making this arrangement permanent."

Grace blinked at him, unable to give any other reply. While Rae had planted the seed over a week ago, she hadn't believed there was any possibility of this happening. But here she was, staring into Jacob's earnest expression and dumbfounded.

"Just say yes," Joe encouraged, stepping up and wrapping an arm around her shoulder. He squeezed it gently and released her quickly. "Glad you were here. Hope to see you next week." He raised his hand to the others and waved his phone. "You know where I'll be. Call me when you're back and ready." Then equally as unassuming, he let himself out the back patio door.

Derek laughed. "You gotta respect a man of so few words."

Carmen waved a peace sign at the group. "Same here. Be safe in Boston next week," she called to Jacob. "Rae, you want a ride?"

The bassist shook her head. "Neh, Grace already offered. I want to make sure she's not going to the vet or the cleaners or anything. She promised."

Carmen chuckled then wrapped Grace in a tight surprise hug. "See ya." She too, exited the kitchen, rolling the patio door quickly shut.

Despite spending the week with the group, she shivered at the invasion of her personal space. "I should've seen that coming by now," she mumbled.

"Oh, if we're doing hugs, it's my turn," Jacob bounced toward her and wrapped her up, lifting her briefly off the floor.

Grace shrieked, not sure if she should hold on for dear life or push him away. Neither option felt appropriate, and she begged him to stop. "Oh dear! Down, down!"

Jacob dropped her unceremoniously, snickering.

Derek smirked. "I promise not to accost you," he pledged. "But I will help you carry your things to the car."

"What a gentleman," she replied, picking up her purse and a stack of papers. Derek had already grabbed her heavy laptop bag and shouldered it with ease. They headed out, and the sound of the patio door slipping shut pinged in her ears.

"If he offers you the job, you should take it," Derek murmured.

Grace took a deep breath as she recalled the proposition. "It's a very kind offer. I'll have to evaluate it if it happens."

He nodded as she opened the car door. "The thing about LA is you have to learn to say yes," he instructed. "You don't usually get a second chance."

"Thank you," she replied as he passed her bags to her.

He stretched his neck and shoulder. "And you should consider traveling lighter. You're gonna break your back."

She grinned. "Or I'll have to hire a sherpa to follow me around."

Derek arched a brow at her. "Good luck with that." He shoved his fingertips into the front pockets of his jeans. "You've really been a great asset to the team," he complimented. "I'm not sure that Meyers knows what he has in you."

"Possibly," she agreed, not wanting to talk about Meyers in that moment. "If I'm honest, I'm dreading going back there. This has been a lot more fun."

"And that is why a lot of people take that job, to find one like this. I respect that you don't complain about it, although I can empathize 'cause I do not miss my days of dog groomers and dry cleaning."

"You did this?"

"Something like it. We all pay our dues."

Her head was spinning with questions, and she bit her lower lip.

Before her train of thought could progress further, the patio door slid open again, and Grace looked past him to see Rae, her bass slung over one shoulder.

Grace sucked in a deep breath, loathe to end the conversation. In the moonlight, with Derek standing a foot from her and giving her career advice like an older brother or mentor, she was wholly content. While her fantasies all centered around a much different relationship with him, she was quite happy to have the easy engagement they had fostered over the past week.

She glanced back at Derek in time to see his hands dislodge themselves from his pockets, and he hugged her quickly.

"You promised not to accost her in the house, D. I heard it," Rae goaded.

Grace's thighs were tingling, and she gripped the car door to keep herself upright. It had been such a speedy embrace, she wasn't convinced it had happened. Except that the warmth of his body lingered against her cheek and where his hands had rested on her back.

"See you next week, D," Rae called as she stowed her gear in the back and slipped into the passenger seat.

Derek lifted a hand to them both then ducked into his own car to clear a path. Grace watched him go until his headlights had completely disappeared.

"You okay there?" Rae beckoned.

Rae's voice cut through the sense of longing that filled Grace at his departure. She dropped into the driver's seat and shut the door.

"What?" She snapped her seat belt into place and pressed the car's start button quickly, pretending nothing had happened.

Rae snorted and clipped in her seat belt. "Forward ho!" she rallied, pointing toward the street.

~ 🎵 ~ DEREK ~ 🎵 ~

Nearly two weeks later, the entire band was playing their asses off, but something was just...*off.* Derek couldn't put his finger on it, and it was making him cranky. He opened a channel to the booth, leaning in and grumbling.

"Sorry guys, but it's not right. Joe, I like what you're doing with the syncopated beat, but can we try it straight once?"

Joe shook out his arms. Before he could count off the beat, five alarms blared across the studio announcing lunch. Last week, Grace had insisted they take breaks and sent reminders that interrupted them three times a day. It wasn't the same as when she would sneak into the space, wait to be acknowledged, and then tell them all it was time for bio breaks. They were all too polite to ignore her in person, unlike the five aggravating alarms going off at once. Derek was tempted to work once everyone had silenced the phones.

However, now that the alarm had interrupted his train of thought, he realized he was hungry. She had figured him out pretty quickly, he realized. He tucked his phone back into his bag and opened the microphone. "You wanna break or keep going?"

Jacob rolled his neck. "Let's stop. We're not getting anywhere anyway. Chinese okay?"

The band grumbled but extracted themselves from their instruments and made their way out of the studio and headed down the hall.

Jacob pressed his head against the wall, eyes closed, as he spoke to the local delivery.

Derek followed the others down the hall.

"This is a fresh new hell," Rae complained, displaying her thumb to Carmen. "There's a blister forming under the one that opened up last week."

Carmen shrugged. "The blister under my blister popped on the last song." She held the weeping appendage out to her band mate. "But who cares if Grace isn't here to nearly upchuck. Now it's annoying and not funny."

Rae agreed, slouching onto the couch in the front room.

"I got some new tape over the weekend," Joe offered, reaching into his nondescript backpack and producing some antiseptic tape. He tossed it to Carmen who grabbed it deftly out of the air.

Joe sat heavily on the other end of the couch, laying his head back and groaning. "I'm starving," he complained. "Grace always had it here waiting at break time."

Derek paced, eyeing each of the members. None of them had been playing poorly, but it wasn't gelling. If he didn't know better, he'd say they were arguing, but they weren't. No one had been happy since they arrived to an empty counter and not even a pot of coffee. Jacob had tried making a pot, but the grounds were old, and he wasn't sure if he put enough in the filter. Rae had broken three strings. Jacob seemed to have some kind of throat issue, missing notes left and right. Joe had sent at least two sticks flying. The only one who'd been hitting all the marks was Carmen, but she couldn't carry the band alone.

"Food's on its way," Jacob announced from the mouth of the hallway. Before anyone could say more, his phone rang.

The others were silent, staring at him with curiosity at the distinct smile that turned the corners of his mouth as he pressed the phone to his ear. "Why hello, Gracie!" the singer caroled.

Rae squeaked, clapping her hands furiously and bumping Carmen's shoulder with her own.

He chuckled and tucked one hand into the crook of his elbow. "Yes, ma'am we're on lunch break as you stipulated."

Everyone crowded the phone, Derek on the outside edge as Jacob tapped the speakerphone button and held it out.

"HELLO, GRACE!" they chorused, leaning into the phone.

"We miss you!" Rae called.

Carmen yelled, "We need some Bactine, Grace!"

"Hey, can we get coffee delivered?" Joe added.

Jacob pulled the phone back and took a few steps away.

Grace's giggle sounded like a cartoon through the speaker. "How is recording?"

"It sucks!" Carmen groused. "And it's your fault. We can't function without an audience."

"She means we value your opinion," Jacob interpreted. "How's it going at the office?"

"Oh, I'm running an errand and thought I'd check in. I didn't want to call from inside the building. Too many ears, you know?"

"I think I do," Jacob concurred. "Any chance you'll be able to swing by when you're done?"

"Well," Grace replied drawing out the word. "I can make that happen. I'll call when I'm close so someone can let me in."

Jacob groaned. "Yes, Grace. The door is locked. We learned our lesson. Maybe I should make you a key."

Grace laughed. "Don't let Meyers find out. He'll say I'm forgetting my place again."

Derek backed out of the conversation, finding the couch with his bottom harder than he had planned when he sat down. The others huddled around Jacob's phone as they chatted, and the girls took turns described their wounds in gory detail with glee and listened to Grace protest. He could practically see the assistant's cringe, face wrinkling into a knot and her slender fingers covering her brown eyes.

He wondered when it had happened that his agent's green wallflower of an assistant had become the opinion that mattered. If he was honest, he had missed her, too. He'd gotten used to her taking up the administrative slack he usually handled. She took care of all the food, handled phone calls, accepted packages, kept notes of their interactions, and so many more tiny things that allowed them to keep working and not run out to buy more water. With a jolt, he realized he had started to think of her as his partner. He frowned and turned his attention back to the conversation.

Grace's tinny voice silenced the others. "You guys could make a girl get a big head. It has been proven I know nothing about music or music history."

"But you know what you like," Jacob replied. "You're a better litmus test than you think. And you're not afraid to say when you don't like something."

Grace laughed. "That's what you think."

"We know you're quiet, Gracie," Rae cooed, "It's..." The bassist waved her hands in the air, apparently lost for words.

"You're so calm," Joe finished. "Somebody has to help me balance out these loudmouths!" He cracked a smile for the first time that day.

Everyone else laughed as Derek continued pondering. They were all right. Grace had literally been there from the beginning. She was part of the magic. She had set the tone at that very first lunch, which would not have gone the same with Meyers meddling. Grace knew enough about him and Jacob to be the perfect blend of helpful and unobtrusive that they needed. Before he had a chance to say anything, the call was over. Everyone was energized and laughing in the wake of the call, and he hadn't said a word.

The food arrived shortly thereafter, and he followed Rae into the kitchen to retrieve plates and utensils.

"We need her back," he muttered.

"Agreed," Rae exclaimed.

Carmen joined in, taking the utensils from Derek as Rae passed him plates. "If we eat fast maybe we can fix what's wrong with that last track before Grace gets here, or if not, maybe she can put her finger on it with that fart expression she does when something's not right," Carmen suggested.

Jacob barked a laugh. "She would not like that description."

"I never said we should tell her," Carmen cooed, taking a container from Jacob and running to the table.

"Voting for the secret," Derek approved, raising a hand before he took a seat. "Where's the Kung-Pao chicken?"

The band virtually inhaled their food, debating what they could do differently, then zoomed down the hall into the studio.

~ ♫ ~ GRACE ~ ♫ ~

Paused in the mouth of Jacob's driveway, foot firmly on the brake, Grace reached for her phone to text the group chat to unlock the door. The message whooshed away, and she rolled down the slight hill and around the back of the house to park in her usual place. Her heart thrilled at the sight of Derek's car ahead of her.

She chucked off her suit coat, tossing it in the back seat, then untucked her shirt. She took a moment to stretch, reveling in the glorious sensation, before collecting her handbag and locking the car door. She couldn't remember the last time she'd done something on her way home from the office that she actually looked forward to.

The patio doors slid open, and she spun around to face them. Derek leaned out, balanced on the door frame. His hair was getting a bit longer, and it gleamed in the setting sunlight.

"Hey," he greeted. His mouth quirked into a smile as he swung gently. The breeze lifted the corner of his shirt, giving her a glimpse of his stomach, and her brain filled in the rest. It was a completely innocent pose, she knew. Something her friends in high school might have done, or something she'd been guilty of as well. But with Derek, everything was sexy.

She stumbled as she approached the threshold, eyes drinking in his taut body. She'd fully expected Rae or Carmen to meet her. In hindsight, she realized of course it would be Derek who spent most of his time manning the controls. His hand shot out inches from her, presumably to catch her in case she fell, and she cleared her throat.

"Oh, hi!" She smoothed her hands over her smart slacks. "I'm good," she assured as she breezed past him.

He locked the door behind her. "Come on back. They're wrapping up another take. It's been a long day," he explained.

Grace glanced around the kitchen. "Have I got five minutes before they're finished?"

He craned an ear toward the studio. "Maybe."

She nodded. "I'll be back in a minute. Don't let me distract you."

Derek opened his mouth to reply, but no sound followed, and he closed it again. He waved a hand and sprinted back down the hall to the studio.

Grace shed her handbag and shoes before cleaning up the dining table and kitchen. Her mind played over the events of the day. Meyers had been frigid when he wasn't grilling her about setting up an appointment with Rae to get her to sign with him. He had reminded her three times to make the phone call.

She dreaded the conversation she had planned to have during a break tonight. She knew Rae would react badly given the way she'd been talking the week before.

When she'd finished, she loaded her arms with bottled water before hurrying to the studio. Given how much food they'd left on their plates, not to mention the table, she assumed they could use some tending. The control room door was open, and Derek was poised against the console, hands braced on its edge with his ass in the air. She was afraid the others would catch her, and she tore her gaze away to look at them. The musicians were virtually frozen, their eyes glued to Derek. He pressed a button and dropped the headphones from his ears.

In the next moment, Rae and Carmen began screaming, high fiving each other before hugging and jumping, barely managing not to tangle their instruments together in their excitement.

"That felt right!" Jacob exclaimed.

"Playback!" Joe begged. "Play it back!"

Derek seemed equally excited, tapping a series of buttons before the song filled the room.

Grace was motionless in the doorway, clutching the water as music oozed out of the speakers. Joe was bopping his head to the beat and twirling his sticks as the chorus began, air drumming to his own work. Rae and Carmen had deposited their strings into waiting stands and were dancing like they were at a club. Jacob's feet were tapping as he joined them.

To her delight and horror, Derek darted into the tracking room and bumped Jacob's shoulder lightly with his own.

And then, right before her eyes, Derek began to dance, hips jutting forward, feet keeping perfect time with the song, and arms pumping rhythmically. Within a split second, Jacob matched the footing, and they were in lock step. Derek's confidence was intoxicating, and she imagined him stalking toward her with that same swagger in a far more private setting.

Every last bottle of water slipped from her arms as Grace's body puckered, and her arms closed over her chest to hide her flashing headlights. The bottles bounced across the control room floor.

"Oh, shit!" she yelped.

Terrified one was going to burst, she chased after them. The fumble gave her a perfect distraction, and she dropped on her haunches to collect them. She barely even noticed that everyone had stopped reveling to stare at her.

Rae rushed in to help.

"I got it, I got it. Nothing broke," Grace declared with one hand in the air, and making no eye contact. Forcing the images of Derek from her mind required conjuring dirty drains and sewage, and some really strange pimple popping videos that were flooding the internet. However, it did the trick, and as she pulled herself to her feet, the tickling sensation of loose hairs fluttering around her cheeks and chin the only indication that she was flustered.

"I brought water," she offered, holding one out to Rae sheepishly.

The others joined her accepting the proffered plastic with a smile.

"So, was it so bad you just lost your grip?" Joe teased before sucking down half the bottle in a single pull.

She shook her head, grateful when the last bottle had been dispersed. "No. Just a klutz," she covered. "I thought you said it was going badly, but it was great! I really loved the tempo. So positive."

Carmen curtsied. "Thank you. That was Derek's idea. It was pretty dark and slow this morning."

"Group effort," Derek corrected. "We're in this together."

"Whatever. You got skills. Accept the compliment," Rae scolded.

"Well, I like it," Grace stated. She watched as Jacob stretched, and Joe emptied his water bottle. "You guys look whipped."

"I know, right?" Carmen grumbled, yawning for emphasis. "My fingers are toast for today." She stuck her wet bandages near Grace's face, grinning when Grace pulled back, lips curled up in disgust.

"Play it again," Rae begged. "I want to hear it all from the couch."

"Sit," Jacob insisted to Grace, motioning to the seating.

Derek restarted the track, and the band settled into whatever seat they could find.

Grace closed her eyes to focus. Instead, her brain treated her to the memory of Derek dancing, his torso and hips rolling fluidly. As a teen, when he'd danced, she'd always been enamored by his skill and wished to have his timing. Nothing she had ever done looked as cool as he did dancing. She'd never seen him dance in person before. All she could do now was translate his moves to other, more mature applications. She prayed that her tapping foot would keep anyone from noticing.

EIGHT

The following week, Derek was fighting not to lay his head on the diner table as he waited for Peter to arrive. Nancy wanted her husband out of the house for a few hours, and Derek had agreed to meet him for lunch at their favorite dive restaurant. The food was delicious, but it wasn't especially healthy, and they had once agreed to never ask about the cleanliness of the kitchen. A goodly amount of deep frying killed everything.

He watched bubbles forming around the straw in his cup as the striped plastic tube tried to float over the edge and onto the Formica tabletop.

Peter was suddenly across from him, dropping into the booth unceremoniously. He was dressed casually in a T-shirt and ripped jeans. The shirt may as well have been painted across his six-pack abs. A random stranger would have thought he'd done it on purpose, but Derek had spent long enough sharing a roll of toilet paper with him from neighboring apartments to know that Pete was simply outgrowing his clothes. He spent nearly all his time in the gym these days, and his muscles were out of control.

"Look who I found wandering the parking lot like a lost valet," Peter announced, throwing his arms left.

Derek jumped from the booth when he spied their friend Leo standing beside him.

They hugged tightly, thumping each other on the back before Derek slipped back into the booth, and Leo crushed in beside Peter till the other man was squished against the wall. They relented and finally sat still.

It was like being back on the tour bus with them, and he smiled at the memory. "Man, it's good to see you. It's been a lifetime."

Leo nodded, his dark hair curling around his jaw. His smile was the same as always despite the salt-and-pepper beard framing it. There was no faking happy for this passionate man. Leo was all in or all out.

"I know, right? It sounds weird, but I had to get back to LA to relax after being in New York for so long."

"I know what you mean," Derek chuckled. He looked at Peter. "I thought you wanted to get out of Nancy's way for a bit."

Peter shrugged. "I did. And Leo called last night to say he was in town, so I invited him. You're completely impossible to get a hold of lately, or I'd have told you in advance."

"It's good to see you," Derek replied. "Keeping busy hopping coasts it sounds like."

Leo launched into details of the project he'd been working on lately, until a young waiter shuffled to the table to take their orders then headed toward the kitchen.

Derek fussed with his escaping straw, chuckling at the litany of items Leo had ordered.

"So, what's today's deep thought?" Peter questioned once they were alone.

Derek blinked at his friend. "Not a thing. I'm wiped out. Never worked so hard in my life."

Peter chuckled. "I thought that's what you lived for."

Derek shrugged. "Yeah, but it's good we have a break today. I think we went like, eleven days without a break. I needed time to sleep in my own bed."

"What do you mean your own bed?" Leo queried, leaning over the table.

"The client has this massive house, and we're there till like 4 a.m. a lot of times, and then he tells us to stay the night. Super generous. Comfortable digs. Just…"

"Weird," Peter finished. "That's never happened before, has it?"

Derek indicated that it hadn't. "It's really going well. We've got at least five in the can. Not that he can leave them alone. We say we're going to sleep on it, and then I come back, and he's changed it, and it's like starting from square one."

"Wait, so you're working with someone pickier than you?" Leo feigned horror, then smirked at his friend. "I thought you were the biggest perfectionist."

"Apparently not," Derek countered. "At some point, you have to stop. I'm all for letting it rest and then tweaking, but one of them we've rewritten twice. And it's good still—I'm not convinced it's better. It's hard to see the forest for the trees. Thank God Grace comes in and settles arguments for us still."

"Wait—Grace?" Peter balked. He turned to Leo to fill him in. "She's his agent's assistant and a *fan*."

"You're hanging out with a fan?" Leo gasped.

"Why is she still around?" Peter added.

Derek threw up his hands in dismay. "Jacob likes her. Meyers let him borrow her for a week to get us started, and now they're all addicted to keeping her around."

"Why?" Leo questioned. "I know you, man. You don't keep fans in your circle."

Peter arched an accusatory brow, seconding the remark.

"She's really good at admin work. She set up auditions in a day. Like, she started in the morning, and that afternoon, we were holding auditions with ten people."

Leo drew back. "Do you call her Wonder Woman?"

Peter barked out a laugh, pointing. "Look at you, picturing her in nothing but that leotard, you nerd."

Derek rolled his eyes. "It's weird. She has no music background, but we've all somehow agreed that if Grace doesn't like it, it's back to the drawing board."

Their waiter returned with two drinks and a side of onion rings for Leo who grabbed one without pretense, hissing around the hot batter as it touched his lips.

Peter stirred his drink with a straw as he inspected the glass. "Well, from what I remember, she's a fan of both of you and knows all your work. So, maybe she is uniquely qualified."

"Maybe," Derek allowed begrudgingly.

"For the record," Peter explained, turning to Leo, "We like this girl. D brought her over to the barbecue you missed out on because you're like famous or something. He's in denial."

"We as in Nancy approves too?" Leo quizzed, blowing on another onion ring.

Peter nodded, reaching for one of the fried circles.

Leo fixed Derek with a look and gave a slow shake of his head. "You are toast, bro."

"Stop," Derek protested. "You're worse than Carmen."

"Who's Carmen?" Peter retorted, dropping his hand to the table, half eaten onion ring still lodged between his thumb and forefinger. "Is she hot?"

"Smoking," Derek answered. "She's our guitarist."

Peter glanced at Leo and back then narrowed his eyes. "How long have you been working with these people?"

Derek's eyes flew up as he did mental calculations. "Going on three weeks now."

"And you're just now mentioning that there are people other than the client and Rae?"

"So?" Derek snapped. "I shouldn't have even told you who my client was. I don't tell you everything."

"Who's the client?" Leo grumbled. "Pretend I haven't been in town lately, and I don't know anything."

Derek frowned at himself. "Sorry, man. There's Grace and me and my studio tech Rae that I told you was a big fan of yours. And Carmen, our guitarist, and Joe, our drummer. And the client that I can't name."

"But you've included Grace before any of them. Grace with no musical credentials. And someone you met a month ago. And I saw the way you looked at her at my barbecue. Like a puppy you wanted to take home."

"I do not have time for a puppy," Derek replied as their food arrived.

"You have time for whatever you want to have time for," Peter scolded, unfolding a napkin into his lap. "And maybe I think you should make time for something like this."

Derek pretended nothing had been said and took an enormous bite out of his burger, chewing it slowly.

Leo shuffled plates around then glanced at Derek. "A puppy would be good for you. You can't take home strays all the time." His brows furrowed. "I think I've lost the metaphor."

Peter swallowed his bite hastily. "See, the way you're avoiding just makes me want to push more. What is it about her that's under your skin? Why are you avoiding? I've seen you pounce on people far less appropriate."

"Appropriate?" Derek recoiled. "What's that supposed to mean?"

"She's the right age. She obviously likes you, and she's got her own job and supports herself." He glanced at Leo. "You remember that one he took back to our hotel who was way older than you and had no money."

Leo nearly choked on a mouthful of food. "The leopard print ass!" he exclaimed. "Yes!" He wiggled his hips on the seat, and the whole booth shimmied.

"I know you ain't that picky," Peter accused, looking directly across the table.

"I don't know what you're talking about." He reached for his straw and sucked up some diet cola to avoid their line of questioning. He remembered her too. He thought he was something being able pull a woman so much older on his nineteenth birthday. She was the boldest woman he'd ever talked to, not afraid to show him that women wanted it as badly as men did.

"Don't even try to deny it," Peter pressed. "None of us will ever forget the sight of that walk of shame leaving your room that morning.

Like, how drunk were you?"

"We're done with that," Derek insisted. "That was almost twenty years ago, man. Pick another story."

Peter grinned. "Forget it. Any story that includes a leopard printed ass is for keeps. Seriously—what's wrong with Grace? I'm not saying marry the girl—but ask her out. Maybe there should be some alcohol. She's kind of tight-lipped."

Derek frowned. "That sounds like a lot of work."

Leo set down his fork. "Excuse me? You, Mr. Workaholic, are afraid of work? Wait, lemme get out my phone and record that for your baby book."

"What's the big deal? Between you guys, Rae, and Carmen, I'm getting it non-stop." His nose wrinkled as he realized that Jacob and Joe were no better. Each one of them was constantly engineering some way to force the two together.

"Because you won't admit what we all clearly see. You're attracted to her. So? You're a red-blooded male, and she has all your favorite parts." Peter laughed at himself.

Leo lifted his roast beef sandwich. "Dude—you are the prime example of protesting too much."

"Maybe," he grumbled. Derek refused to admit his friend was right, but the woman had been consuming a lot more of his thoughts than was normal. "But what if it's some lingering nostalgia because she's a fan? She's good for my ego."

"You're both in your thirties, man. So what if it is? And you won't know till you try."

"What's wrong with a little...*ego* stroking?" Leo pressed. He and Peter shared a laugh.

Derek grumbled and took another exceedingly large bite followed by two bundles of fries which barely fit in his mouth.

"Dude, if you're trying to turn her off, she's not here, and we were already turned off," Peter harassed. "Slow down before you trigger a cranky over-thirty digestive system."

Realizing what he'd done, Derek eased back in his seat and

swallowed his food. "How did we get this old?"

"Who are you talking about?" Peter waved him off as he struck a pose. "I'm in my prime."

"For dad-bod," Derek countered.

Leo threw a French fry at him.

~ ♪ ~ GRACE ~ ♪ ~

When Grace arrived at Jacob's place on Thursday afternoon, Carmen and Rae met her at the door. They crowded close to brandish their blisters and woes about being ugly handed in the tropics as she headed toward the studio.

Grace shied away, squeezing her eyes shut. "I brought some Bactine and Neosporin," she soothed, pulling the items from her purse.

"Let the woman breathe, ladies!" Derek reproached, stepping into the middle of the trio. He lifted his arms to force the strings section to back up then lead Grace by the hand to the console where he pulled out the chair next to his and took a seat.

She stared at the back of his head, putty in his hands. He had released her when he pulled out the chair, but her hand was still tingling at the contact.

He continued as though nothing had happened. "So, we're thinking the current song is off somehow, but we aren't sure if it's in the mix…"

"More bass!" Rae interrupted, impishly.

Derek shot her a glance, and she smirked, quieting down.

"Ahem," Derek cleared his throat before continuing. He pinned Carmen with a look of warning, and she held up her hands, giggling. "Okay, so…something is missing either in the mix or in the music itself. Would you listen for us?"

"Anything for you," Grace replied without thinking. Her eyes widened, and she looked around at everyone else in the room. "You're my band. You don't even have to ask."

Her pulse was racing. Derek leaned across her to press a few buttons and flip a switch, and she nearly leaned closer to inhale his aftershave but stopped herself in time.

Jacob's voice emanated from the speakers, clear and strong. It was a catchy beat on first listen; the instrumentals were smooth. She kept listening, understanding what they meant about something being missing. The catchy beat and the dark lyrics didn't match.

"It's hard to say," Grace mused, watching the way Derek watched her every move as she tried to articulate herself. "It's like everything is bouncy and light, but there's nothing anchoring it. I think Rae was right. Needs more bass. More drums, too," she responded as the last few notes drifted out of the speakers. "In my opinion..."

"Huh, you were half right, Rae-Rae," Joe chuckled. "Gracie put her finger right on the pulse."

"Hang on," Derek announced. His eyes flickered around the screen, hands were already moving over the console and reaching for his headphones.

"It's happened before, me being right," Rae countered, sticking her tongue out at him.

"What about this?" Derek pressed a button, and the control room filled with the song again, but it sounded different. This time, Rae's syncopated rhythm led the track, Joe's drums punctuating the end of each of Jacob's lines. The rearrangement brought the whole song together, and she felt her shoulders beginning to twist to the beat.

Before they reached the chorus, Jacob was pointing at Grace. "That's it. You're the man. Woman, I mean."

Derek was shaking his head at the console with a smile, giving her a sidelong glance. "You are the magic, Grace," Derek uttered quietly.

Her insides melted at the sound of her name on his lips. Her instincts told her to get up and run to the back yard to squeal like Tinkerbell. Instead, she folded her hands in her lap pinching her wrist discreetly to confirm she was awake.

Derek was already focused on the band again. "I still think the opening needs a little love. Jacob, your voice cracked a little, so can we record that bit again?"

"I want another take in the second verse," Carmen added. "I think it should be a little punchier right before the chorus to match the bass and drums."

Everyone else agreed, talking through the changes they still wanted to make.

"Let's play through it and make sure it's the right direction," Derek called to the others. He turned to Grace. "See this button?" He pointed to the screen. "When I give you the signal, press it. When we stop playing, press it again," he instructed.

Grace nodded dumbly, thinking he had a lot of faith in her as he joined the others in the tracking room, taking position behind a synthesizer. It faced the band but put his back to her, and she watched him wriggle his shoulders before holding a thumbs up.

She pressed the button and sat back, terrified she would accidentally touch something else and ruin the recording.

From her position, she could see Derek's fingers sliding over the keyboard. His touch was light but precise, as though it was no more difficult than breathing. Afraid to get caught staring, she looked around the room. They sounded like a finely tuned machine. Each was in their own little world, but they were connected musically. She heard the flourishes that Carmen had mentioned and felt the bass and drums as they aligned.

When the tones had dissipated to silence at the end of the song, Grace pressed the button again. She leaned into the microphone, remembering the trick Derek had taught her. "Recording stopped. I'm getting a drink. Anyone else want one?"

Carmen raised her hand, but the others ignored her.

Grace ran from the room, fanning herself the moment she reached the hallway. "Get it together," she cautioned herself.

She was halfway in the fridge, digging out a flavored water for herself and Carmen, when she heard the tapping at the patio door. She pulled back, hand wrested on the fridge door with two bottles clutched to her chest. She was afraid she would see her boss who had tailed her to Jacob's home.

The last thing she had expected to see was Jacob's former band mate, Danny, hands cupped around his face and peering into the kitchen. He was almost as tall as Jacob, but considerably thicker now, his scruffy beard splayed unattractively against the glass. His friendly smile and big eyes landed on her, and she hurried to let him in.

"Sorry to keep you waiting," she apologized.

The older man smiled, waving her off. "I didn't expect his door to be locked."

Grace growled, remembering her boss's intrusion as though it had been five minutes ago and not weeks. "We had some trouble with people letting themselves in. Nosy agents and the like. Took me a minute, but I have him locking the doors now."

"Impressive," Danny stated before extending his hand in greeting. "Danny. You must be Grace."

She blinked at him, accepting his greeting. "I suddenly feel famous."

He chuckled as he released her hand. "Jacob told me what good care you're taking of everyone."

"That's generous. Just doing my job." She glanced toward the studio. "I think they're doing some final recording now if you want to watch. In fact, you could take Carmen her water if you want."

"I'd be happy to." Danny accepted the water and jogged down the hall.

From her spot at the kitchen island, she heard the collective applause as he arrived.

About ten minutes later, they broke for dinner, and Jacob grew serious as he ushered them into the dining room. Grace started for her seat between Derek and Rae and saw that Danny had already pulled it out and was about to sit.

"Danny, grab a chair from the bar, man. That's Grace's seat," Jacob instructed.

She blinked in surprise and started to protest when Jacob looked furtively between her and the chair.

"Sorry," Danny apologized, and within moments, he settled next to Jacob at the head of the table with an additional chair.

"No big," Grace mumbled. It was a big deal though, and the idea that Jacob wanted her at the table instead of his band brother made her eyes a little glossy. When he spoke to her again, she was not expecting the direct address.

"So, Grace, we need your help," Jacob requested.

Her dark eyebrows arched up. "Oh?"

"We were talking earlier about us all needing a vacation, and we were hoping you'd set it up, because you're so good at it."

After being so welcomed to the table, the invitation to work released the wind from her sails. They wanted her to work for them. For free. She had set herself up in this role, and she shoved down the reaction. "Oh."

"I still think I should get to go," Danny interrupted, waving his arm around the table and stopping with Jacob. "It's not fair that you make me listen to the plans, and all of you get to go, but not me."

Jacob rolled his eyes. "Don't start that again," he begged.

Grace stared at Jacob for more information. "All of us?" she scanned the table.

"All of us," Jacob replied. "Including you." He smiled and winked. "But not him." He pointed at Danny.

Danny crossed his arms over his chest in an exaggerated pout.

Panic rose in her throat at the thought of asking permission from Meyers to take a vacation so soon after being hired. "Where and when would you like to go?"

"Derek suggested Tulum. And we're in. My treat," he added hastily. "I think we should finish the album first, so that puts us out till when, guys?"

The group discussed the details with her until long after their salads and pizzas were history. They settled on Independence Day weekend, asking her to make plans for a five-day excursion. Grace's concern as she left that evening, was how she was going to get the time off from work.

She wondered if Meyers could smell her dread the moment he walked in the door the following morning. He lit right into the sore spot that had been festering all night.

"How's it been going with Hunter and Reed?" Meyers asked as he flipped through the pile of mail she'd left in his inbox. He was seated in one of the chairs in front of her desk, and if she didn't know him better, she'd have considered his question merely casual—even friendly. But he'd burned her more than once with this tactic, and she locked her mental barriers into place.

"Good as far as I know," she replied.

"You still hanging out with their bass player?"

Grace swallowed before answering. "Sometimes. I have better laundry facilities at my complex, so she comes over when she needs them."

"Still a free agent?" he prodded.

"Yes, sir." Grace searched her computer screen. If he was going to pretend not to have an agenda, she could pretend as though she didn't have one either. "How did your son enjoy the honeymoon? Didn't they go somewhere exotic?"

"Not very. The Bahamas. Seems like they had a nice time."

"Planning anything with the family for the summer?" she asked.

"Oh, the wife hasn't said anything, but she's always got something up her sleeve."

"So," Grace plowed forward boldly. "I know I'm still pretty new, and I'm not entirely sure how the vacation policy works, but I was hoping I could take some days off a few weeks from now. I understand if I need to take it unpaid..."

Meyers cut her off. "We can work that out. Where you going?"

She hesitated, excited at the prospect, but hesitant to share details. "A beach, I think. Wanted a little R&R."

He smirked. "Tired of me already, are you?"

"Hardly," she replied with a brief chuckle. "I had an opportunity."

He folded his hands behind his back casually and assessed the view from her windows. "Who you going with? New boyfriend?"

Grace's face wrinkled involuntarily. "Not that kind of girl," she answered. "But I love a good beach."

"Well, make sure I'm not out of the office. I like it better when you're here, and that week you spent with Hunter was awful."

She frowned. "Sorry. I have no idea what made him ask for that. Does this happen often?"

He shook his head. "Not this. I get a lot of weird requests. Celebrities are needy. And they need some weird stuff, but this was new."

She smiled. "It was certainly interesting."

"Get me the details for the trip. We can make it work."

"Thanks," she replied, her stomach relaxing at his shockingly amiable acceptance. "By the way, accounting brought over the monthly credit card statements. They were hoping you might get them signed this morning so they could close the books."

"Is it on my desk?"

"Yes, sir. In your inbox. In the red folder from accounting." He ducked into his office, returning with the aforementioned folder. He splayed it open across her desk and proceeded to sign them all. He slipped the pen back into his front shirt pocket, smiling at her proudly.

Grace reached for the unkempt pile before gravity could pull it over the edge.

"So, who are you going with?" he continued.

Her shoulders clenched as she straightened the stack. Hadn't she skirted this question once already?

"Oh, some friends. They offered to pay for it if I'd set it up." She bit her tongue. Why had she shared that detail? It invited more questions.

"Well, that's a bargain," he chuckled. "You've got some generous friends. Anyone I know?"

Grace did her best not to cringe. She wanted so badly to lie to him. But she knew she couldn't. Her body was already fully clenched talking around the elephant in the room.

"Well, yes, actually. Mr. Hunter and his new band," she confessed. "They wanted to relax after the album's done and before they start gigging."

Meyers stared at her hard. "I thought we'd talked about this."

She could barely draw breath to answer. "It's not work. I swear. I'm friendly with Rae, and Jacob said she'd have more fun if I went. It's purely a vacation. That's why I want to take some time off."

He continued staring. "This is hard for me, Grace. And it's unusual because you've worked with many of my other clients, and you've never shown any interest in them or their offers."

She nodded her agreement. "Yes, sir. That's true. I've treated them like I do everyone else at the office. You know celebrities aren't really my thing."

"Let me think about this a bit."

"Yes, sir." She stood, bundling the accounting folder against her chest. "I'll get these back to the money people. Best to keep them happy." Grace didn't wait for permission to make her exit.

He let her stew in worry until Friday evening when she dropped off his family's laundry at the house to tell her she could go to Tulum. He'd called her to the dining room where his family was having a rare and clearly awkward dinner to make the announcement, claiming that his wife had threatened him with bodily harm if he told her no. Then he dismissed her from the house, and Grace escaped with most of her wits intact.

Before she went to bed that night, she emailed itineraries to the rest of the band.

~ ♫ ~ D E R E K ~ ♫ ~

Five weeks later sometime after midnight, Derek held his breath, sound dissipating around him in the ethereal afterglow, and he tapped a button on the console.

"I think that's it," he announced. The little icon spun on the screen as it saved the file, finally stopping to Derek's relief. With a few more nights alone with the tracks, he would have it remixed from very good to studio gold.

"Really?" Jacob questioned, gasping after the last take. He edged closer, leaning on the edge and stared at the screen.

Derek nodded. "And just in time for vacation."

Jacob cheered, Joe joining him unapologetically. Carmen waved a finger around in the air tiredly, and Rae produced a weak smile, but neither whooped or hollered.

"I knew a deadline would help," Jacob proclaimed.

"You're right about that. Three days to spare. Plenty of time to pack," Derek replied, standing and stretching. His tight shoulders twitched under the manipulation, and he felt air brush along exposed flesh above his waistband. He dropped his arms, tugging his shirt back into place.

Grace was half asleep beside him at the console, but she roused at his words to lift her arms over her head, waving them around lethargically. He jumped at the volume of her yawn and fought the urge to join her as she treated him to a view of her tonsils.

Derek's eyes locked onto her long fingers curling gently over her mouth. Her eyes squinted shut, crinkling at the edges. She seemed oblivious that she had shoved her chest out when she stretched, elbows back. If she had, she would have realized the lacy edge of her silvery bra peeked at him around the neckline.

"Not much of a night owl, eh?" He chuckled.

She shook her head. "Too many early mornings."

He nodded, yawning as well.

Grace straightened, the V-neck of her blouse sliding sadly back into place.

"Great work, guys! I'm very excited that it's done, but it is past my bedtime," she explained. She gathered her bags from their spot under the mixer and extracted keys.

"I'll walk you out," Derek offered.

"Thanks," she replied. She trudged sleepily through the studio door. "I'm kinda glad I got to be here for the end," she commented as they meandered down the hall and toward the patio door.

"That's always a cool moment, and you're never sure when it's coming," he answered. "I've got plenty more mixing to do, but the recording's done, which is the hardest part." He wasn't sure why he was telling her this. They reached the cars a moment later, and she wobbled as she turned to face him.

"You really okay to drive?" he asked.

She rolled her eyes. "Are you kidding? I've got this driving sleepy thing down pat."

He smiled. "Well, I guess I'll see you on the plane to Mexico," he added.

"Yeah. You got the itinerary right?" she asked.

"I did. Thank you. I'm getting spoiled."

"It was fun to plan," she replied softly. "I'm glad to help."

He squeezed her shoulder gently. "Be safe," he added. "I'll make sure the door is locked."

"Thank you. Goodnight."

Derek waited till she was safely in the car before he closed the patio door then locked it with an exaggerated gesture and shot her a thumbs up. The moonlight lit her grin through the car window as she backed out of the drive.

When Derek returned to the studio, he found the band disengaging from their instruments. Jacob was absently unplugging cords, and Derek joined in, breaking down the mics first as the ladies packed up their equipment.

"Okay, guys," Jacob announced, clapping his hands lightly to get everyone's attention. "Sleep time. Guest rooms for everyone. You know the drill," he insisted.

Like a mini horde of zombies, they groaned and shuffled to their respective guest rooms.

Derek woke to giggles from all the way down the hall. He recognized Rae's voice and wondered when she had turned into a morning person and who she was talking to. He strained an ear toward her, but hers was the only voice.

He rolled over in bed, staring at the ceiling and wondering if Grace had gotten home safely. She had probably still been driving when they all collapsed last night. Staying in Jacob's guest room had become so normal, he'd kept a change of clothes with him at all times. He wasn't sure he was ready for Rae this early in the morning, and he pulled on a pair of running shorts and shoes to escape.

As anticipated, he found Rae in the kitchen. She was twirling about the space, pulling out stacks of silverware and plates on the counter.

"Good morning!" she hailed.

He offered her a wordless greeting and stole out the patio doors for a jog around the neighborhood to clear his head. He wanted to ask if she'd heard from Grace, but he could already imagine her derision as she would tease him for thinking about the secretary in bed.

She wouldn't have been wrong. Derek rarely dreamed, and when he did, it was unusual for him to remember the plot lines. But he'd woken with the feeling of her mouth on his and having his arms under her rear with her thighs wrapped around his torso. Anything beyond that was a mystery.

He smelled the flowers in the air, listened to birds chirping, and focused on the sweat trickling down his back as the sun bared down on him. It wasn't uncommon to have sexual dreams about coworkers, he rationalized. It didn't mean he wanted to have sex with them. It was more about the balance of power. He skidded to a halt as he reached the patio doors, spying Grace's car as he knocked to be let in.

Rae bounded over to open the door. "We're celebrating," she announced, stepping clear.

Grace was pouring orange juice into champagne flutes, and she wiggled her fingertips at him as he rounded the counter.

"I see you made it home safely," he greeted.

"And back," she added with a smile. "It's like I never left."

"It's like we all live here," Derek continued, closing and locking the door behind himself. "And since we practically do, I'm going to shower before this all gets cold."

"THANK YOU!" Rae called after him, waving her hand in front of her nose.

"Shut up, Shorty. This is youth coming out my pores," he countered, running a finger over his wet muscle like a bad cologne commercial.

"Whatever it is, go wash it off. It stinks," Rae demanded.

Grace offered him a champagne flute. "Mimosa?"

Derek accepted the glass and lifted it to his mouth. The bubbles tickled his nose, and he sipped. "Thank you."

"Shower!" Rae yelled, pointing down the hall. She pinched her nose with the other hand. "I'll push you in there myself if I have to."

Any lusty feeling he'd been having toward Grace dissolved at the warning. "Yes, Drill Sergeant!" he shouted before jogging down the hall to the safety of the bathroom.

When the van doors opened, a thick rush of humid air rolled in. Grace sucked in a breath. The flora and fauna of Mexico were thriving in this space, and the lush greenery seemed to wrap itself around all of her senses. Her eyes roamed over the bustling open-air hotel lobby outside their transport, and she wondered if the rooms were going to be similarly equipped. Were they going to last for four days without air conditioning? Grace was rooted to her seat.

Derek, however, had burst out of the van seemingly before the doors slid open. He flashed his pearly whites at his companions as he spun around to face the others emerging.

"Welcome to paradise!" he greeted, arms aloft showcasing the blue skies, palm trees, and marble-lined atrium behind him as though he had single-handedly built the place for them.

Jacob was next out of the van, returning an easy smile to his friend. "Great choice," he complimented.

Derek smiled, stepping back to the van to help the others out. "Tulum does not disappoint when you need to relax and clear your head." He reached in a hand to Grace.

She accepted, easing herself out. The humidity was immediately replaced by a gentle, sweeping breeze.

"Thank you," she murmured, releasing his hand and placing her wide-brimmed hat on her head. Her eyes darted around the facility, searching for the front desk and an indication of where she would need to go next. Her people were exiting their transport now and luggage was piling up next to them as the driver unloaded.

Carmen bounded out next, extending a hand to Joe who was barely awake.

He looked around with one eye. "I can work with this."

"It's gorgeous!" Carmen enthused, twirling then placing one hand on Joe and one on Derek to stabilize herself as she stopped. "I've got to start earning this kind of money."

The others were chuckling at Carmen's antics, but Grace was worried about Rae who seemed far less enthusiastic. Jacob extracted her from the van, and the breeze picked up tendrils of her hair from around her sticky neck till it floated around her pinched face.

Grace squeezed her forearm lightly. "I'll get us checked in as fast as I can. Will you be okay?"

Rae's ashen pallor stood out starkly against her rosy cheeks, but she nodded and waved Grace off, gripping Jacob's arm.

Grace tipped their driver generously then skipped up the steps into the lobby proper. Her sandals clicked against the tiles as she wound her way to the desk. A staff member smiled and greeted her in English. After a brief exchange, Grace was ushered to a separate concierge desk roped off from the rest where she handed over all six passports and started filling out forms. She handed Jacob's credit card warily to the man, relieved when he did not bat an eyelash. Grace was a little shell-shocked when she rejoined the party, a frozen pink beverage in one hand and five leather corded wristbands in the other.

"Something wrong?" Rae fretted.

"No, it was just...so easy. Here, wristbands for all." She held them out to the others, giggling as they disappeared in a tangle of grabbing fingers. "These are your room keys and give us access to literally everything at the resort," she explained.

"Frosty beverages too?" Rae asked, eyeing the dripping affair in Grace's hand.

"Yes, that too. In fact..." She looked over both shoulders. A hotel staff member had nearly reached them bearing a tray full of frozen drinks the same as hers.

"Welcome to Tulum," the young man smiled.

Carmen wasted no time snatching a glass for herself and for Rae.

Derek looked up from putting on his wristband as Jacob helped Rae with hers. "Ah! The welcome drink! Our adventure begins." He plucked his drink from the proffered tray and held it up in salute.

The others followed suit. Jacob lifted his glass slightly higher. "To a well-deserved break after many sleepless weeks!" he toasted.

"Amen," Rae heralded, clinking her cup to the others.

With a sip, they stared at Grace expectantly. Remembering her role, she straightened up.

"They're bringing a cart up for us to take us to our rooms. We essentially have a hut to ourselves. Derek, Joe, and Jacob are on the odd side, while Rae, Carmen, and I are on the even. We're on the *privileged* side of the resort, so we have access to a special a la carte restaurant near our rooms as well as the private beach. We are free to use any pool or facility at the resort. We have our own concierge next to the restaurant in the hospitality room to handle any special requests including spa treatments, excursions, and motorized water sports."

"So basically, they will be playing the part of Grace for the trip," Joe heckled.

"Pretty much," Grace chuckled.

"Good! It's your turn, too," Jacob insisted. "Don't think we didn't see you nod off at midnight all those nights we were recording. Meyers made it clear that this is your vacation time. And we're going to talk about that while we're here."

"But not right now," Derek interrupted with one hand on Grace's shoulder and the other on Jacob's as two six-person golf carts rounded the driveway. He turned them both to face the vehicles then ambled down the steps, lifting his drink. "Now, to the carts! I fully expect everyone to be toes in the sand by the end of an hour. That means you!" he ordered, pointing at each of them and making eye contact.

"Yes, dad," Rae moaned, following after him.

Jacob smiled, lifting his cup in acknowledgment. He turned to Grace, "I mean it."

"Yes, sir," she saluted, failing to subdue the heat in her cheeks.

"And no more of this 'sir' business," he laughed. They piled into one cart, chatting to the friendly driver as he wound through the resort, and the second followed with their bags.

~ ♪ ~ D E R E K ~ ♪ ~

Despite his rush to get to the beach, Derek spent a moment staring out his window once he was alone. Tropical plants and palm fronds swayed in a gentle breeze. He inhaled for a long moment and exhaled slowly.

Creatively, the last few weeks had been amazing. He hadn't played keyboards for anyone in a very long time. Adding his flourish in a live performance had woken something in him he thought he'd left in the past. He and Jacob had clicked in a major way. Jacob took his input well, and he believed he had taken the artist's work to a whole new level.

It had been exhausting though, and Derek had to admit he wasn't as young as he used to be. His back and neck ached. The bones in his hands and fingers throbbed, and his eyes felt gritty. If Grace hadn't been looking after them, they might have starved to death.

His eyes roamed past the palapas and swimming pools, and he practically heard the ocean calling his name. Pent-up energy resulting from wrapping up a project was thrumming through him. He threw his suitcase onto the bed. In no time, he was decked out in nothing but bright trunks and sandals. As he divested himself of his watch, a now vintage leftover from his fifteen minutes of fame, he caught sight of himself in the mirror. The multi-colored tiger print across his hips showed off his toned thighs and flat stomach. He flexed and grinned at himself. Gym time had paid off. Now all he needed was a tan.

His hair was starting to brush his ears, he realized. He had been so caught up in the work, his buzz cut was starting to look more like a haircut. When he had buzzed it years ago for a movie roll, the drastic change had been startling. But the military cut worked for his new physique and for his budget. LA wasn't known for its affordable hairdressers, and as a producer, he convinced himself that the cut didn't matter. He grumbled, reaching for a comb to tame it before he rejoined the group.

Derek emerged from his room, finding Jacob waiting on the porch outside. The younger man looked almost asleep, sporting a gray, long-sleeved sun shirt and matching board shorts that capped his knees. Jacob looked up as Derek joined him, lifting his sunglasses.

"My God!" Jacob exclaimed. "You're shaming every man here, bro! What are you made of? Marble?"

"This is what I do when I'm not making music," Derek laughed, flexing his biceps. As he flexed, the third door opened, revealing Joe in a baggy black *Journey* T-shirt and black and white checkered board shorts.

"Well, there goes anyone else's chances at being noticed," Joe grumbled.

"I know, right?" Jacob agreed. "Put a shirt on, dude. The girls might blow a gasket."

Derek scoffed. "Let's go find out."

Jacob rose, dropping his sunglasses back into place. "I'm not picking them up if they pass out. You've shown all your cards."

Derek was still chuckling as they rounded the building's corner to collect the ladies. Carmen was seated outside her room, using a straw to coax the last of her beverage out of the cup. She waved a hand in greeting as she saw her bandmates. "Please note my compliance with the order to have fun in the sun." She set her glass on the outdoor table and rose to do a turn in her crocheted, white bikini.

Derek had not paid much attention to Carmen while they were working. She was young and attractive, but they had been focused on the work, and he hadn't noticed. Now, in a revealing bikini, tawny skin glimmering in the sunlight, he realized the band was going to need extra security to protect her from all her admirers.

"Bravo." Derek nodded his approval. "I respect the dedication." From the way she twisted her hips under his appraisal, Derek got the distinct impression that she knew what she was doing, and he passed her to knock on Rae's door. There was no answer.

She had looked piqued on the ride in, and he'd heard her complain about heat enough times to be worried now at her silence. Derek waited then knocked again.

"Rae," he called. "You okay?"

"Go away, D," she replied.

Undeterred, he knocked again. "You said you'd come. You're cutting into my beach time."

As he did so, Grace emerged from her room covered in a short dress, sandals, and a giant straw tote. She pressed a straw hat onto her head, shifting her ponytail out the back. She looked a little like a pack mule.

"Can't I stay here?" Rae protested through the door. "We can do lunch later."

"Don't make me call the front desk to tell them you're unresponsive, and we need a health check," he threatened.

"You wouldn't dare!" she huffed. At this, the lock tumblers turned, and the door opened to reveal Rae in a white beach robe which hinted at the red bikini beneath. To his dismay, she was still barefoot.

"That is obscene!" she shrieked, touching the tip of a fingernail to his chest. "Put that away."

Jacob laughed. "That's what I said."

"Daddy needs a tan," Derek grumbled, running both his hands from his stomach to his chest. "Get shoes and let's go!"

Sighing, Rae complied, stepping into a pair of white wedge sandals and closed her door behind her. "What about towels?"

Grace's reaction time was startling as she jumped into the conversation. "On the way to the pool there is a cart with towels. We're supposed to use and exchange as needed."

Rae turned to Carmen. "We have to find her off switch."

"Good luck finding it under the layers," Carmen ribbed.

Derek chuckled his agreement under his breath.

"What?" Grace cried. "You asked me to plan! I looked up everything I could to be prepared. I'm an organizer. I can't help it!"

Rae took hold of her arm and began leading her away from their rooms. "And you did an exceptionally good job, Honey. Let's put that knowledge to use."

"Best thing anyone's said today," Derek agreed. "This way!"

He jogged ahead of the group toward the pools and stopped when he saw the aforementioned cart. Rows and rows of neatly rolled white beach towels were piled on a bamboo wagon under a small palapa. Derek grabbed one and turned back. "Heads up!" He lobbed one back to Jacob as though it were a football.

Jacob picked it out of the air deftly. "Good throw." He passed the towel back to Rae then called for more. Derek complied, then grabbed one for himself and trotted to the beach.

He dropped his towel then shucked his shoes before sprinting toward the shore slowing down when the water was up to his calves. The crystal turquoise waters were cold upon entry, and he shivered as he plowed deeper into the ocean. He heard Jacob behind him and waited for him to catch up.

"I am so glad you suggested this. I didn't realize I needed it until we got here," Derek called over his shoulder.

"You have to play hard after you work hard so you don't burn flat out," Jacob replied, walking beside him.

They were chest deep now, and Derek dropped into a sitting position. The salt water carried him effortlessly, and he allowed himself to drift in the gentle roll of the current. He turned his gaze to the shore, watching as other guests went about their vacations. He focused on a woman pulling her cover-up over her head. She was struggling a little, and her body jiggled temptingly for his perusal. A dark purple one piece hugged her curves in a way he wouldn't mind mimicking. The fabric popped over her head, and long dark hair spilled out over her shoulders.

"So that's what she looks like under those business suits," Jacob mumbled.

"What?" Derek asked, cocking his head toward his friend.

"Dude—that's *Grace*. You were just hardcore checking her out," Jacob pointed out. He glanced at Derek through the glass-like water. "And you'd better do something about *that* before she gets here. If you thought she freaked out about sexy *music*..." he trailed off.

Derek didn't have to look down to know what Jacob meant. He cursed himself softly. "Quick! Tell me about your mom."

Jacob answered by splashing him hard.

~ ♪ ~ GRACE ~ ♪ ~

On the shore, Grace was slathering her face with sunscreen from her tote. "I brought plenty for all of us," she indicated her straw bag.

"Is that what all the luggage was? Packing for six? Does that make you our mother?" Carmen mocked.

"In a way." Grace shrugged and began covering herself in a cloud of spray lotion.

Joe's gaze was focused on the water where Jacob and Derek were causing a ruckus. "For guys trying to stay under the radar, they sure know how to draw attention."

"No kidding either," Grace grumbled. She dropped the spray bottle into her bag and reached for her cell. Her eyes roamed over the incoming messages she'd missed while in transit.

"Are you seriously working right now?" Rae scowled, making her own cloud and kicking a toe of sand in Grace's direction.

"Always on the clock," she replied. "I'll be quick. I need to let him know we're here. I want to remind him about the meeting he has tomorrow and the one with you on Tuesday."

"Would he really forget?" Carmen questioned, settling into her beach lounger.

"Probably not," she answered, scrolling through messages. She knew Meyers wouldn't forget, but he was petty, and she knew the tactics he used with other agents or people on his shit list. Anything to be in control. "I'll be quick."

Rae gave a head shake, patting her shoulder to ensure full coverage of sunblock. "Alright, but if you're not, I'm telling Jacob. So you pretty much have until I get out there."

"Yes ma'am!" Grace saluted before going back to typing her email. All she wanted to do was send a note saying they'd arrived and there was nothing to report, but autocorrect kept changing the words, and she was terrified of dropping it in the sand and ruining the expensive device. She finally got the words in the right places and was re-reading it one more time when a shadow fell over her.

Carmen was cackling, slapping Joe's arm. "Here it comes," she announced.

Pressing send, Grace laid the phone on her lap, covering it with her hands as she looked up to see Jacob come to a stop behind her. He was sopping wet pushing the hair out of his eyes.

"Grace, are you working?"

"No," she answered quickly. "This is my vacation, remember?"

He narrowed one eye, arching the other one. "I remember. Do you? Do you realize I've marched all the way back to shore on day one because you're breaking our covenant?"

"Covenant?" Grace repeated. "That sound serious." She heard Carmen gasp behind her and sat up a bit straighter, reaching for her bag. She slipped her phone inside discreetly and pulled out a tube of sunscreen. "You don't want me to burn, do you?"

"Rae said you were working on emails," he scolded.

"She was," Carmen agreed. "I saw it."

Grace whirled to glower at her. "Snitch," she grumbled.

Carmen blew her a kiss then laid back in her chair.

"I know that you made arrangements for this trip, and you feel obligated to take care of us, but this is your vacation too. At this point it feels like you're spying," Jacob accused.

She sucked in a sharp breath. "I...I'm not..." Grace protested.

Jacob held up his hands. "I know you're not. It's not in your nature.

Come on. Get screened up and get in the water with us. Derek misses you," he prodded.

Carmen and Joe burst out laughing, reaching for a high five from the tall singer.

Grace dropped her sunscreen. "He does not," she snapped.

Snickering, Jacob crouched beside her. "Got any more sunscreen?"

"Enough to protect an army," she answered. She pulled the pack of protection from her oversized tote. "Want some?"

He nodded, accepting the kit from her and squealing when he spied a tube of zinc. "Okay, you are officially the best even if you're taking advantage of my hospitality by working on the beach."

She sighed. "Fine. Fine. I take your point. I wanted to plant a seed about your meeting with him on Tuesday."

Jacob was spreading a thick glob of zinc across his nose, grinning like a child who'd been given their favorite toy. "Okay, but consider the seed planted and let's go," he replied, rubbing what was left of the zinc over his hands until it thinned out.

"Did you get enough there?" she teased, closing up her bag and kicking off her sandals.

He beamed. "Exactly the right amount," he announced. He looked at the others. "Are you joining us?"

"Nope," Carmen announced, reclining in her chair. "I'm content right here."

Joe roused himself, standing. "I'm up now. You have a limited amount of time to start moving that direction before I go back down."

Grace joined them, heading to the shore.

"We love having you around," Jacob continued gently as they paused to let the surf rush past them. "We all looked forward to showing you our work at the end of the day. But," he paused dramatically, "We need to know your team..." He paused, drawing out his last word.

"Team us," Joe finished.

Grace looked between them both. "I'm definitely team you."

"We so need a name," Jacob complained. "I'm saying that maybe when you're with us… we'd prefer it if you weren't with him."

She frowned, stepping up alongside him. "After all this time, I know that," she groused. "Despite my better judgement because if Meyers knew I was hanging out with all of you at night and ordering dinner and stuff, he'd can me on the spot. I hang out with you guys because you're fun to be around. And I like the music."

Jacob opened his mouth, presumably to argue, but he said nothing.

Joe intervened. "I think she probably gets scolded enough from Meyers."

Grace considered hugging him for a moment, but Jacob found his voice.

"It's a fine line we're walking. And if we have our way, you won't be working for him much longer." His gaze on her felt intense, and she felt the promise behind his words.

She took another step forward. "Is this the talk?"

"Oh, if this is a talk, I'm leaving," Joe grumbled.

"We're not talking," Jacob replied.

Grace grabbed Joe's arm. "You have to at least walk me out there till there are more witnesses to make sure he doesn't harass me."

Joe laughed, dragging her along with him until they were deep enough to wade and join the others. Rae and Derek were mid-splash fight but stopped at their approach.

"What did we miss?" Jacob asked.

Derek burst out laughing. "What happened to your face, bro?"

Jacob touched his white-streaked nose. "This? Grace had a bag of bliss. I do not want to burn, so I used half the zinc."

Grace chuckled. "I've never seen anyone so excited about zinc before."

"I grew up with this stuff. Life saver. You all can mock me for my shirt—"

"Nobody is mocking you for that skintight shirt," Rae drawled.

Grace snickered as Rae's gaze turned somewhat sinister, her

tongue flicking over her lip as she eyed Jacob, red-faced beside her.

"Well," the singer coughed. "Skin cancer is no joke, plus, it's saved me from many a scrape back in the day. Boys and ocean sports spell blood. Thank God I never chipped a tooth." Jacob spun in the water, dunking his head back to wet his hair.

"There's plenty more sunscreen in my bag if either of you want some," Grace offered looking between Rae and Derek. She tried not to stare as his bare shoulders bobbed in and out of the water. Since she had emerged from her room loaded with sun gear, she had been finding it difficult to rip her eyes from him. She had seen how his shirt sleeves strained against his biceps, but the sight of his perfectly sculpted torso put her imagination to shame.

"Maybe later," Derek declined. "I need all the vitamin D I can get right now."

"Vitamin D!" Jacob crowed. "That is your new nickname."

Rae screamed, "Yes!"

"No!" Derek protested.

Jacob continued, throwing his hands up and splaying his fingers. "I can see it now." He peered into the distance, the corners of his mouth pointing to either side and showing every tooth. His hands slowly parted as though reading a marquee high in the sky. "Tonight, for one show only—Vitamin D!"

Derek's perfect arms swept a wall of water toward Jacob, catching Rae and Joe in the crossfire.

Not to be outdone, Jacob returned the volley.

Grace and Rae squealed, putting a little distance between themselves and the boys.

Joe paddled after them. "I thought Vitamin D meant something else," he mumbled.

Rae screamed with laughter, losing her balance while the guys continued to play fight behind her. Grace's face boiled beneath the sunscreen at the innuendo, and she turned away from the pair for a moment to stare at the horizon while she collected herself.

"Sorry," Joe apologized when she turned back around.

She shook her head. "No apology required. You're right, and that's pretty funny," she confessed.

"TRUCE!" Derek spluttered behind them.

They turned as Jacob pulled both hands off Derek's head to allow him to fully surface.

"If you guys are going incognito, this is not the way," Grace admonished.

"Yes, mom," Jacob replied, laughing and relaxing into a floating position.

Derek flicked his fingers against the water in the singer's direction for one final sprinkling, before slicking back his hair.

"You guys are too young for me," Joe whined. "I'm going to hang with Carmen." He pushed himself toward the shore.

"We'll be good," Derek promised.

Joe smirked as he backed away toward the shore. "I really wanted to drink without sounding like an alcoholic."

"By all means," Derek conceded as they watched him go.

A comfortable silence took over as the waves rocked them gently. Grace was relieved to see everyone smiling, including Rae who for the beginning of the trip looked like she might not survive the tropical temperatures. It wasn't long before Rae followed Joe in search of a drink.

Once the bassist was gone, Jacob lifted a hand and motioned Grace toward them. When she didn't respond immediately, Derek pointed at her, hooking a finger in his direction.

Grace hoped she was far enough away that they didn't see her shiver. She sucked in a calming breath and hopped along the sandy ocean floor.

Jacob spoke first. "So—I've been promising you this talk for a while, and I wanted Vitamin D here as a witness."

Joe's comment was still fresh in her mind, and she giggled, covering her face. She did not want to be thinking about his boy parts when he was so nearly naked in the water a few feet away.

"I know that you do not understand your value to this group beyond doing our admin work," Jacob began. "But bands don't play without food in their bellies, and tours don't move without people coordinating. It might be us on stage, but we don't get to a stage without you."

"I think that's a little dramatic," Grace scoffed. "I haven't planned any tours. You don't even have a name yet."

"It's not dramatic," Derek countered. "All it takes is one person not paying attention in an autograph signing, and it's chaos."

Jacob groaned. "Been there. It is not pretty. Until you've had a *group* of perfect strangers ripping off your clothes and pulling your hair in public, you cannot begin to appreciate the person protecting you from all of that."

"I'm not a bodyguard," she disputed. Their praise made her squirm. While she enjoyed their company, Grace still felt like more of a hanger on than a contributor to whatever magic they were creating. Whatever she had done for them could've been done by anyone.

"The fact that you're already thinking about bodyguards is proof of what we've been thinking," Jacob pointed out. "I'm not sure why you're fighting me on this."

Grace felt two pairs of eyes staring her down, and she gulped. She focused on the gentle wave of arms balancing them in the water as she considered her reply.

"I don't mean to," she murmured. "I guess I don't feel like I'm doing anything extraordinary. I don't even have any connections."

"And you still managed to get us a venue for auditions with nearly zero turnaround time," Jacob argued.

"With *Rae's* connections," she emphasized.

"The fact is you recognized the connection. You saw that Rae worked for a bar, and you knew enough to ask. That's instinct," Derek explained. "You can't be taught that."

She warmed under his compliment. "Well…"

"Well, nothing," Jacob interrupted. "He's right. And when this thing gets big, we want you to look after us. It's a big job. A really big job. But I feel like you're already doing it, whether you realize it or not. You think you're being friendly, but you're filling in gaps without us even thinking about it."

"Guys, I really appreciate the compliment, but I've never done this before. If this is really going to be as big as you hope it will, don't you want someone more experienced?"

"We want someone we trust," Jacob answered. "Experience will come."

"We can hook you up with the right people," Derek added. "Figuring the rest out won't be hard with your skills."

"How are we going to know when it's time?" she questioned. "If you guys grow as fast as we think, I won't be able to keep up with Meyers and you. I swear sometimes he throws me extra chores because he thinks I have time for a lunch break."

Jacob and Derek shared a few furtive glances before Jacob answered. "When we get a record deal, I think it's time. And we've got a meeting with Meyers to set up the label appointments. So, soon."

"What you're saying is I have to finish mixing the album as soon as we get home," Derek noted.

Grace grinned at the break in the tension. "You need a band name, too."

"See? You're already doing it. Let us pay you for it," Jacob encouraged. "I need to know if you'll say yes."

"Come with us," Derek encouraged. "I know it seems like you're going from a sure thing to a risk, but I promise that if this doesn't blow up, we still have the means to get you a position with someone better than Meyers. What have you got to lose?"

Presented that way, Grace wasn't sure how she could say no. "Okay, yes. I would love to work with you guys. But let's hold off on promises about anything till we know more, okay?"

"I don't like it," Jacob stated.

Grace shrugged. "If you want me to look out for you, you're going to have to trust me to always have your best interest at heart, even if you can't see it. What is it you actually want me to do?"

"What you'd be doing is managing us more than the tour," Derek detailed. "You call the label, and they do most of the arrangements.

You'd be the one receiving paperwork, making sure it gets signed and returned—"

"And making sure there's no red M&Ms on the table in the dressing room," Jacob interrupted. "We want to officially make you our band manager. And, honestly, I think we're all about to find a new agent anyway, so we want to make sure you stay part of the team."

Grace stared at them. Working with them had been a lot of fun and far more rewarding than working for Meyers, but she had never imagined it would turn into a job interview.

"Meyers will kill me if he catches wind of this," she mused.

"I'm putting you on notice," Jacob insisted. "I'm going to ask Meyers to let you coordinate our first gig at *The Oubliette*, and I want you to put out some feelers for other venues that may be open to letting new bands play."

Before more could be said, a wave swept over them, pressing all three of them toward the shore, and Grace lost her footing. Her arms flew out immediately to catch her balance, and she grabbed for purchase on something to keep her upright. She spluttered to the surface, wiping hair and salt water off her face with her free hand while she caught her breath.

The solid thing under her hand twitched, and Grace released instinctively. She found Derek standing beside her.

"Sorry," she mumbled.

He didn't even acknowledge the word, keeping his arm steady until she let go.

"Admit it," Jacob continued. "You are wasted on dog groomers and dry cleaners. Think of it like a promotion."

"Well, that does sound more exciting than scary," she admitted.

"And let's go shopping when we get back," Derek suggested. "Band needs to find a look, and so do you. You look great for a Fortune 500, but a band manager needs a little more edge."

Grace laughed. "Hey—I wrestled Bruce Romano out of a bar in broad daylight sporting a suit and heels. I think I'll manage."

"What Vitamin D is *trying* to say is that we want you to be comfortable. Wear whatever you want. And I'll make sure you get paid enough to make it worth your while."

She arched a brow. "You have my attention. I promise to give it a fair shake when the time comes. But when it does, I'll need something in writing."

"Done," Jacob agreed.

Grace twisted in the water for a moment, noticing the pink on her arms. "I think I need to re-up." She rubbed the spot on her arm lightly. "I'll be back."

Neither protested as she headed toward shore.

Carmen was snoring in her chair and stirred slightly as Grace approached. "Tell me you're not coming back to work."

The answer surprised her as she looked at the beautifully tan guitarist who was glistening prettily in the sun. "Actually no. I'd forgotten about it for a few minutes."

Carmen shifted her hips in her chair to get a better angle and slipped her glasses off. They dangled stylishly from her fingers. "Good. You work hard enough to make us tired. And life is short. No one's going to talk about your sorting skills at your funeral. Give them something else to talk about. Like our hot keyboard player," she recommended.

Grace wasn't sure how to take the remark. "You should go for it," she encouraged, trying not to picture Derek and Carmen tearing up the dance floor like a celebrity power couple. They would be gorgeous together.

"Not me, silly," Carmen scolded, waving a hand. "I'd be like setting off a roman candle inside his apartment—unstable and burning everything to the ground. I don't mean to be, but I am. D doesn't need that kind of upset in his life. I was talking about you."

Grace gulped. "I'm pretty sure I'm not what he's looking for either." She settled into her chair, slathering more lotion onto her legs.

"Honey, he doesn't know what he's looking for," Carmen sassed, "but someone who believes in him is certainly a start. Did you not see the way he wanted your opinion on everything he did?"

Grace looked at her but didn't answer. She certainly hadn't seen that.

"Oh, come on. Anyone in those sessions with eyes can see that Jacob and Rae are music banging as they play, and Derek's fawning after you like a boy with his grade-school teacher."

Grace burst out laughing. "Well, that got creepy fast."

Carmen smirked impishly at her. "It's okay to accept it. You don't seem like the one-night stand kind of girl, but honestly, there's something to it. Ride it while you can. Life's short."

Forcing a radiant smile, Grace focused on her sunscreen. "Thanks for the advice."

Carmen gave her a thumbs up, leaning back in her chair and pulling her sunglasses over her eyes.

~ ♫ ~ D E R E K ~ ♫ ~

From his spot at the table in the corner of the privileged restaurant that evening, Derek spotted Jacob and Joe walking through the doors easily. They looked beach worn but clean in their polos and khaki shorts, and he waved an arm to draw their attention.

Seated at the head of the table, he couldn't fight the grin stretching from one ear to the other as he surveyed his dinner guests. On his left was Carmen with her barely-there shiny green dress showing off her shimmering skin which was already darker in barely six hours. On his right was Grace in a flowing turquoise strapless dress covered in palm fronds. Next to her Rae, squirmed in a knee-length garnet halter dress. The girls on his right were slightly pink, but neither looked uncomfortable.

As the remainder of the party filled in the empty spaces, Derek greeted them. "Please join my table with the bevvy of sun-kissed beauties."

"Dial it down, sun-god," Joe smirked. "Not all of us are so excited about the fireball frying us all to death. You know it comes up all over the world."

"But not like it does here," Derek replied, beaming at them all. "You cannot be mopey in a place like this. The resort is beautiful, the view is beautiful, the people are beautiful, and the drinks are flowing."

"Drinks!" Joe exclaimed, flagging the nearest server. "That's what's missing."

Their concierge welcomed them, a flurry of staff swarming the table with drinks and suggested appetizers in his wake. When dishes arrived in the center of the table with much fanfare, the group stared at the unfamiliar dish apprehensively.

Derek rolled his eyes, reaching to sample a shrimp. Carmen joined him next, and the others followed suit cautiously. He was frustrated at everyone's fear of the unknown. It wasn't like they were really in a local restaurant sampling the goods. They were in a resort mostly full of Americans with carefully curated dishes for their palates.

Jacob and Rae played a game of reach for the appetizer simultaneously without touching, and therefore spilled half what they pulled from the shared plate.

The table was unnaturally quiet, and it set Derek's teeth on edge. After the day in paradise they'd had, with staff waiting on them hand and foot, they should all be mellow and delightful like he was. He stared at his companions. Jacob and Rae were studiously looking anywhere that wasn't each other. Joe seemed like he'd rather be asleep. Carmen was quiet, looking across the table at Grace. It was as if without the music, they didn't know how to talk. Which was exactly why they needed to spend time together before they considered touring.

His eyes swung toward Grace. She had clearly showered, her hair falling soft across her bare shoulders. He allowed his eyes to trace her white tan lines to where they disappeared into her rayon halter dress. The fabric draped around her figure, and he remembered her pulling off a cover-up at the beach earlier. He wondered what was underneath now.

Derek waited until the first course had arrived before he addressed the melancholy blanketing their dinner. He snapped his linen napkin before dropping it over his lap.

"Okay, guys. What's with the silence?" Derek challenged.

"Um? Maybe we're all tired?" Rae mumbled.

Joe lifted his drink to her statement.

Derek stared at the sullen woman at the end of the table. She was picking at her sundress uncomfortably, adjusting the straps repeatedly.

"So, jet lag? That's all?" he prodded.

Rae groaned, looking up from her food and meeting his gaze head on. "It's been an eventful day, alright?" Her eyes narrowed.

"It was a long flight," Grace agreed, "and I think the heat took a lot out of us at the start."

Derek scowled. What could Rae possibly complain about now? She was in the middle of a beautiful place about to become the rock star she always said she wanted to be. Maybe she needed a little friendly joshing like at the end of their long recording sessions. If he could make her giggle, she might revert to her usual ray of sunshine.

"Being tired has never stopped you from running your mouth before!" he taunted.

Rae shot virtual darts at him as her fingers formed a fist around her fork. "I have a lot on my brain, if that's okay with you." She steeled him with her gaze, head tilted, and one brow arched.

He took a bite of his salad, relieved she was at least speaking. He looked away, knowing her shields when he saw them, and swallowed his food. He softened his tone.

"It feels like something's wrong. Tell me," he encouraged. "Maybe we can help."

Rae groaned, her response echoing across the room. "Drop it. Drop it right now, Reed, if you don't want to ruin the whole trip."

"This is juicy," Carmen remarked, leaning on the edge of the table, head flicking between the pair. "Exes, right? I knew it—I see your chemistry." Her mouth made a delighted O, and she squealed.

Derek and Rae glowered at her in unison. Joe leaned away from the guitarist, pulling the remainder of his whiskey close to his chest.

"Not lovers. Ever," Carmen sputtered. "Gross, why would I say that?" She stared intently at the remainder of the appetizers.

A tiny snicker from Grace tickled Derek's ear.

"This isn't funny," Rae admonished, looking squarely at Grace.

Derek was amazed at his friend's hearing, barely having heard it himself. He looked between Carmen and Joe.

"We're supposed to be having a good time," Derek placated. "Maybe it is funny."

"I am not having fun," Joe interjected.

Grace frowned. "Sorry, man. We'll be better. Won't we?" she asked first Rae and then Derek.

He recognized the assistant's attempt to smooth over the situation, but he cringed anyway. Any time Rae had been geared up for a fight in the past, the tipping point between boiling rage and averting the crisis was always someone trying to pull her off the ledge.

"Why do *I* have to be better?" Rae's voice rose. Her fork clanked on her plate, and she folded her arms over her chest.

"She said that to both of us," Derek pointed out. "Don't feel singled out."

"Well, isn't it nice to be you?" Rae retorted. "I'm so glad you've all got the means to drop everything and run off with this little hobby."

"Rae, that's not fair," Derek countered.

"We're all taking a risk," Carmen commiserated from across the table. "It's cool to be scared. It is scary. But that's why we do big, audacious things like this to release the tension. Don't let the pressure get to you, honey."

A growl emanated from Rae's throat, and she began drumming her fingers on the table. "For the record, in the last two months, I gave up two good jobs that I liked to start playing with you. *Two!*"

Derek had staked a lot on including her in this deal. Up until now, she had been a bright ball of energy, soaking up all the experience and riding this roller coaster with her arms in the air, squealing through the corkscrews. This was how she repaid him? Throwing a tantrum in the middle of this beautiful trip? He was not about to let this continue.

Resting his silverware on his plate, he eased forward, meeting her gaze without trepidation.

"For the record, you got laid off from the one, so don't blame that on us," he corrected, daring her to defy him.

Rae's eyes turned the size of saucers, and he swore he could see a vein throb in her neck from across the table. But he didn't give her a chance to retort.

"I, for one, am happy you lost all those other jobs," he admitted. "You were never going to take the leap on your own, and now you're all ours! No more divided loyalties between band and club!"

Grace and Jacob winced audibly sucking air through their teeth. Joe drained his glass as Carmen latched onto his arm.

Rae pushed her plate toward the center of the table as she snarled, "You want to talk about divided loyalties? At least I don't jump from job to job like you jump from woman to woman!"

He straightened in his chair, jaw dropping. This was a very personal attack, he thought, totally unrelated to the conversation. He gripped the chair arm under the table as she continued.

"Why is it you're almost forty and still single, hmm? Would a relationship divide your loyalties, Mr. All-About-the-Job? Isn't that why you won't even let yourself look at a woman who could make you happy?"

Derek saw the near imperceptible bow of her head toward Grace, and his jaw twitched. He did not want this to turn into a mudslinging contest, and he realized it was on him to tamp down the flames he had fanned, and he felt like a parent as he used her whole name.

"That is not the same, Desirae."

Grace's knee bumped his beneath the table.

Rae's face contorted into an evil smile as she blew straight past his roadblock.

"Oh, we're telling secrets now?" Rae growled. "How about how hard up you are for Grace, hmm?"

Derek slammed his napkin on the table and stood, the chair scooting three inches behind him, plate rattling at its edge. "Walk away right now," he hissed.

"Or what? You'll fire me from the only goddamn job I have left thanks to you?" She turned to Jacob. "And you're going to let him? Who's in charge anyway?"

Jacob raised his hands in mute surrender and shook his head.

Rae jumped up as well, the screeching of the chair legs scraping against the floor. She glared at everyone around the table before pivoting and storming out of the building.

The others stared in silence until the restaurant doors drifted shut in her wake.

"What the hell was that?" Carmen stage whispered.

Their concierge intervened immediately, clearing their plates for the next course, and offering more drinks.

Jacob apologized to their host and followed her silently.

"Nothing pairs better with seafood than drama," Joe stated.

Carmen burst out laughing, and Derek joined in softly.

"Sorry. I maybe shouldn't have picked that fight," Derek apologized, scratching the back of his head.

"Maybe?" Grace repeated.

"Okay, definitely. I know something's up, and Rae has to explode before she can move forward. Maybe a walk will do her good."

"Let's hope so. You better not have run off our bassist," Carmen cautioned.

"Neh. We're like siblings. We'll be okay after we sleep it off. I'll apologize. I promise."

"Good," Joe replied. "Let's eat. I am actually starving, and it smells really good."

They tucked into their meals, pretending they hadn't lost a third of their dinner party, discussing instead the food and service and all the amenities they'd discovered in their rooms.

He noticed Grace's lack of contribution to the conversation. Since they'd boarded the flight, she hadn't shut up about what they could expect from the transit to the lounges spread across the resort. Now she was pushing food around her plate. When he attempted to draw her out, she provided one-word answers. Carmen had slightly better luck, but after the disaster of picking the last fight, he decided to leave Grace to her own devices.

After dinner, Derek made his way to Rae's room when the others parted ways. He owed her an apology. He didn't regret what he'd said to her. But calling her out in front of the group had been unkind at best. He was better than that. He had been so focused on not being embarrassed in front of his client, he had ignored their friendship.

Jacob was closing the door to her room softly, as he approached.

The ugly expression on Jacob's face was intense, and his words slurred together as he glared. "She's asleep, no thanks to you."

"I was coming to apologize," Derek defended. "I realize I screwed up."

"Save it for tomorrow," Jacob barked. He stalked toward the other side of the building to his own door, footsteps ungainly.

Derek followed closely behind him, hoping he didn't trip on something in the dark and break his nose or worse.

However, the singer arrived at his room without mishap then shot a pointed look over his shoulder.

"I thought better of you, man. That was NOT cool at all," Jacob reprimanded. He shut the door sharply in Derek's face.

Derek stared dumbly at the door. Since when had Jacob made himself Rae's protector? He hadn't done anything unforgivable at dinner. Apology worthy, perhaps, but nothing deserving of this drama. He should go to bed after such a long day, but instead, he turned back toward the resort where the "disco" should be gearing up. He doubted it would be much of a club, but there would be women there, he was sure of it. Nobody would know him amidst the throbbing beat and eager bodies. He had nothing to lose.

As expected, their version of a club was a dark, sparse room with flashing lights, loud music, and small high-top tables. What the club did have was bodies and a bar, and he desperately wanted both.

In no time, he slammed down three shots of rum and wiggled his way into the dancing bodies. Dinner had been a disaster. Joe could barely stay awake, Carmen wanted to pretend it was spring break, and he didn't even know why Grace was there. But screw them! He was young and needed to let off some steam.

He focused on the beauty in front of him, backing up against his pants. She didn't seem to have a care in the world, and in that moment, he didn't either. He lost himself in the rhythm, dancing with whoever was in front of him.

He and Rae were going to talk, and everything would be fine. Or it wouldn't. If he couldn't trust her to have his back amongst friends, he might have to find a new sister.

TEN

As the sun rose the following morning, Grace finally opened her eyes to stare at the ceiling. She'd barely slept. In her mind, she was still sitting at the privileged dining table listening to Rae yell out that Derek had the hots for her and was too chicken to make a move. No—she corrected herself. Rae had said, "Hard up."

He hadn't denied it.

Her mind drifted back to the luncheon where she'd introduced Jacob and Derek. Derek had walked her to her car. They had talked about her being his fan, and he had held her arm the whole time. Had he been winding her up ever since because he could? Or was it something more?

The concept sent her into another frustrated flip, sheets tangling around her torso. It wasn't difficult to conjure images of a romantic relationship with Derek. She had done it her whole life. And now, she'd been sitting next to him for weeks, getting used to the way he spun in his chair between takes, memorizing the way his long fingers fiddled with console knobs, and distracted by him clicking a mouse as he navigated software. She knew what he smelled like. She'd shared an ocean with him and touched his bare skin.

At this very moment, he was a mere wall away. In fact, their headboards were back-to-back, leaving inches between them. She closed her eyes, imagining him sleeping in less than he'd worn to the beach, sprawled out on his bed. The ceiling fan brushing his skin with cool air, sunlight doodling patterns on his body, and before she realized it, she'd touched the headboard.

She flipped over again roughly and yanked the pillow down over her head to scream. Being so close to something she couldn't have made her want to cry.

She forced herself up to shower. The warm water stung her pink shoulders, and she promised to wear more sunscreen.

When she emerged from her room, she was alone on the porch. Her stomach had started to twist itself into hungry knots, but she didn't want to go alone. Grace eased into the lounger outside her door and sent a group text to the others about their breakfast plans.

Her stomach growled again as she waited for a reply. From the corner of her eye, she saw Carmen picking her way toward their rooms. Her green dress was askew, leaving the underside of one breast dangerously exposed, and her skirt was hitched high on her hip. Her expression was serene as she made her way to her porch, sandals dangling from one finger.

The guitarist smirked at Grace, holding up her arms and twirling toward her door. "This ain't no walk of shame, baby. I am proud of every minute." She giggled as she fumbled with her wrist band at the door.

"Coming to breakfast?" Grace asked.

"Maybe lunch. Don't wait on me," she cautioned.

"I'm going to schedule some spa treatments today. You in?"

"As long as it's not before two, I'm you're girl." At this Carmen opened the door and stumbled inside without preamble.

She was in the middle of wondering where Carmen had spent the night when Derek jogged around the corner of the building. He was sweating rather profusely, face red from exertion.

"Walk of shame, huh?" he asked, nodding toward Carmen's room as he caught his breath.

"Not according to her," Grace replied. "I was debating whether I should wait for everyone to wake up or go to breakfast alone."

"I'll go with you," he offered. "As long as I have time for a shower. I swear I'm fast."

"Take your time. I'll wait. Maybe the others will join us too."

Derek disappeared around the corner to his room. The room that shared a wall with hers. And he was about to strip down and get soapy. Oh, to be suds!

While she waited, Jacob texted that he was skipping, but neither Joe nor Rae replied before Derek returned. He sported a button up shirt covered in a miasma of palm trees and flamingos, with a hula girl peeking through the leaves sporadically. The buttons strained over his muscular chest, and his navy-blue shorts stopped mid-thigh. Grace tore her eyes away from them.

"I don't think we're going to see any of them 'til way later," Derek speculated. "I saw Jacob last night—dude was plastered. Pretty sure we all were at least a little." He offered her his elbow which she took as they started toward the restaurant.

The sun highlighted the red in his hair as they walked, and Derek talked about the running trail he'd found, going into great detail about the bridge he'd encountered. She was grateful he was chatty to cover her quiet.

Without Jacob in tow, they opted for the main dining hall. Conversations from other guests filled the space with a gentle hum punctuated by silverware and servers replacing dishes at the buffet. She couldn't expect him to do all the talking, and between the people around them and trips to the buffet, there should be no awkward silences while they waited for food to arrive.

Grace was a little embarrassed when she returned to the table with a full plate. Derek was already plowing through a yogurt. At his elbow was a plate of fruit, a single slice of bacon, and a scoop of scrambled eggs. His meal looked so healthy, she was embarrassed to let him see the myriad of samples she'd piled on hers.

He paused in his attack on the dairy product, scraping the sides of the container as he told her, "I asked them to bring you water. I wasn't sure what you'd want."

"Thanks." She adjusted her napkin in her lap and picked up a fork. "I'm not sure how you avoided the pastries," she admired.

He laughed, setting down the empty container and spearing a bite of pineapple with his fork. "I don't look. I got off processed sugars a while ago. Not like, hardcore or anything, but it's too slippery a slope. One muffin, and you're off the wagon, kicking the habit again with night sweats and pancake dreams."

Grace giggled at his description and enjoyed the resulting smile that lit his face.

He schooled his features as he looked back at his plate, but one cheek was stuck northward in amusement. "First time in the tropics?"

She nodded. "I've been out of the country before, but to Europe. Nothing like this. You?"

"This is maybe my fifth trip to the area?" His face contorted in concentration, and he shrugged. "I hope you're all cool with me suggesting it."

"Absolutely," she assured. "I know we all live in California, but getting to a beach is insanely difficult."

"And, let's face it, they are not created equal," Derek added.

Grace agreed, taking her first bite of stewed meat from her plate. The savory spices awakened her tongue. Her hand flew to her mouth to suppress the groan of delight that slipped out.

Derek looked at her face, and then her plate. "What was that? Anything that makes you make that noise is worth trying."

She swallowed sadly. "No idea. It was next to the beans. Who eats beans for breakfast?"

"The British…and the Latin cultures," he replied with a smirk. "You should try it. Whole nations might not be wrong."

She laughed again. "You've got a point." Conversation faltered for a few bites, and she scrambled for a new topic. "Hey, so maybe can I pick your brain?"

"About?"

"The proposition from Jacob to work for the as-yet-unnamed band.

It's super flattering. But it feels..." she hesitated, searching for the word.

"Risky?" he suggested. He waited for her nod before he continued. "It is risky. No matter how you feel about Meyers, he's a sure thing. And it sounds like the only trouble you've had with him to date has been us."

Grace looked away and popped an entire mini tart into her mouth. Initially, she had done it to avoid agreeing with him, but then the creamy lime flavor wrapped around her tongue, and she moaned in delight, eyes rolling back in her head.

"I am so sorry," she apologized the moment she swallowed, covering her lips with her hand to hide her tongue darting greedily to get every last crumb. He was staring at her intently, and heat flushed her body in embarrassment. "I feel rude, but this food is shockingly good. Please continue."

"You're not rude," he assured her. "It is refreshing to watch a woman enjoy food. Most of you pretend you exist on air."

She smiled, quieting the dialogue in her head. She suspected he liked the kind of girl that lived on air, and she couldn't blame him. However, discussing his ideal type of woman was not a conversation she wanted to have. She could imagine the dialogue and be disappointed some other time.

"How do you do it?" she inquired, returning to their conversation. "Living on project-based work?"

He shrugged. "It's definitely a leap. You have to pace yourself. Jacob will offer you a big payment that will be paid out in equal parts for the length of the tour, or he'll offer you a percentage of what the band makes, or some combination of the two. It will be spelled out in your contract. It will sound like more money than you can shake a stick at, but this is no 9-5 job. This is seven days a week for months. And even though we say there's down time—you won't ever really be down. It will drive you crazy with quadruple checking things. And you're going to have some screw ups because you're human."

He paused, and Grace was grateful as she absorbed his words.

"But it's still an opportunity of a lifetime," he advised.

"Well, and I hate to be indelicate, but what happens when the tour ends? What do I do then?"

"Find another gig. Trust me—if you're as good as we think you'll be—you'll get plenty of offers to leave us while we're still on the road."

"And if I'm terrible, I'll have to find another day job before the money runs out."

He shrugged. "Yes, but the reason to take this gig is for the experience," he reasoned. "You'll gain a reputation, which you know is currency in this town."

She sipped her water. "Thanks. You've given me a lot to think about."

"Hey, maybe you'll get lucky, we'll be a mega success, you won't be driven to murder us in our sleep, and you can stick with us forever."

She laughed, thinking that a lifetime tied to this man would be no burden. No matter how it worked out, maybe not working for Meyers wouldn't be the worst thing.

"So, what's on your agenda, Mr. Healthy-Eating-Jogger-Man?"

He blinked, mouth opening and closing like a koi before he chuckled. "Wow that is possibly the worst description of me I've ever heard."

Grace grinned at the look of bewilderment on his face. "But accurate," she agreed.

He waggled a hand in semi-concession. "I might rent a jet ski. Or maybe an excursion. There're all kinds of zip lining tours nearby."

She arched a brow. "Ziplining is not on my list. I am terrified of peeing all over everyone."

Derek laughed loudly enough for other guests to glance their way, but he did not hide it. "I can see it," he laughed harder, eyes closing. "That's awful."

"Vivid imagination," she confessed, tapping her forehead. Her cheeks warmed, remembering visualizing him in the shower.

"What about you?"

"Spa appointments," she answered, trying to stop picturing him naked, under a towel getting a massage. She gulped, terrified he would know and began rambling to cover it up. "If I can get one after two o'clock. Carmen says she won't be available till then. And of course, I hate to book anything without talking to Rae or the others first. Not that I can really picture Joe getting a mud wrap." Her brain treated her to another image of Derek rolling naked under a towel held up by a masseuse. She licked her lips, rested her face on her palms, and stared at him. "Any interest?"

He shook his head. "Not high on my priorities."

"Fair enough. If you change your mind, let me know. I, for one, cannot wait for someone to work the tension out of my shoulders." She had work to do and a brain to wash out with soap. And suddenly her brain returned to soap suds trailing down his torso into places she wasn't supposed to think about. She needed a serious time out.

Plates empty and conversation dwindling, Grace placed her palm on the table. "Thanks for coming to breakfast with me." She stood slowly and smiled. "I'm off to the spa concierge."

Derek waved. "I'll see you around. I think we should try dinner again tonight as a group. I swear to be on my best behavior."

She smiled. "I'll make the reservation while I'm there. Do you want the steakhouse, Hibachi, or Italian restaurant?"

"Hibachi," he answered. "It'll be harder to start a fight when a guy's flinging shrimp at you and there are literal flames separating us."

"I like where your head's at," she agreed, stepping toward the door. "See you then. I'll group text the info." Grace hurried out into the intense sun, feeling the air flowing around her again.

"Calm down, you floozy," she mumbled under her breath as she climbed the stairs toward the concierge.

~ ♫ ~ DEREK ~ ♫ ~

Derek watched Grace race out of the restaurant. Her shapely calves flexed as she ascended, and his eyes trailed upward, stopping when they reached her behind. Left foot, right foot, left cheek, right cheek. He gulped and reached for his coffee, unsure why he was attracted to this woman. He'd seen her fall asleep on couches at midnight in the control room and sat next to her at the console for ages. She was the one who didn't know a fader from a pan! She ordered their lunches and cleaned up after the band. Why now, was he giving her a second look?

Ever since he'd seen her yank that swimsuit cover up over the top of her head, his body was responding to her every signal. Signals he knew were accidental. She was far too casual with remarks about having the tension worked out of her body and moaning in front of him. He wondered if she'd even had sex. Surely, she had. All women her age had. One thing he was fairly sure of was that there was no such thing as a casual relationship with Grace.

After breakfast, Derek rented a jet ski and headed into the crystal waters. The loud machine drowned out all the chaos in his head, and for a few brief moments, he forgot he'd been picturing her on his lap all through breakfast, legs wrapped around his back, her soft flesh bouncing as she finally let go.

The thrill of sluicing through the waves, sending out a giant plume of water began to lose its glamour. His heart wasn't in it, and he slowed to a stop. He twisted around leaning back against the handlebars and staring at the shore. His mind went back to breakfast, allowing himself to have the full daydream far from prying eyes.

The jet ski bobbed on the water as he focused on the resort. He realized he was scanning the spa watching people coming and going. He was looking for her. He wanted to show off for her. Okay—he was attracted to Grace. He could admit that to himself. Did this mean he had to tell Rae she was right? He frowned. Grace was worth fessing up to.

Like lightning piercing his brain, his world went white with a singular possibility. What if she lived up to his fantasy? Derek relished the challenge of finding out exactly how "corruptible" she was. It wouldn't really be fair, he mused. She would never see him coming.

As he started toward shore, he spied Grace exiting the spa with the girls and Jacob. It was a sign from the universe to seize the opportunity, and he gunned toward the rental dock.

The group was ambling slowly away from the spa, and Derek slid close enough to see their faces. Jacob brightened at his approach and waved excitedly.

Derek watched Grace stop behind the others who raced to meet him at the dock's edge.

Jacob reached him first. "Jet skis, dude? That's a great idea!"

The craft drifted closer once Derek killed the engine. He was grateful for the assist as Jacob reached out to pull him in, and they tied the ski up to the dock. In the next moment, he'd clambered up to the pier to greet the others.

"You're all looking very relaxed," he noted.

"Like well-pulled taffy," Rae sighed.

Jacob jumped down to sit on the motorized vehicle. "I totally want to do this." He turned to the others. "Any interest?"

"I'll take a ride," Carmen called back.

Jacob pointed out Rae and Grace who hadn't answered as he hoisted himself up. "Ladies? My treat. Jet skis are the bomb," he encouraged. When they shook their heads, he jogged to the rental counter.

Derek jaunted toward the ladies. "No interest?"

Rae stared at him coolly. "No thanks. I'm not going to ruin a perfect massage with getting jerked all over the ocean."

He should have expected that seeing as how he hadn't apologized yet. Derek waved her off. "It's a smooth ride, I promise."

Carmen shrieked with laughter bumping shoulders with the other woman. "Derek wants to give you a smooth ride, Gracie," she teased.

Derek waggled his brows. He was glad to hear Rae join in the laughter, covering her mouth and turning to both people in question. Her hazel eyes stopped on him. He wondered if she noticed he hadn't denied it and simply prayed that she wouldn't pick at him like he deserved.

Jacob returned, jangling keys at the group. His face wrinkled up.

"Grace, I think you need some sunscreen. You're really red."

It took all Derek's composure not to pick at Grace either. He stared at her openly, keeping his eyes locked onto her cherry face. It was time she found out that he had skills outside the studio.

Rae shook her head. "She's fine."

"Go get your vests, and let's go." He turned to Grace. "Come on. We'll get you a vest too, and you can try it. Totally safe. You guys have abandoned me out here all day. You owe me."

Grace sucked in a sharp breath and turned to Rae briefly. Her tote slipped down her arm, and she held it out toward the bassist. "Would you mind taking this ba—"

Rae grabbed the bag before she could finish the sentence. "Go. Have fun," she encouraged.

Derek hesitated. "You might want to lose the cover up, too. It'll be uncomfortable under the vest."

Grace froze for a moment, then turned her back to the group and divested herself of the cover up which she stuffed into the bag now in Rae's possession. Arms wrapped around herself, she turned back to Derek. "I guess I'm ready."

Derek touched her elbow lightly, leading her to the rental counter to get her a life vest. She kept pace easily, but as she tried to wrap her arms around her body, he realized he was in for a challenge.

The man behind the counter handed him a vest, and before she could protest, Derek helped her slip it over her shoulders. He smirked as her entire body twitched with each click of the plastic safety clasps. He tugged each strap tight, purposefully eyeing her face and not her cleavage. As tempting as it was, if he played his cards right, he'd be able to help himself to more than a look when the time was right.

"I think you're ready," he announced.

She followed him to the dock where he slipped expertly onto the bobbing machine. He straddled the ski and held up a hand to guide her down. Fear gripped her, eyes darting from him to the moving craft.

"Take my hand," he encouraged, waving it at her. "Then step down on the seat."

She blinked but then grabbed hold of his hand. Her fingers were trembling in his palm, and he tightened his grip. She pointed her toes, and one long leg stretched toward him. Her foot landed at the right moment. Seemingly more confident, the rest of her followed, and Derek pulled her down to sit behind him.

Her lifejacket squeaked against his, and he felt her thighs wrap around him. He smiled over his shoulder and pulled her hands around his waist.

"Ever been on a motorcycle?" he asked, turning the machine on. It purred beneath them, the motor making the slightest vibration. He felt her thighs quiver, and her knees tightened on him.

"No," she replied, her arms were squeezing around his waist, hands sliding underneath the base of his life-jacket.

He was grateful she couldn't see the effect her touch was having on him. She seemed nervous enough without springing this on her too. "Okay well, this is a lot alike. Stay with me. Lean when I lean, and don't be rigid. If you're unsure of yourself, close your eyes. Got it?" At her nod, he smiled and patted her hands. "I've got you. Now hang on tight."

He maneuvered the ski until they were facing the right direction before goosing the engine. Her hands tightened on his stomach, and he felt the delightful warmth of her body as she glued herself to his back. If it wasn't for the pesky life-jackets, he'd have gotten to feel all of her molded against his bare skin. He turned a careful circle until they were facing the shore, barely moving at all.

He chuckled, reaching for her hands. "You okay?"

She hummed ascent against his shoulder, then her body relaxed. She was breathing in deeply against his ear. Her reply sounded more confident than her body felt.

"I'm good," she called back. "No hot dogging, please."

"Yes, ma'am." He carried on, making gentle circles in the water until he felt her head lift from his shoulder. As he rounded the next turn, he hollered back to her.

"I'm gonna give it a little gas," he warned.

Grace sucked in a breath as he completed the turn. As promised the jet ski practically skipped over the water, and she squealed, squeezing him tighter.

He loved how reactionary she was to every change in their movement. He heard her squeal behind him as he picked up speed. It was good to know she was capable of letting go. He slowed to make another turn then without warning, skipped back over the water, listening as Grace screamed again. Her arms were relaxing, but he felt her thighs gripping him tighter.

He slowed as Jacob approached, Carmen behind him screaming with one hand over her head. He threw a thumbs up at them.

"I thought you got lost," Derek taunted when the other craft was within earshot.

The grin on Jacob's face was wicked, and he met Derek's eyes.

"Race ya!" he challenged, then roared away, with Carmen cheering behind him.

Without hesitation, Derek sped after them, Grace clinging to his hips while laughing. He prayed his shorts stayed in place as they bounced across the ocean.

~ ♪ ~ GRACE ~ ♪ ~

By the time Grace was hauling herself onto the deck, far less charmingly than her name implied, her legs were jelly. Once she had released her death grip, the ride had been exhilarating. Soaring across the water as though they were weightless was as fun as promised. The engine and roar of the water as they flew had been too loud for any conversation. Instead, she had squealed and screamed, noticing how her reactions seemed to fuel their speed or direction. When Jacob and Carmen joined them, the pressure of being alone with him eased.

They had shifted into competition mode, and as soon as she figured out that she wasn't going to fall, excitement filled her. Even when Derek added a little pizzazz into the ride, she trusted him to protect her.

Jacob had tipped himself and Carmen into the water. Neither were injured, but Grace was grateful to be spared the indignity of heaving herself onto the craft in open water. Carmen had nearly lost her bottoms in the process, but she didn't seem to mind. Grace didn't have the confidence to trade places with the guitarist, she knew.

Derek had patted her calf while the others were dragging themselves back onto the jet ski, and Grace mumbled a thank you against his ear.

The others had followed them to shore, Carmen and Jacob cheering. Derek turned to them. "I think I'm done for the day," he announced.

"Me too!" Carmen squealed. "But that was great! Gracias!"

Standing on the dock, watching him hop onto the deck, her nerves were entirely scrambled, and she didn't trust herself to speak. She wished the cart of fresh towels was closer. She retreated to the safety of the sand into the shade of a palm tree. She stretched her back and shoulders. Derek joined her in the shade as he unsnapped his life vest.

"Wanna relax in the pool?" he suggested. "I could use a few drinks after that."

"Sure," she agreed. She gulped, reaching for her own clasps under his watchful gaze then passed the vest into his waiting hands. "I'm gonna rinse off first if that's okay?"

"Of course." He gestured toward the resort. "I'll meet you at the pool next to the bar?"

Grace gave him a thumbs up then searched the beach for Rae and her cover up to no avail. She started weaving through other guests to find the shower. Between the electrifying sensation of being near him and the water acrobatics, she needed a minute to herself.

She was grateful for the semi-private stall near the pool. The chilly water instantly warmed over her head, and she squeezed her eyes shut, letting it draw her into the present. She concentrated on the feel of her hair slicked back on her head as she ran her hands through it and stilled her breathing. She turned several times, lifting her arms and pulling the suit discreetly from her body to let the water clear out the trapped sand and salt. She was stalling. The moment she stopped, she was going to have to be on again. Without a cover-up; nearly naked in front of God and everybody…most importantly, in front of Derek.

~ 🎵 ~ D E R E K ~ 🎵 ~

Derek leaned back on the edge of the bar as the bartender arranged their drinks. Even the brash blender did not distract him from watching Grace at the outdoor shower. She rinsed her hair thoroughly, and it smoothed into place over her head like silk as it coalesced over her shoulders. Her neck arched, and she ran her fingers over it lightly chasing away the sand. The cascading water gathered around her back side, and her suit had ridden up, displaying distinct tan lines. His tongue swiped out over his lips as she modestly ran her fingers under the edges to pull everything back into place.

The bartender tapped his elbow to alert him that the drinks were ready. With a smile and a thanks, he carried them to where Grace was wringing excess water from her hair poolside.

She thanked him and sipped happily. "Refreshing."

He eased into the pool and reached a hand to help her down. This time, Grace took it without hesitation.

"I hope I'm not monopolizing your time," she fretted. "The whole point of this vacation was for you to gel as a group. And you haven't really spent much time together."

"Nonsense. I like to think you're part of the group, and…" He wasn't sure if it was the lingering feeling of her legs on his or the alcohol, but he was feeling bold. He plunged forward. "…I like to think *we're* gelling along nicely."

She smiled at him, sipping more of her drink. "I think so."

"Favorite movie?" he called out.

Grace didn't hesitate. "*The Princess Bride*."

He arched a brow. "Good choice."

"You?"

Derek crossed his arms to deny her question. "Uh-uh. You know all about me, and I know very little about you. It's your turn to be the celebrity."

Grace's head tilted. "I'm not sure how I feel about this—but go on."

Derek leaned back against the edge of the pool, thinking up his next questions rapid fire: Favorite color, favorite restaurant, favorite season and so on.

"Past boyfriends?" he asked.

Grace swallowed three quarters of her daiquiri before she answered. "Well...one, I suppose."

"One?"

"Well, I'm not sure you'd be able to relate to this, but I've spent an awful lot of time on making sure that my career is going the right direction even if it's a snail's pace."

"Oh, sure. The old work excuse," he jeered, swallowing the rest of his drink and setting it aside. "I don't know anything about that."

"I didn't think you would, that's why I prefaced my statement." Grace drained the rest of her drink, plunking her cup next to his. "In truth, guys don't notice me. I'm shy, and work is easier than figuring out what to say to strangers, so I sort of...blend into the background. Shuffle papers. Because it's what I know."

Derek listened, his understanding of her snapping into focus. He remembered having the feelings she described when he was a teen. A dance teacher had simply dissuaded him of all that nonsense, throwing him into an all-girls dance troupe. Grace must never have had that person.

"How long were you together?" he prodded.

She grimaced. "Three years. In hindsight, it feels so stupid. I never said I loved him."

"Did you?"

She laughed. "No. Not at all. I feel stupid for wasting the time. I thought all the red flags were challenges I was supposed to learn to work through. Like an obstacle course for life."

He smiled. "Don't feel bad. I was in a two-year relationship once.

One day you realize it's not worth the effort to push it uphill anymore." Derek realized that the conversation was veering into dark territory, and he steered them back. "Live and learn, right?" he asked.

"Exactly. I moved here about a year after that. I decided to claim the life I wanted, so here I am."

"No regrets?"

"None. If I hadn't taken the chance, I would have missed this moment in the Caribbean in this pool. And *that* I would regret."

"Is that so?" He relaxed against the pool's edge. Her lips hinted at a smile, and she did not look away. "I feel like we should be drinking to this, and here we are, empty handed. I'll be right back." He waded towards the bar as quickly as the water's resistance allowed.

The bartender must have seen him coming and was already prepping a pair of drinks. Derek saluted him happily.

"Doubles," the man told him with a sneaky grin when Derek reached him. He waved two fingers in the air for clarity.

"My man." Derek sniggered and slapped a high five before collecting the drinks.

The bartender winked before Derek started back, studying her. She was leaning her head back against the pool's edge, eyes closed, legs flicking up and down gently. The water buoyed her up, and he wished she was wearing a bikini so he could see the sunlight glinting off her belly button. However, his eyes trailed upwards to appreciate what he could see. On the surface, she appeared relaxed, but the twin peaks pointing skyward told another tale. He imagined pouring her frozen drink over her and licking it off. He nearly tripped to fulfill his fantasy but kept his footing and held out a drink to her.

"Cheers," he greeted, plopping unceremoniously into the water beside her.

She sipped it happily. "So, thanks for tolerating a novice rider today. I would never have tried that without the encouragement," she explained.

"I like to be part of a new experience for people—coax them out of their comfort zone." He was finding it more difficult to look away as she sucked on the straw in her drink.

A speaker crackled somewhere nearby, and a brisk beat thumped out over the speakers. Within moments, Grace's eyes lit up. "It's you!" she squealed.

Derek recognized the song as well. It was his first big hit—a turning point in his musical career. When the performing artist had bought his song, everything had changed. It was appropriate that it played now as he beamed at the woman across from him.

"It is!"

He set both their drinks on the pool's edge, pulling her by the hand deeper into the water and dancing along with the music. Grace couldn't keep up, but she tried, and he liked the feel of her small hands in his. She was willing to try at least. He lifted his arms overhead to shake the goods at her. He was rewarded by her eyes traveling his body, and he bit his lower lip.

Other girls in the pool filled in the gap between them, and he watched Grace float gently back to the edge, drinking quite steadily as she watched. He recognized a few of the girls from the club the previous night. Their bikinis were even more revealing than their skimpy dresses, but he ogled Grace. She swayed along from the shallow end. It was strange to be making his initial play for a woman and be surrounded by other people.

She was grinning from ear to ear as a server replaced her empty drink. She kept one hand on the cup, the other toying with the straw she kept flicking between her lips. She wasn't like the bombshells he'd scored in the past. He wondered if she knew what it was doing to him, watching her lips close around the straw as her cheeks sunk in.

When the song ended, the dancing continued, but Derek extracted himself from the party to join her.

She giggled. "I'm tired just watching you." She looked into the bottom of her empty cup. "Or perhaps from this."

"Whoa," Derek replied. "You're going through those pretty fast."

"They're tasty," she explained, pointing at a person across the pool. The staff member waved at her. "And that little waiter keeps bringing them to me."

Derek chuckled, taking her by the arm, and she leaned into it, setting her cup aside. Her inviting smile was a little too wide, her eyes dilated slightly. She was sauced, and he refused to take advantage of her, despite how easy it seemed it would be. Despite how much she looked like she wanted him to. He'd much rather wake up with her without regrets.

"You know, I think there's enough time before dinner to squeeze in a nap," he suggested.

Grace reflected for a moment. "No. I'm good."

Derek rubbed his chin with one hand. "Well, I'm bushed, and as Rae so kindly pointed out last night, I'm pushing forty," he stated, leaning in, "and I need a nap. Would you walk me to my room?"

She smiled sweetly at him. "I'd be delighted."

Derek pulled himself out of the pool, helping her out as well. He positioned Grace next to an empty beach chair and made eye contact with one hand on her upper arm. "Stay right here. I'll get some towels."

"Yep, yep. I can do that." She waved her finger lethargically in the air as though she was proving a point.

He chuckled, leaving her to grab towels from the cart. When he returned, she was yawning, poorly covering it with a hand.

"Welcome back," she murmured with a smile, wiggling the tips of her fingers at him.

"Hello." He wrapped the large towel around her shoulders and tucked it into her hands. "You got the towel?" he asked.

"I do," she answered, her fist closing around the fabric. She started snickering then and wobbled.

Derek led her back to their cabin, her hand tucked gently into his. She was surprisingly lucid as she swiped her wrist over the door lock and pushed it open.

"Thanks for walking me back," Grace replied softly.

"It was my pleasure. Now you can tell everyone I took you to bed," he tormented, walking her into the room, leaving the door open. He eased her to a sitting on the bed's edge, holding her forearms to steady her.

She laughed, grinning up into his face. "Why, Mr. Reed! I do—do declare." She giggled then, with one hand over her mouth.

"You do do?" he repeated. At least she was a happy drunk.

"Apparently so." She yawned again, exposing all her teeth to him before relaxing into a doe-eyed smile.

He smiled. "Why don't you take a nap too, and I'll see you at dinner?" He feigned a yawn.

"Are you asking me to dinner, Mr. Reed?" she questioned as she rested on her side. Her hair spilled over her pink shoulders as she snuggled up to her pillow.

Derek smiled at her. "Yes, I think I am." He took a few steps to the open door. "And maybe I'll treat your shoulders to some aloe later."

She hummed in delight, eyes already closed. "Sounds good," she mumbled.

Derek returned to the doorway. "Sweet dreams," he called as he shut the door. He stared at it for a long moment, quite pleased with himself. His body was singing for attention, but it stopped abruptly as he turned, spying Rae's room next door. He had acted a fool the night before, and given their exchange at the jet skis, it was time to make amends, so he knocked on Rae's door. His parents had raised him better than that.

The bassist looked confused and mostly annoyed as she answered, raking her eyes none too gently over him.

"Hi?" she asked after a moment. One hand was braced on her hip as if daring him to speak. She wasn't going to make this easy, but he shouldn't have expected sympathy.

"I shouldn't have picked a fight last night. I'm sorry." He paused, allowing his words to sink in. Truthfully, he was only sorry she was upset. He firmly believed everything he'd said about being glad she was fully committed to the band.

"Thanks," she finally accepted. "And I overreacted. I'm sorry I made such a scene."

Derek studied his feet, hands instinctively shoving themselves into his pockets. "We're cool. But I'm glad you're finally committed to this band because I think you'll be successful. I want good things for you, sis."

Her mouth quivered for a moment, and she snarled, "I'm not crying; you're crying."

Sensing that the argument was behind them, Derek pulled her gently into a hug. Her tears were wet on his chest, and he was fairly certain some nasal fluids were mixed in, but he did his best to ignore it, grateful when she pulled away.

"I'm super vulnerable right now, Reed. I could use some kid gloves, please." She wiped her eyes, sniffing and returning to her doorway. When he didn't leave, she tilted her head. "Is there something else?

At this, Derek scratched the back of his neck and squinted at her toes. "Well, I was actually hoping you might do us both a favor."

She crossed her arms over her chest. "And here I was thinking you came to mend fences."

"I can't multitask?"

She chuckled. "Go on."

"I left Grace in her room. She's...well, she might need some tending in a couple hours. Think you could bring her to dinner?"

"Why does she need tending?" she worried, arms falling slack. She took three steps out of the doorway to look at Grace's room.

"Well, I fed her at least three daiquiris, and someone slipped her a few more. Pretty sure she's already asleep."

Rae chuckled, unsuccessfully hiding it behind her hand. "So, Gracie is drunk? Why do I feel the need to record this for posterity?"

"You'd be bored. She's a sleepy drunk," he added. "Maybe a little giggly."

Her expression did nothing to hide her amusement as she assessed him again. "So...you and Grace? Finally?"

Talking to Rae would be an excellent way to harsh his mellow. And while he was itching to talk, Rae was not his first choice.

"Not a word," he warned.

She rolled her eyes and groaned, throwing one hand up in

frustration. "I don't know why you're so prickly. I fully support this."

"Thank you?" he asked.

"I'll get Grace to dinner," Rae promised. "But I'm going to treat you like the best reality TV show never made."

He sighed, waving, and hurrying to his room. As he rounded the corner, he spotted Joe relaxing on the couch outside.

The drummer held up a hand in greeting. "Don't wanna worry you, and I hope nothing's wrong, but your phone has been blowing up."

Derek thanked the drummer and darted inside, making note of how thin the walls must be. He scrolled through the missed texts and calls. They were all from Peter. And they were all about Grace. He dialed his friend back.

"How did you know something was going on?" he prodded. "I won't believe you if you say ESP."

"Rae texted me. Something about a jet ski. What is going on?"

Derek flopped on his bed. "Why did you give her your number?"

"It's fine," Peter assured him. "I think she's hoping we can team up and talk you into Grace."

The room was swimming in the corners of his vision. He'd nearly kept pace with Grace's drinking, and he'd been on the water for longer than the others.

"Figures she would tattle." He splayed one hand over his face to shield him from the world. "I don't know, man. I don't know if it's the tropics or the liquor. I can't keep my eyes off her."

"You said you didn't want to mix business with pleasure," Peter reminded.

He flopped an arm over his eyes to block out everything but the conversation. "I don't. I don't know what I'm thinking."

"I do," Pete asserted. "You're thinking that you're ready to stop being alone."

"Or I'm just horny," he grumbled. The alcohol was definitely reducing his ability to keep his mouth shut.

"D, I know you. If you wanted tail, you'd have already sampled the entire buffet. Women love you—and some of the men, too."

He chuckled. "Maybe."

"I know you don't want to admit it, but you like this girl. I'm with Rae on this one, bro. Why are you so against this?"

Derek didn't answer.

"It's okay to try and fail. At least you'll know. And she's not really part of the band. So, if it doesn't work, you don't blow up the band. What have you got to lose?"

"That's what I've been thinking today. Rae kind of outed me at dinner last night. So, I may as well capitalize on it."

"That's the spirit. Way to take all the romance out of it." Pete's tone was harsher than teasing, and the reprimand was not lost on him.

"Not fair, Pete."

"So, what did you do today to remedy this no-lose situation?"

"Rented a jet ski. And then took Grace for a ride on said rental."

"Ooh," Pete said. "Respect. That was a bold opening move."

"It was the only move," Derek explained. "I don't think she understands subtle."

"She does seem pretty conservative," Pete agreed. "But it's the quiet ones you've got to watch out for."

Derek chuckled, remembering all the indelicate positions he'd been imagining her in since breakfast. "I'm hoping so."

"And how did the bold move work out?"

"I followed it up with drinks at the pool. And dude, they played one of my songs, and she knew it right away."

"Feels good to have your ego stroked too, bro. It's your turn."

"Thank you, man." He ran a hand through his hair, thinking he needed a good shower and some of the after-sun lotion he'd offered to rub all over Grace. He barely kept a happy noise from escaping.

Pete interrupted his fantasy. "If it went so well, why are you not with her now?"

"She's sort of passed out. Didn't hold her daiquiris well."

They shared a laugh before Pete sobered. "That means she's not a drunk. Be careful, man. She sounds like a keeper."

"That's what I'm afraid of," Derek confessed.

ELEVEN

Grace jump-started awake at the sound of a knock on her door. Her hip slipped off the silky sheets, unbalancing her. She scrambled for purchase on the mattress, pulling at the pillows until her lower body had dragged her to the floor. Her reaction had been completely inappropriate. Rationally, she knew the knock wasn't especially loud, but in her current state, it could've been a rocket launch.

She cursed as her bottom slammed against the hard floor, and she ran a hand over the sore spot feeling for any damage beyond her pride. Then she cracked the door open a few inches to find Rae holding out a bottle of water.

"I've come to help," she announced.

Accepting the offering, Grace allowed the other woman entry. She focused on uncapping the water and taking a long drink while Rae settled into a chair.

The ache growing in her head eased. At first, she'd assumed the pain was from falling out of bed, but as she regained more consciousness, she realized it was a mild hangover. She eyed Rae suspiciously.

"How did you know I'd need this?" Grace rasped, easing back onto the bed. Her bathing suit felt knotted indiscreetly around her body, and a scowl twisted her face as she tugged the drying fabric into place.

"A little bird said you might need looking after," Rae replied gently. "And yes, we made nice. Now, go take a shower. I'll wait."

Grace did not like the authoritative tone in the other woman's voice. Of course, in the brief time they'd known each other, she realized that Rae probably had a lot more life experience. Maybe she would do well to listen. It took more than one try to get back on her feet and shuffle toward the shower.

The day's events flooded her head as she stepped into the hot spray. She'd spent over an hour plastered to the back of the boy that fueled all her teenaged fantasies. But he wasn't that boy anymore. He was a man. And she'd had her hands on his bare stomach, boldly slipped beneath his life jacket. He had allowed it. She pulled her hands up to her shoulders, feeling slightly naughty washing away the sand, and chlorine, and probably some of his sweat dried to her skin. He had woken a part of her long dormant in her pursuit of staying afloat in the city of angels. A part of her she had written off.

She scolded herself for the errant thoughts. Why did she have so much to drink? If she had stayed sober, they might still be sunning in the pool, and she could be evaluating the way different parts of his body glinted in the rays, memorizing his face as he laughed and letting the sound of it tickle all her senses. Instead, she was wasting daylight sleeping it off. And Rae was in the other room bossing her around.

She couldn't deny when she finally emerged that she did feel physically improved. She realized her mistake, as she wrapped herself in a towel. All her clothes were in the other room with her guest. She wished for a larger towel but did her best to cover herself before making a bee line for her suitcase.

"Apparently, my limit is three daiquiris." Her stomach rumbled, and an ugly belch emerged. "Make that two."

"Duly noted," Rae smiled. "So, how was the pool? Vitamin D seemed incredibly pleased with himself when he stopped by to tell me he'd over served you."

"Oh, he did?" Grace squeaked, then shrugged and pulled a strapless dinner dress from her case. She ran back to the bathroom to put it on. "All we did was ride the jet ski and have cocktails at the pool. Oh! They played one of the songs he wrote, and an impromptu dance party broke out!" She sighed, thinking how perfect he looked in the middle of a throng of women rocking out to him with no idea who he was.

"Aw I bet that was sweet," Rae called back.

Suitably covered, Grace wrapped the towel around her wet hair and rejoined Rae. She searched the comb out of her bag and plopped on the bed.

The smile had disappeared from her companion's face, and she was studiously picking lint off her bare knees.

"I'm really sorry about yesterday," Rae apologized. "I have no reason or excuse for—"

"Stop," Grace interrupted. The entire exchange had been inexcusable for them both. Their history did not give them the right to subject the whole table to their outburst. However, the perfect storm had been brewing since Rae set foot on the tarmac and began wilting in the heat. Mostly, Grace wanted to forget it had happened. "You'd been sick all day, and he kept prying."

"Well thank you. And something good came from it at least. D finally accepted his feelings for you."

Grace drew back. That could not be true. Derek had his pick of women regardless of his fame. She had seen herself in a mirror, and he could absolutely do better. She pulled the towel from her head and began combing the damp locks. She grimaced at the thought of food.

"Are you seriously so naive that you can't see it?" Rae confronted when she didn't respond.

"I'm not sure naive is the word. Maybe realistic," Grace quipped.

"So, when you were on the back of that jet ski clinging to him for dear life, it didn't do anything to you? You felt nothing?" Rae prompted.

Grace rolled her eyes. "Of course I felt something. I'm not dead. I've explained to you what a fan I am. Every time he says hello to me, it's a little nugget of gold. But a jet ski and drinks don't make feelings for *both* parties. Women all over the world have the hots for guys that do not reciprocate every day," she reasoned.

"Okay—I'm going to do you a favor and save you a bunch of time. Dude is into you. I have known him longer than you, and I've never seen him walk anyone to their car more than once except for you. And since we've been here, he's been popping boners like a teenage boy with a girlie mag."

Grace choked, dropping her comb. "You did not say that out loud."

"I did," Rae squealed. "And now you can think about his boner all night!" She laughed wickedly.

"That is not funny," Grace groaned as she combed out her hair. She squeezed her eyes shut to push away the heat climbing her skin and failed. And while her eyes were closed, Rae's words painted a picture in her mind.

"NO!" she shrieked, running for the bathroom. She hung her towel over the shower door and dug out the leave-in conditioner from her toiletry bag.

Rae laughed from the other room. "Come out here so I can talk to you."

Grace emerged, shoulders slouching in her long strapless dress as she rubbed in the hair cream. "Don't guys get that way because the wind changes direction?" she countered.

"Not at his age," Rae replied.

Grace sat on the edge of the bed again, working the conditioner through her wet hair. It was still tangled, and she reached for the comb.

"Do you not like him back in a sexy way?" Rae questioned.

"Of course I do. I don't want to believe it's real. Because if I'm wrong, I'll be heartbroken." The truth tightened her chest.

"And if you're right?"

The proposition made the room swirl. "I'm not sure I can live up to it." What did she have to offer him beyond exceptional filing skills?

"He hasn't proposed," Rae rationalized. "We're talking about the potential for a relationship."

Grace shook her head sadly. "I understand that. But even if he has caught feelings, if we try and it doesn't work, I'll be heartbroken. Every scenario ends up there. I'm ruined for him."

"Unless it does work out and you pop out six beautiful, pale children," Rae encouraged. "Seriously, you need to invest in a sunscreen company. You'll be rich."

She grimaced at having one baby, let alone six. "Oh, that sounds painful," Grace laughed. She needed to stop being so dramatic. "I should roll with it. If fourteen-year-old me could see me hemming and hawing, she'd slap me straight."

"I would be happy to play the role of fourteen-year-old you," Rae offered, hand poised in the air.

"No thank you," Grace replied with a gentle smile. "Present day me worries the main reason I'm excited is because of that old fantasy." She moved back into the bathroom, eyeing herself in the mirror. "Is this okay for dinner? I feel like I need a bra with it."

"It's perfect for dinner. And if I were you, I wouldn't wear one. You haven't worn one all day. Why start now? It's not like he's not seen your headlights by now."

Grace spun to face her, crossing her arms over her chest. "Well, now I have to wear one!" she squeaked.

Rae stood in the bathroom doorway. "Girl, it's time to start using what you've got. If you wanna seal the deal, go without. I don't know what you're shy about now after riding a jet ski."

Grace blinked in shocked silence.

To her dismay, Rae grinned wickedly. "Besides, you don't want straps with that dress. It's designed to be worn without. Go free range!"

Picking up her round brush, Grace turned on the hair dryer, effectively ending the consultation. It took less than ten minutes with her trusty round brush to make everything soft and glowing, ends turned slightly under. She knew the minute she stepped out of the bathroom it would all go straight again, but at least for the moment, when she looked in the mirror, she'd seen uglier women have feelings for a man as attractive as Derek.

The ladies spent the rest of their time discussing Rae's feelings for Jacob and the near dalliance she'd had on the beach while Grace had been busy getting plastered in the pool.

"Is it me, or does it feel like being in high school, and we're waiting to be asked to prom or homecoming or something?"

"I'm worried Valley is going to beat us in the big game," Rae replied.

Grace laughed, collapsing on her bed, and Rae followed suit. In the midst of their laughter, both their phones dinged. It was a group text from Joe.

Joe
I can hear Rae and Grace cackling. Is it time for dinner yet? I'm starving

Rae shot back a reply to meet on the pathway outside their bungalow to head toward the restaurant in five minutes.

Unlike the previous night, dinner was a pleasant affair. It helped that they were squeezed in around a hibachi table, and an animated chef was putting on a spectacular show. Food and drinks were flowing, but Grace refrained from imbibing, sipping water to abate the afternoon's dehydration. Tonight, she wanted to be clear headed. Once the show had ended and the eating began, conversation revolved around a series of bad and worse band names. Grace threatened to call them Fart Bandits if they didn't make a decision by the time of their gig at *The Oubliette* in a few weeks.

As the party was breaking up, she felt Derek's hand tugging gently at her pinky, and he absconded with her to meander the grounds. She squealed as the local critters darted across their path, oblivious to their interruptions. With the distant sound of the surf and the moon to light their path, his fingertips stroked hers gently against his arm as they walked.

Over the last two months, she would never have described Derek as standoffish. He was professional, cordial, but not interested. Despite her best efforts, every time she saw him, a little thrill slipped uncomfortably through her body no matter that they saw each other almost daily. Usually, she still froze up around him. But today, he hadn't allowed her to shy away.

The breeze toyed gently with his collar, and she was mesmerized. She allowed her eyes to roam over him as they walked, as he steered them toward the main lobby where the resort disco resided.

She broke the silence. "I'm happy to go wherever you want as long as you know that I cannot dance. I was born completely without rhythm," she confessed.

Derek laughed. "I saw you at the pool," he admitted softly. He bumped her hip lightly with his as they continued toward the disco. "I thought we could catch a drink, and maybe, we could at least sway to the music."

"I can sway. I think." She chuckled.

"I have faith."

As they approached, the music spilling out of the club made conversation more challenging. He beamed as they reached the door. "Hey, this is my song too!" He sped up the pace, pulling her toward the dance floor.

Grace picked out some of the lyrics as he tugged her into the fray on the floor, and she flushed at the sexual overtones. There was nothing unclear about this song of lust and desire. No shame either, she realized. She loved his enthusiasm as he sang along. She kept pace with the beat but wasn't sure what to do with herself besides bopping from side to side.

The music was intoxicating, and she watched him relinquish himself to it. It was an instantaneous and wholly natural thing for him. His body rolled in perfect time and without hesitation. Even Grace could see how it had turned him on, and she cursed Rae in her head for drawing her attention to it.

However, as he bit his lip, dancing toward her, inches from her body, Grace could barely breathe. His heat rolled over her, and she wanted to inch closer till they were touching and every movement of his body would be connected to hers. They were consenting adults, she rationalized. His hips were hypnotic, and his words through the song washed over her.

Derek beckoned her closer with his arm extended, fingertips drawing her closer.

She wanted to lose control right there on the dance floor.

He popped his hips in her direction as she took his hand, and he yanked her closer till their bodies aligned.

Grace sucked in a sharp breath, eyes fastened to his. His hands slid down her hips, and she gasped. Her eyes slipped shut, and she gave herself over to his control. He guided her expertly as she succumbed to the beat. She wished suddenly she'd worn a short dress as his hand gripped her behind tightly against himself. A tiny, strangled cry slipped from his lips as she became intimately aware of his interest pressing against her hip bone. She felt like a marionette gliding gracefully against him.

If this was a dream, Grace didn't want to wake up. His grip was firm without being restrictive, and she allowed herself to be led. Her whole body felt alive, tingling and reacting in ways that would normally have embarrassed her, but with him, she wanted more.

All too soon, the song changed, and Derek stopped singing along. They danced through two more songs, Derek turning her forward and backward, always moving, until Grace could barely catch her breath. She was unused to the exertion of dancing, but truthfully, her body was thrumming, and panting was the only response she could muster.

Derek finally released her, leading her from the dance floor to the bar. "Water or daiquiri?" he inquired.

"Water," she yelled back. She was still tingling from all the small touches across her body, and maybe she should have asked for the rum to calm her nerves.

Derek ordered their drinks and immediately turned his attention back to her. He leaned against the counter, pulling her to his hip and leaning down to speak close to her ear.

"You were great out there."

She shivered at the contact. His breath on her ear, his arm wrapped around her, and the dancing they'd done had Grace's body ready to explode. She was strangely aware of her chest heaving as she looked at him, heart galloping.

"I have never felt that good on a dance floor before," she complimented. "You're a good partner."

Her breath caught in her throat as she looked up, and he winked.

It felt like a kiss was imminent, and Grace was sure she would have a heart attack.

The arrival of their drinks saved her from a quick death as he released her to accept them. Grace exhaled deeply as he handed her the cup, and she chugged half of it in one swallow.

He grinned, licking his lips. "I'm good with my hands," he replied.

Grace choked a little and turned away to try to compose herself. She wiped the water off her chin and dropped her empty cup on the bar. She turned back to him lightly. "It's warm in here. Could we go outside?" she asked.

In response, he reached for her hand, and they wove toward the patio beyond the doors. The warm evening air washed over them, and while it wasn't actually cooler than the disco, Grace sighed relief at the quiet that greeted them.

The music and flashing lights faded slowly as they moved away from the building, Derek's fingers still wrapped around hers. He stroked the tip of her pinky with his thumb.

"How is it I haven't had any alcohol since my nap, and I feel completely buzzed?" Grace wondered.

He laughed. "I think you maybe aren't familiar with the sensation," he joked, sipping at his drink. "And maybe it's the Caribbean."

"And my day of firsts," she teased. "Because I have most certainly never been that coordinated or slutty on a dance floor." As soon as the words popped out, she inhaled sharply and looked away.

"Slutty?" He laughed, tugging at her hand. "Were you slutty? I didn't see it. Come on, let's go back. Do it again."

Grace barked a laugh and stared at him. The beginning of a grin tugged at one corner of her mouth, the rest forming an "O" of shock. She tried to form words at least three times before she stopped.

He smirked and stopped to lean against the wooden railing along the path. She propped herself beside him, face to face.

"You didn't seem to mind while we were dancing," he murmured, meeting her gaze.

Grace forgot to breathe, but then whispered, "I didn't." She stared at his blue eyes, searching for any form of mockery but found none.

"It wasn't slutty," he asserted. "It was sexy." He set his cup on the railing.

Waves were crashing against the shore as the tide bore down, and Derek extracted his hand from hers, pulling her closer until their bodies were smashed together. His hand was still cold from the drink and damp as he pressed it gently against her cheek then crushed his mouth to hers.

Her eyes shut as their lips touched, and a whimper emitted from the back of her throat as she kissed him back. They parted briefly, eyes searching for permission to continue. His hand slipped from her cheek to behind her neck, and she arched up to meet him as they kissed again.

Derek pressed his forehead to hers as the kiss ended. "There are some loungers closer to the beach," he suggested, his voice breathy against her mouth. "I think we'd be more…comfortable."

Grace nodded, sucking in air as she pried herself away, and they scurried toward the shore.

This was not Grace's first kiss, but it was certainly the first one that made her heart jump into her throat and caused her despair of living if it had to stop. On the privileged side of the beach, about six canopied platforms lined the shore, natural canvas covering the tops with sheer netting fluttering against the four posts on the corners.

They were beds, Grace realized. Beds! Not *loungers*. But in the dark, with Derek's hand in hers, her lips still wet from his, she raced alongside him, giggling until they reached their destination.

He pressed against her with another kiss, scooping her up enough that they tumbled onto the mattress side by side.

Grace's breath came in shallow bursts. Whenever she fantasized about making out with him as a teenager, the logistics of limbs had never come to mind. Now, in the heat of the moment with the Caribbean breeze caressing them, the one arm pinned beneath her presented a challenge.

Fortunately, Derek did not seem overwhelmed, and the moment his hand began roaming her side, she went back to getting lost in the way his knee instinctively locked around hers to keep her close as he kissed her more gently than before. Exploring. She reciprocated, running her hand up his chest.

His kisses trailed across her jaw, down her neck, and then back to her mouth. She hoped no one was nearby to hear them, but when she felt his teeth graze her collarbone, she didn't care if the entire resort gathered to spy as long as he didn't stop.

They paused again several minutes later, staring like teenagers into each other's eyes, catching their breath. Derek was shifting his hips, pulling away slightly, and Grace started to pout until she felt his hand on her bare thigh. Her skirt was pooled beneath his palm, and his fingertips were making first small circles, then larger ones. He exhaled slowly, his eyes closed, and Grace studied his face, her hands frozen to his torso.

She shifted to rest her head below his chin, listening to his heartbeat as he moved again until he had both arms wrapped around her. Grace nestled into his embrace. She wanted to peel his shirt off and feel his skin beneath her teeth. Wanted to kiss him in all the unseemly places. Instead, she took a moment to collect herself. She realized she'd been dangerously close to stripping off her dress and hopping astride him right there in the middle of the beach with the moon as their witness. Something about him brought out her aggressive side.

"I'm glad I met you, Gracie," he said softly. "Again." He followed it with a single chuckle.

She realized he was referring to their first fan meeting. "Me too," she replied. "Although this is certainly not what I was expecting the first time we met."

He shifted gently until they were nose to nose. "You'd have turned me down back then? I know I was better looking."

She laughed. "I would have been terrified. I might have said no. I had more principles then."

He snorted. "Principles?"

"Oh, I don't know what I'm saying," she groaned. "You can't ask me hard questions *now*. You've sort of swept me off my feet."

He wiggled one foot between hers. "I see that."

She snickered, brushing her nose lightly against his. "You're looking a little proud of yourself."

"Maybe," he conceded. His hand roamed up her thigh, over the fabric of her dress, and Grace wondered briefly how much of it was still in place. At this point, with Derek, she didn't care. She'd give him everything.

She shifted her head to his shoulder, not sure if she more enjoyed the sound of the waves or his pulse. What felt like moments later, she felt Derek's lips on her forehead. She yawned, realizing she'd dozed off.

"Grace?" he asked softly. "Wake up, sweetheart. Let's go back to our rooms."

She blinked groggily, patting his chest and sitting up slowly. Her top had inched down, but the delicates were still covered, and she twisted the fabric back into place as Derek stretched.

He rose first, then helped her up, eyes glued to her cleavage as she stood. His lower lip slipped briefly between his teeth before he pulled her in for a languid kiss. Standing, squished together on the sand, Grace's heart raced again, and she stilled her hands to keep from stripping them both and pushing him down in the sand.

He hummed, pulling away, and led her back toward the resort. They walked silently, his arm wrapped around her shoulders, until they reached their building. He walked her to the door, then kissed her slowly, one hand cupping her cheek.

"Goodnight," he whispered, forehead to forehead.

Grace grinned at him, unable to speak as she watched him go, staring even after he had disappeared around the corner. She had no idea how she was going to sleep after that.

"Your headlights are on," announced a voice in the dark.

Grace whirled around, nearly tipping over as her eyes landed on Carmen slouched on the lounger on her porch.

Still sleepy and in the haze of her recent encounter, she shook her head at the guitarist. "What?"

Carmen moved a hand to either side of her chest. "Your headlights are on." She flicked her index fingers like flashing headlights.

Realization dawned on her, and Grace clutched her chest with one forearm. "Really?" she asked.

Carmen chuckled softly. "Mine would be too after a kiss like that." The guitarist fanned herself obnoxiously.

Grace sighed wistfully, looking over her shoulder. "It was pretty good," she agreed. Her attention rolled back to the other woman. "Were you out here waiting for me to come back?"

Carmen laughed. "No. Just airing out before bed." She paused, standing as Grace swiped her wristband over the door lock. "Hey, the walls are pretty thin, and I think our girl might need some love, but she didn't answer my text. You up for checking on her? Or are you too atwitter after that?" She pointed in the direction of Derek's room.

Grace's brows furrowed, and she closed her door. "Let's go," she agreed.

The pair hurried to Rae's room, and Grace pressed an ear to the door. She didn't hear anything and looked to Carmen for more details.

"She was hardcore sobbing," Carmen explained, hands on her hips as she pressed an ear to the door. "Shower stopped about twenty minutes ago."

"What happened at dinner after we left?"

Carmen shrugged. "Nothing. It was great. Then she and Jacob took off after, and I went to the disco, and I don't know where Joe went. But when I got back, I heard her crying."

Grace knocked lightly at the door, wondering how bad the crying must have been for fearless Carmen not to check in alone. There was no answer, so she tapped again. "Rae, sweetheart? It's Grace and

Carmen. You okay?"

"Fine," came the reply, but Rae's tone was clipped and offered no more explanation.

"Can we come in?" Carmen pled.

After a minute or so, Grace called again. "Rae?"

"See you at breakfast," she replied.

Grace turned to the other woman, frowning. "I guess we'll see her at breakfast."

Carmen shrugged. "She's talking. You're an early bird. Get me when you get up, and we'll grab her and get private beach service for breakfast and pry it out of her with no one else around."

Grace agreed, and they parted ways. A piece of Grace wanted to bang on Jacob's door and demand an explanation, but she resigned herself to waiting. Tomorrow morning would have to be soon enough.

TWELVE

race and Carmen were pacing the porch outside Rae's room in the morning, waiting for the woman to show her face.

"Good morning," the bass player caroled when she saw them.

Carmen wrapped Rae in a sideways hug. "We're having a boy-free chat so you can quit pretending," she proclaimed. She tucked Rae against her left side then hooked Grace with her right arm and headed down to the beach. Carmen tried to skip, but Grace let go quickly, unable to match their pace. Rae leaned into the activity, and they skipped ahead to the first beach bed.

Grace felt her pulse begin to race as Rae grabbed hold of the post and tried to twirl herself onto the mattress.

"Keep up, Gracie," Rae taunted.

She was instantly transported to hours ago when Derek had briefly rolled on top of her to better access a spot right below her ear, one hand stroking the side of her torso. Her insides twisted immediately, and she gulped, gesturing to the other beds.

"Maybe we can use the one down there. It looks fresher," Grace requested, already walking past them relaxing when the others followed. She set her bag on the bed three stations down, claiming one corner of it and crawling in.

Rae and Carmen exchanged confused looks but followed suit. It was still early, but already a staff member was at their side, offering to bring breakfast and drinks.

Carmen shook her head when they were alone, looking after the staff member who had already disappeared from view. "How are we ever going to go home and live without this service?"

"I know, right?" Rae agreed.

Grace reminded herself that they were there to find out what had happened to Rae the night before. Unexplained crying could not be left unanswered, but it was hard to be unhappy while being fawned over by the staff in the midst of blue skies and palm trees swaying gently in the never-ending breeze.

"Okay, you two are going to spill about your evenings," Carmen demanded.

"Nothing happened," Grace and Rae chimed in on cue.

Carmen fixed them both with a gimlet glare and rose to her knees to lean into both their faces. "You liars!" She pointed at Rae first, the shadowy light of the canopy filtering over her perfect figure. "You first," she pointed at Rae.

"There's nothing to tell," she promised.

"I heard you last night crying. From my porch," Carmen prodded. "Something happened."

Rae paled, her normally rosy skin taking on the hue of old paper. "You did not," she whispered worriedly.

"Oh, I did," Carmen snapped. "And I'm sure he and Joe did too because they were both in their rooms." Jerking her thumb at Grace, she added, "You're lucky this one and Reed were out gettin' busy, or we'd have all listened."

Latching onto the shift in topic, Rae raised an eyebrow. "Busy? What were—"

"Nope!" Carmen interjected, bodily inserting herself between Rae and Grace. "You first, Missy."

Rae sighed. "Jacob and I...we had a conversation," she began.

"What part of '*go for it*' did you not understand?" Carmen accused. "Joe and I *both* told you to get after that boy who, I might add, would do anything you asked. And after we set you up to be alone, I hear you sobbing outside your room. That is literally a cry for help, and you wouldn't let us in." She pointed between herself and Grace.

Rae scowled at the guitarist for a moment before her glare morphed into a sheepish expression. It took her more than a minute to reply, the swell of the ocean filling in the gap.

"I can't...it's..." she trailed off, tears springing to her eyes and choking her up further. "Please, not yet," she whispered.

"Honey," Carmen cooed, hugging the bass player tightly.

Grace patted Rae's knee gently. She heard other people and noticed three servers approaching. She extracted herself from pile to receive the incoming treats to cover Rae's vulnerable state. The smell of bacon, the sight of beautifully arranged plates of fruits, and glasses of juice were the distraction the ladies needed. She thanked the staff as they deposited the food on the bed.

"Bacon?" the bassist sniffled.

"Okay, I'll let you off for a minute, but only because it smells amazing, and I'm starving." Carmen sighed, grabbing a piece of the bacon and virtually inhaled it. "I'm going to gain like twenty pounds by the time we go home."

They set to demolishing breakfast, and Grace waited until about half the food was gone before she pried again.

"Are you okay?"

"Yes," Rae answered, nibbling on a piece of bacon. "I am now."

"Then explain to me what this crying jag was about," Grace demanded, a little sharper than she intended. She looked at her own plate, seeing the fruit, and her brain was back on Derek and watching him eat breakfast the day before. She set the plate down and turned her full attention to Rae.

Carmen shrank back at the intensity and turned to the bassist. "I think you'd better tell her before she gets snarly."

Rae looked like she was close to barfing but finally started speaking. "We agreed that we didn't wanna be Fleetwood Mac. All that inter-band romance with Stevie and Lindsay destroyed them! So, we've decided that we'd stay friends. We're colleagues. We're okay."

"You so are not," Grace refuted. She reached for her drink. "What I truly don't understand is why you're both fighting it so hard. I mean, I get not wanting to put the band at risk, but let's be honest. You don't even have a name yet. So, what are you suffering for?"

Carmen squealed, looking between the pair. "Note to self: Do not fuck with Grace 'cause she will straight up lay you out."

"Because," Rae whined.

"Look, I get that you're afraid," Grace continued, "but there's no fear of rejection at this point. You're scared of something that may never happen. Isn't that what you told me yesterday?"

Rae frowned at her. "I may have buggered it all up," she worried. "I told him the Stevie Nicks thing."

"You didn't," Carmen groaned. "Honey, I told you that to show you that relationships don't make or break bands. Fleetwood Mac was mega successful! You can have it *all*."

Rae set down her bacon sadly. "Can we talk about Grace now? This is making me tired."

"Yes, let's!" Carmen grinned. "Because she came home late last night all pew, pew, pew," she described, shooting pistols from her ribcage, "And Vitamin D just kissed the crap out of her right there in front of me. I thought I was going to have to look away."

Grace covered her face with her hands, crushing her elbows against her chest. "Why do you have to tell it like that?" Grace cried. "It sounds like porn!"

"It's so much more exciting that y'all didn't know I was there watching you make out like a creeper," she laughed.

"Tell me more! I have to live vicariously through you," Rae prompted.

"I'm not sure what there is to tell," Grace replied, face hot as the words escaped her lips.

"Well, first," Carmen tattled, "They went to the club, 'cause I saw them there. And Vitamin D had this one wrapped around his pinky, all slinky bumping uglies on the dance floor."

"What?" Grace squawked. "Did you like follow us all the way back here? Are you actually a creeper?"

Carmen burst out laughing. "No. I saw you both dancing, but after a couple songs you disappeared and when you resurfaced, you looked you'd stuck your head out the window of a car on the Audubon and you were attached at the mouth."

"Was there tongue?" Rae prompted Carmen conspiratorially.

"No. It was all chaste," the guitarist grumbled, smoothing a hair behind one ear. "But what I need to know is where you were between the disco and the rooms."

It was Grace's turn to feel their gaze on her, and she didn't like it one bit. "Stop. It was…personal." She reached into her bag for sunscreen and slipped off her cover up to start slathering it on. That was her mistake.

"Is that a hickey?" Rae yelped.

Grace looked all around her, as though she were about to swat a bee away.

Carmen clapped. "Where? Where?"

Rae reached forward, pulling Grace's arm away and touching her collarbone.

Grace cursed, covering the spot immediately. "It's not funny."

"This is a good thing," Rae assured, squeezing Grace's knee. She grinned wickedly, looking around the resort. "You must've found a good, secluded corner to find time to do that."

"Yeah, where? I know you weren't in the room," Carmen agreed.

"We were on the beach," Grace confessed, pulling her knees to her chest.

"But you were dry. I saw…" The words died on Carmen's lips as she looked around them. "You were here!" She pointed to the bed that Rae had tried to jump into, then gaped at Grace. "In that first bed! That's why you wouldn't stop. You sly dog!"

"What? No," she protested.

Rae hugged Grace from one side, and Carmen joined from the other. "Good for you," they chorused.

Grace wriggled, pushing them away, but they kissed her cheeks and squeezed tighter.

"Wow. Can anyone join in?" a familiar voice asked.

Derek clapped his hands over his ears at the resounding mixture of laughter and cackling he inspired. He was clad in an athletic T-shirt and shorts sweating quite noticeably. He took a deep swig from the water bottle he was carrying, some of it spilling down his chin.

"Girls only, you gross boy!" Rae scolded.

Derek pouted. "I saw a pile of ladies on a bed, and it looked like something I wanted to be part of," he hassled, waggling his eyebrows at them. "Especially when I saw this one," he added, taking a lock of Grace's hair between his fingers.

Grace listed toward him, nearly forgetting the others were there.

"Gross!" Rae groused. "You're all sweaty too."

Derek let go of her hair and waved Rae off. "Last good morning run. Not sure I can squeeze one in before the flight tomorrow."

"I hate how fit you are," Carmen teased. "We're on a vacation, and you're exercising."

He held out his arms in a T-pose and managed to flex his muscles. "All this isn't by accident," he smirked, eyeing Grace for a moment before addressing the others. "What am I interrupting?"

"We were admiring how you signed your work," Carmen replied, running a finger over Grace's collarbone.

Grace drew back, pulling Carmen's hands away. "Everyone's so touchy this morning," she groused.

Derek grinned, reaching out to run a single fingertip over the bruise. "A hickey from Kenickie is like a Hallmark card: When you care enough to send the very best." He reached for a strawberry off Grace's plate, making no effort to be subtle as he sucked it between his lips.

Derek wiped his hands together in triumph. "My work here is done." He eyeballed Grace for a moment. "Lunch?" he asked.

She nodded mutely, already enthralled by him all over again. She watched as he jogged away and heard Carmen whisper behind her. "Pew, pew, pew!"

~ ♪ ~ DEREK ~ ♪ ~

Derek reached his room in no time, thinking of Grace as he ran. He had seen the way she'd pulled away at Carmen's touch. When he'd touched the same spot, she'd practically displayed herself for his perusal. He hadn't expected it to be difficult—she was a fan after all. The way it pleased him was unnerving.

He spied Jacob at Rae's door, hand raised to knock, as he passed. "The girls are at the beach," Derek called out to him. He slowed down, noticing that Jacob looked off. His shoulders were slumped, and his usually bright demeanor was distinctly gray. "Woah, what did she do?" he breathed.

Jacob growled.

"Okay, buddy," Derek murmured, hands out as if he were approaching a wild animal. Thinking back to the beach, he realized Rae's eyes had been bloodshot like Jacob's. Her eyes had been filled with despair while the man in front of him looked like an angry tiger stalking prey. "Let's go talk this out over breakfast, hmm?"

Jacob's stomach grumbled at the mention of food. "Yeah, okay."

The pair walked in silence to the restaurant and took a table in the corner, out of sight of most of the dining room. Once breakfast was ordered, Derek spent a moment looking at his friend. He didn't think he had ever seen him so angry...or angry at all. He grimaced.

Jacob's gaze fell somewhere in the middle distance behind Derek's head.

Derek busied himself adjusted his silverware to give the other man space to unload.

Sighing, Jacob confessed, "I was going to tell her...everything." His eyes were glassy as he whispered softly. It took him several stuttering starts before he strung a sentence together. "She cut me down like it meant nothing to her. I mean, I get it, the band comes first..."

"But?" Derek could guess how it had gone. He had seen the drama wrought in Rae's life over her ex who had been gone for several years now. He didn't want to think about the upset that would cause in their fledgling group. He knew other bassists, but he didn't want to lose Rae or deal with the drama that would bleed into his own life when he didn't abandon the project for her. He was relieved when his friend spoke again.

"But she refuses to even listen to me." His lips snarled as his pitch raised to mimic Rae's words. "She doesn't want anything from me, and that we wouldn't work out. And then…" His hands were flat on the table as he stared back. "…she gets to her room, and I hear her crying in the shower from my room." He paused then relaxed back in his chair, tapping the butt of his fork on the edge of the table. "And I couldn't do anything because she doesn't want me. I had to sit there and listen. Helpless…"

Derek went silent as their food was delivered. The quiet remained as Jacob stabbed at the food on his plate more viciously than necessary.

Derek mumbled a curse and scooted closer to the table. "You're in love with her," he accused.

"What an idiot, right?" Jacob scoffed. "You warned me, man."

Having no words for him, Derek focused on his food. It was hard to look at him in this state. "I'm sorry, man."

Jacob relinquished his silverware, straightening the napkin on his lap. "And why the hell did I give her the power to end this before it started?"

"Because you're a feminist," Derek answered easily.

Jacob arched a brow, stirring his coffee. "Don't we at least deserve a chance?" he pleaded.

Derek shrugged, sipping his OJ.

"So go get her," came a familiar voice, startling both men. Joe pulled a chair from a nearby table and sat down, ordering a coffee.

"But she said—"

"Jacob," the drummer cut in. "In what world did that sob fest sound like she doesn't want to be with you? Go. Get. Her," he instructed, fixing the younger man with a friendly glare. "Don't make me speak more than my daily quota."

The singer laughed. "Okay, after food."

"Now, what about you and Grace?" Joe grinned, saluting Derek with his coffee cup. "You seal that deal?"

Derek smirked. "There may have been a hickey involved."

"Way to go, Kenickie," Joe congratulated, holding up his hand for a high five.

Derek returned the gesture happily and speared more fruit. He used it to point towards the beach. "Little tip since it's our last night and all—lot of privacy on the beach beds," he suggested, eyeing Jacob. "After you persuade her in your most respectful way."

"Of course," Jacob veritably purred in reply. He tucked into the food in front of him. "So, speaking of it being the last night, I'd like for all of us to hang out for at least a little tonight. I haven't been to the disco yet. Any good?"

"It's good," Derek answered. "Small, but good. We can have fun there."

"It's a plan," Joe agreed. He pressed his shoe against Jacob's shin. "You've eaten enough. Go find that woman and make her listen to reason," he encouraged.

Jacob slugged back the remainder of his coffee. "We'll see you at the club. You're on your own for dinner."

The group spent their last day as tourists in a private van. They toured a dozen tourist shops, where Derek kept begging Grace to buy a coconut bra and any other slinky outfit he could find. It became a competition to find the most outrageous outfit based on print, lack of fabric, or both. Carmen out-sauced them all, teasing that she would wear it on stage at their first gig. Everyone was ready for a nap after their adventures.

They reconvened at the club where Grace acquired the holiest of holies: a corner booth. Joe climbed over everyone to settle in the center, making himself "unable" to get out and dance when asked.

"Shots!" Carmen cried, headed to the bar. She returned with a server and a platter of twelve brightly colored concoctions.

Grace looked warily at the two placed before her.

"One for each hand," Rae explained.

"To one last night of obscurity," Jacob saluted, raising his glass. The others joined, and everyone slammed first one drink then the other. Carmen and Rae raced to the dance floor in the direction of the DJ.

"Well, we're in trouble now," Derek drawled, draping an arm across Grace's shoulders, eyes sparkling. "Shall we?" he purred.

Grace giggled. "Other than my exceptionally bad dancing? Why not?" The pair wriggled out of the booth, Derek pulling her by both hands to the dance floor.

"I'll hold on to the table," Joe offered, lifting his drink to the others with a smile.

When Derek had her in position on the dance floor, he slipped his hands to her hips, moving them in time with his and meeting her eyes. He couldn't stop smiling at her. She seemed to be suffering the same affliction, managing to look shy as she did so.

"Got it?" he asked.

She nodded, and his hands slowly slipped up her sides, lifting her arms overhead. He liked the way she kept moving as instructed, trailing the tips of his fingers up her arms. She trembled under his touch until he reached her hands and twined them together. He pressed his forehead to hers, the tips of their noses aligning. He felt her moving against him and watched her chewing her lower lip, losing the beat for a moment as she began singing along.

He couldn't hear her, but she was wrapping her mouth around every word, and he had no trouble reading her lips. The lyrics were sexy, and her eyes gave every indication that she was doing this purposefully. His throat tightened, realizing that she was actively attempting to seduce him.

Her efforts were not lost, and Derek felt himself rising to the challenge, encouraging her and licking his own lips. His hands splayed over her hips, thumbs stroking her hip bone, fingers gripping her backside. Her chest heaved against the blissfully risqué v neck of her dress, and her eyes slipped shut, moving on pure instinct. The tone of the song changed, and her hands slid down his body. It felt like an eternity from his shoulders to his chest, down his stomach, until she pulled his hands from her body. She put her back to him, chin over her shoulder. He was mesmerized by her lashes flirting over chestnut eyes. And then she rolled her hips till they grazed the front of his pants.

He worried his zipper was going to burst, and he grunted, trying not to lose control over the small gesture. She was completely out of her comfort zone, and he felt his inner caveman taking over. He spun her back to face him and yanked her hips tight against his own. He wanted her to feel what she had done to him. Her eyes widened as he clamped one arm up around her lower back to hold her there as they moved. The other, he snaked up her spine until he tangled his fingers in her hair.

She curled both arms around his neck, and he felt her gasping against him before he crushed his mouth to hers. He pulled lightly on her hair, exposing her neck to him. This time, he knew was about to leave a mark, and this one she wouldn't be able to hide. She was his. He felt her whimpering as he trailed his tongue across her neck. Her body bowed against him when he first nibbled her earlobe then kissed her deeply.

Her fingers were crawling through his hair, holding him close. He wondered if she was kinky enough to let this display of affection continue more intimately in a nearby bathroom…or against a wall…or maybe in their rooms if they could wait that long.

And then like a lightning bolt, he felt an ice cube slip into the back of his pants, freezing a path down the crack of his behind, and his whole body convulsed, releasing Grace as he whirled to find the culprit.

Rae was already a step away, incriminating cup in hand and Grace's wrist in the other.

He scrambled to retrieve the offending cube from the back of his pants, watching as Rae dragged Grace back to the booth.

It took him far too long to grip the ice and free himself of the shock to his overheated body before chasing after them.

"Not cool, Rae," he yelled, rubbing the small of his back as he caught up.

"It was precisely cold enough. You're welcome" she countered, then pivoted toward the bar to get drinks.

He scowled at her before sliding in next to Grace who was flushed and panting. A faint sheen of sweet covered her face. He could already see marks forming on her neck, and he stroked them gently. There was heat in her eyes as she canted her neck toward his touch.

Carmen threw a straw at them. "Hello! We're a band, not a porn cast!"

"Are you sure?" Joe questioned, holding up his thumbs and forefingers to frame the couple.

"Oh, stop," Derek defended. "Consenting adults."

Grace shivered, folding her hands on the tabletop. She shifted until she was facing the others, leaning back against his chest. "We'll be good," Grace slurred.

Derek pressed a kiss to the top of her head and curled and arm around her waist. There was something liberating about giving into rising tension between them. He wondered if this was how Pete felt with Nancy in his arms. Quiet, not overtly sexual, and like home being seen together. He was grateful when Rae dropped a whiskey in his hand.

"Neat, like you like it," Rae offered. Her eyes darted to Grace's repose, and she gave him a wink. "One for you too, Gracie." She placed a peach-colored frozen drink on the table then passed out the others and slipped in beside Carmen.

"Thank you, guys, for going into town today," Jacob yelled, leaning in to be heard. "It meant a lot to me. You're my family now, and I'm honored to be making music with you."

The collective aww at the table was cut short by everyone sipping their drinks.

Grace was halfway through hers when she started yawning,

twisting in Derek's lap to rest her head on his shoulder.

"Lightweight," Joe badgered.

She smiled sleepily at them. "I promise I'll work up my tolerance, but I may never be able to keep up."

"Two's your limit," Rae added. "And this makes three. You look like you're out for the count, girl."

Derek felt Rae's eyes on him even though her words were directed to Grace.

"Why does that feel like weaponized information?" Derek asked. Why would she intentionally sabotage his last night on the beach with this woman he liked very much? Despite the literal ice down his pants, his brain was still firmly settled on taking Grace somewhere and ravishing her until neither of them could walk.

"I have no idea what you mean," Rae replied, twirling the straw in her cup and watching the ice race laps around the edges. "Better to be the tortoise and win then run the race like the hare."

Her eyes were boring holes through his, and he turned his attention to Grace pressed to his side. Her cheeks were rosy, and she looked sleepy and languid beside him. He tickled his fingers against Grace's rib cage, and she squealed, sitting up to sip her drink.

"I'm not plastered yet," Grace denied. "But I can't have any more so I won't be."

Carmen thrust her drink up at the center of the table. "To riding that line between good and bad decisions," she toasted.

The others clinked glasses, draining their contents within the next moment.

"Let's make this our official battery recharging station," Jacob suggested.

Joe raised his empty glass in agreement before the others had even gotten a grip on theirs, and they laughed as they approved.

THIRTEEN

Tuesday morning, Grace was wrapped up in securing lunch reservations for her boss at a swanky restaurant touting the most encompassing view of the city. The host was being particularly fussy about both the time of the meeting and the size of the party when the other line beeped from reception. She knew who was waiting at the front desk, but hanging up on this pedantic maître 'd now would put the final nail in her coffin, and she'd never get a table. She would explain the delay to Jacob and Derek that evening, and they would understand. Once she finished up, she called the receptionist back.

"Sorry I missed your call. How can I help?"

"Mr. Meyers' ten o'clock appointment is in the lobby."

Her heart raced, but she remembered her place. "Thank you. I'll be right there." She hung up the phone and stood, straightening her skirt and jacket before tapping on the jamb of Meyers' door. "Your ten o'clock is here. I'm going to the lobby to get them."

He nodded to her and started straightening his papers.

Grace tried not to run to the lobby, pretending this was any other client. But she knew on the other side of that door was the man who was responsible for her restless nights alone since they'd parted ways in the Caribbean. They'd gotten in late Sunday night, and Monday she had been so consumed with catching up at the office she'd barely noticed he hadn't called. But the memories of the last two days of their vacation were still fresh, and she'd reveled in it non-stop. She pushed the frosted glass door open that separated the lobby from the offices.

When her eyes landed on the two men waiting, her knees went weak, and she laid a hand on the reception desk to steady herself. Heat crept up her neck to her cheeks, and her skin puckered. She swallowed hard, looking away from Derek's well-groomed appearance to meet Jacob's eyes. He looked so professional she almost didn't recognize him, but she caught herself before giving either of them a compliment.

The receptionist spoke up quickly. "Misters Hunter and Reed for Mr. Meyers."

"Thank you, Cindy. Good morning, gentlemen." She nodded at each of them in turn. "I hope we haven't kept you waiting long," she offered.

"Not at all," Jacob answered with a kind smile.

She gestured for them to follow her. "Mr. Meyers is waiting for you in his office. If you'll walk this way," she offered.

She started away, purposefully slowing her gait. She was afraid if she said anything to either of them, the jig would be up and everyone in the office would notice how tan all three of them were. She'd been hearing about it all day and received the compliments with as much aplomb as she could muster without spilling all the glorious details.

She listened to their footfalls behind her, glancing at their reflection in the glass walls as she passed. They looked like kings striding behind her, and she saw Derek adjusting his collar from the corner of her eye. She stopped at the entrance to Meyers' adjoining office.

Derek and Jacob strolled inside like they owned it.

She snatched up a tablet and pen, tucking it behind her back, awaiting an invitation to the meeting.

Meyers was on his feet in an instant, shaking both their hands and gesturing to the meeting table as they exchanged pleasantries.

"Help yourself to a water," he offered, taking a bottle from the glass tray in its center. "Or if you prefer coffee or tea, Grace would be happy to get that for you."

She waited in the doorway for answers. "Anyone?"

"Not necessary for me," Jacob replied.

Derek shook his head as well.

"If you change your mind, say the word," Meyers offered. He turned to Grace. "You'll be taking notes?"

"Yes, sir." She hurried into the room, closing the door then taking a seat on Meyers' right side. She straightened her back, making neat notes at the top of her sheet and scrawling the attendees' names.

Meyers got straight down to business.

"So the album's almost ready," Jacob explained. "We'd like to start shopping it to some labels, and we'd like you to help us find some. We brought a track to sample so you can guide us to the ones likely to be most receptive. In the meantime, we're going to book a few gigs and get the band dialed in live. Generate a little buzz."

"We already have a venue for our first gig. It's called *The Oubliette*," Derek announced.

Grace was glad she was taking notes, because it was the first time he'd spoken since he'd arrived, and his confidence gave her a chill.

"I know it. That place doesn't have near the capacity—" Meyers began.

"It was part of our obligation when we used the club for audition space," Jacob pointed out. "And it happens to be perfect for our album launch. Invite-only for our VIP friends. They'll be more comfortable, and they can hype it up. And we'll fill it up with press and label execs. It will be a very grass roots approach."

"We'd have to hire security," Meyers mused. "That would certainly cause a splash. Alright, I'll see what I can do on that front. How about House of Blues to follow up? It holds twice as many people."

"Good," Derek agreed.

"And we can get the word out to my street team," Jacob added. "They do wonders. We'll get buy-in from the top all the way down to the consumer."

"I've already seen some buzz on a few minor websites," Meyers added. "I've had a few calls from morning radio asking about interviews and singles. I think your next step once you secure a label is to get a band manager to deal with the minutiae."

"Oh, we've got a bead on that," Derek replied with a shark's smile. "We're going to use the internet to promote ourselves for now. I think social media is the way to get the word out fast and nearly free. The benefits of modern technology." He reached for a bottled water from the center of the table, his long fingers circling the lid.

Grace nearly forgot what she was doing and looked at her tablet. She made a hasty note: *bead on band manager.*

"You do? Anyone I know?" Meyers pressed.

Grace swore she felt Meyers' eyes pass over her, but she made no indication that she knew anything, simply glanced around the table waiting for someone to say something else she could write down.

Jacob frowned. "It's too soon. I don't want to jinx anything talking about it. We'll need a label first. I was hoping you could give us some connections today."

Grace felt sweat form in the small of her back, and she focused on writing furious notes. She almost didn't feel Derek's foot press against the side of her shoe, and despite her best efforts, a smile turned up her mouth as the conversation progressed. She fixed her eyes on the table, her hand shaky as she wrote the words *label contacts* under the next bullet point.

"Are you getting this, Grace?" Meyers asked.

She looked up then, nodded. "Yes, sir." She held up the notebook slightly for him to see the outline and notes she'd been making, neat purple ink filling the page. "*Oubliette*, House of Blues…"

He waved her off. "Good. Get details for these gentlemen for the labels," he instructed. He reached back to his desk to pull a handwritten note from its surface and passed it to her. Without waiting for a reply, he turned back to his clients.

Grace scanned the note, then walked back to her office. She noticed Derek's eyes begin to trail after her as she breezed past him.

"I didn't want to set an appointment until I knew your schedules,"

Meyers continued.

Jacob coughed before answering. "Naturally."

She tuned them out, pulling up contact information from Meyers' address book and creating a sheet. She printed three copies of the details, then popped the same into an email to all three. When she returned, she saw them staring at their phones looking at their calendars.

"Thank you, Grace," Meyers offered. "What would I do without you? She keeps me so organized."

Grace offered a smile and took her seat. His compliments were reserved for impressing his clients with the quality of his staff. She knew it wasn't especially sincere, but it did feel good in the moment.

"Yes, she's great. She set up all these alarms for our phones so that while we were recording, we stayed within union guidelines for breaks and everything," Jacob praised then laughed. "Now if I can figure out how to turn them off..."

"I'd be happy to help with that." She turned to Meyers, who looked at her suspiciously. "It's a recurring calendar appointment. I set it up that first week. I can cancel them." She stood. "In fact, I'll go do that now."

Grace listened to them batting around dates until they finally settled on one. She jotted it into Meyers' calendar, adding the guys to the invitation.

"Did you get that, Grace?" Meyers yelled from his office.

"Yes, sir." She repeated the date back to him and turned just as Jacob stood, Derek rising a moment later. She couldn't help but eye the back of his black slacks. Instead of the usual ventilated jeans she'd grown accustomed to at Jacob's house, today he wore a pair of charcoal chinos that showed off the perfect curve of his backside.

"We'll look for those appointments," Jacob offered as he started toward the door, Derek on his heels.

Meyers launched out of his seat to chase them out of the room as they passed into Grace's office. "Good to see you, both."

"Thank you for everything, Grace," Jacob greeted.

"My pleasure," Grace replied, returning his wave.

Derek lifted his hand at her and winked quickly before strutting out of the office.

Grace sighed. There was that heat flushing her neck again, and she fanned herself as she watched them walk back through the reception door.

<h3 style="text-align:center">~ ♪ ~ DEREK ~ ♪ ~</h3>

"Oh, my God! That man is awful. A hundred bucks says that Grace is making those appointments right now," Jacob blurted once they had cleared the lobby and were back on the street.

Derek smirked. "You know that's her job, right? Making appointments and getting water. It's honest work, and she's good at it."

Jacob scowled. "Okay, yes, but he treated her like a piece of furniture. Cut her off while she was talking and everything."

"You're not wrong," Derek agreed as they walked to his car. He hadn't liked it either. But he'd had several epiphanies about her behavior now seeing her in her natural habitat.

He rehashed the meeting as he navigated the streets toward Jacob's house. At first when they walked into the office area, he'd been confused. Grace, who had been so intimate with him less than forty-eight hours ago, had barely even looked at him in the lobby, and he knew he was looking the part today. He'd texted pictures to Rae to confirm.

She'd been nothing but professional, but there was no cute smile or overtly friendly greeting. She hadn't even met his eyes before she'd led them to her boss's office. The other employees were spread out in a giant cube farm comprised of four-foot fabric partitions. He felt their eyes assessing them both—mostly Jacob. He was definitely the more famous party.

It was incredibly intrusive, but such was the nature of celebrity. Everyone wanted to be fame adjacent. And as per usual, they tried to look bored, or uninterested, but at least half a dozen of them had their mouths hanging open. One was eating a donut, three had been gossiping, sitting on someone else's desk and giggling with foam cups in hand. His memory painted him a bleary picture of the dull faces. He imagined what it must be like to work in a dreary building like Meyers Talent Agency.

He remembered letting his eyes roam over the back of her shapely calves up to her behind covered in a navy pencil skirt. It was such a sensible article of clothing that he wanted to rip off of her. He couldn't be faulted for checking her out. He was a guy, after all. They didn't know he knew exactly what it felt like. He tucked that secret in the back of his mind and sat a bit taller in the driver's seat.

A smirk lit his face as he recalled what she was wearing to the office: a simple navy suit with a silky shell beneath her jacket. It was at that moment that he realized how her suits set her apart from the cattle at the office. Everyone was in khakis and polos and Sunday dresses. But Grace, in her fishbowl office next to the owner of the company looked like royalty. Her suit screamed that she was too important to remember their names because she was the boss's right hand. Her suit at their first lunch and Jacob's studio made sense, and he regretted judging her for it.

His reverie was interrupted by Jacob.

"I was impressed by your restraint in there," Jacob complimented. "I fully expected you to maul her the way you two were acting in Tulum. Especially when Meyers was being such an entitled dick."

Derek laughed. "Thank you. That was ridiculously hard work," he replied. "Let's not go back there for a while. I'm not sure I could pull that off again."

Jacob laughed too. "It was weird," he agreed, "Not being able to act like we know her."

"Yeah, especially after the vacation. Which got me to thinking," Derek trailed off.

"Don't hurt yourself," Jacob interrupted.

"I walked right into that one." He rubbed his fingers over his mouth, not wanting to be distracted and forget his question. "You remember

Pete and Nancy, right?"

Jacob nodded.

"So, I don't like to make a big deal of it," Derek continued, "But my birthday's coming up, and they want to throw me a little party. They've invited my old band mates, and they suggested I invite my new ones."

"Is that so? Big birthday?"

"Big birthday adjacent. So… you in?"

"Hell, yeah," Jacob smiled. "I should introduce you to my guys at some point too. You're going to be their hero."

"Why?"

"Because you are Team Jacob in the Jacob and Rae saga. Danny blabbed to them all about her, and now they're all up my ass about it."

"I have a couple of those. Peter and Nancy have threatened me with bodily harm if Grace isn't on the guest list."

They chuckled, and Jacob adjusted his sunglasses jauntily. "If they could have seen you in Tulum."

Derek grinned wickedly. "That was such a good trip, man. Thank you so much for taking us. That was incredibly generous."

Jacob shook his head. "Money is there to be spent. It doesn't do any good sitting around. And besides, this could pay big dividends in the end." He paused. "I know we already talked about commitments, but…" Jacob trailed off. "While we're alone…I was thinking about it, and I kind of feel like this project belongs to you and me. With bands, someone needs to have the final say, and I think that's really us, dude. Are you okay with that?"

"Where does that leave Rae and Carmen and Joe?"

"Oh, definitely part of the creative team. But I feel more like they water ideas that you and I plant."

"As long as they don't get cut out. I don't want them to feel like less."

Jacob frowned. "They won't. I think we'll save a lot of time and hurt feelings if we go into with an understanding that if we were the Beatles, you and I are Lennon and McCartney."

No one had ever compared him to Lennon or McCartney before,

and he liked the appraisal.

"Okay. Let's approach it carefully with the others. We're really coming together. I don't want to fracture us over rights. And we can always renegotiate if things change."

"Of course. I didn't want to surprise you when I have my lawyer start drawing up the contracts. I'll make sure everyone gets a fair portion. I want to keep our catalog and make sure we have it set in stone who's going to have the final say."

His back straightened like a ram rod, and it took far too much concentration for Derek not to grin like a schoolboy. He'd played significant roles in so many projects now and had taken charge of his own career. In that moment, he knew this was the start of his very own origin story.

"Thanks, man. I appreciate it."

FOURTEEN

Grace had melted when Derek invited her to his birthday party. She got a text roughly an hour later from Rae asking for a ride to the same event. Apparently, he'd invited the whole band to the soiree. She spent the next three weeks fretting over what to wear and what she could possibly bring as a gift.

She pulled up to Rae's apartment complex, pleased when she spotted the bassist leaning against the fence surrounded by cases of soda with a brightly wrapped gift bag dangling from her fingers.

Rae actually jumped and clapped as Grace hopped out of the car to help put the goodies in the trunk.

"I can't believe how excited I am to hang out with y'all again," Grace sighed. "It's been weeks without anyone making fun of my headlights."

Rae cackled as she closed the trunk lid, and the ladies settled into the car.

"I haven't seen Vitamin D since we got back or anyone else for that matter."

Nodding, Grace checked traffic and pulled into an opening. "Derek's been tied up with projects and producing your songs in between."

"Have you even seen him since you got back?"

Grace considered how to answer the question. "Not really." He had been sending her the craziest selfies in various states of undress to prove he still existed. He hadn't sent her any nudies, thankfully. Some part of her wanted to save her first sight of that for an in-person exchange. "He usually calls around lunch, but it's hard to talk for long in the office. We've resorted to texting."

"You mean sexting," Rae clarified.

"I do not," Grace yelped. "He has not sent me any pictures I couldn't show you."

"Don't want to see them," Rae protested. "He's like my big brother. It was bad enough with those short shorts in Tulum."

Grace snickered, thinking she hadn't minded them at all. "At any rate, I'm looking forward to seeing the gang again."

"I can't wait to see Pete again and extract more embarrassing stories!" Rae agreed. She sighed, leaning her elbow on the passenger door. "Although...I bet Big D would answer anything *you* asked him at this point."

Grace bit her lips together and shrugged. "Maybe."

Rae's face blossomed with wide eyes and an eager smile. "You have secrets?" she pressed.

"Maybe," she answered, noncommittally. "But I don't think they're the kind you want to know."

Instantly, Rae clammed up, waving her hands and tucking her knees to her chest. "No. You're right. Forget I asked."

She wasn't sure where the wild streak came from, but Grace couldn't pass up the opportunity. She picked an innocuous detail about his gym schedule then arched a brow and leaned conspiratorially closer. "Because he really likes—"

"No!" Rae yelled. "I beg of you, say no more!"

Grace snickered. "Well, don't say I didn't offer."

They arrived early and wasted no time in extracting tasks from their hosts to help in any capacity they could. Pete handed out jobs happily, refusing to let Nancy lift a finger even though she was barely showing.

"I'm not an invalid," Peter's wife huffed.

"No, of course not, but you are carrying precious cargo, so let us spoil you a little, please?" Rae asserted, smiling widely. There was a reluctant acquiescence, and Nancy followed Peter around, instructing him on how to manage each task. As they worked, Jacob and Joe arrived. Joe was assigned cooler filling duty while Nancy oohed at Jacob's height and roped him into looping streamers from the light fixtures to the ceiling, creating a tent-like effect.

As they were hanging the last of the streamers and balloons, the back door slammed again, and they startled at the loud entry. "Is this the party place?" boomed a cheerful voice.

Rae and Grace gasped, exchanging looks as Leo Gomez walked in the back door carrying a huge sheet cake. Leo had been one of Derek's bandmates back in the day. Grace had never met him before and wondered if the others had been invited too.

"Leo!" Rae squealed, grabbing Grace's arm and giggling. "Is this *my* birthday?"

Grace felt frozen to the spot in the doorway between the kitchen and the dining room, head whirling.

"You must be Rae," Leo beamed, setting the cake down on the dining table and opening his arms for a hug.

Rae threw herself into his embrace and pressed her head to his chest like a child with a teddy bear. He looked over her head and winked at Grace. "That means you must be the incomparable Gracie my brother has fallen for."

"Um..." Grace blushed and smiled as he tucked Rae against his side and held out a hand. She gathered her wits and returned the greeting. "Mr. Gomez," she nodded at him. "And it's just Grace."

"Not the way Alfalfa tells it," he retorted. Leo didn't release her hand and led both women into the living room where Nancy was finally resting on the couch, pointing out places for Jacob to adjust his work.

"Nance," Leo greeted. He let go of the ladies and enveloped Nancy in a gentle hug. Grace and Rae slipped out of the way, backing into a corner of the dining room to watch.

Leo gave her a long hug, mumbling against her ear. He doled out another for Peter, slapping him on the back. "Thanks for inviting me, guys. Does D know I'm coming?"

Peter shook his head. "Yeah. I'm terrible at keeping secrets. I haven't heard back from Ryan—he said he might have one of his wrestling things with his daughter. Fingers crossed."

Leo held up his crossed fingers then turned to Jacob. "Leo Gomez," he introduced, holding out a hand.

"Jacob," the younger man replied and shook the proffered hand stiffly. "Hope I'm not intruding."

"No such thing," Leo assured. "Some days I think he likes to forget it all happened with us. But there are some people you can't forget," he offered. "Looks like you have all this under control. I've got two more things in the car. Could you give me a hand, Gracie?"

She managed a nod, setting down the napkin she had been fretfully shredding. She followed him out to the back end of a Camry and bit back a laugh at the practicality of it.

"Quick," Leo asked. "Jacob. Boyband, right?"

She nodded.

His face pinched it in thought. One eyebrow arched carefully as though he was about to step on a land mine. "Harmonizers?"

Grace nodded again.

Leo blew out a sigh of relief. "Thank God," he groaned, popping the trunk. Inside was a wrapped gift and an enormous aluminum pan covered in foil. It was cossetted in a hefty looking cardboard flat that had once housed strawberries with a tatty looking bath towel sandwiched between the cardboard and the pan for insulation.

A delicious, spicy aroma wafted out, and Grace voiced her delight. "That smells good—but spicy, which is bad for me, but tasty," she rambled.

Leo laughed. "My Tia made tamales. There's no way my freezer can even hold all these, and my students get tired of them. Spoiled."

She laughed, taking the gift box and shutting the trunk for him once he had the delicate cargo in hand. They started walking back toward the house when a car horn blared at them repeatedly. The pair stopped, looking behind them to see a BMW slowing down in the street. The window rolled down, and Derek leaned toward the passenger side to call out.

"Hey, party people!"

Grace recognized the car immediately. She hadn't seen his face outside of a phone screen since they'd returned, and she leaned down to see in the car. Another woman was seated beside him, looking entirely too comfortable for Grace's liking. She was relatively unadorned, but attractive in her natural state. She was younger than Derek and dressed in an edgy green top. Grace couldn't see the rest of her, and she flagged as conspiracies began forming in her head.

"Hey, birthday boy!" Leo greeted. He hefted the tray in his hands. "Park that lux monster and get your ass inside. This shit's heavy."

"See you inside!" Derek called back with a grin. The window whirred up, and he sped away.

Leo and Grace passed through the back gate, headed toward the house. "That's his sister," Leo informed her. "So don't get your panties in a twist." He chuckled. "I hate having friends with hot sisters."

The laugh that burst out of Grace's lips at the top of the steps surprised her and everyone nearby as she held the door for Leo. She covered her mouth to finish her giggle. "Sorry! And also Derek is here."

"With Cassie," Leo announced, placing the tray on the stove top. He checked to make sure the oven was empty then set the temperature and slid the covered dish inside.

Nancy darted over to him. "Is that what I think it is?" When Leo nodded, she squeezed her hands together. "Please tell me you brought the raisin ones."

"And the mild ones," he confirmed.

Squealing, Nancy threw her arms around his neck and kissed his cheek. "Why are you still single?" she sighed.

"I'm married to the dance," he answered, performing a quick spin. "And also, I don't cook."

"And you should not. I will never forget that thing with the hot dogs and cinnamon," Peter laughed.

Everyone in hearing distance groaned.

"Bro, you got no room to talk," Leo laughed. "You can't even make a bowl of cereal."

At least ten minutes passed before Derek and his sister entered the house with Carmen in tow.

"You may now begin to pay me tribute," Derek announced.

A cheer rose from his friends, and the hugs started first with Leo then their hosts.

Grace and Rae trilled as Carmen threw her arms around them both.

"I've missed you guys. Life has been so boring since we got back from the Caribbean," Carmen enthused.

"We were just saying that on the drive here," Rae commented.

"I ran into Derek and his sister on the way to the house," Carmen explained. She opened her mouth to say more but froze as her eyes slipped past Grace. "Who. Is. That?"

Grace looked over her shoulder to follow the guitarist's gaze. "Oh, that's Leo. He was one of Derek's original band members."

"He's pretty."

"Let me introduce you," Rae grinned, pushing through the crowded kitchen.

Grace wanted to join but was stopped as Derek reached her.

Derek dropped his sister's wrist before touching Grace's cheek and leaning down to kiss her chastely.

"My sister *surprised* me by coming down from San Francisco for my birthday," Derek explained to Grace as he wrapped an arm around her waist. "Grace, this is my baby sister Cassie. Cassie, this is Grace."

Grace did her best to make small talk, asking about her travels, but she was incredibly grateful when Nancy called for everyone to settle around the table.

"Food first! Then gifts," she announced. "The pregnant woman has spoken."

"We'll be right there," Derek called. He touched Grace's elbow. "Come with me."

She followed him to the front room by the surprisingly large pile of gifts. They were relatively hidden for the moment.

"That was not a good hello kiss," he apologized. This time, he folded his arms around her and kissed her slowly. "Better," he murmured.

"Much," she concurred. She had snaked her arms around his waist and contemplated slipping them lower.

"I missed you."

She felt suddenly shy. "I missed you, too," she whispered.

Needing no further encouragement, he kissed her again.

"DJ! We cannot celebrate you without you!" his sister called from the dining room.

Derek chuckled against Grace's mouth and pulled away. "Busted. Come on. My audience demands a performance." He pulled her by the hand to the table, pushing his sister to the next chair so he could sit with Grace.

Pleasantries dispensed, the food began veritably flying from hand to hand, and Grace found herself serving from the pan nearest her. It was utter chaos, but she couldn't stop grinning as she looked around the room.

Mid-meal, there was a knock at the back door, and a voice called out. "Is this a private party or can anyone join?"

Rae's fork clattered to her plate, and she shot a look at Grace.

Grace recognized this voice as well, belonging to Ryan Wier, another member of Derek's band, and she glanced at him. "You didn't tell me everyone was coming," she whispered.

Derek grinned wickedly as he swallowed a bite of food. "I wanted it to be a surprise since you missed the last two reunions." He placed a kiss on her forehead as he backed away from the table to greet the newcomers.

"Ryan! Come in!" Peter called, standing. "Let me find some more chairs."

Derek hugged the two new guests. "Ryan, Gina, let me introduce my new friends." He gestured around the table. "This is Grace, these are my new partners in crime: Rae, Carmen, Joe, and Jacob."

Ryan and his wife Gina waved at each person in turn, and Gina was the first to speak.

"We know who this is," she cooed, reaching across to shake Jacob's hand. "We have two girls. We have been to the shows and listened to your albums on repeat for hours." She laughed. "Pleasure to meet you."

"Partners in crime?" Ryan questioned. "New album?"

"Yeah. In fact, we brought the demo if anyone wants to hear it," Derek offered.

"Hell yes!" Cassie cried, swallowing her food in a rush. "How have you let us sit here and have boring conversation all this time when there's new music?"

"Because we were all groaning over the food, and I don't want our music to sound like a porn track," he explained. Derek retrieved the backpack he'd left at the door and extracted a CD in a blank jewel case.

Peter ordered Derek to get the music cranking while the newcomers took their seats.

"Oh my God—are those Tia's tamales?" Ryan asked, eyes landing on Leo. "I haven't had these in like twenty years!" He frowned. "Fuck we're old. When did that happen? Where was I?"

"Making babies and wrestlers," Gina replied patting his hand.

"Baby wrestlers?" Jacob asked.

The table burst into laughter, discussing tiny luchador costumes and potential baby wrestler names.

Conversation stopped as music filled the house. Heads began bopping to the beat, and Leo jumped out of his chair. He pointed at his plate and looked around the table.

"I am not done with this," he warned.

He squeezed around chairs until he reached the open living room where Derek was evaluating everyone's reaction. A moment after Leo began dancing, Derek joined, matching him step for step.

Grace veritably choked at the sight and leaned into the table, nearly dunking her chest in her plate. The way they moved together was like magic, perfectly in sync with each other. Tears trickled down her cheeks, and she clapped a hand over her mouth. A wave of nostalgia washed over her, and she stopped caring if anyone noticed.

"Pete, get over here," Derek encouraged.

Peter laughed, waving his hands. "No chance. Ryan?"

He shook his head. "Tamales," he indicated, taking another from the center of the table.

"Ah, Pete! Come on—we'll do something you know," Leo offered, changing up the steps. Derek fell in line easily, and Peter groaned.

"Fine. Fine. I'll try. But don't anyone laugh when I suck. I haven't done this in like twenty years, guys." He joined the others, and after a few missteps kept pace.

At this, Rae rushed to fill Derek's empty chair between Grace and Cassie.

"Pinch me!" she whispered to Grace.

Without hesitation, Cassie obliged, and Rae squealed. To Grace, it was all background noise, and she couldn't tear her eyes from the dancing trio.

"Jacob?" Derek called. "It's our song, man. You should get in on a piece of this."

Jacob scoffed. "Old school? Sure." The younger man rolled his eyes, stepping into sync with them. After a few beats, he dove forward, hand extended toward the floor. The moment his palm touched down on the wood floor, it slipped out from beneath him. He went down hard, chest smacking against the floor. A panicked wheezing noise blared over the music, and the others rushed to check on him.

Rae flew from her seat like a lightning bolt, shoving Derek, Peter, and Leo out of the way to reach Jacob's side.

"Are you okay?" she fretted, patting his cheek as she assessed his head.

Cassie's warmth drew Grace's attention as the woman leaned toward her.

"How long have they been together?" Cassie muttered.

"They're not," Grace whispered back conspiratorially. "Yet. It's a project your brother and I have, but she's really stubborn."

Cassie chuckled but remained close. "So...you and my bro?" Cassie quizzed.

"Um...yes?"

Cassie smiled at the timid reply. "Not sure about him?" she asked. "'Cause I guarantee he's good deep down under the hair gel and hustle."

Grace snickered at the description. "No. He's gold. I hope I'm worthy."

Cassie touched the other woman's arm reassuringly. "He said you met at a business lunch. What is it you do?"

The statement gave Grace pause. It meant they'd been talking about her. "I work for his agent. Part secretary, part gopher," she explained.

Cassie nodded. "Good. It's about time he found someone real. He's been grumpy and single for way too long. I'm glad for him. But if you hurt him—"

"If that were even possible," Grace scoffed.

"Oh, it is. For all his swagger, big bro is pretty fragile." She leaned in and lowered her voice. "He looks at you the way Pete looks at Nancy...the way Leo looks when he's dancing. Trust me, he's sprung well and truly."

Grace clutched imaginary pearls around her neck and sighed. "I would never hurt him. I want him to be happy. And if by some accident I did hurt him, you'll be first in line after me," she promised.

Rae's voice escalated from the living room, drawing Grace and Cassie into the drama.

"Excuse me," Grace mumbled to Derek's sister then joined the fray. Jacob didn't seem to be injured, but Rae's tirade had yet to cool off as she continued to berate him for the blunder.

Grace touched Rae's arm gently, her words rolling out like honey. "Come outside with me," she advised, leading Rae out to the back porch.

Aggravation roiled in her throat as the door closed behind them, and they navigated the steps carefully. Rae's arm was trembling in her grasp. A tiny part of her worried why the other woman had flown so far off the handle, but in the moment, she was mainly irritated that the outburst had happened during Derek's birthday party. It was supposed to be about him.

Rae paced the small backyard, grumbling. Grace hoped if she got it out of her system, the woman would come to her senses. When her pacing slowed, Grace stepped bodily in front of her and took her by the shoulders.

"Everyone is in that house," she reminded the bassist. "And you're out here being furious over things completely out of your control, and frankly something that's not a big deal. If you think that Jacob is impressed by your level of concern, you're wrong."

Rae's chin dropped, and her eyes narrowed. She shoved Grace's hands from her shoulders.

Sensing an oncoming attack, Grace defended herself. "And might I remind you, it's Derek's birthday. So can you pull it together long enough for presents, and then I'll take you home?"

She couldn't believe she was going to have to leave Derek's party because Rae was throwing a fit. But as she'd told Cassie, if it would make his party happier, she'd do anything, including leave.

Rae blinked at her several times, then exhaled. The fists at her side relaxed, and she flexed her digits as her gaze dropped to the ground.

"You go in," Rae sighed. "Tell Derek I'm sorry, and I'll be in shortly."

"Are you going to be okay?" Grace worried. "I didn't mean to get so sassy."

Rae lifted a hand to stop her. "I deserved it," she replied.

With stumbling steps, Grace hurried back inside, taking a seat beside Derek and his sister at the table.

He pulled her to his side, kissing her temple. "Hey, it's not a real party without some drama, right?" he chuckled. "Thank you for putting yourself in the line of fire. Angry Rae is scary!"

"So that's my replacement?" Cassie smirked.

"Funny, Pipsqueak," Derek countered.

"I'll go check on her," Carmen offered.

Jacob was already pushing in his chair. "I got this. I started it anyway." He lifted an apologetic wave to the group and slipped out the back door.

Derek pushed his plate away, and Grace began clearing dishes. She was pleased to see her casserole dish empty, and she started carrying it back to the kitchen with their plates.

"What was that?" Gina asked. "I didn't get any."

"You snooze you lose," Leo ridiculed. "It was like lasagna only not. So good. You've got to get that one to places on time," he told Gina, pointing at Ryan.

"After a decade, I gave up," she laughed.

"How many of those things are you going to eat?" Peter badgered as Ryan reached for another tamale.

"How many are there?" Ryan laughed. "And don't hate on me. You all had an earlier start."

Peter laughed. "I'm ready to give gifts. We're waiting on you, man."

Ryan sighed. "Fine. But I'm having a raisin one after."

The group moved to the living room, pulling chairs out of the dining room and gifts were passed to the birthday boy.

Grace did her best not to fidget as he revealed gifts from the others, hoping he would like her gift. When his sister handed him the box from Grace, he beamed. He pulled a black bag out of the case, brows furrowed as he investigated.

Grace gulped, tucking her fingers under her knees as she explained. "It's a special media bag. There's a place for headphones and pockets for jewel cases—I checked to make sure they're the right size. To you know, keep you organized and protect your stuff."

"Really?" He pulled the zip open immediately then reached in to see the surprise she'd stowed inside. "What's this?" He extracted a handful of glossy school folders, emblazoned with his own face.

Peter leaned in, squinting. "Is that our band stuff?"

"Yeah," Derek answered. His voice was low, mouth hanging open as he turned them over. "And I have never seen these before." He looked up with a grin and passed them to Peter.

Grace smiled shyly. "I hope it's okay. You said you had never seen the folders before or the T-shirt you and Peter autographed for me all those years ago. I sort of out-fanned you."

"Wait, you've met before? Didn't you meet a few months ago?" Leo questioned.

"Grace was at the very first reunion back in '99. Pete and I went. You guys were busy or something," Derek explained.

All eyes were on Grace, and she shifted uncomfortably.

"There is a T-shirt I haven't signed? Where is this shirt?" Leo demanded.

Grace groaned. "At home. And also—totally inappropriate to ask for signatures on Derek's birthday."

"I'd sign a T-shirt. You should've worn it," Ryan added.

"Okay—that's it," Derek declared. "You're coming by the house after this so I can add these to the collection. It's only fair that you witness the installation."

Cassie linked her arm through Grace's. "I support this plan."

"Where's my invitation?" Carmen pouted.

"It's lost in the mail with Rae's," Derek retorted.

Staring between the brother and sister team, Grace desperately wanted to leave with them, but her promise to Rae surged to the forefront of her mind. "I'm supposed to take Rae home."

"Nonsense!" Carmen denied. She gestured between the remaining members of their band. "One of us can take her home, can't we?" She looked pointedly at Joe and Jacob.

"Sure, sure," Joe and Jacob chorused.

The rest of the party passed in a blur for Grace. They sat around the table and living room laughing and noshing, but all she could think about was going to his place for the first time. She had been dreaming about seeing his collection for more than a decade, but it took second place to seeing where he slept. Given the announcement he'd made upon arrival about his sister's visit being a surprise, she suspected he had similar ideas of what he'd like to show her at his place.

Once the food was gone, the party started to break up. Ryan and his wife were the first to announce their departure.

"Last in, first out," Gina teased the group.

"You barely got here," Derek protested. "Am I not celebratory?"

Ryan rolled his eyes and shoved him lightly. "We're here, aren't we? I do make an appearance around these parts sometimes."

"Not often enough," Pete agreed.

"Just because you two never stopped living out of each other's pockets doesn't mean the rest of us don't have stuff going on. And you're so far away!" Ryan complained.

"I promise to visit a lot more often," Leo vowed, hand over his heart. Grace could have sworn his eyes landed on Carmen as he made the promise.

Peter patted Leo on the back. "Lead by example," he complimented.

"Trust me. I'll be around."

"You guys should come to our show at *The Oubliette*," Jacob invited.

"A show?" Nancy balked, eyes swinging fully on Derek. "You're performing again? Not just recording?"

Derek nodded. "Yeah. Date's not set yet, but Grace can send out the details."

"Hell yes," Leo volunteered. "And can I please have the CD you played? I want to use it in class this week. We'd kill for some new music."

"No, man. That's the only copy," Derek exclaimed, holding the disc to his chest.

Jacob's face scrunched in confusion. "That's not the master, is it?"

Derek pouted. "No—but I wanted to listen to it in the car on the way back," he pouted. "I'll give you one at the show, okay?"

"Not gonna help me in the studio tomorrow," Leo derided.

"Give the man the CD," Jacob ordered.

With a roll of his eyes, Derek handed it over. "Fine. It's my birthday, but I'm glad *you* got what *you* want."

Grace felt a poke in the small of her back, and she glanced to see Carmen staring at her. The guitarist's eyes darted at the group.

Realizing what she was hinting, Grace spoke up, infusing her voice with more boldness than she felt. "I guess I need everyone's contact info," she requested.

Peter passed junk mail to Ryan and Leo to write on, then scribbled his email address on one to hand to her. Ryan and Leo gave her their information as they left, hugging her swiftly with jovial threats about taking care of their brother as a parting gift. Carmen pinched her cheek as she ran out to her car behind Leo.

Derek leaned on the counter beside Cassie. "Well, should we leave your car here and go to my place?"

"I could drive your car home if you wanted to ride with Grace," his sister offered.

"Not a snowball's chance, squirt," he rebuffed. "And no, you can't drive her car either."

"Oh, I can follow you over," Grace offered. "It's no problem."

Derek pouted. "But I wanted you to be in the car with us. And today's my actual birthday."

"Let her drive," Cassie insisted. "In fact—I want to ride with Grace."

Derek arched a brow. "I'm not sure I'm comfortable with that."

Cassie poked his side. "I'm not sure you get a choice." She spun on her heels and began gathering her brother's gifts.

"I see now how you handle Rae so easily," Grace harassed.

Derek smirked watching her go. "She's a good sister. I wasn't expecting her, but I'm glad she's here." He trailed off then turned his eyes on Grace. "You don't mind coming my way, do you? Even though I have company."

Grace balked. "To see the great collection?" she asked. "Not remotely. I've been dying to see it ever since Peter mentioned it in '99."

Derek sucked in sharp breath. "Oh, I'm not sure it will live up to your expectations."

She shrugged. "As long as you're there, it will be perfect."

"Why, Grace, if I didn't know better, I'd think you're attracted to me," he murmured, stepping closer to her.

Grace licked her lips and looked away demurely for the briefest moment. "Well, it's certainly possible," she spurred.

He placed a hand on her hip, stepping forward again until they were touching. "You're saying you need more convincing?"

She considered his words, pursing her lips and wrinkling her forehead. "It couldn't hurt."

Derek bit his lip, watching her face. "I'm up for it," he whispered against her ear.

"Gross. Keep your hands to yourself," Cassie grumbled, flicking her brother's ear as she walked past the pair, Derek's new media bag over her shoulder. "I've got your gifts. If you want to see them again, keep up," she encouraged.

Derek laughed, caressing Grace's cheek as he pulled back. "We'd better go, or she's going to nab the cars too."

"Both of them?" Grace asked, trailing after him.

"I wouldn't put it past her. Follow me. I promise not to lose you at a light. But if I do, Cassie will have the details."

"See you there," she promised.

The ride to Derek's place was short, and she enjoyed Cassie's banter as they drove. She discovered that they were the same age, and that Cassie had a crush on Leo when she was younger but had grown out of it by the time she was a junior in high school and she had witnessed him eating like a starving man. She told Grace about their brother who was even younger and finishing up his veterinarian degree. Their parents were retired. Their father was an artist, and their mother loved the challenge of gardening in Phoenix. She apparently grew the most beautiful succulent garden.

Grace slipped into the spot next to Derek at his complex. It was nothing extravagant, and nothing to set it apart from the thousands of apartments around the city. He had a second-floor walkup with a narrow balcony, barren of any adornments.

Derek ushered them in, welcoming Grace with a smile. Cassie

flopped down on the couch, kicking off her shoes under the coffee table. He offered them both something to drink but had little more than water or light beer. "I wasn't really expecting company," he apologized.

Cassie belly laughed, taking him up on the water. She turned on the TV and reached for a gaming controller.

Grace stood awkwardly near the front door, memorizing the room. It was so—sparse was the word that described it. The dove gray walls were empty. A modest television sat on a smoky oval glass cabinet designed for this very purpose. A gray gaming system and other electronics filled the shelves, all neatly aligned. The coffee table was covered in a monitor and several tiny control panels like baby versions of Jacob's studio.

Derek handed a bottled water first to Grace and then to his sister. "What are you doing?" he asked.

Cassie shrugged. "Trying not to be a third wheel," she answered. "Have you got anything besides Halo?"

"I think there's a driving game in there if you check the bottom shelf," he answered.

Cassie was immediately on the floor, scouring the cartridges lined up like books.

Derek squeezed Grace's fingers and led her into the hallway. There were three doors. She assumed one must be a bathroom. He opened the first door on the right and motioned her inside. Mostly, it was full of cardboard boxes and totes, but Grace could barely tear her eyes from the four industrial shelving units displaying memorabilia she had read about. She spied the board game, dolls in boxes, lunchboxes and thermoses, and many more collectibles. The walls were lined with framed posters, and the bottom shelves were filled with periodical boxes stuffed with hundreds of magazines.

She squealed. "I've had dreams like this where I walk into a store, and everything I've ever dreamed of is there. But I can never find someone to sell it to me, and I never have enough money to buy it all, but I want to."

Derek laughed as she dashed from shelf to shelf. She was terrified of touching anything, but she wanted to fan out all the magazines on the floor and roll around reading them like she had done as a teen. Of course, why read about the man when he was in the room with her and had already kissed her?

She spun to face him, putting her back to all the distracting goodies. "I'm sorry. I feel incredibly rude and weird fawning over this stuff when you're standing right here."

He waved off her apology. "It's good to be appreciated."

"I am so glad that you didn't let the network stop you from acting and making music," she began. "I spent a lot of time wondering what you were doing after that, and you were the first thing I looked up when I found the internet. I wanted to know you were having a good life and were happy. Thank you for sharing this with me."

"It was my pleasure." He held out his hand, beckoning her closer. "I was actually hoping we might end up here tonight, but I didn't expect it to be with my sister."

Grace's whole body flushed at the suggestion. "I'm glad I got to meet her. She's very nice, and she adores you."

He shrugged. "Of course. I'm her big brother."

Grace looked over her shoulder. "So—I have a weird question... being that it's your birthday and all."

He narrowed his eyes but smirked. "Go ahead."

"So—when we met at lunch with Jacob, you told me you'd give me a copy of the demo CD you made for him."

Derek's eyes searched her face. "You're going to hold me to that?" he questioned. "After all the hours you spent sitting in the studio with us?"

She nodded. "You can't make a girl a promise like that and then renege."

After a long pause, Derek replied slowly. "There is a condition to this exchange."

"Condition?" she questioned. "After I accepted your promise in good faith?"

He lifted his chin, challenging her to refuse. "Next weekend, I have a charity event to attend, and they keep pushing me for my plus one. I would like that to be you."

Grace blushed. Despite the fact that everyone who knew them had already labeled their relationship as a couple, she realized this would really be their first date.

"Wish granted."

He pulled her close in the doorway, and Grace's arms looped around his neck without thinking. He kissed her languidly as though they had all the time in the world. Her insides twisted happily, and she forgot that anyone in the world existed besides the two of them. He didn't rush the kiss or grope her excitedly, but his palms roamed slowly up and down her back.

Cassie's voice broke through their moment. "You're too quiet! Come watch me race cars!"

Derek pulled his face away, turning toward the hallway with Grace still snugged close.

"SPOILSPORT!" he called back.

Grace giggled in his embrace. "I should probably go."

He sighed. "Must you always be right?"

"It's a curse," she teased. "I'll try to be wrong more often."

He groaned his distaste for the sentiment. "Don't be wrong. But you could make it up to me…"

Grace buried her head in his chest to muffle her squeal. "You bring out the wickedest things in me," she explained.

"Perfect," he whispered, pecking her lips again. With a heavy sigh, he disentangled them. "I'll go burn your disc if you don't mind hanging out with Cassie."

"Your wish is my command," she replied. "And thank you."

FIFTEEN

As Grace pulled up Blake Marlin's number, she couldn't believe the phone numbers she had accumulated. Somehow she'd managed to get all the phone numbers of The Legends, plus there was Jacob and two members of his old band, such as Blake.

In addition to having a wildly successful pop idol career, Blake had become a fashion icon. He made everything he touched look cool. Jacob had insisted on connecting the two.

She'd have to make this quick. She was hiding in her car in the parking garage. She wasn't sure this was an appropriate use of her contact, but she wasn't sure what other choice she had. When he answered, Grace was suddenly at a loss for words.

"Grace," he greeted warmly. "What's up?"

"Well, I hope I'm not interrupting…"

"I always have time for you, but only if you say what you mean. I can literally hear a question in there," he badgered.

She sighed. "So, I've been invited to a charity gala on Saturday, and I'm not sure what to wear or where to go for something. I was hoping you might have a hookup."

"Because I'm gay?" Blake questioned.

"No—because you have more style in your little pinky than I have in my whole body," she almost cried. "And the guy I'm going with knows how to work a camera."

"Good save," Blake complimented. "Yes, of course I've got a hook up. I'll send over contact info for you. It's a bit short notice, but I'm sure she'll have something."

While grateful for the information, Grace had never felt so out of place as she did walking into what looked like a warehouse that afternoon. She wondered briefly if Blake was punking her. However, a young woman rushed out within moments of her arrival.

"You must be Blake's friend Grace," she greeted, extending a hand.

Grace accepted the gesture with a smile. "That's me. I'm so sorry for the last-minute notice, but I got invited yesterday."

"No apologies in this town over timing," the woman declined. "Besides, Margo works best under pressure, but you did not hear it from me." The woman offered a kind smile. "I'm Elizabeth, Margo's assistant. She does the fashion; I do the scheduling."

Grace smiled. "Me too."

Elizabeth ushered her toward a large square of carpet—she wanted to say a rug, but it was simply an unbound piece of carpeting roughly ten feet square. Two empty rolling racks lined the space. In the center was an octagonal riser with a three-sided mirror. She spied a pair of comfortable-looking chairs and what must be a changing screen. Suddenly it all felt profoundly serious and almost bridal.

"Margo was finishing up a call. If you'll hop up here for me, I'll take some measurements to get the ball rolling."

Grace followed along as instructed, and before she could recover from having her measurements taken, Margo joined them with a brief greeting. She gave Grace the third degree about the event, her personal taste, who she was going with, and other details. The woman's face pinched in concentration.

"Liz," she called. She glanced at Grace. "Have a seat. This will take some time." With a flick of her finger, Margo disappeared with Elizabeth behind her.

Frowning, Grace took a seat, pushing down her insecurities. Every measurement number felt too large or too small. She wrapped her arms over her chest. If Blake believed this woman would be able to fit her, she must be a miracle worker. This was for Derek. She wanted to look the part so he would not be embarrassed. She wanted to shine for him. And she trusted Blake, she reminded herself.

The women returned, Elizabeth carrying what looked like more than her weight in gowns. She and Margo proceeded to hang them on one of the racks until it was nearly full. The next two hours were a horrifying eternity for Grace, stripping down to almost nothing and donning multiple gowns, trying not to take it personally as Margo commented to Elizabeth about her body as though she wasn't even there. Margo pinched the gowns, finally selecting one and clipping it from behind and tugging indelicately at the neckline and the hips.

"No," the designer grunted before calling to Elizabeth to find some more appropriate undergarments. "And I am guessing you will also need a hair and makeup appointment. Liz, call Raquel and Thomas. Ask them if they can make time Saturday afternoon to meet us here."

Grace blinked, hands clasped over her cleavage. "Oh, I only needed the gown," she rushed.

Margo's head flicked from side to side, rejecting the suggestion. "Blake said it's your first gala. And you want to impress this man. So you will do it right the first time. And then you will know for the next time. We all have firsts," she explained.

In the same instant, the ladies disappeared leaving Grace on the pedestal with binder clips poking out from her shoulder blades. She eyed herself in the mirror nervously and snatched the cell phone from her purse, photographing her reflection. She sent it to Rae then stared at the screen, wishing she would reply.

Her ego had taken such a beating during the fitting she needed validation from someone not selling her a gown. She frowned, dropping the phone back in her bag and studying the mirror. The dress was lovely, but she looked frumpy, and the neckline was crooked. The blue fabric was lined with rhinestones, and it was perfect for the gala. Except that she was wearing it, and she looked like a toddler playing dress up.

Before she could fret more, the designer and her assistant returned. Elizabeth handed her some undergarments while Margo began removing the clips and sent her to change behind the screen. They were dull and nearly flesh toned, and Grace hated them. The mixture of mesh and foam barely covered her, but not in a sexy way that she hoped to show Derek. It was utilitarian and perfunctory.

She emerged clutching the dress over the front of herself and holding back tears at how ugly she felt as Elizabeth closed up the back for her. Margo placed her on the octagon again facing away from the mirror, pinning and tugging everything back into place. There was a nod, and then Margo was auditioning jewelry to complete the look. Elizabeth returned with strappy heels, and finally, Margo stopped working. Judging from the smile on her face, Grace assumed she liked what she saw.

Margo's voice was slow and thick as she mused. "Yes, I think that's it. With the right hair and makeup."

Grace turned to the mirror slowly, and from the neck down, she didn't recognize herself. The rhinestones made her look tall and lean and emphasized her bust line. With each breath, her chest heaved. When had those arrived? The practical unmentionables were surprisingly effective. She hated them a little less now. Maybe she could pull this off.

"When they ask who styled you Saturday night," Margo ordered, "I expect you to remember my name." She clapped her hands. "Okay, street clothes. Be here at two o'clock sharp Saturday. Don't dress up. Barefaced. Don't style your hair. No elastic. Bring perfume. Take a taxi. We'll courier your street clothes to you the next day."

Grace was dry mouthed at the prospect but bobbed her head mutely. She called Blake after she left.

"That was both the most humiliating and upper-class thing I've ever done," she gasped.

He laughed at her. "Fittings always suck. But the reason these people are hard to get into is because they know what they're doing.

You don't have to like it, but you do have to let it happen. Margo has never steered us wrong."

"I'm terrified of the bill. She's got me scheduled for hair and makeup on Saturday at the warehouse."

"She likes you then. She doesn't make appointments for everyone. I'm totally responsible for my own hair and makeup," he complained.

Grace thanked him profusely and promised him a favor if it was ever in her power. She still had to run several errands for Meyers afterwards, and by the time she reached her apartment, she was exhausted. She nearly tripped over the sealed box on her doorstep, marked with express delivery tags. Confused, she carried it inside.

Inside was a bottle of vodka, a box of condoms, and lube. Grace fumbled it to the coffee table. She had definitely not ordered this. She pulled out the vodka and found a note beneath it. She read it slowly.

> *Saw the text of your dress. Amazing. You'll need*
> *these. Be prepared, girl scout.*
> *Love, Rae.*

Grace gasped in horror and called Rae immediately to reprimand her for the prank. "I got your package," she grumbled.

Rae squealed. "Hang on!"

Her jaw was on the floor, and she started pacing the front room, frustration bubbling close to the surface.

When Rae returned, Carmen was with her.

"What have I been dragged into?" Carmen grumbled.

"Vitamin D is taking our girl to a gala Saturday, and she sent me a picture of the dress she's going to wear," Rae explained.

"Why was I not on this text? I want pictures of dresses," Carmen complained.

"I can fix that," Rae replied quickly. "There. Sent. So, after seeing this dress, I had some supplies delivered because I'm thoughty like that."

"Supplies?" Carmen repeated. "Say more words."

The glee in Rae's voice was clear over the phone. "I sent her some vodka for courage, some raincoats for D, and KY for the rest."

There was static on the line, and Carmen's voice sounded far away. "Hang on. Lemme see this dress."

"When I sent that picture, I wasn't asking if it was slutty enough," Grace reprimanded.

Carmen squealed. "Girl—that dress. That is the most thoughtful gift ever. He is gonna unwrap you like a Christmas gift the moment he gets you alone. I hope you sent more than one box, Rae."

Grace knew she was the color of a tomato. "I'm not trying to seduce him," she protested. "I want to look the part. For his sake. I don't want to look like a hooker."

Carmen and Rae laughed for what felt like an eternity to Grace. As soon as the laughter began to fade, it started again afresh.

"No one said you looked like a hooker," Rae soothed. "We merely agree that you look like a million bucks, and he's going to appreciate every penny."

"You only get one life, Grace," Carmen encouraged. "Live it. Man looks like he's got some moves. Let him spoil you with them. And then give us all the gory details."

"No!" Rae yelled. "I don't want to know anything about his moves."

"I do, I do!" Carmen yelled.

"I'm hanging up now," Grace grumbled.

~ ♫ ~ DEREK ~ ♫ ~

Saturday found Derek jittery. He dropped his comb twice, tripped over his shoes, and stared at his watch collection for thirty minutes before he selected one. When he'd told Pete about the date, his friend had insisted he get some new duds for the gig.

"You cannot go in another baggy suit that looks like you borrowed it from someone's dad," Peter had demanded.

Derek knew his style was fine, but he accepted the help anyway. This was, after all, the first time he was escorting someone he actually liked. It was time to take a bolder approach to his appearance as well. His goal was to press the flesh—get photographed as often as he could and maybe make some contacts. These events were filled with people he should get to know. No, he corrected himself, they should know *him*.

As he stepped out of the shower, he was consumed by Grace and how she would react to him. He'd taken starlets and star seekers to work events like this when he was green. But he was their ticket to a star-studded event. Once inside, they disappeared. He told himself that was the game. But Grace…he wanted to be with her…share the event with her.

He had been thinking about his birthday party all week, specifically when she was in full fan-girl mode looking at his memorabilia. She had inspected each item reverently, hands clasped behind her back. She had plenty of commentary, remembering the items she had seen or owned and bouncing when she found something new to her. She had taken her time, unabashedly admiring the collection. And they'd made out in the door frame, her body molded to his as he explored her mouth. It felt like home.

She was still Grace, the band's right hand. The woman who knew his coffee order. Cassie told him after Grace left how much she liked his new girlfriend. They had discussed her until the moment his sister had zipped her bag shut and gone home Sunday afternoon. He had tried to change the subject repeatedly, but Cassie was persistent.

"Derek, I know you," she insisted when he told her it was still new. "I don't know why you insist on letting yourself get used because it's good for your career. This woman is independent, stable, and she has no ulterior motive for being with you. And if you don't tell her how you feel, she's going to back away thinking she's bothering you."

Derek had argued that point with her the entirety of breakfast before she'd left. But as he zipped up his trousers, he wondered if maybe his sister wasn't right. Grace had been nothing but receptive to all of his advances. But each time, she seemed to be holding her breath. Her first instinct in most situations was to back out of a situation. Even the band had spent a lot of energy telling her that she was not intruding and should consider herself part of the group. She had come so far out of her comfort zone in Tulum on the dance floor. He knew she wanted him—would surrender to him if he asked. Tonight—he was going to ask.

It was almost show-time, and he spritzed on an extra dash of cologne. He had chosen a blue-black brocade jacket held closed with a single button at the waistline. His tailor said it made him look taller, and he wanted all the help he could get. Underneath the glitzy jacket, he sported a black silk shirt. He popped his collar in the mirror, unbuttoning an extra button. He didn't care if the cameras on the red carpet liked what they saw. He only cared about driving Grace crazy.

His apartment was immaculate in anticipation of her company. He'd even stocked the fridge to look less like a bachelor. This weekend, he didn't want anything to distract him or Grace from getting to know each other better.

In the backseat of the limo, he poured himself a vodka tonic. He practiced a few breathing exercises to calm his racing heart as the city flew by. He picked at his fingernails, wishing he'd taken the time to file them more or buff them. Surely Grace would be impressed by his well-manicured hands. He searched for scuffs on his shoes, finding none. Finally, his ride slowed to a stop, and he heard the driver exit the vehicle. He texted Grace that he had arrived.

The driver opened his door, and he stepped out. The nondescript two-story building was adorned with a three-foot-tall set of numbers next to the door and a single torch-like sconce. He couldn't find a name anywhere to indicate where she was hiding. He fidgeted to find the perfect pose to make his best first impression. When the door opened, he froze, forgetting entirely about himself.

Grace emerged like a Queen, eyes forward and shoulders squared. She was outfitted in a twilight blue, strapless gown that brushed her ankles. The bodice was fitted from her hips to her bust and a sheer, silvery material floated over her shoulders like a cloud. His eyes trailed over the rhinestones squeezed tightly together in lines up the bodice and spreading out over her chest. His throat transformed into the Sahara. He reached for her.

"Hi," she greeted shyly, resting her fingers in his hand. Grace's eyes roamed him, and he lifted his chin to display every inch.

"Hello, gorgeous," he admired. Derek imagined he towered over her as he pulled her closer for further inspection. Her skirt parted at the thigh exposing her tanned leg, and Derek fought not to groan at the sight. A breeze caught in the soft curls flowing over her shoulders glinting in the waning sunlight. Every spec of her was perfect.

She smiled at him. "You're no sleeper yourself," she complimented. "Shall we go? I'd hate for the wind to ruin this hairdo before we even make it to the car."

He nodded, leading her to the limo's plush seats. As she eased herself in, Derek treated himself to the view down the front of her dress. Once on their way, he offered her a drink.

Grace refused. "I have been sworn to let nothing pass these lips till after we have reached the event and gone inside."

"Well, there goes all my fun," he pestered. "Just the lips?"

Grace slapped his knee playfully. "Naughty," she replied.

He took her hand, stroking the back of it before turning it over and tracing the lines in her palm. Her muscles relaxed under his ministrations as he covered her hand with his. It might be rude to stare, but he couldn't stop himself. He focused on sipping his vodka.

"You really went all out with the limo," she pointed out.

He smirked. "It's practical really. Easier to get in and out. The valet after an event can take hours. Plus, a limo piques everyone's curiosity. Everyone wants to see who's inside. Gets the cameras primed."

She chuckled. "You're good at this game."

He shrugged. "When something's important, you find a way to get good at it." He glanced out the window, seeing the venue ahead and scooted to the edge of his seat. "Speaking of—we're here."

He turned gently to her, and words tumbled out as the car inched forward. "Okay, when this door opens, I'll get out first, and then I'll help you out. We're going to go left to the photo op. We will be called forward; we'll smile and answer questions if anyone asks. They'll probably want to know where you got the dress, and then we'll go inside, and we can relax. It's a little unnerving, but smile and stay close, and it won't take that long."

The driver's door opened and shut.

"Don't you need to be alone?" she asked. "You're the celebrity. I don't want to crowd you."

No one had ever offered to stay behind for him before, and he felt a surge of warmth spread throughout his body. "Very considerate, but no. I'm not a big enough fish. But you are so stunning, people will be wanting to know who you are. And, by extension, me."

"Oh, I see. I'm bait," she laughed.

"You've got my attention," he retorted.

The door opened, and Derek launched out ahead of her then reached inside to extract her from the vehicle. He compared her to Grace Kelly unfolding herself to full height, and he held her fingers tightly, afraid someone else may swoop in and pluck her away. He led her through the photographers, posing with his arm around her, boldly resting his hand on her hip dangerously close to where the slit stopped on the side of her dress. After a handful of questions from some press, it was over.

He ushered her inside, passing his invitation to a host. A team of staff were stationed in the vestibule, gathering payment information from each guest to bid on auction items. He noticed that Grace was registering her information with the agent next to his. His brows furrowed. Was she doing this to impress him? He hadn't invited her to buy anything.

"You don't have to do that," Derek murmured.

She shrugged, glancing at him as the agent handed her a bidding paddle. "I know. But I want to. What if there's something super cool that I simply must have?"

"Maybe I will get it for you," he cooed as they started away from check in.

She squeezed his arm as they roamed. "Thank you, but I am

capable of buying things for myself."

He slipped his arm around her waist again. "You continue to impress me," he whispered.

The event didn't start for another forty-five minutes, and they meandered through the silent auction, reading descriptions and separately bidding on items.

Grace was shaking her head as she read some of the items on offer, and Derek reminded himself that she was a gala virgin. Sometimes the donated items up for bid were ludicrous, risqué, or both. Many of the items were thinly veiled ads. A few were unique opportunities, but he knew the best packages had been reserved for the live auction later in the event.

He spied an interesting auction item and reached for the bidding clipboard. He held it up to her. "I'll get this for you," he offered.

Grace leaned in to read the description of the boudoir photo shoot, and her jaw dropped. To her credit, she stood up straight without a peep then hip checked him gently. She was pink all the way down her neck into the bodice of her dress. "No, thank you."

He smirked, setting the clipboard back down. "You didn't even think about it. And here I thought you'd let your hair down for the evening."

"Perhaps," she baited. "Let's see where the evening takes us."

The promise in her voice left him completely unfocused, and he knew he bid on three more items without remembering what they'd been before he bumped into someone he knew, and the glad handing began. Grace stood by his side, slightly behind him, smiling and virtually silent.

He lost track of time and the number of people he schmoozed before they started toward the dinner tables, and he took her hand.

"You're a real trooper," he said as he pulled out her chair at their table near the back of the room. He had learned early on that seats in the back of the room got the same show as those in the front, and everyone had to walk by him on the way to their tables, so he was guaranteed to get seen. And when it was over, a swift exit was easy. No one wanted a check from *him* after the people in the front had shown how many cards lived in their wallets.

She smiled. "I knew what I was in for when I said yes. Well, at least about the gala itself. Meyers tells me about these events all the time. He comes back with pockets full of business cards and sometimes a goodie bag or three to share."

He groaned unhappily as he took the seat next to her. "Not sure I want you comparing me to your boss."

Her eyes followed him the whole way down. "Oh, trust me," she assured, "I've never thought about the boss the way I think about *you*."

Derek didn't waste the moment, taking her chin lightly in his hand and leaning in for a kiss. "I waited till we were inside as promised. I think I should get brownie points for being such a gentleman when you're wearing that dress."

She smiled broadly back at him. "You can have all the points."

"How long do we have to stay?" he asked, trailing a finger over her arm.

She chuckled. "Darling, you came here for a purpose. Don't let me distract you."

"Then why didn't you wear a potato sack?"

Grace laughed. "Oh, stop it. I look like every other woman in this room. I did what I needed to fit in."

Rolling his eyes, Derek pulled the phone from his inside jacket pocket then pulled her in, chair and all, until they were touching. Grace held onto him for dear life.

"Let's let the girls decide," he insisted then wrapped an arm around her for a quick photo. He sent the picture to Carmen and Rae, sounding out the message as he tapped it into the phone. "Grace thinks she blends in. Send."

"Okay! I'm stunning," she exclaimed, flinging one hand up. She touched her chest with the other and leaned in with an exaggerated drawl. "I am the most special woman in the room."

Her face was inches from his, and he leaned in until his cheek brushed hers. "You are to me," he intoned against her ear. He felt her gulp before he pulled away.

The phone dinged, interrupting the moment. Rae and Carmen sent half a dozen messages before he turned the ringer off and stowed it in his jacket pocket.

Their table began filling up, and Derek greeted the newcomers as they arrived. He knew most of them, and they caught up as other guests took their seats. Grace perked up as he talked about the album, gesturing enthusiastically and complimenting his work. Waiters plied them with wine and food throughout the mission engagement program and live auction. When it was over, Derek helped Grace to her feet.

"Let's go see if we won any of the silent auctions," he suggested, leading her away.

The area was swarming with bidders, and they split up to check on their auctions. Derek spotted his name in a winner's frame, and his shocked laugh drew Grace's attention.

"Well, I did not expect that," he mumbled, reaching for the frame. Anyone looking at the winning bidder's name and all the people he'd beat out on this item knew his name now.

Grace closed the gap between them. "What?"

He laughed, displaying the frame to her. "I won. I'm not sure I've ever won one of these before."

She studied the notice and made a silent clap. "Congrats!"

He scanned the package description again. "How do you feel about a weekend on Catalina Island?"

"I don't know a thing about Catalina Island."

"Would you like to find out?" he asked boldly.

"Sure," she accepted.

Derek growled inside his head. She had promised him a weekend together. Tonight was a sure deal. He texted the driver to collect them.

"Did you win any?" he asked hastily.

She indicated that she had not, and they rushed to retrieve his winning packet certificates before retreating to the safety of the waiting limo.

Derek relaxed into the plush seats with a sigh. "Thank you. I've never had anyone stay with me the whole evening without fighting for the spotlight much less leave with me."

"I feel like saying 'You're welcome' would be insulting."

Derek reached for the champagne in the mini fridge and pulled a pair of flutes from storage. He popped the cork gently, and she flinched at the sound. He held the cork deftly out to her. She was biting her lip as she took it from him, but her eyes never left his as he offered her a glass.

"So glad that's over. To a successful gala," he toasted. "And to a perfect plus one."

He sipped, watching as her lips parted for the glass. He emptied his in one pull and set it aside before tugging her into his lap.

Grace squealed, champagne nearly sloshing out of her flute. Derek plucked the glass from her hand to deposit next to his. He finally placed his hand on her thigh, slipping the other into the hair at the back of her neck. In the next moment, he kissed her fully, and the pair were entangled until they arrived at her apartment and the door to the street opened.

They pulled apart gasping for breath. He wasn't ready for the night to be over. She stroked a palm over the side of his face, her index finger and thumb tugging tenderly at his earlobe.

"Come inside?" she uttered.

"I thought you'd never ask," he rushed.

They raced to her door, Grace fumbling with her keys. Derek pressed himself to her back, kissing her neck and whispering in ear. "Relax—we have all night."

She slipped the key in the lock, turning it more confidently. "That's a tall order," she grinned over her shoulder.

"I'm up to the challenge," he replied, kissing her softly and slipping the shoulder of her dress down. He stroked her stomach, feeling the rhinestones dragging roughly across his palm.

She whimpered against him, pushing the door open and tugging him inside. He felt her stumble under the momentum, but he had crushed her to himself, supporting them both.

"Bedroom," he mumbled against her mouth as he backed her into her apartment.

"Mhmm," she hummed, and her hands snaked down his chest. Squeezing one of his hands, she pulled him down the hall and around the corner. He shed his jacket along the way, working the buttons of his shirt with one hand until they stopped in front of her bed, and he grabbed her to himself to taste her mouth again.

Derek stirred, feeling a light touch on his upper arm. His brows furrowed as he realized Grace was tracing the tattoo there.

He sucked in a breath, his eyes fluttering open as he rolled to face her. "Good morning," he whispered.

She beamed. "Good morning," she replied. "Sorry I woke you. You looked so peaceful."

He stretched, encouraging his body to wake. Sunlight streaming through the window lit her hair like a halo, and he admired the subtle red hues hiding beneath the chestnut locks. She was soft and unkempt after their night together, and so unlike the buttoned-up beauty he'd met at a business lunch. He liked this Grace the most.

"Are you hungry?" she asked after a moment.

He shrugged. At two a.m. they'd stumbled to the kitchen for water, snacks, and round two. "I'm okay at the moment." He gathered her closer. "Why are you so far away?"

Grace squirmed deliciously in his arms settling beside him. "I don't know how I'm awake at all. Not much sleep to speak of."

"I, for one, am not opposed to a midday nap. Except you're distracting me with all this skin." He pinched her side to make her jump against him.

She smacked the back of his hands with her fingertips and clutched the sheet around her body. "I can cover up," she threatened.

"Don't get formal on my account." He ran his fingers through stray tendrils of hair on her cheeks. She wasn't meeting his eyes, and he knew he was being charming. "What are you thinking?"

She pursed her lips, eyes darting back and forth before settling on him. "I really want a shower."

"That can be arranged. But that's not what has your nose flaring every few seconds."

"It is not!" she squealed, clamping her hands over her face.

He pulled her fingers to his lips to kiss the tips. "It is. Out with it. You have nowhere to hide with me now."

She sighed, and her face flushed red. For a moment, her eyes shimmered wetly. "I've never done this before."

He gulped. "Sex?" he stammered. "You didn't tell me…"

She chuckled, splaying her fingers over his chest. "No…just dragged you into bed like a cave-woman."

At this, he laughed, hugging her close. "Oh, Grace," he mumbled against her cheek. He pulled back so she could see his face when he spoke. "Did you have fun?"

"I didn't think you'd need to ask," she replied. "I thought I made it pretty clear."

Memories of her cries returned, and he growled, nipping her chin. "You did, you sexy minx."

"You don't think I'm a hoe?" she whispered, voice cracking.

He shook his head. He wanted to laugh at the absurdity of it, but the set of her jaw told him she was serious. Her eyes were searching his for answers. To laugh at her now would break the fledgling trust between them. Up until this question, she had been like a wet noodle draped over him. He wasn't ready for her to withdraw.

"You have had every opportunity to throw yourself at me from the moment I walked you to your car after meeting Jacob the first time. And even if you had, that wouldn't make you a hoe," he explained.

She made a snuffling noise, clearing her sinuses. "So, what do you do after a one-night stand?"

Both his eyebrows hit his hairline. "One night?" he barked. "You think I'm not going to ravish you for the rest of the weekend?"

"You're…" she trailed off, eyes large as she stared back. "You're not leaving now?"

"Absolutely not. It would take an act of congress to get me out of your life right now." He'd meant to say out of her bed, but the word had slipped out in the honesty of the moment. He waited for her to laugh, but she did not. This time, she nearly leapt on him to kiss him.

He returned it happily, imagining her in the shower as he drew back to speak. "What do you say we clean up, get breakfast, and go to my place?" he suggested.

She cuddled against him with an adorable pout. "But it's a school night," she whined.

He agreed, nuzzling her neck. "I have fresh sheets," he whispered against her ear.

"You should have led with that," she said with a giggle.

~ ♫ ~ GRACE ~ ♫ ~

When Grace floated into the office Monday morning, she swore she heard birds singing. She had never felt more focused or confident in her life. Derek liked her. Derek liked all of her and didn't hesitate to show it whenever the urge struck. The box of goodies Rae had sent as a joke had turned out to be incredibly useful. She licked her lips as she strutted from Derek's front door all the way to her desk.

She almost hummed as she waited for the computer to load but she swallowed it back to avoid questions about why. Her eyes scanned the office as they often did from her fishbowl, but instead of the usual cliques cackling over green juices and interns running back and forth, everyone was still. They were staring back at her...in whispering pairs.

She had to be wrong. Scooting behind her computer monitors to hide, she pulled up Meyers' schedule. It had taken every ounce of her willpower to pull herself out of Derek's bed and not call off sick. There was dry cleaning to collect, and she didn't want to have to explain her tardiness.

The familiar sound of jangling keys drew her attention, and she saw Meyers strutting through the bullpen.

She smiled at him as he tramped by her desk. "I've put your dry cleaning—"

"In my office," he interrupted, not making eye contact. "Now."

Grace shrank at his tone and stumbled a little getting out of the chair to follow him.

Meyers was at his desk, and he threw his keys down on the blotter. "Shut the door," he instructed as he plopped into his chair.

Grace was practically sweating as she closed the door and sat in front of the desk.

"How long have you been working with me, Grace?" he asked.

"Going on nine months," she replied.

"And how many times have we had the conversation about fraternizing with my clients?"

"Fraternizing?" she repeated. She resented his insecurity. She didn't want his job, and she certainly didn't want to steal his clients. She switched gears to reassure him. "I know that you're the agent, and I'm not working for anyone else. I'm not trying to handle your clients for you."

He turned his computer monitor to face her. "Then how do you explain this?"

Before her eyes was a celebrity photo website displaying a series of pictures of Derek at the recent charity event. Amidst them were three photos of her squeezed tightly against his side, hands resting on his shoulder. There was no mistaking his affection or hers.

She gulped. "This isn't any kind of move against you. He invited me to the gala, and I didn't talk to anyone else. Not even at our table."

"You're dating my client. How is that not a direct conflict of interest?" He paused, staring at her for a long moment. When she didn't answer, he sighed. "I thought you had better sense than that." He twisted the monitor back to its original position.

Grace's throat tightened and her vision blurred. "It's just Derek. It's not anyone else. Ask Mr. Hunter how professional I've been."

"It's just Derek until it's the next one," Meyers protested. He shook his head, leaning back in his seat. "Do you know how many other women he's been photographed with on a red carpet? And he's hungry for attention. What better way to get mine than to get my assistant to book him more time?"

Her voice cracked. "It's not like that."

He sighed. "Grace, I can't trust you. Clear out your desk. Leave your credit card and phone with Clarence in accounting."

"But, Mr. Meyers..."

He stood, walking to the door and opening it for her. "That will be all."

To her credit, she managed to hold her back straight as she picked up her purse. She plucked out the cell phone and the credit card from her wallet and marched into accounting. She laid the two items on Clarence's desk without a word and quickened her pace.

It took her nearly an hour to compose herself in the parking garage before she could drive, and she went straight home.

Some Attraction

SIXTEEN

Derek melted into the vinyl chairs in the record label lobby Monday morning, closing his eyes briefly to block out the band's turmoil. His back still ached mildly due to over exertion from his weekend with Grace, but he didn't mind. He was still chuckling over the way she squealed when he smacked her behind as she left his apartment for work that morning in a business suit. He couldn't deny that she made them look good, and he could imagine a few role-playing scenarios. But otherwise, he much preferred her bedhead and the jeans she'd sported Saturday afternoon when she drove them to his place.

He peeked one eye open to survey the others.

The lobby was small hinting that this label didn't invite many acts to visit. He remembered a few lobbies he'd waited in before, and this one was the snobbiest with its minimalist chairs and shin height tables. But Derek wasn't about to be intimidated by furniture.

The others were not relaxed at all, having berated him repeatedly for abandoning them on their wardrobe hunt over the weekend. But he didn't care. He could still feel Grace's fingers running through his hair that morning. He took a deep breath, tucking her away in his mind. He could wait two meetings and a few hours to continue their escapades.

On the settee across from him, Carmen's knee was bouncing, and Rae placed her hand on it. Joe was slumped in a chair drumming a beat silently onto his thigh. Jacob was pacing, chewing a fingernail and eyeing each of the seated members.

"You got the CDs?" Jacob asked.

"Yes," Derek replied calmly, tapping the purpose-built backpack on his lap. The one Grace had given him for his birthday. He smiled in memory.

Jacob sighed. "Nerves," he explained.

Derek gave him a thumbs up.

Carmen jabbed his foot with the toe of one boot. "I can't believe you spent the whole weekend with Grace, and now we can't talk about it," she complained.

"Who says we can't?" Rae beamed.

Jacob stopped, staring at Rae. "Can we focus on the band?" he begged. "Please."

They all nodded, and Jacob resumed his anxious march. Rae jumped up and matched his gait, mimicking him perfectly.

He stopped suddenly. "What are you doing?"

"Trying to cut the tension," she offered. "Is it working?"

In the following silence, Joe's voice was clear as a pin dropping. "Sonic Tension."

The two words hung in the air, and Derek's mind raced. Through all their recording sessions, the push and pull had generated their sound.

"I think that's it," Derek announced, eyes darting to the others.

"Me too," Carmen added.

"Yes," Rae confirmed.

They looked at Jacob, holding their breath. The singer blinked. "Yes! Can we label the CDs before we go in?"

Rae produced a black Sharpie from her back pocket. "I have a marker, but someone else has to write it."

Carmen grabbed the marker while Derek started shoving discs into her hands. They huddled around the coffee table, watching as Carmen scrawled the words artfully across each disc. She finished the last one as a young man in a T-shirt, jeans and a vest entered the lobby.

"They're ready for you," he announced.

The group broke apart as Derek slipped the freshly labeled discs into his bag hoping that the marker would dry before they were passed out.

It was approaching noon when the band exited the building. Carmen linked arms with Rae as Derek, Jacob, and Joe rushed after them. No one said a word 'til they were on the street and half a block away.

Jacob pumped his fist in the air. "Yes!" His long arms spread out wide before clamping down over as many of the band members as he could reach, pulling them into a group hug.

"I have never had a label be so receptive before," Derek huffed, reaching for a high five from everyone.

Joe shook his head. "That was amazing. And it was only the first meeting," he gloated.

"Let's call Grace," Rae suggested.

"She's at work," Derek cautioned. "She can't take that call in front of Meyers." He could picture her hiding the call. It might be cruel to put her through the effort.

Rae grumbled, pouting and crossing her arms.

"Let's text her a picture," Carmen countered. "Jacob—you've got the longest arms."

They squeezed together until everyone's face fit on Rae's phone screen and snapped a photo. Rae tapped out the message in a flash. "Greetings from Sonic Tension."

Mollified that their group mascot was apprised of their status, they raced to Derek's BMW and Carmen's pink vintage Pontiac Astre to find a café.

Derek didn't realize he was hungry until they were all squeezed into the booth, jockeying for elbow room and a dozen plates arrived. After the initial frenzy had passed and an entire plate of onion rings had disappeared, Carmen broke the silence.

"I wish Grace could've been with us today," Carmen mused. "She set us up good for that last one."

Jacob leaned against the table. "So you all know...while we were in Tulum, I told her that I wanted her to be our manager. I know it was a unilateral decision, and I probably should have asked…"

"Thank fuck," Joe replied.

Rae burst out laughing at his response. "I second that."

Carmen and Derek raised their hands as well.

Jacob sighed relief. "Well, first, we're gonna have to land one of these labels. And I want to include her in our contract. Are we agreed?" He raised his hand. The others joined him.

"Has she responded?" Carmen questioned.

Rae checked her phone, pouting. "No."

"She's at work," Derek soothed. "We'll call her after this meeting."

Joe looked at his watch. "We gotta go, guys. I bet we can close a deal today."

"Let's let them stew," Jacob countered. "I'm as anxious as you guys to lock this down, but if that first meeting was any indication…we've got something big, and we can play them off one another."

They bounded from the tight booth to wiggle through LA traffic until they reached the second office.

It was approaching four o'clock when they surfaced from their second meeting, riding another high. Huddled between the two cars in a nearby parking garage, they cheered for the second time that day.

"Oh, that felt good," Jacob moaned.

"So validating," Rae concurred.

"When are we playing this gig, you threw in their faces?" Carmen prodded.

"We're thinking early August," Derek replied.

"The one we promised *The Oubliette* when we held the auditions there," Rae explained.

Derek nodded. "But we need time to practice and get the right playlist together."

"Practice," Joe confirmed. "I know we wrote the songs and all, but if there's one thing I've learned, it's that we have got to practice until we're playing it in our sleep."

"Yes," Jacob said, pointing to Joe with one hand and his nose with the other. "That. We need to practice."

"And not in the studio," Carmen chimed in. "We're going to need practice space. We need a stage."

"Grace to the rescue!" Rae called. "Quick, let's send her another picture and see when she gets out. We should take her to dinner."

They squeezed in around Rae's phone, Joe throwing a thumbs up, Carmen pulling a rock star pose, Rae beaming with Derek holding bunny ears behind her, and Jacob struggling to get it all in one frame. Rae sent the picture, then frowned.

"Well, that's weird. She still hasn't seen the last one yet, look." She passed her phone around. Derek's stomach rolled as he viewed the "Not seen" notification on Rae's screen.

"That's unlike her," Jacob agreed. "She's hella quick on these phones."

Derek pulled out his cell and stepped away from the group to lean against the third-floor railing of the garage. He smirked at the new picture of her that he'd taken that morning that popped up on his phone beside her number. She was still sleep worn and barely awake. He selected her work cell from his contacts and listened to it ring twice.

"Meyers Talent Agency," a low male voice greeted. "How may I direct your call?"

He pulled back the phone to check the number he had dialed and confirmed it was correct. He pressed it back to his ear. "I'm looking for Grace, please. Mr. Meyers' assistant," he explained.

"I'm sorry, but there's no Grace here."

He pressed a finger to his opposite ear to eliminate the noise and squeezed his eyes shut. "You must be confused. She's Meyers' assistant."

There was a pause on the other end of the line. "I'm sorry, sir," the man apologized. His next words were enunciated slowly. "There's no *Grace* at Meyers Talent Agency."

He recognized the emphasis on her name.

"Truer words," Derek mumbled, ending the call. The breeze three floors up was brisk against his cheek as he leaned into it. She didn't work there. Meyers must have found out about him. He'd messed around with the bull and gotten the horns, but Grace was the one gutted. He gripped the railings until his knuckles turned white.

"Uh… D?" Carmen questioned.

Derek didn't answer. He stared across the skyline, replaying the conversation in his head.

He heard footsteps as the group gathered behind him.

"What's going on?" Jacob questioned.

Putting his back to the wind, Derek faced them. "I called Grace's work cell, and I got some guy. He said there's no Grace at the agency."

"What?" Rae exploded. Her whole body poised to leap, but Jacob gently blocked her with a single hand to her stomach.

"Don't hurt the messenger," the singer instructed.

"Do you think she'd quit?" Joe asked.

Derek shook his head. "No. She left early this morning all dressed for the office. We skipped breakfast so she could pick up his dry cleaning. That doesn't sound like someone planning to quit." He lifted his phone again, this time dialing her personal cell. Without so much as a ring, her dulcet voice calmly asked him to leave a message after the beep.

"Voicemail," Derek replied, launching himself from the railings. He stalked toward the driver's side of his car.

"Where are you going?" Jacob questioned, chasing after him.

"To her place and hope that's where she is," he snarled.

"I'm going too!" Rae demanded.

"Fuck that," Carmen growled. "We'll all go. Hop in whoever's going with me," she announced then looked at Derek. "Hit the gas. I can keep up."

Within moments, the pair of cars was speeding across town. Rae beat him up the stairs, banging on her door without hesitation.

"Grace, let us in," she demanded. "I saw your car. I know you're in there."

The five of them squished in together on her balcony, waiting and exchanging worried glances. When she didn't answer, Derek cupped his hands around his face on her window, peering inside. He saw her on the love seat, dressed in her business suit, sound asleep.

"Grace!" he called through the glass. He rapped a knuckle against the pane.

Rae pounded harder on the door, and the others joined in, calling her name.

Inside, she startled on the couch, and Derek watched as she hauled herself first to a sitting position and then to her feet. He slipped behind Rae, planning to be at least the second in the door when she opened it. Several minutes passed before there was a collective gasp of relief as the tumblers turned in the locks.

Grace poked her head out, squinting against the sunlight.

"Hi," she greeted softly. Her face was splotchy red, eyes swollen. She was running her fingers through her hair, smoothing out the tangles on one side. She cleared her throat. "What are you all doing here?" Her voice was raspy.

Rae barreled into the apartment, pushing past Grace, accusation in her tone. "Why aren't you at work? D called, and they said there's no Grace there."

Grace stumbled in her wake, clinging to the door. Derek was the next to enter, and he collected her gently, pulling her back toward the couch for the others to file in. He could smell the sickly-sweet scent of alcohol on her breath. She hadn't ignored their calls or their pleas to open the door; she hadn't heard them because she'd been passed out, not asleep.

"You said I worked too much," Grace slurred.

"I called the office to tell you how the meetings went," Derek expounded, keeping his voice low. "And they said you don't work there in so many words."

Her lips quirked into a bright, interested smile. "How did the meetings go?"

Derek guided her the rest of the way to the couch and sat her down with his arm still snugly around her waist. Rae scooted Grace's laptop aside then perched on the coffee table facing her, kneecap to kneecap. Carmen took a seat on Grace's other side while Jacob and Joe stood behind Rae.

"What happened?" Derek asked softly.

Grace didn't speak. Instead, she pointed at the laptop next to Rae. The screen was filled with a photo from the gala. Derek hadn't even remembered to check the usual websites for his photo after an event. He'd been too busy focusing on her. But there she was in her beautiful blue dress that hugged all her curves, his hand clutching her hip on the red carpet. It was the most natural he had ever looked at one of these events.

Meyers must have seen the photos. Derek had been so enraptured with her that night, he hadn't considered the consequences of being seen together. He was a fool! This was his fault.

When she did speak, her voice was wispy, and he strained to hear.

"It's the best picture I've ever taken." Tears clogged her throat again, and she blew a shaky breath into her lap.

"A photo?" Carmen looked from Grace to the open laptop. "Sexy," she cooed, poking Grace's knee.

Grace shrugged, laying her head on Derek's shoulder.

Jacob and Joe peered at the screen now from opposite sides of the coffee table, and Derek was feeling crowded. He couldn't imagine what Grace with her giant space bubble had to be feeling. He pulled her protectively deeper into the couch and his embrace.

"The good news is, it's just a job," Jacob consoled gently as he straightened up.

"Yes," Grace agreed. "I've been telling myself that all day. It's just a job."

"And a shit one," Joe added.

Grace snickered.

"And," Jacob added. "Now you don't have to face him to quit. I know you were worried about that."

Joe eased down on the corner of the table next to Rae. "We'll be better to you than Meyers," he vowed. "I don't even *have* a dog."

Grace burst out laughing, uncharacteristically loud. She clamped one hand over her mouth.

Jacob yanked his phone from his pocket and paced toward the kitchen with the device to his ear. "Meyers," he greeted. "Jacob Hunter."

Grace jumped to her feet. "No," she stage-whispered, shaking her hands at Jacob. "Oh, please, no!"

Jacob faced her, arching a brow, and steeled her with a look. He turned away and continued his conversation.

She froze, one knee in the air as she tried to step over the corner of the table. Rae and Joe were blocking her escape, and her bare toe swung toward the laptop, making contact with the corner of the screen. She swayed, and Derek grabbed her around her waist. She leaned into him, slowly drawing her leg back and taking a seat, face covered in an exaggerated pout beneath the hair that fell over it.

Jacob's reply bordered on harsh, and Grace shuddered at the sound.

"No. I've decided to find another agent," Jacob commanded. "I'd like the paperwork to my lawyer by morning." He paused. "No, I'm not interested in discussing it." He paused again. "Frankly, it's none of your business. I want the paperwork by morning." Jacob's finger smashed the red button at the bottom of his screen.

Grace blanched. "That wasn't necessary," she whispered.

"It was," he countered, dropping the phone into his side pocket. His eyes landed on the half bottle of vodka on the counter then lifted them to Grace. "Have you been drinking?"

She shrugged. "Nowhere else to be," she replied.

Rae followed Jacob's gaze. "Is that the bottle I sent you?" she asked.

"Yes, thanks. I ran out of Diet Pepsi, though." She sighed.

"Did you open this today?" Carmen pressed.

Grace nodded, leaning back on the couch.

The tone was starting to sound accusatory, and Derek didn't like it. He knew what it felt like to drown his sorrows in a bottle, and the current line of questioning could easily throw her into a tailspin.

"Okay, I think Grace needs a little air," Derek asserted, standing. He lifted his arms to usher them out.

"Yes," Rae agreed.

Derek looked at their guitarist. Usually, it was Derek's job to take Rae home, but in this instance, he couldn't leave. "Carmen, do you mind…"

"Say no more," Carmen acquiesced. She hugged Grace for a long moment. "I'm sorry you had such an ass for a boss, but his loss is our gain." She pulled away, grinning brazenly at the laptop. "You should frame that." She winked and headed out the door.

Joe followed suit, joining Carmen on the front porch. Jacob was next, holding her gaze as he promised to put her on his payroll until the label contracts came through.

"Hang in there. It'll get better," he encouraged and started for the door. "You coming, Rae?"

"No, I'm going to stay and look after Grace." She wrapped her arm around the woman, hugging her from the side.

Derek removed Rae's hands gently, leading her toward Jacob. "I've got this," he soothed.

Rae's face wrinkled. "But I want to make sure she's okay."

"Then trust me," Derek persuaded. He handed her the vodka. "And maybe take this."

"No." Grace shook her head, reaching for the bottle. "I need more soda," she said.

Rae held onto the bottle firmly out of Grace's grasp. "I'll send you over some soda." She looked at Derek.

He recognized the betrayed expression on her face, but after the weekend he'd spent getting to know Grace, he was confident that he was the person she needed. She could have her girlfriend later when the initial crying jag had ended, and she'd sobered up.

Jacob touched Rae's elbow. "Carmen's waiting," he said softly.

"Call me later?" she pleaded.

Derek nodded, closing them out. Once alone, he gathered Grace in his arms, gently stroking her hair as her cheek pressed against his shoulder.

"I'm so sorry," he murmured. The moment his fingers laced together behind her, a fresh batch of tears soaked his shirt. He crooked his cheek against the top of her head, holding her tight.

"I'm sorry," she choked out.

He shushed her, clucking his tongue lightly and closing his eyes. If she needed him to stand there, holding her next to the front door all day, he would do it.

"You have no reason to apologize. Losing a job is hard," he commiserated.

He let her cry for ten minutes before deciding that letting her free fall wasn't productive. With a lingering kiss to the top of her head, he placed a hand on her cheek to draw her mascara-streaked gaze up to his.

"Come on," he encouraged, leading her to her bathroom. "I can't believe you're still dressed for him." He began unbuttoning her blazer, watching her face as he removed it and hooked it over the doorknob. "I'm throwing out all your suits tonight." He started the water in the bathtub.

Her tears had slowed, and she was catching her breath. Piece by piece, he stripped her down, gauging her reaction with each, but she didn't fight him. She shivered as he removed the last vestige of her proverbial armor.

He tugged off his own shirt, shimmying out of everything else quickly, then stepped into the tub. He helped her over the edge in front of him and settled her between his legs, her back against his chest as the water thundered into the space around them. Her breathing was finally still, and somehow, the silence was more unnerving than the tears.

Usually, Grace was untouchable. Derek would go so far as to call her intimidating. She had opened up to him on the weekend, liberated from her battle gear. But wounded Grace pricked a part of his heart that he wasn't aware existed. The protective side that looked at any threat to her as a challenge to him. She was... *his.*

When the tub was full, he reached out a toe to stop the faucet. After a minute, Grace shifted to her side in his embrace.

"It's just a job," she repeated. Her voice was clear, and her nose wrinkled as she continued. He wasn't even sure she was talking to him as she mused, "And a stupid job. Why in the world am I so upset about losing a job taking a stupid dog to a stupid groomer?"

"Good question." At least her reasoning was still sound.

"I mean, I have a degree for fuck's sake," she complained, anger raising her voice.

He bit his lip, fighting the urge to chuckle. Something about her spewing these foul words gave him another peek behind the proverbial curtain, and his heart squeezed happily.

"And I get photographed at an event with this amazing man, and the asshole fires me?" She let out strings of expletives that would've made a sailor blush. Before he could respond, she rolled over fully, water splashing over the edges.

"And who the fuck does he think he is anyway?" she groused, meeting his gaze. "I did everything he asked. *All you have to do is introduce them and pay the bill,*" she mimicked Meyers' voice then pouted, resting her cheek on his chest.

Derek caressed her face, thumb rinsing away the mascara on one cheek. He hated to see her so defeated, but he couldn't ignore the compliment she'd given in the midst of her diatribe. He wouldn't have been surprised if she'd called him a teen idol or a heartthrob, or any of the other myriad names that he'd read in teen magazines. But she called him an amazing *man.* If he had any doubts that she was with him because of his stardom, it died in the bathwater.

"Did you call me amazing?" he asked quietly.

She lifted her face to grin at him, and he stroked the other cheek clean as he stared.

"I might have," she flirted, resting her chin on his sternum. She sighed. "It was such a perfect morning. I woke up next to you, and then..." She smirked, nipping at his chest gently.

He jerked at the playful attack, rubbing the spot with a fingertip.

"Careful," he cooed, "or you'll wake the beast." He took several deep breaths to calm himself. His mission was to soothe her, not bed her.

She sighed again, eyes slipping shut before she recounted the event. "I was even cheery when that monkey's butt hole stalked in and pulled me into his office." She twisted her face, mimicking her former boss. "*How many times have we talked about this, Grace? I just can't trust you. It's just Derek now until it's the next one.* Like I'm some kind of star collector."

Derek winced. "What a dick," he agreed.

They lay in silence, Derek stroking her back, and she melted against him. "It's a stunning picture."

"We should buy it," he suggested.

She laughed. "I already saved a copy for my files—watermark and all."

"I have an account," he confessed. "I get a discount."

She laughed, squeezing him around the middle. "Okay, you are officially the best."

He beamed at her. "I'm supposed to be comforting you." He felt a little guilty about how good her words felt in the moment. The transformation from how the band had found her till now was stark, and he knew he was the catalyst for the speedy recovery. His inner caveman was beating a stump against his chest and howling.

She smiled so wide, her eyes disappeared into her cheeks. "And you are. Saying good things about you is one of my favorite pastimes."

"Then by all means, don't let me stop you." Half his mouth quirked left as he snugged his arms around her.

Grace shifted to lay back against him and tilted her head back for a view of his chin. Her upside-down grin was goofy and completely defenseless, evoking a matching grin in him. She rested her palms on his knees as she began ticking off his best traits.

"Well... you are kind, and generous, and smart. And you are so talented—the singing, the dancing, and frankly, I think you are a great actor—shit movie, great acting. You really gave more to that director than he deserved."

He let out a pained cry, pinching the bridge of his nose. "I'll never live that down."

She shook her head. "But you took it seriously, and you can't be ashamed of that. You did the best you could with what you were given."

He laughed now, hugging her with his thighs. "Grace," he purred. "Where have you been all my life?"

There was a long moment before she answered. "Doesn't matter. We're here now."

Derek couldn't wait any longer and pulled her in for a long kiss and proceeded to spoil her for the rest of the day.

SEVENTEEN

Grace did not expect to feel the calm she did as she walked through *The Oubliette's* front of house toward backstage, where Sonic Tension was getting ready to perform. So much had changed since she'd officially started working for Jacob. The pay was actually better, and while she was making phone calls all day long and working more than she ever had for Meyers, the atmosphere was different. When she called vendors and venues, she knew that her decisions were respected by the others.

It didn't hurt that Derek was at her side most of the time either. They had been shuttling back and forth between their apartments, and it was becoming incredibly clear that neither of them had the right space. She had begun discussing their leases when they had free moments. It would certainly make things easier.

She nearly collided with a server running across the room with a stack of freshly washed trays, drawing her attention back to the moment. One of the new guitar techs she had hired was on stage testing the wireless system on Rae's bass, and she scurried to deflect a fight when the bassist discovered a stranger touching her equipment.

She had already put out a dozen fires, but none of them critical. The band was in house. The club was ready. And from what she could see, the valets were already getting a workout. Dozens of Jacob's hard-core fans had been lining up at the doors since the sun came up, and they had waved to her when she tried to sneak in the back door. Jacob had leaked a picture of Sonic Tension on his website, including a picture of them in the studio where Derek had pulled her into his lap at the mixing board. She had expected running into his fans was going to be time consuming, but so far, they had waved and called out thanks for getting him back onto the stage.

She let herself into the changing room where Rae and Carmen were holed up. Carmen was inches from the mirror applying what Grace thought might be an entire tube of eyeliner. Rae was pacing, and she swirled around as the door closed, her red vinyl pants squeaking in protest.

Grace clapped in their direction. "The stage gear looks amazing on you," Grace complimented.

"Doesn't it?" Carmen called from her corner. "I still think she's going to die of heat stroke on stage, but she'll look like a cover model doing it."

"I didn't want my ass hanging out for any rando to see," Rae countered, pointing at Carmen's denim mini skirt with rips over the back pockets.

Grace agreed with them both, but she was their manager, not their wardrobe consultant, and if they were comfortable, she would be too.

Carmen snickered. "Right—only Jacob."

Rae's face turned the color of her pants. She smiled then, dropping onto the small dressing room couch. "And what about you, Ms. Band Manager? Look at these duds!" she praised, gesturing to the asymmetrical hem of Grace's shirt.

"Derek took me shopping," she confessed.

Rae laughed. "If I hadn't seen you two making out more than once, I'd swear he's gay."

"Not gay," she mumbled, suddenly remembering how he'd dressed her that very afternoon in a slinky tank and the low-slung jeans she now sported. His reaction to the outfit negated anyone else's opinion. "Definitely not gay," she sighed.

Rae poked her shoulder. "It's nothing to be embarrassed about.

Whoever you're with should be rocking your world."

Grace cleared her throat, not trusting herself to agree for fear she'd spill all her secrets over the sheer joy of them. She stepped past Rae to a short rolling rack. "I came to tell you to hang your stage clothes here afterwards so I can have them cleaned and ready for the next show."

Rae gave a short scream. "No more dry cleaning," she growled.

Grace laughed and waved her off. "I have people for that now," she replied, waggling her brows. "The VIP section is starting to fill up."

Carmen bounded across the room till she was shoulder to shoulder with Grace. "Is Leo here yet?" she asked.

"Yes. All of Derek's people are already here," she replied, arching a brow. "Why?"

Carmen beamed. "Boy dances like the wind moves, and I want a piece of that," she announced. She danced in place, hips wriggling sensually with her arms over her head. "Aye!"

Taking that as her cue to leave, Grace hugged them both and headed a few doors down the hall. When it was finally showtime, she led the entire band from the dressing area to the back of the stage for them to take their positions.

Jacob sneaked a peek from the edge of the stage, looking back at the others. "Dude, it's full," Jacob mumbled.

With a smirk, the keyboardist peered past him. "We have a lot of friends," he replied.

The sound techs appeared, fitting everyone for microphones and equipment, and Grace beamed at their efficiency. She noticed Derek adjusting his collar when they were finished before he began shaking out his hands, flexing each joint.

"Nervous?" Grace asked quietly.

He smiled at her tightly.

"Whatever you do—they're your songs. There are no mistakes." She leaned in and whispered against his ear. "And you've already started my engine, so luck is on your side."

His shoulders squared, and he licked his lips hungrily. His chin lifted as he turned to the band.

"Let's do this!" he hollered, stalking past the others onto the stage.

Inspired by his cry, the others followed. Jacob lifted his arms to the air as the house lights dimmed and the few stage lights came up. The cheering was instantaneous, and Grace was grateful for her noise blocking earplugs. Her eyes drifted to Derek standing behind his keyboards, settling his custom headphones into place. She felt his swagger from where she stood in the wings.

"Hey, everybody. We are Sonic Tension. Thanks for coming out tonight," he began. Joe was already clicking the downbeat of the first song with his sticks, and they launched into their set.

Grace situated herself on the stairs to the VIP area for a better view. Their special guests were lining the railings. There was no room for her, and she contented herself with a prime view.

A tug on her arm nearly made her lose her balance. She turned to find Pete as the culprit. He spoke behind her ear. "Share our spot," he offered.

Grace couldn't refuse, and she followed behind him. The crowd suddenly parted, making room for her, and Pete slipped her in front of him between Nancy and Leo.

Nancy hugged her shoulders, wiggling her pregnant belly in delight. She mouthed words that Grace couldn't understand, but the two thumbs up she saw were a pretty good indication.

She greeted the rest of Derek's bandmates, grateful for the noise so they wouldn't hear her gasping. In all her life, she had never imagined standing in a VIP section, surrounded by Derek's friends and watching him perform. Tears threatened to fall, but she refused to let good mascara go to waste.

Grace focused on the performance, dancing with the group around her, giggling at Carmen's commentary on Leo's skills. He was cheering beside her like the others, somehow managing to look graceful packed in like sardines. Even from her spot, she felt it when Derek threw a kiss.

Pete reached out a hand, snatching at the air in front of her, giving a silly wave back to his friend, and the crowd seemed to go stark raving mad as the next hour flew by. Grace screamed with the others, applauding till her forearms hurt as they exited the stage.

And then she was in motion, turning on the headset attached to her ear and passing out instructions to the crew to get the gear loaded into Joe's van. She ordered servers to the VIP area and started weaving through the crowd when she spotted Jacob's head cresting the stairs.

Carmen was behind him, followed by Joe and Rae, and then her blue-eyed man at the end of the line.

Her heart thrilled at the sight. His face was a little feral as he stalked past everyone between them, and she struggled for breath as he clamped onto her, kissing her till her lips felt bruised and grabbing her ass audaciously in front of God and everyone.

"Well, hello to you, too," she laughed breathlessly when he released her.

"What am I? Chopped liver?" Leo crowed beside them.

Derek disengaged slowly, spanking her in one sharp whack before he turned to his friend for a high five. He hooked a thumb in Grace's waistband, pulling her with him to talk to his friends.

Grace stayed with him for a minute then excused herself to ensure that the birthday cake she'd arranged for Jacob was on its way. She passed out cake after they sang, but she continued glancing at her watch, making sure everything remained on schedule. So far, everything was going well, but part of her was on high alert. She surveyed the staff, scolding herself when she couldn't remember everyone's names. None of them appeared to need her attention.

It was during her scan that she saw Nigel Davies, the bassist from her now-second favorite band, Rebel Gloss, heading her way. She had passed him and his wife cake not long ago.

"Grace," he called, lifting a hand to get her attention.

She had seen him earlier, but they hadn't been introduced. How had he known her name? She pushed the confusion down and bridged the distance between them with a friendly smile. "Hi," she greeted. "What's up?"

Nigel gestured toward the bar where Jacob was presiding over a group of guests. "I was talking with your singer about the band and how we wanted to know when the album was coming out, and he said I should talk to you about it."

She sighed in relief. "Ah! Well, let me give you my card," she offered, pulling one from her jacket pocket. Jacob had presented her with the cards a week ago in a smart little holder, and now, as she pulled a crisp card from its folds to hand to this man, she stood a little taller. "We're planning for a September release, but we don't have an exact date confirmed. I'd be happy to take any information you're willing to share, and I'll let you know when it's arrived."

Nigel took the card graciously, his finger and thumb rubbing the corner of the stock as his gaze swept over it. "Actually, could I put you in touch with my PA?"

Grace smiled. "That would be great," she replied.

Before the exchange could go any further, a sudden bodily warmth pressed to her side and a hand slipped deep into her back pocket. Recognizing Derek, she relaxed.

"Hi. Derek Reed." He stuck out a hand to the bass player.

Nigel chuckled, shaking it kindly. "Nigel Davies. You were the synthesist?" he asked, squinting.

Derek nodded. "Pleasure to meet you. Did you like the show?"

"It was great. Your singer sent me over here to talk to Grace about getting my wife and I a CD when they're out. I heard you got signed to a label." Nigel reached back to his wife, who took Grace's business card from him. "Have you got one of Leslie's cards for me in your bag?" he asked.

She didn't fish long before she pulled one out for him and slipped Grace's into its place.

Nigel handed the card to Grace then looked at Derek. "My mate will be jealous he missed the show. Part synth, part DJ. I really liked how it worked in the set."

His wife appeared at his side, tucking her hand through his elbow, and the musician nodded. "Good luck, man. I promised your bass player some backstage passes the next time we're in town. I'll have Leslie keep you in the loop, Grace."

She thanked him profusely until his wife tugged him toward the exit. She sighed relief as she was finally able to stop talking then looked up at Derek once they were alone. "Did you grab my ass in front of Nigel Davies?"

"And everyone else," he purred.

She snickered. "Are you jealous?"

"No. No. I just didn't know who was all up in your business."

Grace laughed. "Dear, you're going to have to make peace with the fact that as your manager, I sometimes have to talk to strangers. And I promise, they're not hitting on me."

"Then they're stupid," he grumbled, turning to wrap himself around her. "Because I so want to do more than hit on you."

She laughed, reaching up to press a kiss on his mouth. "Go mingle. You're missing some golden opportunities."

He looked around the room full of people and sighed. "Okay," he acquiesced. "But I'm coming for the rest of this later," he promised, kissing the side of her neck and squeezing both her back pockets.

Grace squirmed and laughed. "I'll hold you to that."

~ ♫ ~ DEREK ~ ♫ ~

Nearly a month later, Derek was shaking out the nerves once more as Grace hurried them down the hall of their record label's office toward a conference room. Sonic Tension had been invited to open for the first three months of Rebel Gloss's tour of the US and Canada. From the way Grace had talked, he'd started to worry she might switch teams once in the presence of pop/rock royalty. Derek knew the group's name, but he hadn't known any of the details that Grace and Rae bandied about the day they received the offer.

This meeting was strictly a formality so both bands could lay eyes on one another and agree to terms. This was the first time he'd seen

Grace in action in an office setting, and her transformation was stunning. Her hair swung in lose waves down her back over the tightest pair of jeans he could talk her into. Her wedge heels echoed in the barren hallway, exuding confidence. She'd even seen a stylist that morning to prepare, taking Rae and Carmen with her. They looked like Charlie's Angels breezing ahead of the guys.

She pushed the door open, and he trailed past her with the group, and squeezed her hip discreetly as he passed.

Three members of the other band stood alternately chatting and looking out the window over the LA skyline, and Derek recognized one of them as the tall man in the VIP lounge who looked like he'd been hitting on Grace at their first gig. The others were seated at the table with a variety of their entourage, and Derek marveled at how sleek Sonic Tension looked in comparison.

The tall, blond man at the window whirled as the door shut.

"They're here," he enthused. "Joe, man! How've you been?" he asked, coming around the table to hug their drummer. The taller man offered a warm handshake for Jacob and Derek and proceeded to hug Carmen, Rae, and lastly Grace. Derek bristled at the affront, shoving his hands in his pockets to keep from forming fists.

"I'm Charlie, the singer," he introduced. He pointed around the room in turn, introducing everyone else at the table. "This is Nigel, Mick, James, and our UK and US managers Miranda and Leslie."

"And you're Sonic Tension," Mick spoke up with a smirk. His voice was shockingly deep despite his diminutive size and platinum blond comb-over. "Great band name."

"Thanks," Jacob replied. "It was Joe's idea."

Mick beamed at his former mate. "Impressive!"

Jacob returned the favor, introducing the band. "I'm Jacob," he began, "This is Rae, Derek, Carmen, and you already know Joe, and our manager Grace."

Nigel stood, arms akimbo with a proud smile on his face. "The album is great, and Grace got it to me so fast. I've been trying to describe the energy at your show to the guys. And I really like how you switch singers depending on the song."

"The album rocks," James piped in. "So, who plays what?"

Grace opened the negotiations skillfully, passing stacks of paper around the room, and Derek watched her work. That morning, she had checked her messenger bag for the fifth time, grumbling and sorting documents. She'd nearly ruined her manicure pulling staples out of one of the piles, and then tossed them in the garbage to print fresh ones.

Her words were like a siren's song, and if he hadn't been involved in the industry so long, he might have been inclined to smile and agree to whatever she said. She broached several of their requests flawlessly, and the two other managers in the room were smiling encouragingly.

He rested his hand on her knee proudly, following along. The other managers spoke in tandem, Grace responding as though she'd been doing this her whole life.

The door opened again, and a team of six lawyers entered the room, gray and navy suits buttoned up to their necks and looking strangled in pastel ties. His eyes darted from the female lawyer who was buttoned up even tighter than Grace had been. He winked at her quickly as the newcomers took their seats, rewarded by the flushing of her cheeks.

They began to hammer out the details of the tour profits in deep legalese. He was grateful three of the attorneys belonged to Jacob and the label. When the topic changed from ticket sales to merchandising, he leaned toward her, whispering against her ear. "We're gonna need a bigger place," he laughed, thinking of where to store the new memorabilia, and most importantly, Grace.

She bit her lower lip to hide the grin that popped up and squeezed his knee.

"So, the tour kicks off in about a month," Miranda explained, flipping through a packet of documentation. "We've sent your label the details of where we'll be staying and what you'll need for transportation. Are you up for it?"

A resounding, "Yes," answered her.

"Excellent!" Charlie agreed, bouncing up to shake hands across the table.

Nigel joined him. "Here's to a great tour," he enthused. "I'm really excited to work with you lot."

"So are we," Derek pronounced.

The corporates flowed out of the room once all the necessary signatures were acquired, the other band on their heels, leaving Sonic Tension alone in the conference room.

Carmen peeking out the door 'til the others were a safe distance and closed it. "We did it! We've hit the big time."

Jacob laughed. "We're big time adjacent, but this is amazing exposure. I'm looking forward to the day when *we're* auditioning opening bands."

The others rambled about the possibilities, and Derek leaned against the table to pull Grace into his arms.

"*We* need a new place, huh?" Grace murmured gently.

Derek tangled his fingers together on her lower back. "Well, yes. I have to have some place to display my latest collectibles."

She laughed. "Collectibles?" she repeated.

"Yes," he replied. "I'm collecting you."

Grace kissed him in the middle of the conference room, as though the entire band wasn't watching.

~ ♪ ~ GRACE ~ ♪ ~

The last full weekend before the band would begin their tour started with blue skies, speckled with wispy clouds, and mild temperatures as Derek slipped his car into his prepaid slip at the ferry parking garage. Sunlight pierced the murky garage interior, and Grace smiled softly as he burst out onto the pavement.

She followed suit, handling the door gently before she met him at the trunk where he was extracting their two rolling bags. She had resisted purchasing them when they were shopping for the tour, but as she looked along the endless, winding pathway leading to the ferry, she was grateful he had insisted. She released the long handle, still amazed at how the bag glided effortlessly. No dragging or struggling to lift it.

"You are so smart," she complimented.

He smirked, closing the trunk. "Don't forget sexy."

She made a slightly obscene noise in the privacy of the garage in agreement. Derek licked his lips, locked the car 'til it beeped, and took her hand in his to lead her away.

"I'm glad we decided to do this now. I didn't want our auction to expire," he rambled as they walked.

Grace tried to take in the sights, but she was wondering if the rest of the band had appropriate luggage, and then she was worrying about the logistics of their stage garb.

Sensing that she was in work mode again, he squeezed her hand. "Everything is squared away," he reminded her. "You proved it to me when you were showing me how unprepared you are," he goaded. "Remember?"

She sighed. "I know you're right. But this is my job and your career. I don't want to half ass anything," she mumbled.

"And you won't," he encouraged. "Look, it's an hour's ferry ride, and a golf cart to the villa, and then I'll switch you into primal mode."

His code word flooded her mind with images of his aggressive caveman approach. She recognized his attempt to quiet her nerves. "I'm sorry. I have a lot riding on this."

He kissed the palm of her hand. "I know." He kissed her wrist next. "We all do. But once we get started, all your work is going to pay off." Another kiss inches lower than the last, moving toward her elbow.

She reached for his cheek as he lifted his head, kissing his lips quickly. "Okay, Gomez. I see what you're doing."

"Do you, Morticia?" he asked, kissing her forearm precisely. He snickered, pulling her to his side. "I don't want you to miss out on this moment because you're lost in another. Enjoy this with me."

She squeezed his hand reassuringly, pointing out different bits of scenery as they made their way to the ferry.

They spent the ferry ride kissing and whispering to pass the time. Between the ocean breezes and his tender attention, Grace's brain stopped whirring, and her muscles relaxed by degrees. She felt safe with him. He would be by her side if things went wrong, like he was now coaxing her into calm with his hand on her thigh.

She let her mind wander as they were transported to the island. It was difficult to think much when one moment he was pointing out a bird, and the next he was kissing her temple or her shoulder, and certainly impossible when he'd pulled her into his lap.

They had come a long way since they met at a restaurant from being outed as a fan to now regular bed partners. He was no longer the boy from her poster. He was the man that she showered with, the man who noticed her car made a funny noise, the man responsible for the red wine stain on her couch, and the one who stayed at his place when Rae came over to use the washer and dryers at her complex. The mystery sort of went out of a relationship when you heard someone fart in the middle of the night, but he was the one she craved when she was happy or sad or…needed some male attention. But all of these things had become the best part of her life.

Once they reached the island, it was as promised. They started with the rental cart, and she watched from the doorway with their bags as he talked to the agent at the counter. This might be one of the last times he'd be able to do something as mundane as renting a vehicle without getting trampled. He turned, wagging a set of keys at her, and she smiled back before chewing her bottom lip. One step closer to primal mode, where nothing else mattered but the two of them together.

The villa was a short drive, Derek weaving around the island and comparing it to their trip to Tulum. When he pulled up to their temporary home, they were both awed at the sight.

"Okay, I feel a little guilty," he said as he slowed the cart to a stop. "It was a charity auction, but I think I got a bargain."

They stared up at the adobe style home with its earthy clay tile roof and hurried inside. The afternoon sunlight streamed through the front windows, highlighting the designer décor. Grace wanted to see the house, but after a boat ride full of kisses, her desire to be close to her man far outweighed the curiosity. Nothing mattered but him, and she waited outside the main bathroom to virtually pounce on him when he reappeared.

Later in the afternoon as the sun was dropping below the horizon, they donned something quick and light, heading to the boardwalk for sustenance and a walk on the beach. They found an oceanside restaurant with open-air dining facing the water and took seats on opposite sides of a booth, Derek melting into his like a satisfied tiger. Sloshing waves on the shore filled the space between them as a waitress offered them drinks.

Grace hummed in delight reading over the menu, setting it down when she'd made her choice.

He captured her hands in his. "Now there's the Grace I know and love."

Her breath caught in her throat, and she assessed the expression on his face. The slight crease between his brows hinted that he hadn't meant to say it, and she waited for him to take it back.

"You do?" she murmured when he didn't.

The wrinkle on his forehead disappeared, and his cerulean blue gaze pierced through all her defenses. "I do," he replied. "I love you."

Grace nearly leapt over the table, pressing against his side and kissing his mouth eagerly.

"I love you, too," she breathed against him.

THE END

EPILOGUE

Opening night of their first official tour was pure chaos. People rushed back and forth around the venue, climbing up ropes, shimmying over catwalks, and ducking beneath the stage for last minute checks. This would become second nature soon enough, Grace reminded herself as she nearly got plowed over by a wardrobe assistant wheeling a cart into Rae and Carmen's dressing room. This was the third near-death incident since they'd arrived.

She knocked tentatively at the guys' dressing room. "Are you decent?" she called out.

"Are you alone?" Derek answered.

She looked around to make sure. "Yes."

The door opened for her, Joe ducked behind it, and Grace darted inside.

Derek was on the couch in nothing but a pair of black boxer briefs. "Hey, baby," he answered as he pulled on socks.

She looked at the other guys. Joe resumed his stretching routine, faded rubber exercise band turning pale as he pulled. Grace made a note to buy him some new ones before this one snapped. Jacob was dressed and slouched in a chair at the vanity, pouring over the set list.

"Why aren't you dressed?" she asked, moving to stand in front of Derek.

"I will be," he promised, reaching out to stroke her calf. He was rewarded when she leaned down to kiss him.

"No!" Joe interrupted, snapping the couch with a band. "I do not need to see that. New rule: You must at least be wearing pants during a PDA."

"I second this rule," Jacob called out.

Grace chuckled, pulling away, then glanced at his lap. "They're right," she mumbled. She darted to the clothing rack, pulling out a pair of his pants and tossing them to him. "Get dressed. Showtime in T minus twenty." She gave Jacob and Joe a thumbs up and left.

"Cruel," Derek called after her.

At three minutes till showtime, she ushered them toward the stage. Techs followed them, tucking their mics and gear under their clothes none-too-discreetly in their haste.

Nigel and Charlie were in the wings, pacing in their pre-concert clothing.

"Hey, guys," Nigel greeted, "We know you're about to go on, but we wanted to wish you luck."

Jacob was already bouncing, and he smiled at the two older men. "Thanks."

The exchange was cut short as techs finished suiting up Carmen and Rae with their instruments.

"You guys are gonna do great," Charlie encouraged. "We have THE best fans. They're going to love you."

"It's time," Grace announced, gesturing for them to go.

Derek grabbed her around the waist, yanking her close and kissing her hard. He released her, slapping her behind and running out after the others as Jacob introduced Sonic Tension to the crowd.

"At least he was wearing pants this time," she mumbled.

Charlie burst out laughing and flung an arm around her shoulder. "You're fun. I'm going to like touring with you."

Nigel chuckled, pulling Charlie free of her. "I wouldn't do that, or he might come back here to make sure you know she's his."

Grace balked, then shrugged. He wasn't wrong.

The opening chords of the show began, and Grace watched from the wings with Charlie and Nigel as her band began winning over the crowd. Jacob's voice wove a spell around their audience. Derek belted out his backup vocals and tried not to laugh as Carmen rode up on him with her guitar. Rae and Joe plugged away at the rhythm section without rushing the beat.

It was arguably one of the best nights of all their lives, and it was only the beginning.

ABOUT THE AUTHORS

Laura Christian was raised in St. Louis, MO but now resides in the great state of Texas with her husband, a Siamese cat and a Jack Russel Terrier. In her spare time, Laura enjoys reading, sewing, knitting, painting, and mostly playing Fortnite with her besties.

Gihan Salem resides in the great state of Texas, making a home with her husband, adopted daughter, grandson, and a bevy of affectionate cats. She has been writing for many years for fun and takes great joy in all things Star Wars. Gihan is a trained audio tech and loves music and the arts. When not writing, she can be found reading, gaming, or following BTS.

To learn more about the author and other publications, please visit www.thelaurachristian.com for more.